Educational Thoughts of Swami Vivekananda

Educational Thoughts of Swami Vivekananda

Dr. Sudharma Joshi

CRESCENT
PUBLISHING CORPORATION

[The responsibility for the facts stated, conclusions reached and plagiarism, if any, in this book is entirely that of the Author. And the Publisher bears no responsibility for them, whatsoever.]

Educational Thoughts of Swami Vivekananda

Edition:2024

ISBN 978-81-8342-157-7

Published by :

CRESCENT PUBLISHING CORPORATION

4806/24, Mathur Lane,

Ansari Road, Darya Ganj,

New Delhi - 110002

Phone : 011- 23244131

Mob. : 9711991838, 9999021668

E-mail : crescentbook@gmail.com

Website : www.crescentpublishingcorp.weebly.com

Typesetting by :

Arjun Computers

Delhi-110051

Printed at :

Roshan Offset Printers

Delhi

Preface

Renowned throughout the world as a patriot-saint of India, Swami Vivekananda was also heralded as a social reformer, religious leader and philosopher. It is within the ambit of these multiple facets of his personality that he is also regarded as a radical educationist, albeit not so well-known. Founding his educational philosophy on the conditions of Indians in both urban and rural areas, and first hand knowledge of the Indian educational scenario his ideology incorporated nearly all the requisites for improving education in India. He once articulated, 'all the wealth of the world cannot help one little Indian village if the people are not taught to help themselves'. This statement, in a nutshell, sums up the educational ideology of the great man.

This book on the educational philosophies of great men looks at the ideological beliefs of Swami Vivekananda pertaining to education, and analyses its relevance within the present context. It looks at his educational thoughts and efforts, including his insistance on development of science and technology, spirituality and morality in education, encouragement of women's education, as well as the efforts of the Ramakrishna mission to propagate his Vedanta school of education and thought. In addition, the book compares his ideology with those of his contemporaries, and assesses its relevance to contemporary times.

Dr. Sudharma Joshi

Contents

1

Swami Vivekananda

Swami Vivekananda (January 12, 1863 - July 4, 1902), whose pre-monastic name was Narendranath Dutta, was one of the most famous and influential spiritual leaders of the philosophies of Vedanta and Yoga and a major figure in the history of Hinduism and India. He was the chief disciple of Ramakrishna Paramahamsa and the founder of Ramakrishna Math and Ramakrishna Mission.

While he is widely credited with having uplifted his own nation, simultaneously he introduced Yoga and Vedanta to America and England with his popular lectures and private discourses on Vedanta philosophy. Vivekananda was the first known Hindu Swami to come to the West, where he introduced Eastern thought at the World's Parliament of Religions, in connection with the World's Fair in Chicago, in 1893. It was there that he was catapulted to fame by his by wide audiences in Chicago and then later elsewhere in America.

BIRTH AND EARLY LIFE

Narendranath Dutta was born in Shimla Pally, Kolkata, West Bengal, India on January 12, 1863 as the son of Viswanath Dutta and Bhuvaneswari Devi. Even as he was young, he showed a precocious mind and keen memory. He practiced meditation from a very early age. While at school, he was good at studies, as well as games of various kinds. He organized an amateur theatrical company and a gymnasium and took lessons in fencing, wrestling, rowing and other sports. He also studied instrumental and vocal music. He was a leader among his group of friends. Even when he was young, he questioned the validity of superstitious customs and discrimination based on caste and religion.

In 1879, Narendra entered the Presidency College, Calcutta for higher studies. After one year, he joined the Scottish Church College, Calcutta and studied philosophy. During the course, he studied western logic, western philosophy and history of European nations.

Questions started to arise in young Narendra's mind about God and the presence of God. This made him associate with the Brahmo Samaj, an important religious movement of the time, led by Keshub Chunder Sen. And along with his classmate and friend Brajendra Nath Seal, he regularly attended meetings of the breakaway Sadharan Brahmo Samaj. Later they would part ways with Dutta aligning himself with Keshub Chunder Sen's Nava Vidhan and Seal staying on as an initiated member. During this time spent together, both Dutta and Seal sought to understand the intricacies of faith, progress and spiritual insight into the works of John Stuart Mill, Auguste Comte, Herbert Spencer and G.W.F. Hegel.

But the Samaj's congregational prayers and devotional songs could not satisfy Narendra's zeal to realize God. He would ask leaders of Brahmo Samaj whether they have seen God. Their answers did not satisfy his quest for knowledge. It was during this time that Reverend William Hastie, the Principal of the Scottish Church College told him about Sri Ramakrishna of Dakshineswar.

With Ramakrishna

Narendra met Ramakrishna for the first time in November 1881. He asked Ramakrishna the same old question he has asked others so often, *"Mahashaya (Venerable Sir), have you seen god?."* The instantaneous answer from Ramakrishna was, *"Yes, I see God, just as I see you here, only in a much intenser sense." " God can be realized," he went on; "one can see and talk to Him as I am seeing and talking to you. But who cares? People shed torrents of tears for their wife and children, for wealth or property, but who does so for the sake of God? If one weeps sincerely for Him, he surely manifests Himself."*. Narendra was astounded and puzzled. He could feel the man's words were honest and uttered from depths of experience. He started visiting Ramakrishna frequently. At first he did not believe that such a plain man could've seen god but gradually he started having faith in what Ramkrishna said.

Though Narendra could not accept Ramakrishna and his visions, he could not neglect him. It had always been in Narendra's nature to test something thoroughly before he could accept it. He tested Ramakrishna to the maximum, but the master was patient, forgiving, humorous, and full of love. He never asked Narendra to abandon reason, and he faced all of Narendra's arguments and examinations with infinite patience. In time, Narendra accepted Ramakrishna, and when he accepted, his acceptance was whole-hearted. While Ramakrishna predominantly taught duality and Bhakti to his other disciples, he taught Narendra the Advaita Vedanta, the philosophy of non-dualism.

During the course of five years of his training under Ramakrishna, Narendra was transformed from a restless, puzzled, impatient youth to a mature man who was ready to renounce everything for the sake of God-realization. Soon, Ramakrishna's end came in the form of throat cancer in August 1886. After this Narendra and a core group of Ramakrishna's disciples took vows to become monks and renounce everything, and started living in a supposedly haunted house in Baranagore. They took alms to satisfy their hunger and their other needs were taken care of by Ramakrishna's richer householder disciples.

Wanderings in India

Soon, the young monk of Baranagore wanted to live the life of a wandering monk with rags and a begging bowl and no other possessions. On July 1890, Vivekananda set out for a long journey, without knowing where the journey would take him. The journey that followed took him to the length and breadth of the Indian subcontinent. During these days, Vivekananda assumed various names like Vividishananda (in Sanskrit, *Vividisha* means "the desire to know" and *Ananda* means "bliss"), Satchidananda, etc., It is said that he was given the name *Vivekananda* by Maharaja of Khetri for his discernment of things, good and bad.

During these wandering days, Vivekananda stayed in kings' palaces, as well as the huts of the poor. He came in close contact with the culture of different regions of India and various classes of people in India. Vivekananda observed the imbalance in society and tyranny in the name of caste. He realised the need for a national rejuvenation if India was to survive at all. He reached Kanyakumari, the southernmost tip of the Indian subcontinent on 24 December 1892. There, he swam across the sea and started meditating on a lone rock. He thus meditated for three days and said later that he meditated about the past, present and future of India. The rock went on to become the Vivekananda memorial at Kanyakumari.

Vivekananda went to Madras and spoke about his plans for India and Hinduism to the young men of Madras. They were impressed by the monk and urged him to go to the United States and represent Hinduism in the World Parliament of Religions. The Raja of Ramnad, who was originally invited for the conference, promoted Vivekananda as the right person to represent the views of Hinduism in the Parliament. Thus, helped by his friends at Chennai, Bhaskara Sethupathi, Raja of Ramnad and Maharajas of Mysore and Khetri, Vivekananda set out on his journey to the USA.

In one of his lectures in California, the swami described about his condition during wandering days as follows:

> "Many times I have been in the jaws of death, starving, footsore, and weary; for days and days I had no food, and often could walk no farther; I would sink down under a tree, and life would seem to be ebbing away. I could not speak, I could scarcely think, but at last the mind reverted to the idea: "I have no fear nor death; never was I born, never did I die; I never hunger or thirst. I am It! I am It! The whole of nature cannot crush me; it is my servant. Assert thy strength, thou Lord of lords and God of gods! Regain thy lost empire! Arise and walk and stop not!" And I would rise up, reinvigorated; and here I am today, living! Thus, whenever darkness comes, assert the reality and everything adverse must vanish. For after all, it is but a dream. Mountain-high though the difficulties appear,

> terrible and gloomy though all things seem, they are but Maya. Fear not, and it is banished. Crush it, and it vanishes. Stamp upon it, and it dies. "

In the West

Vivekananda was received well at the 1893 World Parliament of Religions in Chicago, where he delivered a series of lectures. He also earned wild applause for beginning his address with the famous words, *"Sisters and brothers of America."* A newspaper account described him as "an orator by divine right and undoubtedly the greatest figure at the Parliament." Vivekananda's arrival in the USA has been identified by many to mark the beginning of western interest in Hinduism not as merely an exotic eastern oddity, but as a vital religious and philosophical tradition that might actually have something important to teach the West.

Vivekananda successfully introduced yoga and Vedanta to the West and lectured around America introducing the topics (1894-6). He taught hundreds of students privately in free classes held in his own room beginning in New York in 1895. Later, he started Vedantic centers in New York City and London, lectured at major universities and generally kindled western interest in Hinduism. His success was not without controversy, much of it from Christian missionaries of whom he was fiercely critical. After four years of constant touring, lecturing and retreats in the West, he came back to India in the year 1897.

Back in India

Admirers and devotees of Vivekananda gave him an enthusiastic reception on his return to India. In India, he delivered a series of lectures, and this set of lectures known as "Lectures from Colombo to Almora" is considered to have uplifted the morale of the then downtrodden Indian society. He founded one of the world's largest charitable relief missions, the Ramakrishna Mission and reorganized the ancient Swami order by founding one of the most significant and largest monastic orders in India, the Ramakrishna Math.

However, he had to bear great criticism from other orthodox Hindus for having traveled in the West. In his day there was hardly a Hindu in America and he received criticism for crossing the ocean, at that time a cause for "outcasting." Vivekananda scoffed at these critiques from the orthodox saying "I cannot be outcast - As a monk, I am beyond caste." His contemporaries also questioned his motives, wondering whether the fame and glory of his Hindu evangelism compromised his original monastic vows. His enthusiasm for America and Britain, and his spiritual devotion to his motherland, caused significant tension in his last years.

He once again toured the west from January 1899 to December 1900. He inculcated a spirit of respect and good will for exchanges between the East and the West. He had American disciples whom he brought to India and initiated as Swamis and brought Indian Swamis to America where they and their successors have been ever since.

Principles and Philosophy

Vivekananda was a renowned thinker in his own right. One of his most important contributions was to demonstrate how Advaitin thinking is not merely philosophically far-reaching, but how it also has social, even political, consequences. One important lesson he claimed to receive from Ramakrishna was that "Jiva is Shiva " (each individual is divinity itself). This became his Mantra, and he coined the concept of *daridra narayana seva* - the service of God in and through (poor) human beings. *If there truly is the unity of Brahman underlying all phenomena, then on what basis do we regard ourselves as better or worse, or even as better-off or worse-off, than others?* - This was the question he posed to himself. Ultimately, he concluded that these distinctions fade into nothingness in the light of the oneness that the devotee experiences in Moksha. What arises then is compassion for those "individuals" who remain unaware of this oneness and a determination to help them.

Swami Vivekananda belonged to that branch of Vedanta that held that no one can be truly free until all of us are. Even the desire foı personal salvation has to be given up, and only tireless work for the salvation of others is the true mark of the enlightened person. He founded the Sri Ramakrishna Math and Mission on the principle of Atmano Mokshartham Jagad-hitaya cha (for one's own salvation and for the welfare of the World).

However, Vivekananda also pleaded for a strict separation between religion and government ("church and state"). Although social customs had been formed in the past with religious sanction, it was not now the business of religion to interfere with matters such as marriage, inheritance and so on. The ideal society would be a mixture of Brahmin knowledge, Kshatriya culture, Vaisya efficiency and the egalitarian Shudra ethos. Domination by any one led to different sorts of lopsided societies. Vivekananda did not feel that religion, nor, any force for that matter, should be used forcefully to bring about an ideal society, since this was something that would evolve naturally by individualistic change when the conditions were right.

Vivekananda made a strict demarcation between the two classes of Hindu scriptures : the Sruti and the Smritis. The Sruti, by which is meant the Vedas, consist of eternally and universally valid spiritual truths. The Smritis on the other hand, are the dos and donts of religions, applicable to society and subject to revision from time to time. Vivekananda felt that existing Hindu smritis had to be revised for modern times. But the Srutis of course are eternal - they may only be re-interpreted.

Vivekanda advised his followers to be holy, unselfish and have shraddha (faith). He encouraged the practise of Brahmacharya (Celibacy). In one of the conversations with his childhood friend *Sri Priya Nath Sinha* he attributes his physical and mental strengths, eloquence to the practice of Brahmacharya.

Vivekananda didn't advocate the emerging area of parapsychology, astrology (one instance can be found in his speech *Man the Maker of his Destiny, Complete-Works, Volume 8, Notes of Class Talks and Lectures*) saying that this form of curiosity doesn't help in spiritual progress but actually hinders it.

Influence

Every one of the 20th century Indian leaders of note have acknowledged his influence, from Gandhi to Subhas Bose. The first governor general of independent India, Chakravarti Rajagopalachari, once observed that "Vivekananda saved Hinduism." According to Subhas Chandra Bose, Vivekananda "is the maker of modern India" and for Mohandas Gandhi, Vivekananda's influence increased his "love for his country a thousandfold." Gandhi, who also strived for a lot of reform in Hinduism himself, said: *Swami Vivekananda's writings need no introduction from anybody. They make their own irresistible appeal.* Many years after his death, Rabindranath Tagore (a prominent member of the Brahmo Samaj) had said: *If you want to know India, study Vivekananda. In him everything is positive and nothing negative.* National Youth Day in India is by way of commemorating him held on his birthday, January 12. This was a most fitting gesture as much of Swami

Vivekananda's writings concerned the Indian youth and how they should strive to uphold their ancient values whilst fully participating in the modern world.

Swami Vivekananda is widely considered to have inspired India's freedom struggle movement. His writings inspired a whole generation of freedom fighters including Aurobindo Ghose and Bagha Jatin. Vivekananda was the brother of the extremist revolutionary, Shri Bhupendranath Dutta. Subhash Chandra Bose one of the most prominent figures in Indian independence movement said,

> I cannot write about Vivekananda without going into raptures. Few indeed could comprehend or fathom him even among those who had the privilege of becoming intimate with him. His personality was rich, profound and complex... Reckless in his sacrifice, unceasing in his activity, boundless in his love, profound and versatile in his wisdom, exuberant in his emotions, merciless in his attacks but yet simple as a child, he was a rare personality in this world of ours

Aurobindo Ghosh considered Vivekananda as his spiritual mentor. While in Alipore Jail, Sri Aurobindo used to be visited by Swami Vivekananda in his meditation and be guided by him in yoga.

> Vivekananda was a soul of puissance if ever there was one, a very lion among men, but the definitive work he has left behind is quite incommensurate with our impression of his creative might and energy. We perceive his influence still working gigantically, we know not well how, we know not well where, in something that is not yet formed, something leonine, grand, intuitive, upheaving that has entered the soul of India and we say, "Behold, Vivekananda still lives in the soul of his Mother and in the souls of her children.
>
> —Sri Aurobindo—1915 in Vedic Magazine.

Vivekananda inspired Jamshedji Tata to set up Indian Institute of Science, one of India's finest Institutions.

Abroad, he had some interactions with Max Mueller. Nikola Tesla was one of those influenced by the Vedic philosophy teachings of the Swami Vivekananda.

Above all Swami Vivekanada helped restore a sense of pride amongst the Hindus, presenting the ancient teachings of India in its purest form to a Western audience, free from the propaganda spread by British colonial administators and Christian missonaries, of Hinduism being a caste-ridden, misogynistic idolatrous faith. Indeed his early foray into the West would set the path for subsequent Indian religious teachers to make their own marks on the world, as well herald the entry of Hindus and their religious traditions into the Western world.

Vivekananda and Science

In his book Raja Yoga, Vivekananda writes that practice of Raja Yoga can confer psychic powers such as 'reading another's thoughts', 'controlling all the forces of nature', become 'almost all-knowing', 'live without breathing', 'control the bodies of others' and levitation. He also explains traditional eastern spiritual concepts like kundalini and spiritual energy centres. These phenomena are contradictory to the understanding of modern scientific community. Vivekananda rejected ether theory long before Einstein, stating that it cannot explain the space itself.

However, Vivekananda himself says in the book,

> "It is not the sign of a candid and scientific mind to throw overboard anything without proper investigation. Surface scientists, unable to explain the various extraordinary mental phenomena, strive to ignore their very existence."

He further says in the introduction of the book that one should take up the practice and verify these things for themselves, and that there should not be blind belief.

> "What little I know I will tell you. So far as I can reason it out I will do so, but as to what I do not know I will simply tell you what the books say. It is wrong to believe blindly. You must exercise your own reason and judgment; you must practise, and see whether these things happen or not. Just as you would take up any other science, exactly in the same manner you should take up this science for study."

Death

On July 4, 1902 at Belur Math near Calcutta, he taught Vedanta philosophy to some pupils in the morning. He had a walk with Swami Premananda, a brother-disciple and gave him instructions concerning the future of the Ramakrishna Math. Vivekananda passed away in Mahasamadhi after a session of prayer at Belur Math. He had predicted that he would die before the age of 40, which proved to be true when he died at the age of 39.

2

Sayings of Swami Vivekananda

My ideal, indeed, can be put into a few words, and that is to preach unto mankind their divinity, and how to make it manifest in every movement of life.

Religion is the manifestation of the divinity already in man.

Religion is the idea which is raising the brute unto man, and man unto God.

The secret of religion lies not in theories but in practice. To be good and do good - that is the whole of religion.

Man is higher than all animals, than all angels; none is greater than man.

One may gain political and social independence, but if one is a slave to his passions and desires, one cannot feel the pure joy of real freedom.

Look at the wall. Did the wall ever tell a lie? It is always the wall. Man tells a lie and becomes a god, too.

After so much austerity, I have understood this as the real truth - God is present in every jiva; there is no other God besides that. 'Who serves jiva, serves God indeed.

Cut out the word help from your mind. You cannot help; it is blasphemy! You worship. When you give a morsel of food to a dog, you worship the dog as God. He is all, and is in all.

Unselfishness is God. One may live on a throne, in a palace, and be perfectly unselfish; and then he is in God. Another may live in a hut and wear rags, and have nothing in the world; yet if he is selfish, he is intensely merged in the world.

All nations have attained greatness by paying proper respect to women. That country and that nation which do not respect women have never become great, nor will ever be in future.

With five hundred men, ... the conquest of India might take fifty years: with as many women, not more than a few weeks.

Religion and religion alone is the life of India, and when that goes, India will die, in spite of politics, in spite of social reforms, in spite of Kubera's wealth poured upon the head of every one of her children.

Before flooding India with socialistic or political ideas, first deluge the land with spiritual ideas.

We want to lead mankind to the place where there is neither the Vedas, nor the Bible, nor the Koran; yet this has to be done by harmonizing the Vedas, the Bible, and the Koran.

Mankind ought to be taught that religions are but the varied expressions of THE RELIGION, which is Oneness, so that each may choose the path that suits him best.

Who will give the world light? Sacrifice in the past has been the Law, it will be, alas, for ages to come. The earth's bravest and best will have to sacrifice themselves for the good of many, for the welfare of all.

Truth, purity, and unselfishness - whenever these are present, there is no power below or above the sun to crush the possessor thereof. Equipped with these, one individual is able to face the whole universe in opposition.

Everything can be sacrificed for truth, but truth cannot be sacrificed for anything.

The highest ideal is eternal and entire self-abnegation, where there is no 'I', but is Thou'.

All expansion is life, all contraction is death.

All love is expansion, all selfishness is contraction. Love is therefore the only law of life. He who loves lives, he who is selfish is dying. Therefore love for love's sake, because it is law of life, just as you breathe to live.

The national ideals of India are Renunciation and Service. Intensity her in those channels, and the rest will take care of itself.

Good motives, sincerity, and infinite love can conquer the world. One single soul possessed of these virtues can destroy the dark designs of millions of hypocrites and brutes.

Take up one idea. Make that one idea your life - think of it, dream of it, live on idea. Let the brain, muscles, nerves, every part of your body, be full of that idea, and just leave every other idea alone. This is the way to success.

Sayings and Utterances

1. "Did Buddha teach that the many was real and the ego unreal, while orthodox Hinduism regards the One as the real, and the many as unreal?" the Swami was asked. "Yes", answered the Swami. "And what Ramakrishna Paramahamsa and I have added to this is, that the Many and the One are the same Reality,

perceived by the same mind at different times and in different attitudes."

2. "Remember!" he said once to a disciple, "Remember! the message of India is always '*Not the soul for nature, but nature for the soul*!'"

3. "What the world wants today is twenty men and women who can dare to stand in the street yonder, and say that they possess nothing but God. Who will go? Why should one fear? If this is true, what else could matter? *If it is not true, what do our lives matter*!"

4. "Oh, how calm would be the work of one who really understood the divinity of man! For such, there is nothing to do, save to open men's eyes. All the rest does itself."

5. "He (Shri Ramakrishna) was contented simply to live that great life and to leave it to others to find the explanation!"

6. "Plans! Plans!" Swami Vivekananda explained in indignation, when one of his disciples had offered him some piece of worldly wisdom. "That is why Western people can never create a religion! If any of you ever did, it was only a few Catholic saints who had no plans. Religion was never preached by planners!"

7. "Social life in the West is like a peal of laughter; but underneath, it is a wail. It ends in a sob. The fun and frivolity are all on the surface: really it is full of tragic intensity. Now here, it is sad and gloomy on the outside, but underneath are carelessness and merriment.

   "We have a theory that the universe is God's manifestation of Himself just for fun, that the Incarnations came and lived here 'just for fun'. Play, it was all play. Why was Christ crucified? It was mere play. And so of life. Just play with the Lord. Say, "It is all play, it is all play" Do *you* do anything?"

8. "I am persuaded that a leader is not made in one life. He has to be born for it. For the difficulty is not in organisation and making plans; the test, the real test, of the leader, lies in holding widely different people together along the line of their common sympathies. And this can only be done unconsciously, never by trying."

9. In explanation of Plato's doctrine of Ideas, Swamiji said, "And so you see, all this is but a feeble manifestation of the great ideas, which alone, are real and perfect. Somewhere is an ideal for you, and here is an attempt to manifest it! The attempt falls short still in many ways. Still, go on! You will interpret the ideal some day."

10. Answering the remark of a disciple who felt that it would be better for her to come back to this life again and again and help the causes that were of interest to her instead of striving for personal salvation with a deep longing to get out of life, the Swami retorted quickly: "That's because you cannot overcome the idea of progress. But things do not grow better. They remain as they are; and we grow better by the changes we make in them."

11. It was in Almora that a certain elderly man, with a face full of amiable weakness, came and put him a question about Karma. What were they to do, he asked, whose Karma it was to see the strong oppress the weak? The Swami turned on him in surprised indignation. "Why, thrash the strong, of course!" he said, "You forget your own part in this Karma: Yours is always the right to rebel!"

12. "Ought one to seek an opportunity of death in defense of right, or ought one to take the lesson of the Gitâ and learn never to react?" the Swami was asked. "I am for no reaction", said the Swami, speaking slowly and with a long pause. Then he added " — for Sannyâsins. Self-defense for the householder!"
13. "It is a mistake to hold that with all men pleasure is the motive. Quite as many are born to seek after pain. Let us worship the Terror for Its own sake."
14. "Ràmakrishna Paramahamsa was the only man who ever had the courage to say that we must speak to all men in their own language!"
15. "How I used to hate Kâli!" he said, referring to his own days of doubts in accepting the Kali ideal, "And all Her ways! That was the ground of my six years' fight — that I would not accept Her. But I had to accept Her at last! Ramakrishna Paramahamsa dedicated me to Her, and now I believe that She guides me in everything I do, and does with me what She will. . . . Yet I fought so long! I loved him, you see, and that was what held me. I saw his marvellous purity. . . . I felt his wonderful love. . . . His greatness had not dawned on me then. All that came afterwards when I had given in. At that time I thought him a brain-sick baby, always seeing visions and the rest. I hated it. And then I, too, had to accept Her!

    "No, the thing that made me do it is a secret that will die with me. I had great misfortunes at the time. . . . It was an opportunity. . . . She made a slave of me. Those were the very words: 'a slave of you'. And Ramakrishna Paramahamsa made me over to Her. . . . Strange! He lived only two years after doing that, and most of the time he was suffering. Not more than six months did he keep his own health and brightness.

"Guru Nanak was like that, you know, looking for the one disciple to whom he would give his power. And he passed over all his own family — his children were as nothing to him — till he came upon the boy to whom he gave it; and then he could die.

"The future, you say, will call Ramakrishna Paramahamsa an Incarnation of Kali? Yes, I think there's no doubt that She worked up the body of Ramakrishna for Her own ends.

"You see, I cannot but believe that there is somewhere a great Power that thinks of Herself as feminine, and called Kali and Mother. . . . And I believe in Brahman too. . . . But is it not always like that? Is it not the multitude of cells in the body that make up the personality, the many brain-centres, not the one, that produce consciousness? . . . Unity in complexity! Just so! And why should it be different with Brahman? It is Brahman. It is the One. And yet — and yet — it is the gods too!"

16. "The older I grow, the more everything seems to me to lie in manliness. This is my new gospel."

17. Referring to some European reference to cannibalism, as if it were a normal part of life in some societies, the Swami remarked, "That is not true! No nation ever ate human flesh, save as a religious sacrifice, or in war, out of revenge. Don't you see? That's not the way of gregarious animals! It would cut at the root of social life!"

18 "Sex-love and creation! These are at the root of most religions. And these in India are called Vaishnavism, and in the West Christianity. How few have dared to worship Death or Kali! Let us worship Death! Let us embrace the Terrible, because it is terrible, not asking

that it be toned down. Let us take misery for misery's own sake!"

19. "The three cycles of Buddhism were five hundred years of the Law, five hundred years of images, and five hundred years of Tantras. You must not imagine that there was ever a religion in India called Buddhism with temples and priests of its own order! Nothing of the sort. It was always within Hinduism. Only at one time the influence of Buddha was paramount, and this made the nation monastic."

20. "The conservative's whole ideal is *submission.* Your ideal is struggle. Consequently it is *we* who enjoy the life, and never you! You are always striving to change yours to something better; and before a millionth part of the change is carried out, you die. The Western ideal is to be doing; the Eastern to be suffering. The perfect life would be a wonderful harmony doing and suffering. But that can never be.

    "In our system it is accepted that a man cannot have all he desires. Life is subjected to many restraints. This is ugly, yet it brings out points of light and strength. Our liberals see only the ugliness and try to throw it off. But they substitute something quite as bad; and the new custom takes as long as the old for us to work to its centres of strength.

    "Will is not strengthened by change. It is weakened and enslaved by it. But we must be always absorbing. Will grows stronger by absorption. And consciously or unconsciously, will is the one thing in the world that we admire. Suttee is great in the eyes of the whole world, because of the will that it manifests.

    "It is selfishness that we must seek to eliminate. I find that whenever I have made a mistake in my life, it has always been because *self* entered into the calculation. Where self has not been involved, my judgment has gone straight to the mark.

"Without self, there would have been no religious system. If man had not wanted anything for himself, do you think he would have had all this praying and worship? Why! he would never have thought of God at all, except perhaps for a little praise now and then, at the sight of a beautiful landscape or something. And that is the only attitude there ought to be. All praise and thanks. If only we were rid of self!

"You are quite wrong when you think that fighting is a sign of growth. It is not so at all. Absorption is the sign. Hinduism is a very genius of absorption. We have never cared for fighting. Of course we could strike a blow now and then, in defense of our homes! That was right. But we never cared for fighting for its own sake. Every one had to learn that. So let these races of newcomers whirl on! They'll all be taken into Hinduism in the end!"

21. "The totality of all souls, not the human alone, is the Personal God. The will of the Totality nothing can resist. It is what we know as law. And this is what we mean by Shiva and Kali and so on."

22. "Worship the Terrible! Worship Death! All else is vain. All struggle is vain. That is the last lesson. Yet this is not the coward's love of death, not the love of the weak or the suicide. It is the welcome of the strong man who has sounded everything to its depths and knows that there is no alternative."

23. "I disagree with all those who are giving their superstitions back to my people. Like the Egyptologist's interest in Egypt, it is easy to feel an interest in India that is purely selfish. One may desire to see again the India of one's books, one's

studies, one's dreams. My hope is to see again the strong points of that India, reinforced by the strong points of this age, only in a natural way. The new stage of things must be a growth from within.

"So I preach only the Upanishads. If you look, you will find that I have never quoted anything but the Upanishads. And of the Upanishads, it is only that One idea, strength. The quintessence of the Vedas and Vedanta and all lies in that one word. Buddha's teaching was non-resistance, or non-injury. But I think this is a better way of teaching the same thing. For behind that non-injury lay a dreadful weakness. It is weakness that conceives the idea of resistance. I do not think of punishing or escaping from a drop of sea-spray. It is nothing to me. Yet to the mosquito it would be serious. Now I would make all injury like that. Strength and fearlessness. My own ideal is that saint whom they killed in the Mutiny and who broke his silence, when stabbed to the heart, to say, 'And thou also art He!'

"But you may ask, 'What is the place of Ramakrishna in this scheme?'

"He is the method, that wonderful unconscious method! He did not understand himself. He knew nothing of England or the English, save that they were queer folk from over the sea. But he lived that great life: and I read the meaning. Never a word of condemnation for any! Once I had been attacking one of our sects of diabolists. I had been raving on for three hours, and he had listened quietly. 'Well, well!' said the old man as I finished, 'perhaps every house may have a backdoor. Who knows?'

"Hitherto the great fault of our Indian religion has lain in its knowing only two words: renunciation and Mukti. Only Mukti here! Nothing for the householder!

"But these are the very people whom I want to help. For are not all souls of the same quality? Is not the goal of all the same?

"And so strength must come to the nation through education."

24. The Puranas, the Swami considered, to be the effort of Hinduism to bring lofty ideas to the door of the masses. There had been only one mind in India that had foreseen this need, that of Krishna, probably the greatest man who ever lived.

The Swami said, "Thus is created a religion that ends in the worship of Vishnu, as the preservation and enjoyment of life, leading to the realisation of God. Our last movement, Chaitanyaism, you remember, was for enjoyment. At the same time Jainism represents the other extreme, the slow destruction of the body by self-torture. Hence Buddhism, you see, is reformed Jainism; and this is the real meaning of Buddha's leaving the company of the five ascetics. In India, in every age, there is a cycle of sects which represents every gradation of physical practice, from the extreme of self-torture to the extreme of excess. And during the same period will always be developed a metaphysical cycle, which represents the realisation of God as taking place by every gradation of means, from that of using the senses as an instrument to that of the annihilation of the senses. Thus Hinduism always consists, as it were, of two counter-spirals, completing each other, round a single axis.

"'Yes!' Vaishnavism says, 'it is all right — this tremendous love for father, for mother, for brother, husband, or child! It is all right, if only you will think that Krishna is the child, and when you give him food, that you are feeding Krishna!' This was the cry of Chaitanya, 'Worship God *through* the senses', as against the Vedantic cry, 'Control the senses! suppress the senses!'

"I see that India is a young and living organism. Europe is young and living. Neither has arrived at such a stage of development that we can safely criticise its institutions. They are two great experiments, neither of which is yet complete. In India we have social communism, with the light of Advaita — that is, spiritual individualism — playing on and around it; in Europe you are socially individualists, but your thought is dualistic, which is spiritual communism. Thus the one consists of socialist institutions hedged in by individualist thought, while the other is made up of individualist institutions within the hedge of communistic thought.

"Now we must help the Indian experiment as it is. Movements which do not attempt to help things as they are, are, from that point of view, no good. In Europe, for instance, I respect marriage as highly as non-marriage. Never forget that a man is made great and perfect as much by his faults as by his virtues. So we must not seek to rob a nation of its character, even if it could be proved that the character was all faults."

25. "You may always say that the image is God. The error you have to avoid is to think God is the image."

26. The Swami was appealed to on one occasion to condemn the fetishism of the Hottentot. "I do not know", he answered, "what fetishism is!" Then a lurid picture was hastily put before him of the object alternately worshipped, beaten, and thanked. "I do that!" he exclaimed. "Don't you see," he went on, a

moment later, in hot resentment of injustice done to the lowly and absent, "don't you see that there is no fetishism? Oh, your hearts are steeled, that you cannot see that the child is right! The child sees person everywhere. Knowledge robs us of the child's vision. But at last, through higher knowledge, we win back to it. He connects a living power with rocks, sticks, trees and the rest. And is there not a living Power behind them? It is *symbolism*, not fetishism! Can you not see?"

27. One day he told the story of Satyabhâmâ's sacrifice and how the word "Krishna", written on a piece of paper and thrown into the balance, made Krishna himself, on the other side, kick the beam. "Orthodox Hinduism", he began, "makes Shruti, the sound, everything. The *thing* is but a feeble manifestation of the pre-existing and eternal idea. So the *name* of God is everything: God Himself is merely the objectification of that idea in the eternal mind. Your own name is infinitely more perfect than the person you! The name of God is greater than God. Guard your speech!"

28. "I would not worship even the Greek Gods, for they were separate from humanity! Only those should be worshipped who are like ourselves but greater. The difference between the gods and me must be a difference only of degree."

29. "A stone falls and crushes a worm. Hence we infer that all stones, falling, crush worms. Why do we thus immediately reapply a perception? Experience, says one. But it happens, let us suppose, for the first time. Throw a baby into the air, and it cries. Experience from past lives? But why applied to the future? Because there is a real connection between certain things, a *pervasiveness*, only it lies with us to see that the quality neither overlaps, nor falls short

of, the instance. On this discrimination depends all human knowledge.

"With regard to fallacies, it must be remembered that direct perception itself can only be a proof, provided the instrument, the method, and the persistence of the perception are all maintained pure. Disease or emotion will have the effect of disturbing the observation. *Therefore direct perception itself is but a mode of inference.* Therefore all human knowledge is uncertain and may be erroneous. Who is a true witness? He is a true witness to whom the thing said is a direct perception. Therefore the Vedas are true, because they consist of the evidence of competent persons. But is this power of perception peculiar to any? No! The Rishi, the Aryan, and the Mlechchha all alike have it.

"Modern Bengal holds that evidence is only a special case of direct perception, and that analogy and parity of reasoning are only bad inferences. Therefore, of actual proofs there are only two, direct perception and inference.

"One set of persons, you see, gives priority to the external manifestation, the other to the internal idea. Which is prior, the bird to the egg, or the egg to the bird? Does the oil hold the cup or the cup the oil? This is a problem of which there is no solution. Give it up! Escape from Maya!"

30. "Why should I care if the world itself were to disappear? According to my philosophy, that, you know, would be a very good thing! But, in fact, all that is against me must be with me in the end. Am I not Her soldier?"

31. "Yes, my own life is guided by the enthusiasm of a certain great personality, but what of that? Inspiration was never filtered out to the world through one man!

"It is true I believe Ramakrishna Paramahamsa to have been inspired. But then I am myself inspired also. And you are inspired. And your disciples will be; and theirs after them; and so on, to the end of time!

"Don't you see that the age for esoteric interpretation is over? For good or for ill, that day is vanished, never to return. Truth, in the future, is to be open to the world!"

32. "Buddha made the fatal mistake of thinking that the whole world could be lifted to the height of the Upanishads. And self-interest spoilt all. Krishna was wiser, because He was more politic. But Buddha would have no compromise. The world before now has seen even the Avatâra ruined by compromise, tortured to death for want of recognition, and lost. But Buddha would have been worshipped as God in his own lifetime, all over Asia, for a moment's compromise. And his reply was only: 'Buddhahood is an achievement, not a person!' Verily was He the only man is the world who was ever quite sane, the only sane man ever born!"

33. People had told the Swami in the West that the greatness of Buddha would have been more appealing, had he been crucified! This he stigmatised as "Roman brutality", and pointed out, "The lowest and most animal liking is for action. Therefore the world will always love the epic. Fortunately for India, however, she has never produced a Milton, with his 'hurled headlong down the steep abyss'! The whole of that were well exchanged for a couple of lines of Browning!" It had been this epic vigour of the story, in his opinion, that had appealed to the Roman. The crucifixion it was that carried Christianity over the Roman world. "Yes, Yes!" he reiterated. "You Western folk want *action*! You

cannot yet perceive the poetry of every common little incident in life! What beauty could be greater than that of the story of the young mother coming to Buddha with her dead boy? Or the incident of the goats? You see the Great Renunciation was not new in India! . . . But *after Nirvâna,* look at the poetry!

"It is a wet night, and he comes to the cowherd's hut and gathers in to the wall under the dripping eaves. The rain is pouring down and the wind rising.

"Within, the cowherd catches a glimpse of a face through the window and thinks, 'Ha, ha! Yellow garb! stay there! It's good enough for you!' And then he begins to sing.

"'My cattle are housed, and the fire burns bright. My wife is safe, and my babes sleep sweet! Therefore ye may rain, if ye will, O clouds, tonight!'

"And the Buddha answers from without, "My mind is controlled: my senses are all gathered in; my heart firm. Therefore ye may rain, if ye will, O clouds, tonight!'

"Again the cowherd: 'The fields are reaped, and the hay is fast in the barn. The stream is full, and the roads are firm. Therefore ye may rain, if ye will, O clouds, tonight.'

"And so it goes on, till at last the cowherd rises, in contrition and wonder, and becomes a disciple.

"Or what would be more beautiful than the barber's story?

The Blessed One passed by my house, *my house* — the Barber's! I ran, but He turned and awaited me, Awaited *me* — the Barber! "I said, 'May I speak, O Lord, with Thee?' And He said 'Yes!' 'Yes!' to *me* — the Barber! "And I said, 'Is Nirvana for such as I?' And He said 'Yes!' Even for *me* — the Barber! "And I said, 'May I follow after Thee?' And He said, 'Oh yes!' Even *I* — the Barber! And I said, 'May I stay, O Lord, near Thee?' "And He said, 'Thou mayest!' Even to *me* — the poor Barber!"

34. "The great point of contrast between Buddhism and Hinduism lies in the fact that Buddhism said, 'Realise all this as illusion', while Hinduism said, 'Realise that within the illusion is the Real.' Of *how* this was to be done, Hinduism never presumed to enunciate any rigid law. The Buddhist command could only be carried out through monasticism; the Hindu might be fulfilled through any state of life. All alike were roads to the One Real. One of the highest and greatest expressions of the Faith is put into the mouth of a butcher, preaching by the orders of a married woman to a Sannyasin. Thus Buddhism became the religion of a monastic order, but Hinduism, in spite of its exaltation of monasticism, remains ever the religion of faithfulness to duty, whatever it be, as the path bv which man may attain God."

35. "Lay down the rules for your group and formulate your ideas," the Swami said, dealing with the monastic ideal for women, "and put in a little universalism, if there is room for it. But remember that not more than half a dozen people in the whole world are ever at any time ready for this! There must be room for sects, as well as for rising above sects. You will have to manufacture your own tools. Frame laws, but frame them in such a fashion that when people are ready to do without them, they can burst them asunder. Our originality lies in combining perfect freedom with perfect authority. This can be done even in monasticism."

36. "Two different races mix and fuse, and out of them rises one strong distinct type. This tries to save itself from admixture, and here you see the beginning of caste. Look at the apple. The best specimens have been produced by crossing; but once crossed, we try to preserve the variety intact."

37. Referring to education of girls in India he said, "In worship of the gods, you must of course use images. But you can change these. Kali need not always be in one position. Encourage your girls to think of new ways of picturing Her. Have a hundred different conceptions of Saraswati. Let them draw and model and paint their own ideas.

"In the chapel, the pitcher on the lowest step of the altar must be always full of water, and lights in great Tamil butter-lamps must be always burning. If, in addition, the maintenance of perpetual adoration could be organised, nothing could be more in accord with Hindu feeling.

"But the ceremonies employed must themselves be Vedic. There must be a Vedic altar, on which at the hour of worship to light the Vedic fire. And the children must be present to share in the service of oblation. This is a rite which would claim the respect of the whole of India.

"Gather all sorts of animals about you. The cow makes a fine beginning. But you will also have dogs and cats and birds and others. Let the children have a time for going to feed and look after these.

"Then there is the sacrifice of learning. That is the most beautiful of all. Do you know that every book is holy in India, not the Vedas alone, but the English and Mohammedan also? All are sacred.

"Revive the old arts. Teach your girls fruit-modelling with hardened milk. Give them artistic cooking and sewing. Let them learn painting, photography, the cutting of designs in paper, and gold and silver filigree and embroidery. See that everyone knows something by which she can earn a living in case of need.

"And never forget Humanity! The idea of a humanitarian man-worship exists in nucleus in India, but it has never been sufficiently specialised. Let your students develop it. Make poetry, make art, of it. Yes, a daily worship at the feet of beggars, after bathing and before the meal, would be a wonderful practical training of heart and hand together. On some days, again, the worship might be of children, of your own pupils. Or you might borrow babies and nurse and feed them. What was it that Mâtâji (Tapaswini Mataji, foundress of the Mahâkâli Pâthasâlâ, Calcutta.) said to me? 'Swamiji! I have no help. But these blessed ones I worship, and they will take me to salvation!' She feels, you see, that she is serving Umâ in the Kumâri, and that is a wonderful thought, with which to begin a school."

38. "Love is always a manifestation of bliss. The least shadow of pain falling upon it is always a sign of physicality and selfishness."

39. 'The West regards marriage as consisting in all that lies beyond the legal tie, while in India it is thought of as a bond thrown by society round two people to unite them together for all eternity. Those two must wed each other, whether they will or not, in life after life. Each acquires half of the merit of the other. And if one seems in this life to have fallen hopelessly behind, it is for the other only to wait and beat time, till he or she catches up again!"

40. "Consciousness is a mere film between two oceans, the subconscious and the superconscious."

41. "I could not believe my own ears when I heard Western people talking so much of consciousness! Consciousness? What does consciousness matter! Why, it is nothing compared with the unfathomable depths of the subconscious and the heights of the

superconscious! In this I could never be misled, for had I not seen Ramakrishna Paramahamsa gather in ten minutes, from a man's subconscious mind, the whole of his past, and determine from that his future and his powers?"

42. "All these (visions etc.) are side issues. They are not true Yoga. They may have a certain usefulness in establishing indirectly the truth of our statements. Even a little glimpse gives faith that there is something behind gross matter. Yet those who spend time on such things run into grave dangers.

    "These (psychic developments) are *frontier questions*! There can never be any certainty or stability of knowledge reached by their means. Did I not say they were 'frontier questions'? The boundary line is always shifting!"

43. "Now on tne Advaitic side it is held that the soul neither comes nor goes, and that all these spheres or layers of the universe are only so many varying products of Âkâsha and Prâna. That is to say, the lowest or most condensed is the Solar Sphere, consisting of the visible universe, in which Prana appears as physical force, and Akasha as sensible matter. The next is called the Lunar Sphere, which surrounds the Solar Sphere. This is not the moon at all, but the habitation of the gods; that is to say, Prana appears in it as psychic forces, and Akasha as Tanmatras or fine particles. Beyond this is the Electric Sphere; that is to say, a condition inseparable from Akasha, and you can hardly tell whether electricity is force or matter. Next is the Brahmaloka, where there is neither Prana nor Akasha, but both are merged into the mind-stuff, the primal energy. And here — there being neither Prana nor Akasha — the Jiva contemplates the whole universe as Samashti or the sum total of Mahat or mind. This

appears as Purusha, an abstract Universal Soul, yet not the Absolute, for still there is multiplicity. From this the Jiva finds at last that Unity which is the end. Advaitism says that these are the visions which arise in succession before the Jiva, who himself neither goes nor comes, and that in the same way this present vision has been projected. The projection (Srishti) and dissolution must take place in the same order, only one means going backward and the other coming out.

"Now, as each individual can only see his own universe, that universe is created with his bondage and goes away with his liberation, although it remains for others who are in bondage. Now, name and form constitute the universe. A wave in the ocean is wave only in so far as it is bound by name and form. If the wave subsides, it is the ocean, but that name-and-form has immediately vanished forever, so that the name and form of a wave could never be without the water that was fashioned into the wave by them. Yet the name and form themselves were not the wave; they die as soon as ever it returns to water, but other names and forms live on in relation to other waves. This name-and-form is called Maya and the water is Brahman. The wave was nothing but water all the time, yet as a wave it had the name and form. Again this name-and-form cannot remain for one moment separated from the wave, although the wave, as water, can remain eternally separate from name and form. But because the name and form can never be separated, they can never be said to exist. Yet they are not zero. This is called Maya."

44. "I am the servant of the servants of the servants of Buddha. Who was there ever like him? — the Lord — who never performed one action for himself —

with a heart that embraced the whole world! So full of pity that he — prince and monk — would give his life to save a little goat! So loving that he sacrificed himself to the hunger of a tigress! — to the hospitality of a pariah and blessed him! And he came into my room when I was a boy, and I fell at his feet! For I knew it was the Lord Himself!"

45. "He (Shuka) is the ideal Paramahamsa. To him alone amongst men was it given to drink a handful of the waters of that one undivided Ocean of Sat-Chit-Ânanda — Existence, Knowledge, and Bliss Absolute! Most saints die, having heard only the thunder of its waves upon the shore. A few gain the vision, and still fewer, taste of It. But he drank of the Sea of Bliss!"

46. "What is this idea of Bhakti without renunciation? It is most pernicious."

47. "We worship neither pain nor pleasure. We seek through either to come at that which transcends them both."

48. "Shankaracharya had caught the rhythm of the Vedas, the national cadence. Indeed I always imagine that he had some vision such as mine when he was young, and recovered the ancient music that way. Anyway, his whole life's work is nothing but that, the throbbing of the beauty of the Vedas and the Upanishads."

49. "Though the love of a mother is in some ways greater, yet the whole world takes the love of man and woman as the type (of the soul's relation to God). *No other has such tremendous idealising power.* The beloved actually becomes what he is imagined to be. This love transforms its object."

50. "Is it so easy to be Janaka — to sit on a throne absolutely unattached, caring nothing for wealth or

fame, for wife or child? One after another in the West has told me that he has reached this. But I could only say, 'Such great men are not born in India!'".

51 "Never forget to say to yourself and to teach to your children, as the difference between a firefly and the blazing sun, between the infinite ocean and a little pond, between a mustard seed and the mountain Meru, such is the difference between the householder and the Sannyasin!

"Everything is fraught with fear: Renunciation alone is fearless.

"Blessed be even the fraudulent Sâdhus and those who have failed to carry out their vows, inasmuch as they also have witnessed to their ideal and so are in some degree the cause of the success of others!

"Let us never, never, forget our ideal!"

52 "The river is pure that flows, the monk is pure that goes!"

53. "The Sannyasin who thinks of gold, to desire it, commits suicide."

54. "What do I care if Mohammed *was* a good man, or Buddha? Does that altar my goodness or evil? Let us be good for our own sake on our own responsibility."

55. "You people in this country are so afraid of losing your in-di-vid-u-al-i-ty! Why, you are not individuals yet. When you realise your whole nature, you will attain your true individuality, not before. There is another thing I am constantly hearing in this country, and that is that we should live in harmony with nature. Don't you know that all the progress ever made in the world was made by conquering nature? We are to resist nature at every point if we are to make any progress."

56. "In India they tell me I ought not to teach Advaita Vedanta to the people at large; but I say, I can make even a child understand it. You cannot begin too early to teach the highest spiritual truths."

57. "The less you read, the better. Read the Gita and other good works on Vedanta. That is all you need. The present system of education is all wrong. The mind is crammed with facts before it knows how to think. Control of the mind should be taught first. If I had my education to get over again and had any voice in the matter, I would learn to master my mind first, and then gather facts if I wanted them. It takes people a long time to learn things because they can't concentrate their minds at will."

58. "If a bad time comes, what of that? The pendulum must swing back to the other side. But that is no better. The thing to do is to stop it."

3

Swami Vivekananda: Paradoxical Prophet

Referred to in newspapers as the "Cyclonic Hindu," he was a dynamo of energy — not restless, but controlled. He came to bring peace and a sword, and was at the eye of many a storm. Praised and cursed, lionized and ostracized, loyally followed and shabbily betrayed, Swamiji in his brief thirty-nine years experienced all the vicissitudes to which a public figure can be exposed ; and he held aloft above it all, the message of a prophet, the mission of a prince and the character of a saint.

The first paradoxical aspect of the Swami's life to be noted here is the fact that although he was monk par excellence, he was also a dedicated patriot . That he was a monk and the embodiment of renunciation and the strict adherence to vows, is obvious to those who know his life. After all, the poem he composed, "Song of the Sannyasin," was the perfect picture of his own nature — the life-style he preferred above all others when he could obtain it. He was the natural-born leader of Sri Ramakrishna's monastic band and counted the founding of the Monastery at Belur on the Ganges as probably his greatest work.

But how he loved India! He thought about her future and her welfare and her people, day and night. One night, in the state of New York, a brother-disciple happened to come into his room and discover him lying on the floor, sleepless. When asked why he did not use his bed he replied, "I could not sleep up there in all that comfort, thinking of the millions of my countrymen who have no place to lay their heads." Page after page of the *Complete Works* is devoted to his visions and plans for the nation.

Jealousy was the national weakness: people would have to learn to pull together if there was to be a nation called India. He did not talk about nationalism in terms of revolution or violent overthrow; rather he believed the Indian people had yet to deserve their political freedom, through the independence of their inner spirit and he would illustrate this with stories of the Rajputs, of the Rani of Jhansi and of Guru Govind Singh, and Sivaji.

Yet of all these heroes, the greatest to him was Buddha. He said, "Buddha is my ishta (chosen ideal)." That calmness, that detachment, that self-forgetful benevolence, the welfare of all creatures. India, he reminded us, must never put politics above religion. "I am no politician," he warned, "and no one must put political implication to my declarations." The monk, he said, has no nationality and belongs to no religion. He did not talk about nationality and nation-making; he talked about "man-making." Yet, says Sister Nivedita, his British Disciple, the resentment he felt at the suffering of his country made him appear to her as one who "wore the armour of the warrior under the habit of the monk."

How can we absorb this very evident contrast in Swamiji's life?

Perhaps we can do so with his own great idea of synthesis: that to renounce really means to conquer. Like Sri Ramakrishna before him, he wanted renunciation to be positive, to come through strength and never through weakness. Strong thinking, strong feeling, strong will, were required. "Our ochre robe," he told Nivedita, "is the robe of death on the field of battle." He put out his whole heart and soul for his own land but when the time came to drop it, he wrote to Miss Josephine McLeod, "After all, Joe, I am only the boy who used to listen with rapt wonderment to the wonderful words of Ramakrishna under the banyan at Dakshineswar....working and activities, doing good and so forth are all superimpositions."

In general, this intensity of Swami Vivekananda's emotion stands over against the rationalism, dispassion and serenity which characterized his behavior, as another of the dichotomies. If one reads his letters and talks, one has a picture of how passionately, how vehemently, this man could feel. "I wouldn't give a straw," he said one day, "for the person who is incapable of appreciating a love song." In that mood he would sing the songs the Gopis sang, or come out with one of the many Persian poems he had memorized in his student days. His great weakness was his own mother: he worried all his life over the grief she had experienced on his account and how he might make up to her for that. When his stenographer and disciple, J.J. Goodwin died of malaria in India, he was all broken up for several days, and he used to lament over the weakness of his feelings for his friends. Most intense of all was his feeling for his Master and the Holy Mother.

A Contrast with his Impersonality

Yet this is the same person who, during a teaching retreat with Western disciples suddenly announced that he would have to be alone, and went off into the forest, remaining there for ten hours at a stretch. "A leader," he said on another occasion, "must be impersonal. I see persons giving me almost the whole of their love. But I must not give anyone the whole of mine in return, for then the work would be ruined." Too much sentiment hurts work, he used to say. In him discretion always came to the rescue and would mercilessly demolish the sentiment which so easily welled up in him. "Often I say strange and angry things," he told a friend, "yet remember that in my heart I never seriously mean to preach anything but love!" Sri Ramakrishna had called him "outwardly a jnani, inwardly a bhakta."

In order better to control his all-too-ready sympathies, he would avoid staying in any one place very long. Swamiji used to say to people, about meditation, "strive to realize yourself there without the slightest trace of emotion." And once again we can find the resolution of this internal struggle in his message to us. This was his prayer for Nivedita: "It is immense power — irresistible — that I pray for you, and, if possible, along with it infinite peace..." To all of us he prescribed the madness of love, but in it no bondage. If people sinned against us, what should we do? We must love them till it is impossible for them to resist us. One suspects that Gandhi must have read that.

Money in the life of Swami Vivekananda

Another paradox was that he was as quick to dispose of money as he was to raise it. Like a child he could gleefully calculate how was coming in through lectures to cover the expenses, and then would forget all about it. In his childhood, his mother would have to lock him up whenever beggars came around, because the boy was likely to hand over to them anything in the house that was valuable. On one such occasion he threw clothes out the window to them. Yet he wanted to accumulate funds — he told Sister Nivedita she would have to go out and raise the money for her school — and he tried repeatedly to get his mother and brothers out of poverty by making special provisions for them from what he could collect.

But money had this tendency to drift through his fingers. It eluded him, as he declared it always would elude a monk. The money for his trip to the West had to be collected by the Rajas and his friends in Madras twice. In fact he several times refused it. The first collection he had distributed among the poor: "Let us test the Lord," he told them; "if He really wants me to go, all the money will come again." Of course it did. Then there were certain close friends, such as Miss McLeod and Mrs. Ole Bull, from whom he did not hesitate to beg if necessary. Later, Swami Vivekananda was to be accused of being poor at taking care of money; probably he admired those who handled it well, for he taught that to go from the perfect utilization of material means to their perfect renunciation, was just a short step. If one can do the one, one can manage the other.

One of the more fascinating of the anomalies in Swami Vivekananda is the scintillating interplay of a god-like bent for austerity and asceticism on the one hand, and a very down-to-earth humanness on the other. This is the man who was shocked by the way his Western friends always gave expression to their feelings — of pain, admiration or surprise — yet who, in his letters to the Hale sisters for instance, bubbled over with fun, teasing and jokes of all kinds. He had a superb sense of humor; we may recall his replies when Christians would ask him if the Hindu mothers threw their baby girls to the crocodiles: "Yes," he replied on one occasion, "and nowadays all the babies are born to men." One day in America he finished the food on his plate, then picked up the plate and licked it clean. "Oh, Swami!" his hostess exclaimed in horror.

"That's the trouble with you people," Swamiji said, "You want to make everything so nice and proper on the outside." Those were indeed Victorian days.

This is the man who trained his own novices so strictly that he threatened with expulsion a lad who had delivered a letter in person, to a house where women renunciates were living. Yet he had an easy forgiveness, and could declare on another day that asceticism was savagery and fiendish, and spoke of the "torture of religion." When the diagnosis of cancer was made, on Sri Ramakrishna's sore throat, at Cossipore, the nature of cancer was not well understood. The doctor had warned the boys nursing him of the danger of contagion. Narendra (the future Vivekananda) came into the room when they were sitting around discussing what to do. At once he picked up the cup of gruel which the Master had not been able to finish and swallowed all of it. This put an end to all the talk and hesitation. Such was the one chosen to be their leader. Yet see how unassumingly he would enter the kitchen of some Western friend and begin to prepare a curry for the devotees, or accept a pipe of tobacco, smoke it and throw all the ashes on the carpet!

Swamiji could tell the devotees in California that the reason for his success at the Chicago Parliament was his lifelong mastery over every form of sexual expression. Still, realizing that Goodwin, his secretary, was living with him in a house full of vegetarians and was not one himself, he had the tenderness to send him out with money to buy himself a restaurant meal. We know that when he visited in the home of Margaret Noble (Nivedita) in Northern Ireland, he went walking one day with her young brother. "My boy," he said, "it is my religion which has deprived your family of your beef. Come on, let us go to this cafe and buy you a steak!" In London people would remark on how relaxed and natural he was, just before giving a powerful and mesmerizing lecture; yet the same man would come back from his periodic retreats in such a lofty mood one would not dare approach him.

In attempting to comprehend this particular paradox we may think of two of the Swami's observations. One is that religion should be the most joyful thing in the world. And the other is that one should look for greatness in the little things of a person's life — what they eat and wear and how they speak to their subordinates. He looked for and saw both of these in his Master's life as well.

His Language

Swami Vivekananda used simple language in presenting to us the profoundest philosophical truths. It makes us forget or ignore what a scholar he was. It would be an injustice to call his style "popular": for it was never shallow. It was clear, direct, uncomplicated and appealing. Wherever he went among his own people, the peasants loved him just as much as the statesmen. Boatmen on the river would watch for his return; servants would dispute with guests for the chance to do him service. Swamiji spoke constantly of how the future would belong to "women and the masses", and described his presentation as an attempt to put the highest Vedantic truths so simply that a child could understand them. This, the speaker who at both Harvard and Columbia was asked to take the position of guest lecturer in philosophy and Sanskrit! We have to realize that he had read widely and so retentive was his memory that he could give the substance of whole pages of his favorite reading — the encyclopedia — or repeat verbatim something he had heard only twice. At Belur Math he urged upon the young trainees the study of the latest researches and critical methods in sciences and letters as well as religion. Because of his popular, unprofessorial style the academic world, East and West, has not appreciated Swami Vivekananda; you would not find his name in the bibliographies of the textbooks on Hinduism, and one is ashamed to say that even great men of the "Hindu

Renaissance", who freely used his ideas and insights, felt, for various reasons, that they could not afford to acknowledge the source.

We come, finally, to that paradox which may be the most important of all, the traditionalist versus the innovator — the orthodox Hindu and the Promethean proletarian. Swamiji was both a preserver of the past and a harbinger of the future; truth for him did not depend on whether it was old or new. You recall that in ancient Greece, mythology told of a monster called Scylla and a whirlpool called Charybdis, with ships having to ply narrowly between the two. Now when Swami Vivekananda returned to India this is what he said: "There are the two great obstacles on our path in India, the Scylla of old orthodoxy and the Charybdis of modern European civilization. Of these two I vote for the old orthodoxyfor the old orthodox man may be ignorant, but he has strength and stands on his own feet." Yet the Swami himself was in many ways unorthodox. He saw the Indians of his day as chained — by superstitions, by political subjugation, by sheer *tamas*. He would shock them by crossing the seas, eating food from a Muslim vendor, bringing Western students into high-caste homes, challenging outmoded ideas. He told pupils of a Calcutta art school, "Why do you always have to represent Kali in exactly the same way: same pose, same ornaments, same expression; where is your creativity?" Asked about socialism, the political rage of the day, he replied, "Why not? Let it be tried. Half a loaf is better than no bread!"

With all that, his reverence for the Vedas is extraordinary, beyond question; his respect for and delight in the *tirthas*, the places of pilgrimage is incomparable; he vehemently upholds homage to the line of teachers, and as a result of his Master's revelations he finally places himself at the feet of the Hindu gods as well. His conversations were filled with new ideas relating to the problems of man — and particularly of woman — for he was a pro-feminist and deeply dyed with Western humanism; yet he could give this message to the women of modern times: "If, in the midst of your new tasks, in office, school or kitchen, you will remember now and then to say 'Siva! Siva!', that will be worship enough."

Yet again, he said, "I am no preacher of momentary social reform. I am not trying to remedy evils. I only ask you to follow the ways of your ancestors and realize more and more fully the Vedantic ideal. But this must be brought down out of the caves and monasteries and into the huts of the cobblers and fishermen." And he felt, you know, that it was in America that Advaita could come into its own.

So let me close by saying that if Swami Vivekananda seems to you to be plagued by contradictions, remember, it is as if he were experimenting with different brands of Hinduism, to the very end. He placed the stress where he knew it was needed. "A foolish consistency, " Emerson reminds us, "is the hobgoblin of little minds." There was nothing little about Vivekananda. Again, he is paradoxical because Hinduism itself is paradoxical, and he was the embodiment of it.

4

Addresses at the Parliament of Religions

At the World's Parliament of Religions, Chicago
11th September, 1893

Sisters and Brothers of America,

It fills my heart with joy unspeakable to rise in response to the warm and cordial welcome which you have given us. I thank you in the name of the most ancient order of monks in the world; I thank you in the name of the mother of religions; and I thank you in the name of millions and millions of Hindu people of all classes and sects.

My thanks, also, to some of the speakers on this platform who, referring to the delegates from the Orient, have told you that these men from far-off nations may well claim the honour of bearing to different lands the idea of toleration. I am proud to belong to a religion which has taught the world both tolerance and universal acceptance. We believe not only in universal toleration, but we accept all religions as true. I am proud to belong to a nation which has sheltered the persecuted and the refugees of all religions and all nations of the earth. I am proud to tell you that we have gathered in our bosom the purest remnant of the Israelites, who came to Southern

India and took refuge with us in the very year in which their holy temple was shattered to pieces by Roman tyranny. I am proud to belong to the religion which has sheltered and is still fostering the remnant of the grand Zoroastrian nation. I will quote to you, brethren, a few lines from a hymn which I remember to have repeated from my earliest boyhood, which is every day repeated by millions of human beings: "*As the different streams having their sources in different places all mingle their water in the sea, so, O Lord, the different paths which men take through different tendencies, various though they appear, crooked or straight, all lead to Thee.*"

The present convention, which is one of the most august assemblies ever held, is in itself a vindication, a declaration to the world of the wonderful doctrine preached in the Gita: "*Whosoever comes to Me, through whatsoever form, I reach him; all men are struggling through paths which in the end lead to me.*" Sectarianism, bigotry, and its horrible descendant, fanaticism, have long possessed this beautiful earth. They have filled the earth with violence, drenched it often and often with human blood, destroyed civilisation and sent whole nations to despair. Had it not been for these horrible demons, human society would be far more advanced than it is now. But their time is come; and I fervently hope that the bell that tolled this morning in honour of this convention may be the death-knell of all fanaticism, of all persecutions with the sword or with the pen, and of all uncharitable feelings between persons wending their way to the same goal.

Why we Disagree, 15th September, 1893

I will tell you a little story. You have heard the eloquent speaker who has just finished say, "Let us cease from abusing each other," and he was very sorry that there should be always so much variance.

But I think I should tell you a story which would illustrate the cause of this variance. A frog lived in a well. It had lived there for a long time. It was born there and brought up there, and yet was a little, small frog. Of course the evolutionists were not there then to tell us whether the frog lost its eyes or not, but, for our story's sake, we must take it for granted that it had its eyes, and that it every day cleansed the water of all the worms and bacilli that lived in it with an energy that would do credit to our modern bacteriologists. In this way it went on and became a little sleek and fat. Well, one day another frog that lived in the sea came and fell into the well.

"Where are you from?"

"I am from the sea."

"The sea! How big is that? Is it as big as my well?" and he took a leap from one side of the well to the other.

"My friend," said the frog of the sea, "how do you compare the sea with your little well?"

Then the frog took another leap and asked, "Is your sea so big?"

"What nonsense you speak, to compare the sea with your well!"

"Well, then," said the frog of the well, "nothing can be bigger than my well; there can be nothing bigger than this; this fellow is a liar, so turn him out."

That has been the difficulty all the while.

I am a Hindu. I am sitting in my own little well and thinking that the whole world is my little well. The Christian sits in his little well and thinks the whole world is his well. The Mohammedan sits in his little well and thinks that is the whole world. I have to thank you of America for the great attempt you are making to break down the barriers of this little world of ours, and hope that, in the future, the Lord will help you to accomplish your purpose

Paper on Hinduism, Read at the Parliament on 19th September, 1893

Three religions now stand in the world which have come down to us from time prehistoric — Hinduism, Zoroastrianism and Judaism. They have all received tremendous shocks and all of them prove by their survival their internal strength. But while Judaism failed to absorb Christianity and was driven out of its place of birth by its all-conquering daughter, and a handful of Parsees is all that remains to tell the tale of their grand religion, sect after sect arose in India and seemed to shake the religion of the Vedas to its very foundations, but like the waters of the seashore in a tremendous earthquake it receded only for a while, only to return in an all-absorbing flood, a thousand times more vigorous, and when the tumult of the rush was over, these sects were all sucked in, absorbed, and assimilated into the immense body of the mother faith.

From the high spiritual flights of the Vedanta philosophy, of which the latest discoveries of science seem like echoes, to the low ideas of idolatry with its multifarious mythology, the agnosticism of the Buddhists, and the atheism of the Jains, each and all have a place in the Hindu's religion.

Where then, the question arises, where is the common centre to which all these widely diverging radii converge? Where is the common basis upon which all these seemingly hopeless contradictions rest? And this is the question I shall attempt to answer.

The Hindus have received their religion through revelation, the Vedas. They hold that the Vedas are without beginning and without end. It may sound ludicrous to this audience, how a book can be without beginning or end. But by the Vedas no books are meant. They mean the accumulated treasury of spiritual laws discovered by different persons in different times. Just as the law of gravitation existed before its discovery, and would exist if all humanity forgot it, so is it with the laws that govern the spiritual world. The moral, ethical, and spiritual relations between soul and soul and between individual spirits and the Father of all spirits, were there before their discovery, and would remain even if we forgot them.

The discoverers of these laws are called Rishis, and we honour them as perfected beings. I am glad to tell this audience that some of the very greatest of them were women. Here it may be said that these laws as laws may be without end, but they must have had a beginning. The Vedas teach us that creation is without beginning or end. Science is said to have proved that the sum total of cosmic energy is always the same. Then, if there was a time when nothing existed, where was all this manifested energy? Some say it was in a potential form in God. In that case God is sometimes potential and sometimes kinetic, which would make Him mutable. Everything mutable is a compound, and everything compound must undergo that change which is called destruction. So God would die, which is absurd. Therefore there never was a time when there was no creation.

If I may be allowed to use a simile, creation and creator are two lines, without beginning and without end, running parallel to each other. God is the ever active providence, by whose power systems after systems are being evolved out of chaos, made to run for a time and again destroyed. This is what the Brahmin boy repeats every day: *"The sun and the moon, the Lord created like the suns and moons of previous cycles."* And this agrees with modern science.

Here I stand and if I shut my eyes, and try to conceive my existence, "I", "I", "I", what is the idea before me? The idea of a body. Am I, then, nothing but a combination of material substances? The Vedas declare, "No". I am a spirit living in a body. I am not the body. The body will die, but I shall not die. Here am I in this body; it will fall, but I shall go on living. I had also a past. The soul was not created, for creation means a combination which means a certain future dissolution. If then the soul was created, it must die. Some are born happy, enjoy perfect health, with beautiful body, mental vigour and all wants supplied. Others are born miserable, some are without hands or feet, others again are idiots and only drag on a wretched existence. Why, if they are all created, why does a just and merciful God create one happy and another unhappy, why is He so partial? Nor would it mend matters in the least to hold that those who are miserable in this life will be happy in a future one. Why should a man be miserable even here in the reign of a just and merciful God?

In the second place, the idea of a creator God does not explain the anomaly, but simply expresses the cruel fiat of an all-powerful being. There must have been causes, then, before his birth, to make a man miserable or happy and those were his past actions.

Are not all the tendencies of the mind and the body accounted for by inherited aptitude? Here are two parallel lines of existence — one of the mind, the other of matter. If matter and its transformations answer for all that we have, there is no necessity for supposing the existence of a soul. But it cannot be proved that thought has been evolved out of matter, and if a philosophical monism is inevitable, spiritual monism is certainly logical and no less desirable than a materialistic monism; but neither of these is necessary here.

We cannot deny that bodies acquire certain tendencies from heredity, but those tendencies only mean the physical configuration, through which a peculiar mind alone can act in a peculiar way. There are other tendencies peculiar to a soul caused by its past actions. And a soul with a certain tendency would by the laws of affinity take birth in a body which is the fittest instrument for the display of that tendency. This is in accord with science, for science wants to explain everything by habit, and habit is got through repetitions. So repetitions are necessary to explain the natural habits of a new-born soul. And since they were not obtained in this present life, they must have come down from past lives.

There is another suggestion. Taking all these for granted, how is it that I do not remember anything of my past life ? This can be easily explained. I am now speaking English. It is not my mother tongue, in fact no words of my mother tongue are now present in my consciousness; but let me try to bring them up, and they rush in. That shows that consciousness is only the surface of the mental ocean, and within its depths are stored up all our experiences. Try and struggle, they would come up and you would be conscious even of your past life.

This is direct and demonstrative evidence. Verification is the perfect proof of a theory, and here is the challenge thrown to the world by the Rishis. We have discovered the secret by which the very depths of the ocean of memory can be stirred up — try it and you would get a complete reminiscence of your past life.

So then the Hindu believes that he is a spirit. Him the sword cannot pierce — him the fire cannot burn — him the water cannot melt — him the air cannot dry. The Hindu believes that every soul is a circle whose circumference is nowhere, but whose centre is located in the body, and that death means the change of this centre from body to body. Nor is the soul bound by the conditions of matter. In its very essence it is free, unbounded, holy, pure, and perfect. But somehow or other it finds itself tied down to matter, and thinks of itself as matter.

Why should the free, perfect, and pure being be thus under the thraldom of matter, is the next question. How can the perfect soul be deluded into the belief that it is imperfect? We have been told that the Hindus shirk the question and say that no such question can be there. Some thinkers want to answer it by positing one or more quasi-perfect beings, and use big scientific names to fill up the gap. But naming is not explaining. The question remains the same. How can the perfect become the quasi-perfect; how can the pure, the absolute, change even a microscopic particle of its nature? But the Hindu is sincere. He does not want to take shelter under sophistry. He is brave enough to face the question in a manly fashion; and his answer is: "I do not know. I do not know how the perfect being, the soul, came to think of itself as imperfect, as joined to and conditioned by matter." But the fact is a fact for all that. It is a fact in everybody's consciousness that one thinks of oneself as the body. The Hindu does not attempt to explain why one thinks one is the body. The answer that it is the will of God is no explanation. This is nothing more than what the Hindu says, "I do not know."

Well, then, the human soul is eternal and immortal, perfect and infinite, and death means only a change of centre from one body to another. The present is determined by our past actions, and the future by the present. The soul will go on evolving up or reverting back from birth to birth and death to death. But here is another question: Is man a tiny boat in a tempest, raised one moment on the foamy crest of a billow and dashed down into a yawning chasm he next, rolling to and fro at the mercy of good and bad actions — a powerless, helpless wreck in an ever-raging, ever-rushing, uncompromising current of cause and effect; a little moth placed under the wheel of causation which rolls on crushing everything in its way and waits not for the widow's tears or the orphan's cry? The heart sinks at the idea, yet this is the law of Nature. Is there no hope? Is there no escape? — was the cry that went up from the bottom of the heart of despair. It reached the throne of mercy, and words of hope and consolation came down and inspired a Vedic sage, and he stood up before the world and in trumpet voice proclaimed the glad tidings: "Hear, ye children of immortal bliss! even ye that reside in higher spheres! I have found the Ancient One who is beyond all darkness, all delusion: knowing Him alone you shall be saved from death over again." "Children of immortal bliss" — what a sweet, what a hopeful name! Allow me to call you, brethren, by that sweet name — heirs of immortal bliss — yea, the Hindu refuses to call you sinners. Ye are the Children of God, the sharers of immortal bliss, holy and perfect beings. Ye divinities on earth — sinners! It is a sin to call a man so; it is a standing libel on human nature. Come up, O lions, and shake off the delusion that you are sheep; you are souls immortal, spirits free, blest and eternal; ye are not matter, ye are not bodies; matter is your servant, not you the servant of matter.

Thus it is that the Vedas proclaim not a dreadful combination of unforgiving laws, not an endless prison of cause and effect, but that at the head of all these laws, in and through every particle of matter and force, stands One "by whose command the wind blows, the fire burns, the clouds rain, and death stalks upon the earth."

And what is His nature?

He is everywhere, the pure and formless One, the

Almighty and the All-merciful. "Thou art our father, Thou art our mother, Thou art our beloved friend, Thou art the source of all strength; give us strength. Thou art He that beareth the burdens of the universe; help me bear the little burden of this life." Thus sang the Rishis of the Vedas. And how to worship Him? Through love. "He is to be worshipped as the one beloved, dearer than everything in this and the next life."

This is the doctrine of love declared in the Vedas, and let us see how it is fully developed and taught by Krishna, whom the Hindus believe to have been God incarnate on earth.

He taught that a man ought to live in this world like a lotus leaf, which grows in water but is never moistened by water; so a man ought to live in the world — his heart to God and his hands to work.

It is good to love God for hope of reward in this or the next world, but it is better to love God for love's sake, and the prayer goes: "Lord, I do not want wealth, nor children, nor learning. If it be Thy will, I shall go from birth to birth, but grant me this, that I may love Thee without the hope of reward — love unselfishly for love's sake." One of the disciples of Krishna, the then Emperor of India, was driven from his kingdom by his enemies and had to take shelter with his queen in a forest in the Himalayas, and there one day the queen asked him how it was that he, the most virtuous of men, should suffer so much misery. Yudhishthira answered, "Behold, my queen, the Himalayas, how grand and beautiful they are; I love them. They do not give me anything, but my nature is to love the grand, the beautiful, therefore I love them. Similarly, I love the Lord. He is the source of all beauty, of all sublimity. He is the only object to be loved; my nature is to love Him, and therefore I love. I do not pray for anything; I do not ask for anything. Let Him place me wherever He likes. I must love Him for love's sake. I cannot trade in love."

The Vedas teach that the soul is divine, only held in the bondage of matter; perfection will be reached when this bond will burst, and the word they use for it is therefore, Mukti — freedom, freedom from the bonds of imperfection, freedom from death and misery.

And this bondage can only fall off through the mercy of God, and this mercy comes on the pure. So purity is the condition of His mercy. How does that mercy act? He reveals Himself to the pure heart; the pure and the stainless see God, yea, even in this life; then and then only all the crookedness of the heart is made straight. Then all doubt ceases. He is no more the freak of a terrible law of causation. This is the very centre, the very vital conception of Hinduism. The Hindu does not want to live upon words and theories. If there are existences beyond the ordinary sensuous existence, he wants to come face to face with them. If there is a soul in him which is not matter, if there is an all-merciful universal Soul, he will go to Him direct. He must see Him, and that alone can destroy all doubts. So the best proof a Hindu sage gives about the soul, about God, is: "I have seen the soul; I have seen God." And that is the only condition of perfection. The Hindu religion does not consist in struggles and attempts to believe a certain doctrine or dogma, but in realising — not in believing, but in being and becoming.

Thus the whole object of their system is by constant struggle to become perfect, to become divine, to reach God and see God, and this reaching God, seeing God, becoming perfect even as the Father in Heaven is perfect, constitutes the religion of the Hindus.

And what becomes of a man when he attains perfection? He lives a life of bliss infinite. He enjoys infinite and perfect bliss, having obtained the only thing in which man ought to have pleasure, namely God, and enjoys the bliss with God.

So far all the Hindus are agreed. This is the common religion of all the sects of India; but, then, perfection is absolute, and the absolute cannot be two or three. It cannot have any qualities. It cannot be an individual. And so when a soul becomes perfect and absolute, it must become one with Brahman, and it would only realise the Lord as the perfection, the reality, of its own nature and existence, the existence absolute, knowledge absolute, and bliss absolute. We have often and often read this called the losing of individuality and becoming a stock or a stone.

"He jests at scars that never felt a wound."

I tell you it is nothing of the kind. If it is happiness to enjoy the consciousness of this small body, it must be greater happiness to enjoy the consciousness of two bodies, the measure of happiness increasing with the consciousness of an increasing number of bodies, the aim, the ultimate of happiness being reached when it would become a universal consciousness.

Therefore, to gain this infinite universal individuality, this miserable little prison-individuality must go. Then alone can death cease when I am alone with life, then alone can misery cease when I am one with happiness itself, then alone can all errors cease when I am one with knowledge itself; and this is the necessary scientific conclusion. Science has proved to me that physical individuality is a delusion, that really my body is one little continuously changing body in an unbroken ocean of matter; and Advaita (unity) is the necessary conclusion with my other counterpart, soul.

Science is nothing but the finding of unity. As soon as science would reach perfect unity, it would stop from further progress, because it would reach the goal. Thus Chemistry could not progress farther when it would discover one element out of which all other could be made. Physics would stop when it would be able to fulfill its services in discovering one energy of which all others are but manifestations, and the science of religion become perfect when it would discover Him who is the one life in a universe of death, Him who is the constant basis of an ever-changing world. One who is the only Soul of which all souls are but delusive manifestations. Thus is it, through multiplicity and duality, that the ultimate unity is reached. Religion can go no farther. This is the goal of all science.

All science is bound to come to this conclusion in the long run. Manifestation, and not creation, is the word of science today, and the Hindu is only glad that what he has been cherishing in his bosom for ages is going to be taught in more forcible language, and with further light from the latest conclusions of science.

Descend we now from the aspirations of philosophy to the religion of the ignorant. At the very outset, I may tell you that there is no *polytheism* in India. In every temple, if one stands by and listens, one will find the worshippers applying all the attributes of God, including omnipresence, to the images. It is not polytheism, nor would the name henotheism explain the situation. "The rose called by any other name would smell as sweet." Names are not explanations.

I remember, as a boy, hearing a Christian missionary preach to a crowd in India. Among other sweet things he was telling them was that if he gave a blow to their idol with his stick, what could it do? One of his hearers sharply answered, "If I abuse your God, what can He do?" "You would be punished," said the preacher, "when you die." "So my idol will punish you when you die," retorted the Hindu.

The tree is known by its fruits. When I have seen amongst them that are called idolaters, men, the like of whom in morality and spirituality and love I have never seen anywhere, I stop and ask myself, "Can sin beget holiness?"

Superstition is a great enemy of man, but bigotry is worse. Why does a Christian go to church? Why is the cross holy? Why is the face turned toward the sky in prayer? Why are there so many images in the Catholic Church? Why are there so many images in the minds of Protestants when they pray? My brethren, we can no more think about anything without a mental image than we can live without breathing. By the law of association, the material image calls up the mental idea and *vice versa*. This is why the Hindu uses an external symbol when he worships. He will tell you, it helps to keep his mind fixed on the Being to whom he prays. He knows as well as you do that the image is not God, is not omnipresent. After all, how much does omnipresence mean to almost the whole world? It stands merely as a word, a symbol. Has God superficial area? If not, when we repeat that word "omnipresent", we think of the extended sky or of space, that is all.

As we find that somehow or other, by the laws of our mental constitution, we have to associate our ideas of infinity with the image of the blue sky, or of the sea, so we naturally connect our idea of holiness with the image of a church, a mosque, or a cross. The Hindus have associated the idea of holiness, purity, truth, omnipresence, and such other ideas with different images and forms. But with this difference that while some people devote their whole lives to their idol of a church and never rise higher, because with them religion means an intellectual assent to certain doctrines and doing good to their fellows, the whole religion of the Hindu is centred in realisation. Man is to become divine by realising the divine. Idols or temples or churches or books are only the supports, the helps, of his spiritual childhood: but on and on he must progress.

He must not stop anywhere. *"External worship, material worship,"* say the scriptures, *"is the lowest stage; struggling to rise high, mental prayer is the next stage, but the highest stage is when the Lord has been realised."* Mark, the same earnest man who is kneeling before the idol tells you, *"Him the Sun cannot express, nor the moon, nor the stars, the lightning cannot express Him, nor what we speak of as fire; through Him they shine."* But he does not abuse any one's idol or call its worship sin. He recognises in it a necessary stage of life. *"The child is father of the man."* Would it be right for an old man to say that childhood is a sin or youth a sin?

If a man can realise his divine nature with the help of an image, would it be right to call that a sin? Nor even when he has passed that stage, should he call it an error. To the Hindu, man is not travelling from error to truth, but from truth to truth, from lower to higher truth. To him all the religions, from the lowest fetishism to the highest absolutism, mean so many attempts of the human soul to grasp and realise the Infinite, each determined by the conditions of its birth and association, and each of these marks a stage of progress; and every soul is a young eagle soaring higher and higher, gathering more and more strength, till it reaches the Glorious Sun.

Unity in variety is the plan of nature, and the Hindu has recognised it. Every other religion lays down certain fixed dogmas, and tries to force society to adopt them. It places before society only one coat which must fit Jack and John and Henry, all alike. If it does not fit John or Henry, he must go without a coat to cover his body. The Hindus have discovered that the absolute can only be realised, or thought of, or stated, through the relative, and the images, crosses, and crescents are simply so many symbols — so many pegs to hang the spiritual ideas on. It is not that this help is necessary for every one, but those that do not need it have no right to say that it is wrong. Nor is it compulsory in Hinduism.

One thing I must tell you. Idolatry in India does not mean anything horrible. It is not the mother of harlots. On the other hand, it is the attempt of undeveloped minds to grasp high spiritual truths. The Hindus have their faults, they sometimes have their exceptions; but mark this, they are always for punishing their own bodies, and never for cutting the throats of their neighbours. If the Hindu fanatic burns himself on the pyre, he never lights the fire of Inquisition. And even this cannot be laid at the door of his religion any more than the burning of witches can be laid at the door of Christianity.

To the Hindu, then, the whole world of religions is only a travelling, a coming up, of different men and women, through various conditions and circumstances, to the same goal. Every religion is only evolving a God out of the material man, and the same God is the inspirer of all of them. Why, then, are there so many contradictions? They are only apparent, says the Hindu. The contradictions come from the same truth adapting itself to the varying circumstances of different natures.

It is the same light coming through glasses of different colours. And these little variations are necessary for purposes of adaptation. But in the heart of everything the same truth reigns. The Lord has declared to the Hindu in His incarnation as Krishna, "*I am in every religion as the thread through a string of pearls. Wherever thou seest extraordinary holiness and extraordinary power raising and purifying humanity, know thou that I am there.*" And what has been the result? I challenge the world to find, throughout the whole system of Sanskrit philosophy, any such expression as that the Hindu alone will be saved and not others. Says Vyasa, "*We find perfect men even beyond the pale of our caste and creed.*" One thing more. How, then, can the Hindu, whose whole fabric of thought centres in God, believe in Buddhism which is agnostic, or in Jainism which is atheistic?

The Buddhists or the Jains do not depend upon God; but the whole force of their religion is directed to the great central truth in every religion, to evolve a God out of man. They have not seen the Father, but they have seen the Son. And he that hath seen the Son hath seen the Father also.

This, brethren, is a short sketch of the religious ideas of the Hindus. The Hindu may have failed to carry out all his plans, but if there is ever to be a universal religion, it must be one which will have no location in place or time; which will be infinite like the God it will preach, and whose sun will shine upon the followers of Krishna and of Christ, on saints and sinners alike; which will not be Brahminic or Buddhistic, Christian or Mohammedan, but the sum total of all these, and still have infinite space for development; which in its catholicity will embrace in its infinite arms, and find a place for, every human being, from the lowest grovelling savage not far removed from the brute, to the highest man towering by the virtues of his head and heart almost above humanity, making society stand in awe of him and doubt his human nature. It will be a religion which will have no place for persecution or intolerance in its polity, which will recognise divinity in every man and woman, and whose whole scope, whose whole force, will be created in aiding humanity to realise its own true, divine nature.

Offer such a religion, and all the nations will follow you. Asoka's council was a council of the Buddhist faith. Akbar's, though more to the purpose, was only a parlour-meeting. It was reserved for America to proclaim to all quarters of the globe that the Lord is in every religion.

May He who is the Brahman of the Hindus, the Ahura-Mazda of the Zoroastrians, the Buddha of the Buddhists, the Jehovah of the Jews, the Father in Heaven of the Christians, give strength to you to carry out your noble idea! The star arose in the East; it travelled steadily towards the West, sometimes dimmed and sometimes effulgent, till it made a circuit of the world; and now it is again rising on the very horizon of the East, the borders of the Sanpo, a thousandfold more effulgent than it ever was before.

Hail, Columbia, motherland of liberty! It has been given to thee, who never dipped her hand in her neighbour's blood, who never found out that the shortest way of becoming rich was by robbing one's neighbours, it has been given to thee to march at the vanguard of civilisation with the flag of harmony.

Religion not the Crying Need of India, 20th September, 1893

Christians must always be ready for good criticism, and I hardly think that you will mind if I make a little criticism. You Christians, who are so fond of sending out missionaries to save the soul of the heathen — why do you not try to save their bodies from starvation? In India, during the terrible famines, thousands died from hunger, yet you Christians did nothing. You erect churches all through India, but the crying evil in the East is not religion — they have religion enough — but it is bread that the suffering millions of burning India cry out for with parched throats. They ask us for bread, but we give them stones. It is an insult to a starving people to offer them religion; it is an insult to a starving man to teach him metaphysics. In India a priest that preached for money would lose caste and be spat upon by the people. I came here to seek aid for my impoverished people, and

I fully realised how difficult it was to get help for heathens from Christians in a Christian land.

BUDDHISM, THE FULFILMENT OF HINDUISM, 26TH SEPTEMBER, 1893

I am not a Buddhist, as you have heard, and yet I am. If China, or Japan, or Ceylon follow the teachings of the Great Master, India worships him as God incarnate on earth. You have just now heard that I am going to criticise Buddhism, but by that I wish you to understand only this. Far be it from me to criticise him whom I worship as God incarnate on earth. But our views about Buddha are that he was not understood properly by his disciples. The relation between Hinduism (by Hinduism, I mean the religion of the Vedas) and what is called Buddhism at the present day is nearly the same as between Judaism and Christianity. Jesus Christ was a Jew, and Shâkya Muni was a Hindu. The Jews rejected Jesus Christ, nay, crucified him, and the Hindus have accepted Shâkya Muni as God and worship him. But the real difference that we Hindus want to show between modern Buddhism and what we should understand as the teachings of Lord Buddha lies principally in this: Shâkya Muni came to preach nothing new. He also, like Jesus, came to fulfil and not to destroy. Only, in the case of Jesus, it was the old people, the Jews, who did not understand him, while in the case of Buddha, it was his own followers who did not realise the import of his teachings. As the Jew did not understand the fulfilment of the Old Testament, so the Buddhist did not understand the fulfilment of the truths of the Hindu religion. Again, I repeat, Shâkya Muni came not to destroy, but he was the fulfilment, the logical conclusion, the logical development of the religion of the Hindus.

The religion of the Hindus is divided into two parts: the ceremonial and the spiritual. The spiritual portion is specially studied by the monks.

In that there is no caste. A man from the highest caste and a man from the lowest may become a monk in India, and the two castes become equal. In religion there is no caste; caste is simply a social institution. Shâkya Muni himself was a monk, and it was his glory that he had the large-heartedness to bring out the truths from the hidden Vedas and through them broadcast all over the world. He was the first being in the world who brought missionarising into practice — nay, he was the first to conceive the idea of proselytising.

The great glory of the Master lay in his wonderful sympathy for everybody, especially for the ignorant and the poor. Some of his disciples were Brahmins. When Buddha was teaching, Sanskrit was no more the spoken language in India. It was then only in the books of the learned. Some of Buddha's Brahmins disciples wanted to translate his teachings into Sanskrit, but he distinctly told them, "I am for the poor, for the people; let me speak in the tongue of the people." And so to this day the great bulk of his teachings are in the vernacular of that day in India.

Whatever may be the position of philosophy, whatever may be the position of metaphysics, so long as there is such a thing as death in the world, so long as there is such a thing as weakness in the human heart, so long as there is a cry going out of the heart of man in his very weakness, there shall be a faith in God.

On the philosophic side the disciples of the Great Master dashed themselves against the eternal rocks of the Vedas and could not crush them, and on the other side they took away from the nation that eternal God to which every one, man or woman, clings so fondly. And the result was that Buddhism had to die a natural death in India. At the present day there is not one who calls oneself a Buddhist in India, the land of its birth.

But at the same time, Brahminism lost something — that reforming zeal, that wonderful sympathy and charity for everybody, that wonderful heaven which Buddhism had brought to the masses and which had rendered Indian society so great that a Greek historian who wrote about India of that time was led to say that no Hindu was known to tell an untruth and no Hindu woman was known to be unchaste.

Hinduism cannot live without Buddhism, nor Buddhism without Hinduism. Then realise what the separation has shown to us, that the Buddhists cannot stand without the brain and philosophy of the Brahmins, nor the Brahmin without the heart of the Buddhist. This separation between the Buddhists and the Brahmins is the cause of the downfall of India. That is why India is populated by three hundred millions of beggars, and that is why India has been the slave of conquerors for the last thousand years. Let us then join the wonderful intellect of the Brahmins with the heart, the noble soul, the wonderful humanising power of the Great Master.

Address at the Final Session, 27th September, 1893

The World's Parliament of Religions has become an accomplished fact, and the merciful Father has helped those who laboured to bring it into existence, and crowned with success their most unselfish labour.

My thanks to those noble souls whose large hearts and love of truth first dreamed this wonderful dream and then realised it. My thanks to the shower of liberal sentiments that has overflowed this platform. My thanks to his enlightened audience for their uniform kindness to me and for their appreciation of every thought that tends to smooth the friction of religions. A few jarring notes were heard from time to time in this harmony. My special thanks to them, for they have, by their striking contrast, made general harmony the sweeter.

Much has been said of the common ground of religious unity. I am not going just now to venture my own theory. But if any one here hopes that this unity will come by the triumph of any one of the religions and the destruction of the others, to him I say, "Brother, yours is an impossible hope." Do I wish that the Christian would become Hindu? God forbid. Do I wish that the Hindu or Buddhist would become Christian? God forbid.

The seed is put in the ground, and earth and air and water are placed around it. Does the seed become the earth; or the air, or the water? No. It becomes a plant, it develops after the law of its own growth, assimilates the air, the earth, and the water, converts them into plant substance, and grows into a plant.

Similar is the case with religion. The Christian is not to become a Hindu or a Buddhist, nor a Hindu or a Buddhist to become a Christian. But each must assimilate the spirit of the others and yet preserve his individuality and grow according to his own law of growth.

If the Parliament of Religions has shown anything to the world it is this: It has proved to the world that holiness, purity and charity are not the exclusive possessions of any church in the world, and that every system has produced men and women of the most exalted character. In the face of this evidence, if anybody dreams of the exclusive survival of his own religion and the destruction of the others, I pity him from the bottom of my heart, and point out to him that upon the banner of every religion will soon be written, in spite of resistance: "Help and not Fight," "Assimilation and not Destruction," "Harmony and Peace and not Dissension."

5

Vedanta of Swami Vivekananda

In one of the lectures he gave in this country Swami Vivekananda said, "A sannyasin cannot belong to any religion, for his is a life of independent thought, which draws from all religions; his is a life of realization, not merely of theory or belief, much less of dogma." Even to call Vivekananda a "Vedantist" is to put a label on him unjustly.

What, then, do we mean by the Vedanta of Sankaracharya or of Ramanuja or of any other *acharya?* We mean the emphasis, something indicated by the Sanskrit word *darshana,* the outlook special to that particular person. We wish to outline and discuss here some nine salient points which could be considered the special features of Swamiji's Vedanta.

Before we do that, let us first point out what seem to be mistakes often made in approaching the life and thought of Swamiji. If we can first clear the ground of these mistaken preconceptions, our step into Vivekananda-land will be more sure.

1) That he was at times unfaithful to what Sri Ramakrishna taught: his message seems to be quite different

— *Reply*: in the first place, the Master never told Narendra that he was to be a "clone" of himself. He often stood in awe of the height and breadth of his disciple's mind. Secondly it must be remembered that they had very different audiences. Ramakrishna spoke to the western-educated, but still very Indian in background, Calcutta residents, whereas Vivekananda addressed crowds of Americans and Europeans, products of the Renaissance, of science and of western philosophy and theology. In Vedanta the message is guided by the nature of the recipients.

2) That Swamiji got his humanism, socialism, organizing methods etc. from his experience in the West.

— *Reply*: by reading his life in detail one soon discovers that he was studying, and thinking about the ideas of Hamilton, Herbert Spencer, Tyndall, T.H. Huxley and others and how to use them, long before he left for the West. He was, even in his college days, familiar with philosophers like Hume and Hegel, and an avid reader of John Stuart Mill.

3) That he was "only" the Master's messenger, not a spiritual power in himself.

— *Reply*: Nothing could be further from the fact. Sri Ramakrishna gave him the power accumulated by his own sadhana, on one fateful day at Dakshineswar, remarking afterwards, "Now I have become a mere fakir." Swamiji too, challenged by one of his brother-disciples, declared unequivocally, "While I am on earth Sri Ramakrishna is working through me, have no doubt."

Now let us turn to what I would call Vivekananda's most significant and distinctive teachings. We shall put them under nine headings:

That Truth is Brahman Alone

This differs a bit from Sankara's "Brahman alone is real; the world is false." Swami Vivekananda said that the greatest name man ever gave to God was Truth. "My mission," he explained to an interviewer in London, "is to show that religion is in everything and is everything." He told us that drama and music and art are by themselves religion; that any song, love song or whatever, will lead to liberation if one's whole soul is in that song.

Most surprisingly, he said "I am a materialist in a certain sense, because I believe that there is only One. That is what the materialist wants you to believe; only he calls it matter and I call it God, Brahman." He knew from his own experience, when, after the touch of his Master, he went into the streets and saw that everything before him was God.

So much for nature. As for the soul, "There is only one individual," he said, "and each of us is That." Atman is Brahman.The ultimate realization is identity with Brahman

Here he shows himself the orthodox Advaitan. No compromise can be accepted. "Stop not until the goal is reached," he urged. What is the goal? That pure identity, attained only by fearlessness, which is why he talked so much of fearlessness. "That God, for whom you have been searching all over the universe is all the time yourself — your self, not in the personal sense but in the Impersonal." And when others appealed to Ramakrishna that this sounded like egotism, the latter replied, "Naren can say that."

"The eternal, the infinite, the omnipresent, the omniscient is a principle, not a Person. You, I and everyone are but embodiments of that principle and more of it is embodied in a person, the greater is he, and all in the end will be the perfect embodiment of that, and thus all will be one, as they are now essentially..." He told us we are born monists; we cannot help it, because we always perceive the One.

All Paths are Grounded in Advaita and Fulfilled in it

This is what will prevent us from being fanatics: that man goes not from error to truth, but from lower truth to higher truth. When Swamiji spoke about Sri Krishna and the Gita he cautioned, "You must worship the Self in Krishna, not Krishna as Krishna." He shows the all-inclusive nature of Advaita when he says that it accepts dualism and all systems that preceded Advaita. This is the universal solvent into which all philosophies must merge at last. This is not "inclusive-*ism*" nor triumphalism as is sometimes alleged.

Religion Should be Presented Rationally

This is just what Swami Vivekananda did in his speeches at the Parliament of Religions in Chicago in 1893. It captivated the audience, which was tired of emotional harangues from sectarian prelates. Vedanta of all persuasions has always prescribed *shravanam, manamam, nididhyâsanam* — hearing the truth, mulling it over, and meditating upon it; here was Vivekananda telling us not just about his own faith, but about all faiths. Had anyone done this in this way before? "If one religion be true," he pointed out, then all the others must be true." "What happened once in history must happen again..." That was the scientific attitude. He said that the study of religion can and should be pursued on exactly the same basis as the pursuit of any other science. "Everything religion claims must be judged from the standpoint of reason," and when people replied that human reason was weak, he told them "a body of priests would be even weaker!" He dared to say to his own disciples at the head monastery in India, "Only those portions of the Vedas which agree with reason are to be accepted as authority," and also warned them, regarding the Guru, "Worship your Guru as God, but do not obey him blindly; love him all you will, but think for yourself."

All Truths should be made available to All People

> "What I want to propagate," Swamiji said, in his lecture "The Ideal of a Universal Religion," "is a religion that will be equally acceptable to all minds; it must be equally philosophic, equally emotional, equally mystic and equally conducive to action... and this ideal will be the nearest approach to a universal religion." Particularly he dinned this into the ears of his fellow Indians. "The most wonderful truths confined in our Upanishads, in our Puranas, must be brought out from the books, brought out from the monasteries, from the forests, from the possession of selected bodies of people and scattered broadcast over the land, so that these truths run like fire, all over the country."

"Advaita," he said, ..."shall no more be a secret... it must come down to the everyday life of the people." It has to enter the palace, come from the cave to the cottage, to the beggar — everywhere. The oppressed — the outcast and the woman were to fear no longer. "Let the new India arise, from the man who grasps the plough, from the huts of the fisherman, the cobbler, the sweeper..." And in London he made this prediction: "The power of religion, broadened and purified, is going to penetrate every part of human life ... it will live in our every movement, penetrate every pore of our society, and be infinitely more a power for good than it has ever been before."

EVERYONE SHOULD EMBODY ALL PHASES OF TRUTH

By this the Swami did not mean that there would no longer be specialists: he meant no more exclusiveness. What the age needs is the all-rounded person. "Would to God," he said, that all the elements of philosophy, mysticism, emotion and work were equally present in full! That is my ideal of the perfect person. Everyone else ...is one-sided, and this world is almost full with these 'one-sided' people, with knowledge of the one road only in which they move; anything else is dangerous and horrible to them. To become harmoniously balanced in all these directions is my ideal of religion." On rare occasions he would point to his Master as the example of this: e.g., "It was given to me," he told the Madrasis, "to live with a man who was as ardent a dualist, as ardent an Advaitin, as ardent a bhakta, as a *jñâni* Swamiji fortunately provided his own fine example: another such well-rounded prophet is difficult to discover. He was a master at stating accurately the views of another. He was a musician, and in the West took lessons in painting and in the French language. "We are of a new type," he told his listeners; "sometimes dressed like gentlemen, we are engaged in lecturing; at other times, throwing all aside ...ash-clad, we are immersed in meditation and austerities in mountains and forests." This same idea he applied to the form his work was to take: "I haven't been born," Swamiji remarked, "to found one more sect in a world teeming with sects."

ALL PATHS ARE TO BE MADE ACTIVE IN THE SERVICE OF MAN AS GOD

Suppose we want to do charitable work; in that case what Swami Vivekananda tells us is: "Never approach anything except as God." "It is our privilege to be allowed to be charitable, for only so can we grow. The poor suffer that we may be helped; let the giver kneel down and give thanks, let the receiver stand up and permit." "Feel that the receiver is the higher one. You serve the other because you are lower than he, not because he is low and you are high." The relation of all this to the overcoming of ego is obvious. "Philosophy and yoga and penance... —all these constitute the religion of one person or one country; doing good to others is the one great universal religion." Swamiji told his own disciples, "Know this for certain: he who will work will be the crown on my head." "What is India, or England or America to us? We are the servants of that God who by the ignorant is called MAN."

Now if this activity of service is to be expressed through all paths, then we are again reminded of our first point: that drama, music and art are by themselves religion. What Vivekananda preached he carried out. In his lecture to an American audience in San Francisco, entitled "Is Vedanta the Future Religion", he confided: "You are the Personal God. Just now I am worshipping you (in speaking). This is the greatest prayer."

That Man-making was his Religion

What does he mean by a man? A human being, of course. "Great men," Swamiji said, "are those who build bridges for others with their heart's blood." That was the austerity for this age, not so much the forest penances and meditations, but the building of character through karma yoga, is what is needed today. What India in particular now wanted was "muscles of iron and nerves of steel", which nothing could resist, which could penetrate the mysteries of the universe, and accomplish their purpose in any fashion, even if meant going down to the bottom of the ocean and meeting death face to face. Quoting or paraphrasing some verse of poetry he said, "We shall crush the stars to atoms and unhinge the universe. Don't you know who we are? We are the servants of Sri Ramakrishna!" One can sometimes feel that Swamiji's God was Man; "Read Man," he said, "he is the living poem." It is not humanism. It has a much larger definition.

Worship the Terrible

This, in a way, is the most "personal" of these distinctive accents in the message of Vivekananda. He used to say, when speaking of Kali, that She, whom at first he could not accept, had become the Power that now moved him. "Two or three days before Sri Ramakrishna's passing away She whom he used to call 'Kali' entered this body. It is She who takes me here and there and makes me work... I feel that that Power is constantly directing me." Aside from being personal to him, how is it an injunction for all of us? "Each is responsible for the evil anywhere in the world." No one can really "shut the door where evil dwells"; everyone has to face, eventually, that Being whose hands hold good and bad, sweetness and terror. She, the even-handed Mother, was the chosen Ideal of Ramakrishna, and Swami Vivekananda had to make out the significance of it and carry this to the world. "Worship the Terrible," meant for him and us, no fear even of death; to see in the world of today the tremendous play of energy, showing its splendors in every way, understanding it as the Power of Brahman Itself.

6

Swami Vivekananda and America

Every Indian schoolchild seems to be told that an Indian *sannyasin,* Swami Vivekananda, went to America and made a sensation at the Parliament of Religions in Chicago in 1893, and that this has something to do with the rejuvenation of India. About the antecedents of Vivekananda they may know almost nothing — his Western-type education, the years of preparation at the feet of Sri Ramakrishna and the wanderings through nearly every part of India to gain his practical experience; nor do they know much of what happened in the rich remainder of his brief life. If you are one so deprived, you may want to know that volumes have been written detailing all of the above.

The average resident of the U.S.A. today has never even heard his name nor knows what the Parliament of Religions was. Such is the fate of a minority faith, in a society raised totally on secular lines. We do not teach our people the history of ideas or philosophies, generally: only of battles and presidents and movie stars. If any ordinary American knows Swamiji's name, it is likely to be from reading his only widely-known book, *Raja Yoga* — one of the least typical and representative of his productions.

He came by ship to the west coast of Canada and arrived in Chicago in the summer of 1893. He discovered that the Parliament, his only fixed engagement, would not begin until September. What to do? He had very little money. So he bought a train ticket to New England (where living was said to be less expensive) and on the train happened to meet a cultured lady who became interested in Swamiji and took him to her house, showing him off to her friends! There he met a Dr. Wright, professor at Harvard, who, much impressed, wrote on his behalf to the Parliament authorities. (He had no formal papers.) The sessions of the Parliament, an adjunct of the Chicago World's Fair ran from Sept. 11 to 27, 1893. Swami Vivekananda made his first public speeches and was a sensation. That part of his story is well known in India. About it he rightly wrote: "Never before did an Oriental make such an impression on American society."

After the Parliament a lecture bureau signed him up and from the fall of 1893 to the end of 1894 he toured the eastern sections, getting invited as far north as Canada, and south as Memphis. At times Swamiji gave fourteen lectures, class talks and "parlor talks" in a week. Not all of the early lectures were on religion, and we will mention those later. At the beginning of 1895 he took an apartment in New York City and began weekly classes and discourses on the four Yogas, setting the patterns for the present Vedanta Societies.

Naturally he had some funny experiences with his Western students. Once he had to proceed to the lecture hall through a vestibule where there was a full-length mirror. The lady who was assisting him at the time saw him stop, look into the mirror, proceed a few paces, return and look again; this happened twice. "Oh my," she thought to herself, "he too is not above vanity!" Vivekananda turned to her and said, "You know, Ellen, it's a strange thing: I cannot remember what I look like;

the moment I leave the mirror that image is totally gone from my mind!"

All the time his mind was occupied with the problems of his homeland and their solution; he was writing to his brother-disciples in India: "Come out of your self-absorption! Stop all the rituals. Travel. Get organized for the worship of Man through selfless service! After a long hard spring season, he was off to retreat at Thousand Island Park, New York for five weeks with a select twelve disciples, speaking with them "off the cuff" day and night for nearly six weeks. The notes, titled "Inspired Talks", are some of his most dramatic utterances and it was there he composed the poem, "Song of the Sannyasin." One afternoon , meditating in the woods, he went into samadhi. Then came a European interval in which he lectured in England and traveled on the Continent . He observed on the differences between Europe and America, saying to someone that in America alone there is a certain something in the air which brings out the best in everyone. Another time he called this a "sympathy." But after three months in England Swamiji felt that his work there was very successful.

He returned to New York and with almost no holiday, picked up the thread of the work and began his most productive year in the West, 1896. Between December 1895 and February of '96 he gave seventy classes and ten public lectures, along with interviews, initiations, translation, writing and editing. He made trips to Boston, Chicago, and other cities and towns in the midwest and east, and again set sail for England. Teaching in London for nearly seven months, he left at last for home, for India, in December.

After enormous welcomes all the way from Sri Lanka to Calcutta, Vivekananda did not do public teaching in India. He set himself to the work of establishing the monastic base, Belur Math, near Calcutta, and the Ramakrishna Math (Order) and Mission. Yet only two-and-a-half years later all the signals were for making a second visit to the West. His American students were calling for him; he was known to have diabetes and his doctors urged him to regain his health through travel.

Therefore in the summer of 1899 he did return to America, eventually carrying his message to California where he worked both in Los Angeles and San Francisco. In the latter city he founded the second Vedanta Society, in 1900 (the first had been formed in New York, in 1894.) In the spring of 1900 he made his way back to his homeland via a tour through Europe and Egypt, and arrived at Belur Math. What followed was two years of semi-retirement and the consolidation of the Math and Mission. Swami Vivekananda gave up his body at the age of only thirty-nine, on (his choice) the great day of freedom, July Fourth.

Motivation

What motivated Swami Vivekananda to come to America? It is usually thought that he had a command from his Master, Sri Ramakrishna, to do so, or that he came to "bring the message of Vedanta to the Western world." But that was not his view of it at the time. Rather, it is our reading, our understanding as we look back through history. "I did not go to America for the Parliament of Religions," he wrote; "I wanted to get experience and mix." And that he did. He met some of the prominent figures of that day, whose names would mean little to us now. His most important contacts with the famous include those with philosopher and psychologist William James; Nicola Tesla, engineer and inventor; Mme. Calve, an opera soprano; actress Sarah Bernhardt; poet Ella Wheeler Willcox and Robert Ingersoll, the country's most popular orator and agnostic.

Vivekananda learned only gradually about his mission. He came here, as he saw it, to try to raise funds for his new monastic plans in India. He saw that no one in that land would give such money and he hoped to make new friends and followers of Ramakrishna who would. The outcome? He got very little money for India. It was a case of serendipity, one could say. Slowly he realized that he was being used as a tool by the Divine Power — he was Mother's child, made to play here for the sake of an act of the Divine Drama. At the end of 1894 he wrote to his Indian friends, "I find I have a mission in this country too." Not only that. He saw how it would bring benefit to India in her enslavement to foreigners. "One blow struck outside India," he wrote, "is equal to 100,000 within."

It is quite clear, then, that Swami Vivekananda spent his best energies in this country. During his first twenty-nine years in India he was gathering the experience and the resources for his mission; and the last two years, also over there, he was polishing the Indian work and retiring from it. The whole middle period, his best seven years, he gave to the West. "I had to work," he wrote to Mary Hale, the one he regarded as a sister, "till I am at death's door and had to spend nearly the whole of that energy in America, so that the Americans may learn to be broader and more spiritual."

Even his second visit was undertaken, not so much with this consciousness of a mission, but with the same frank and avowed purpose of raising funds for the Mission's service work, this time, education. It always has to be so, that a great prophet like the Swami does his best work unconsciously. Good work is seldom done in the mission field if one is too conscious of being a missionary. He lived and breathed Vedanta: it came from every pore of his being and rubbed off on all who encountered him. He said once: "What I am is written on my brow. If you can read it you are blessed!" But when he goes to work he forgets this; he must, for other purposes come to the fore.

We mentioned that the Swami used to give some lectures on subjects other than Vedanta. Among them were, curiously, Persian art, the gold standard, Indian women. When one American woman made some remark to him about his teaching religion, he turned to her and said, "Madam, I am not teaching religion; I am selling my brain for money to help my people. If you get some lesson out of it, that is your benefit, not mine."

Fruits of the Labor

Now, as we look at it from this distance, what was the result of these years Swamiji spent working in our land? We, as his students and followers — what judgments do we make about the total effect upon our culture and our society? This is the main question to be addressed. He was speaking at the Brooklyn Ethical Society in 1896 when a reporter mentioned to him, perhaps critically, that Hinduism was not called a proselytising religion. This drew from him one of those flashes which epitomized the meaning of his entire life. He said, looking off into the distance: "I have a message for the West as Buddha had a message for the East." Do we understand the implications of this? Is it not that Hinduism needs a "shaking up" from time to time and this time it would be via the West?

Other amusing things happened to him over here. One eager devotee, trying to help with the cure of his sporadic illnesses brought to him the services of a "magnetic healer" of the day — a woman who rubbed and rubbed his flesh till he was nearly raw, "drawing the *prana*." Oh, how he described it! "Now I know what hell is: it's being flayed alive by Mrs. Melton !"

Swamiji fell in love with America. He said it was where his heart was, and he loved the "Yankee-land" as he called it. He said he liked to see new things, not the old ruins of Europe. He felt that America was the place, the people and the opportunity for everything. He may have upset the reporter, when in London he said, "The American civilization is in my opinion, a very great one. I find the American mind peculiarly susceptible to new ideas, nothing is rejected because it is new. It is examined on its own merits." He told people in Calcutta: "America is where, more than anywhere else, the feeling of brotherhood has been developed. An American meets you for five minutes on board a train and you are his friend, and the next moment he invites you as a guest to his house and opens his whole home to you. He spoke particularly of our women: "Their kindness to me it would take me years to tell. "They are the life and soul of this country" he remarked, and said he could never repay his debt of gratitude to them.

Cultural Criticism

Swami Vivekananda did not, however, see only our virtues! He saw many other things besides. He saw for instance that American men profess to worship women, but behind all the chivalry was lust. "They simply worship youth and beauty, they never fall in love with wrinkles and gray hair! "His message to the West was dynamite! It turned our whole self-appraisal upside-down. Swamiji wrote in a letter to India: "Nowhere have I heard so much talk about freedom — 'life, liberty and the pursuit of happiness' — and nowhere is it less understood." Ingersoll, popular orator of the day, much given to ridiculing religion, told Vivekananda: "If you had come to this country fifty years ago, you would have been hanged."

Swamiji is quite correct in saying that the West never had the true idea of soul until they got it through Sanskrit philosophy in the 1870s. From the time of the Greeks, Plato and Aristotle, "soul" in the West has been confused with mind. His clear expositions of Vedanta philosophy made a very great impact on his listeners. To the shame of America, the jealous missionaries, fearful of their revenues, lit into him with a vengeance. That is a sad story which we do not like to tell. The letters columns in Detroit papers were full of the lies and half-truths concocted by missionaries to discredit him. "There is not one black lie, he used to say, "they did not cook up to use against me."

Swami Vivekananda's character shone through it all. No one who knew him believed the slanders. But he also fought back in his own way. He praised Jesus Christ — and Christians when he found them faithful to Christ; but he "told them off" when he did not, and drew a line between Christ and Christianity. "Christianity," he told a large audience, "wins it prosperity by cutting the throats of its fellow-men." "Go back to Christ!" he thundered, "stop worshipping this almighty dollar!" He was a prophet. He saw the West in 1900 as living on a volcano and predicted the first and second World Wars.

Touched the Heart and Brain of America

In a very few sentences: Swami Vivekananda took his Master's message to a foreign world; there he learned the language of that world; then gave the universal message for the Age in that language of education, science, research and experiment. Moreover, he demonstrated, in himself, a new kind of person to the American people: the universal man, so to say, the man for all ages, all nations, all faiths — a new breed. He spoke of "the new American," who would accept all from the past and be open to all of the future. Do you know what he said? He said, "I must touch the brain of America and stir it up if I can." He did.

His was a universal message, his Vedanta. "Do you think people in this country would be much attracted if I talked about Hinduism?" he asked his brother monks in India. "The very name of narrowness in ideas will scare them away! The real thing is the religion taught by Sri Ramakrishna, let the Hindus call it Hinduism, let others call it whatever they like." "I do not want to convert you to a new belief," he told us; "I want you to keep your own belief; I want to make the Methodist a better Methodist, the Muslim a better Muslim, the Hindu a better Hindu." "I do not say to the West, 'take up our method.' My message in life is to ask East and West not to quarrel over different ideals, but to show them that the goal is the same."

Finally, he told his brother-disciples that Indian spirituality must conquer the West, and he sowed the seeds of that conquest. He told those whom he had sent here to carry on the work begun, "If you live for some time in places where I have sowed the seeds of our Master's ideals and develop those into plants, you will be doing a much greater work than I did."

American Independence

The Fourth of July has a special significance for those of us who follow Swami Vivekananda, and the Fourth of July had a special significance for him. In four of the years he spent in this country, being present in July, he celebrated the holiday with his companions and friends. Moreover, while spending the summer in London, he was guest of honor when the American community there celebrated it, in a gala occasion hosted by a high society American lady who had married a British banker.

More notable still, in the valley of Kashmir, where he had taken some of his close followers to live on a houseboat on that gorgeous lake, he insisted on observing the Fourth when the day approached, with a party and decorations; his friends even hired an Indian tailor to make what might pass as an American flag!

It was in 1902 that he looked in an almanac a few months ahead and apparently chose deliberately to leave this earth on the evening of July 4th. We take this as a symbol. Vivekananda, who had all his thirty-nine years chafed under the burden of an unwell body, found his independence from it at last, his mission accomplished, now achieving his well-deserved rest. He gave out certain signs on the late days of his life that, his work being over, he would accept now the mergence in Freedom which his Master had promised. Lying on his cot in the evening, he sent away his attendant, entered into a deep meditation and did not return to our world.

About 400 people turned up and were fed, then entertained with speeches by the Swamis and the special guest, playwright John Van Druten, and by music composed and sung by members of the monastery. Here is Swami Vivekananda's poem to the Fourth, which he composed on that houseboat in Kashmir and read, or had someone read, at the early morning breakfast. As he did in everything, in this symbol of American freedom too, he saw divinity:

> Behold, the dark clouds melt away,
> That gathered thick at night, and hung
> So like a gloomy pall above the earth!
> Before thy magic touch, the world
> Awakes. The birds in chorus sing.
> The flowers raise their star-like crowns—
> Dew-set, and wave thee welcome fair.
> The lakes are opening wide in love
> Their hundred thousand lotus-eyes
> To welcome thee, with all their depth.

All hail to thee, thou Lord of Light!
A welcome new to thee, today,
O Sun! Today thou sheddest Liberty!

Bethink thee how the world did wait,
And search for thee, through time and clime.
Some gave up home and love of friends,
And went in quest of thee, self-banished,
Through dreary oceans, through primeval forests,
Each step a struggle for their life or death;
And worship, love and sacrifice.
Fulfilled, accepted and complete.
Then thou, propitious, rose to shed
The light of Freedom on mankind.
Move on, O Lord, in thy resistless path!
Till thy high noon o'erspreads the world.
Till every land reflects thy light,
Till men and women, with uplifted head,
Behold their shackles broken, and
Know, in springing joy, their life renewed!

This great poetry was the heartfelt expression of a prophet, a great and reverential man. It starts in the dawn in which it was composed, with the victory of day over night, light over dark, and goes on in that victorious vein; but this is not battle-victory; it is the triumph of ideas. It is typical of its day (1898)—flowery, Victorian; today we might hum high violins in the background—but it is also typical of Swamiji: positive, optimistic, prophetic.

He loved the United States as if it were his native country. What he gave especially to his American listeners and followers will be mentioned later. On his arrival in Chicago he lived with a midwestern American family and from them he had much to learn and learned it most willingly; only then was he ready to teach.

In the Declaration we asserted our political independence from the land of origin. But it is important to realize that we have gone on declaring it ever since: in George Washington's speeches, in the Monroe Doctrine, in our relatively small involvement in European and Asian internal conflicts. It is reflected again in the furor felt by many citizens at the idea of a third, and a fourth, term for Franklin Roosevelt. Swami Vivekananda saw this as an ongoing process and appreciated it and praised it, for his own reasons. His conception of freedom came from his immersion in the ideas and ideals of the Upanishads and the *Bhagavad Gita*. He knew and tried to convey to us that men would never be content with a partial, a temporal and temporary, image of freedom. Let us hear some of the things he said:

Neither the Declaration nor its framers had absolute freedom in view. Jefferson had said, "The greatest freedom is the right to use our reason." If this be true, we have much to do yet in exercising that right, in ever more significant ways.

He asked us to take a good look at the contrast between the freedoms we profess and our actual behavior, in gender, race and religious prejudice. He commented on the bondage our desires create for us, notably when we talk of our "work time" and our "free time," and the dislike we often cherish for the former, and even hate our work; on how our emotions and passions make us slaves to one another, positively or negatively. Swami cited the traditional examples of the Pandava brothers, Yudhishthira and Arjuna, both of whom complained to the Lord, "I know what I should be doing, but am unable to do it, and what I should not do, but am unable to prevent myself." "What sort of freedom is this?" asks Vivekananda.

Often, it seems, we do not really want freedom. A classic and popular book titled, *Escape from Freedom.* was written by Erich Fromm. Many thinkers write in that way, using that language. Swami Vivekananda never did.

He told the true story of a Chinese prisoner incarcerated for long years in a cave with no light at all, who was suddenly freed, when the government changed. The man could not stand the pain of light, and retreated to remain in his darkness.

But in defining liberty as the soul's total independence from bodily demands and mental stagnation, Swamiji did not negate nor devalue our relative freedom. "Liberty is the first condition of growth," he says. "Just as a man must have liberty to think and speak, so he must have liberty in food, dress and marriage, and in every other thing, so long as he does not injure others." Even a high degree of this "human" freedom, however, does not guarantee success. Power does not always mean happiness—certainly not perduring—as Pharaohs and emperors know, as well as the worker on the assembly line. In prosaic illustration of this, we know of a worker who, achieving a long-sought promotion to inspectorship, found herself now faced with decisions, thick and fast, and stress she had never known farther down the line.

> "Where is true independence?" Vivekananda asks. "It is not freedom of the senses; it is freedom from the senses." Bound in the habits and demands of our physical and vital energies we are and ever will be, only slaves. His Master, Sri Ramakrishna tells us, echoing the Buddha, "What you think you are, you become. Think constantly of the spirit and spirit you become, for freedom and bondage are of the mind."

Swamiji made us realize, by constant reminder and example, that freedom from death must mean freedom from life. "No covering the corpse with flowers." This world of our senses cannot be made a sorrowless playground where only the good and the perfect have sway, and the door be sealed where evil dwells. We know the one only by the other, in this spinning miasma of the pairs of opposites. Give up "Life" and "Death" goes too, leaving us where we always are: pure Spirit. "He is free, he is great," he said, "who turns his back upon this world, who has renounced everything, who has controlled his passion, and who thirsts for peace. One may gain political independence," Swamiji added, "but if one is a slave to ones passions and desires, one cannot feel the pure joy of real freedom."

Let us look at some of the specific kinds of freedom Swami Vivekananda admired in our society.

— Freedom from arbitrary authority. A modern example will be the Supreme Court's decision on the Nixon tapes: even the President cannot have absolute immunity.

— Freedom to worship as we please. This was not, in his time, nor is it now, complete. Certain minorities can point to places where they may not operate, rituals they may not perform, acts they may believe in but cannot carry out. But this was a cardinal point settled in the war between Great Britain and her American colonies: that the churches should be free from state control. The social and prestigial differences which are created in statecraft merely by church affiliation or lack of the same.

— Freedom to assemble. The difference between the United States and Communist Poland before "Solidarity", for example, and other countries behind the Iron Curtain, or in the theocratic governments of the Third World, in this right of the common people to gather, combine and protest or promote, was clear to Vivekananda in 1900.

— Freedom to have a speedy public trial. Contrast this with the situation in his native India, where suspects can languish in prisons and jails for months and years with no trial. But today we too are falling behind on this freedom, as crime increases and courts become glutted.

— Freedom from excessive bail or fine; to have defense counsel; to have military justice subordinated to civil justice. These are our judicial freedoms.

Swami Vivekananda regarded dignity as a hallmark of the human species, and encouraged what he called "strength" or "manliness" as the desideratum for a society. Our founding fathers built our political, and to some extent social, system on several convictions: some on a brand of humanism, some on theological convention, but seeing man generally as a biological creature. The message of the Vedanta of Vivekananda is to see his divinity.

7

Swami Vivekananda and Yoga

Yoga comes from the Sanskrit root *yuj*, which means to yoke or unite. This union describes the goal of yoga, to unite us with the Ultimate consciousness, which is sometimes called the Absolute, the Self, God, or the Creator.

Vivekananda's Pronouncements on the Yoga of Work

In this age special stress should be laid on Karma Yoga.

— By work alone men may get to where Buddha got largely by meditation or Christ by prayer.

— Doing work is not religion, but work done rightly leads to freedom.

— We have to work, for it is the only way to get out of maya.

— Buddha is the ideal karma yogi, acting entirely without motive.

What our attitude toward work must be, to make it yoga:

— Ordinary mankind, driven everywhere by false desires, what do they know of work? He works who is not propelled by his own desires, by any selfishness whatsoever... He works who has nothing to gain from work. Who enjoys the picture, the seller or the seer?

— If you want to help a man, never think what that person's attitude toward you should be. Those who want to help mankind must take their own pleasure and pain, name and fame, and all sorts of interests and make a bundle of them and throw them into the sea, and then come to the Lord.

— Perfect sincerity, holiness, gigantic intellect, and an all-conquering will. Let only a handful of men work with these and the whole world will be revolutionized.

— But if we are to renounce the fruits (of work), what inducement is there, to work?

— (Reply): One must learn, sooner or later, that one cannot get salvation if one does not try to seek the salvation of his brothers.

— You work best when you work for others. "Out of the fulness of the heart, the mouth speaketh" — and out of the fulness of the heart the hand works, too. There is no engine which can pull against the human heart. Feel, my children, feel: feel for the poor, the ignorant, the downtrodden; feel till the heart stops and the brain reels and you think you will go mad.

— In this battlefield of ours, the dust of mistakes must be raised. Those who are so thin-skinned that they cannot bear the dust, let them get out of the ranks.

— Constant defeat — let that not unnerve thee.

— He who is the servant of all is their true master.

— Know for certain that he who will work will be the crown on my head!

— You may be astonished to hear that as practical Vedantins the Americans are better than we are.

What our conception of ourselves must be, to make it yoga.

— The great thing is to have faith in oneself. You cannot believe in God until you believe in yourself. Animals can do charitable work... see the bees, the ants, dogs; men can be masters of themselves.

— You have yourself manufactured your body, bit by bit... Nobody eats for you... All the responsibility for good or evil is on you.

— Say, it is my nature, never say it is my duty. All the work you do is subjective, it is done for your own benefit. God has not fallen into a ditch, for you and me to help him out.

— Try not to know that you work. The true man is he who is strong as strength itself yet has a woman's heart. Whether or not you know it, through all hands you work, through all feet you move....

Ways we must work, to make it yoga.

— Every ounce of muscle in excess of what is beyond the needs of one's physical work is that much less of brain. Do not exercise too hard; it is injurious.

— The best work is done by alternate repose and work.

— The ideal man is he who, in the midst of the greatest silence and solitude finds the intensest activity and in the midst of the intensest activity finds the silence and solitude of the desert.

— Standing on Market Street, waiting for the car, with all the rush going on around you, are you in meditation — calm and peaceful?

— Three things are necessary: purity, patience and perseverance. And there is a fourth, even more important: love.

— Condemn none; if you can stretch out a helping hand, so much the better. If you want to reform John Doe, go and live with him. Don't try to reform him. If you have any of the divine fire, he will catch it. Vedanta only preaches the principles, and the method it leaves to you.

— A time comes when one understands that to serve a man even in the smallest way is far greater than millions of meditations. Please everyone without being a hypocrite and without being a coward.

Wisdom consists in carrying on the work cleverly keeping all in good humor. Many feel, but only a few can express. It is the power of expressing one's love and appreciation and sympathy for others that enables one person to succeed better in spreading the idea than others. Our teacher and Lord was so original, and each one of us will have to be original or nothing.

Even the greatest fool can accomplish a task if it be after his heart. But the intelligent man is he who can convert every work into one that suits his taste.

Get rid of the fundamental superstition that we are obliged to act through the body. We are not. You will be able to work for the good of the world when you know for a fact that this work is all illusion. Be bold and face the truth! Be one with it

> Let visions cease,
> Or if you cannot, dream but truer dreams
> Which are Eternal Love and Service Free!

The conception of those we work with which we must have, to make it yoga.

— Have faith in man (If he is pursuing the false, it is because he cannot get the true. Put it in front of him and let him judge, he must see.)

— If you do good at all, you do it to yourself; feel that the receiver is the higher one. You serve the other because you are lower than he, not because he is low and you are high. Give as the rose gives perfume. A man should not be judged by the nature of his duties.

— When you serve a *jiva* the idea that he is a *jiva,* it is *daya,* not *prema,* but when you serve him with the idea that he is the Self, it is *prema..* It is very difficult to superimpose divinity, but one is sure to succeed by repeated efforts; God is in every man whether man knows it or not; your loving devotion is bound to call up the divinity in him. Do not pity anyone; look on all as your equal.

— It is our privilege to be allowed to be charitable, for only so can we grow. The poor man suffers that we may be helped; let the giver kneel down and give thanks, let the receiver stand up and permit.

— Do not create illusion by "helping" anyone.

— Help another because you are in him and he is in you.

— Learn to feel yourself in others' bodies.

— The individual's life is in the life of the whole.

— Love makes no distinction between man and man, between white and black, between brahmin and pariah, nor even between a man and a woman. Love makes the whole universe one's own home.

Vivekananda's Raja-Yoga

The fire of Yoga burns the cage of sin that is around a man. Knowledge becomes purified and Nirvana is directly obtained. From Yoga comes knowledge; know ledge again helps the Yogi. He who combines in himself both Yoga and knowledge, with him the Lord is pleased.

Those that practise Mahayoga, either once a day, or twice a day, or thrice, or always, know them to be gods. Yoga is divided into two parts. One is called Abhava, and the other, Mahayoga. Where one's self is meditated upon as zero, and bereft of quality, that is called Abhava. That in which one sees the self as full of bliss and bereft of all impurities, and one with God, is called Mahayoga. The Yogi, by each one, realises his Self. The other Yogas that we read and hear of, do not deserve to be ranked with the excellent Mahayoga in which the Yogi finds himself and the whole universe as God. This is the highest of all Yogas.

Yama, Niyama, Asana, Pranayama, Pratyahara, Dharana, Dhyana, and Samadhi are the steps in Raja-Yoga, of which non-injury, truthfulness, non-covetousness, chastity, not receiving anything from another are called Yama. This purifies the mind, the Chitta. Never produc ing pain by thought, word, and deed, in any living being, is what is called Ahimsa, non-injury. There is no virtue higher than non-injury. There is no happiness higher than what a man obtains by this attitude of non-offensiveness, to all creation. By truth we attain fruits of work. Through truth everything is attained. In truth everything is establlshed. Relating facts as they are this is truth. Not taking others' goods by stealth or by force, is called Asteya, non-covetousness. Chastity in thought, word, and deed, always, and in all conditions, is what is called Brahmacharya. Not receiving any present from anybody, even when one is suffering terribly, is what is called Aparigraha. The idea is, when a man receives a gift from another, his heart becomes impure, he becomes low, he loses his independence, he becomes bound and attached.

The following are helps to success in Yoga and are called Niyama or regular habits and observances ; Tapas, austerity; Svadhyaya, study; Santosha, contentment;

Shaucha, purity; Ishvara-pranidhana, worshipping God. Fasting, or in other ways controlling the body, is called physical Tapas. Repeating the Vedas and other Mantras, by which the Sattva material in the body is purified, is called study, Svadhyaya. There are three sorts of repetitions of these Mantras. One is called the verbal, another semi-verbal, and the third mental. The verbal or audible is the lowest, and the inaudible is the highest of all. The repetition which is loud is the verbal ; the next one is where only the lips move, but no sound is heard. The inaudible repetition of the Mantra, accompanied with the thinking of its meaning, is called the "mental repetition," and is the highest. The sages have said that there are two sorts of purification, external and internal.

The purification of the body by water, earth, or other materials is the external purification, as bathing etc. Purification of the mind by truth, and by all the other virtues, is what is called internal purification. Both are necessary. It is not sufficient that a man should be internally pure and externally dirty. When both are not attainable the internal purity is the better, but no one will be a Yogi until he has both. Worship of God is by praise, by thought, by devotion.

We have spoken about Yama and Niyama. The next is Asana (posture). The only thing to understand about it is leaving the body free, holding the chest, shoulders, and head straight. Then comes Pranayama. Prana means the vital forces in one's own body, Ayama means controlling them. There are three sorts of Prana yama, the very simple, the middle, and the very high. Pranayama is divided into three parts: filling, restraining, and emptying. When you begin with twelve seconds it is the lowest Pranayama ; when you begin with twenty-four seconds it is the middle Pranayama ; that Pranayama is the best which begins with thirty-six seconds. In the lowest kind of Pranayama there is perspiration, in the medium kind, quivering of the body, and in the highest Pranayama levitation of the body and influx of great bliss.

There is a Mantra called the Gayatri. It is a very holy verse of the Vedas. "We meditate on the glory of that Being who has produced this universe ; may He enlighten our minds." Om is joined to it at the beginning and the end. In one Pranayama repeat three Gayatris. In all books they speak of Pranayama being divided into Rechaka (rejecting or exhaling), Puraka (inhaling), and Kumbhaka (restraining, stationary). The Indriyas, the organs of the senses, are acting outwards and coming in contact with external objects. Bringing them under the control of the will is what is called Pratyahara or gather ing towards oneself. Fixing the mind on the lotus of the heart, or on the centre of the head, is what is called Dharana. Limited to one spot, making that spot the base, a particular kind of mental waves rises ; these are not swallowed up by other kinds of waves, but by degrees become prominent, while all the others recede and finally disappear.

Next the multiplicity of these waves gives place to unity and one wave only is left in the mind. This is Dhyana, meditation. When no basis is necessary, when the whole of the mind has become one wave, one-formedness, it is called Samadhi. Bereft of all help from places and centres, only the meaning of the thought is present. If the mind can he fixed on the centre for twelve seconds it will he a Dharana, twelve such Dharanas will he a Dhyana, and twelve such Dhyanas will be a Samadhi.

Where there is fire, or in water or on ground which is strewn with dry leaves, where there are many ant-hills, where there are wild animals, or danger, where four streets meet, where there is too much noise, where there are many wicked persons, Yoga must not he practised.

This applies more particularly to India. Do not practise when the body feels very lazy or ill, or when the mind is very miserable and sorrowful. Go to a place which is well hidden, and where people do not come to disturb you. Do not choose dirty places. Rather choose beautiful scenery, or a room in your own house which is beautiful. When you practise, first salute all the ancient Yogis, and your own Guru, and God, and then begin.

Dhyana is spoken of, and a few examples are given of what to meditate upon. Sit straight, and look at the tip of your nose. Later on we shall come to know how that con centrates the mind, how by controlling the two optic nerves one advances a long way towards the control of the arc of reaction, and so to the control of the will. Here are a few specimens of meditation. Imagine a lotus upon the top of the head, several inches up, with virtue as its centre, and knowledge as its stalk. The eight petals of the lotus are the eight powers of the Yogi. Inside, the stamens and pistils are renunciation.

If the Yogi refuses the external powers he will come to salvation. So the eight petals of the lotus are the eight powers, but the internal stamens and pistils are extreme renunciation, the renunciation of all these powers. Inside of that lotus think of the Golden One, the Almighty, the Intangible, He whose name is Om, the Inexpressible, surrounded with effulgent light. Meditate on that. Another meditation is given. Think of a space in your heart, and in the midst of that space think that a flame is burning. Think of that flame as your own soul and inside the flame is another effulgent light, and that is the Soul of your soul, God.

Meditate upon that in the heart. Chastity, non-injury, forgiving even the greatest enemy, truth, faith in the Lord, these are all different Vrittis. Be not afraid if you are not perfect in all of these ; work, they will come. He who has given up all attach ment, all fear, and all anger, he whose whole soul has gone unto the Lord, he who has taken refuge in the Lord, whose heart has become purified, with whatsoever desire he comes to the Lord, He will grant that to him. There fore worship Him through knowledge, love, or renun ciation.

"He who hates none, who is the friend of all, who is merciful to all, who has nothing of his own, who is free from egoism, who is even-minded in pain and pleasure, who is forbearing, who is always satisfied,, who works always in Yoga, whose self has become controlled, whose will is firm, whose mind and intellect are given up unto Me, such a one is My beloved Bhakta. From whom comes no disturbance, who cannot be disturbed by others, who is free from joy, anger, fear, and anxiety, such a one is My beloved. He who does not depend on anything, who is pure and active, who does not care whether good comes or evil, and never becomes miserable, who has given up all efforts for himself ; who is the same in praise or in blame, with a silent, thoughtful mind, blessed with what little comes in his way, homeless, for the whole world is his home, and who is steady in his ideas, such a one is My beloved Bhakta." Such alone become Yogis.

There was a great god-sage called Narada. Just as there are sages among mankind, great Yogis, so there are great Yogis among the gods. Narada was a good Yogi, and very great. He travelled everywhere. One day he was passing through a forest, and saw a man who had been meditating until the white ants had built a huge mound round his body - so long had he been sitting in that position. He said to Narada, "Where are you going?" Narada replied, "I am going to heaven." "Then ask God when He will be merciful to me ; when I shall attain freedom." Further on Narada saw another man. He was jumping about, singing, dancing, and said, "Oh, Narada, where are you going?" His voice and his gestures were wild. Narada said, "I am going to heaven." "Then, ask when I shall be free." Narada went on. In the course of time he came again by the same road, and there was the man who had been meditating with the ant-hill round him. He said, "Oh, Narada, did you ask the Lord about me?" "Oh, yes." "What did He say?" "The Lord told me that you would attain freedom in four more births." Then the man began to weep and wail, and said, "I have meditated until an ant-hill has grown around me, and I have four more births yet!" Narada went to the other man. "Did you ask my question ?." "Oh, yes. Do you see this tamarind tree? I have to tell you that as many leaves as there are on that tree, so many times, you shall be born, and then you shall attain freedom." The man began to dance for joy, and said, "I shall have freedom after such a short time!" A voice came, "My child, you will have freedom this minute." That was the reward for his perseverance. He was ready to work through all those births, nothing discouraged him. But the first man felt that even four more births were too long. Only perseverance, like that of the man who was willing to wait aeons brings about the highest result.

Benefits of Yoga

Following are the benefits of yoga when practices regularly:

Flexibility and Strength

Yoga postures stretch and strengthen muscles and ligaments and put joints through their full range of movement. Good posture and better look. You develop the postures which are beautiful to look at. Firm muscle tone, bright eyes and clear complexion contribute to the radiant appearance of the person. This, combined with good posture and grace of movement, makes for a pleasing outward appearance.

Breathe smoothly and efficiently

Yogic breathing strengthens the diaphragm and encourages deeper, freer breathing.

Sleep well

Scientific relaxation helps in sound sleep and refreshing the body and mind.

Concentrate well

Yoga Posture, yogic breathing, relaxation and meditation all help to calm and still the mind. When your mind is calm and still you develop higher concentration for your work.

Cope well with stress

The improvements to your health and the ability to relax deeply that come with yoga make you more resilient. Even in times of crisis you can learn to cope well without getting much stressed. Massaging of all organs of the body – It massages all the internal glands and organs of the body in a thorough manner.

Benefits of yoga for sports professionals

— Gentle hatha yoga can be used to lubricate joints and relax muscle tensions.

— It can help in correcting muscle imbalances resulting from high impact training, strengthening the spine to prevent pain and injury.

— Yoga can help to balance your lower body strength. Healthy movement requires less expenditure of energy, so you will have greater reserves to take longer, faster strides.

— Standing yoga postures correctly align the knee.

— Dynamic yoga develops stamina and upper body strength without tightness in the shoulders also prepares the cardiovascular system and muscles for peak performance.

— Yoga and breath work can benefit the mind in competition to improve confidence and concentration.

— Yoga has numerous benefits however, the benefits of yoga depends on how regularly you are practicing and also how you are practicing (example are you practicing only yogasana or also along from yogasana, you are combining it with pranayama,

Yoga for breast cancer patients

Yoga, the ancient Indian therapy for exercise and meditation of the mind and the body, has for long been known to help people cope against ailments.And now, the age old therapy is providing healing touch to patients suffering from breast cancer by reducing pain and trauma.

The University of Texas MD Anderson Cancer Centre and the Swami Vivekananda Yoga Anusandhana Samsthana, have announced a research collaboration to scientifically validate the belief that mind-body interventions have a beneficial impact on the health of cancer patients. The University of Texas, MD Anderson Cancer Centre is the world's largest cancer hospital and Research Centre.

Dr HR Nagendra, the President of "Swami Vivekananda Yoga Anusandhana SamsthanaSamsthana" has said that the research on breast cancer patients through specially developed Yoga technique helped control their agony, adding that the MD Anderson Centre has accepted the theory.

Yoga is an effective agent and it can bring a lot of improvement for the patients. For the last 25 years we have been doing extensive research, findings of which are published in nearly 75 research papers in the top reading journals. What we have been able to show is that yoga is effective by systematic protocols, which are acceptable by international standards. The MD Anderson Centre has also come forward and for the first time seen how yoga can be useful for cancer patients. They are very much impressed," said Dr HR Nagendra, President, Swami Vivekananda Yoga Anusandhana Samsthana.

The ten-year research at Bangalore Institute of Oncology on Yoga therapy on more than 400 breast cancer patients has given a positive output and it is based on this research, that the MD Anderson Centre has accepted Yoga as a therapy for elieving pain in breast cancer patients. Researchers from both institutions are currently studying the effects of yoga on breast cancer patients undergoing radiation treatments.They are also exploring whether participating in a yoga programme diminishes patients' fatigue and sleep disturbances, while improving the overall quality of life, mental health, stress hormone levels, and aspects of immune function.

Presently, the randomised-controlled trial is aimed at monitoring the patients' physiological responses to yoga as determined from blood and saliva samples, lung function tests and goniometric (joint motion) measurements.

Few of the most popular Branded Hatha yoga style has been mentioned below:

Ananda Yoga is a relatively gentle, and not an athletic or aerobic practice. Its object is to awaken, experience, and begin to control the subtle energies within oneself, and use these energies to harmonize body, mind, and emotions, and above all to attune oneself with higher levels of awareness. One unique feature of this system is the use of silent affirmations while in the Asana as a means of working more directly and consciously with the subtle energies to achieve this attunement. It was developed by Swami Kriyananda, a direct disciple of Paramhansa Yogananda, author of the spiritual classic, Autobiography of a Yogi.

Ashtanga Yoga This style of yoga is physically demanding. It is not for Beginners or anyone who's been taking a leisurely approach to fitness. Participants move through a series of flows, jumping from one posture to another in order to build strength, flexibility and stamina.

Ashtanga Yoga Practice involves performing challenging sequence of poses. This Yoga Style uses a system based on six series of increasing difficulty The so called power yoga is based on Ashtanga yoga developed by K. Pattabhi Jois.

Iyengar Yoga style is famous for great attention to details and precise alignment of postures. The Yoga Poses are held much longer than in other schools of yoga and repeated several times .He also popularized the use of Yoga Props such as blocks and belts. This great attention to details, posture, and alignment has also become the notable characteristics of Iyengar Yoga and was named after B.K.S. Iyengar.

Sivananda Yoga This Style of Yoga focuses on the Pranayama, classic Asanas, Relaxation, Diet and Meditation. Sivananda Yoga practice consist twelve Yoga Poses that seeks to increase strength, flexibility, Proper Breathing, and Meditation. It was developed by Vishnu-devananda .He named Sivananda Yoga after his teacher, Swami Sivananda who is also one of the greatest Yoga gurus in the world.

Viniyoga rooted from the principle practiced by Sri. T. Krishnamacharya - the teacher of well-known contemporary masters B.K.S. Iyengar, K. Pattabhi Jois and. His son, T.K.V. Desikachar, continued this principle and developed the practice of Viniyoga. Viniyoga make use of modified Yoga Poses that are designed to meet the specific needs of an individual and to enhance healing, flexibility and strength of joints. The emphasis of Viniyoga practice is on coordinating breath and movement.

Bikram Yoga is practiced in a room with high temperature and thus lots of sweat. Bikram students perform a series of 26 Asana. Each posture is usually performed twice and held for a certain period of time. Their Yoga Sessions start from Standing Postures, then the Backbends, Forward Bends, and Twists. Bikram Yoga may be practiced by people who are already in good shape however you should ask for your physician's advice before getting involved into any exercise activity in case if you are suffering from any ailment. It is named after its founder - Bikram Choudhury.

Scientific Yoga is a style which is systematic and has yoga exercise from simplest yoga asana to strength building posture step by step, which are being practiced considering, body strength and participants comfort level. It includes postures for flexibility. It is good for strong workout. It includes the Scientific sleep, practiced by many great leader of the world. It includes breathing exercise for balancing energy level in body and relaxing mind.The emphasis in this style of yoga is to understand scientifically every step and then experience the same. The Truth is what you experience. Its founder -Subodh Gupta

Anusara Yoga: A new style developed by John Friend, Anusara Yoga is described as heart-oriented and spiritually inspiring, yet grounded in a deep knowledge of outer and inner body alignment. It is a combination of Hatha Yoga and biochemical principles. Each student's various abilities and limitations are deeply respected and honored. According to the practice of Anasura Yoga, one must keep one's heart open and flow with grace as one do the postures. Anasura Yoga practice is based on three principles: attitude, action and alignmen.

Kali Ray TriYoga :It was founded by Kali Ray. On practicing styles of Yoga benefits which one gains are Posture, Breath, and Focus together to create dynamic and intuitive flows. The Tri Yoga exercises combine flowing and sustained postures following a spinal wave like movement, economy of motion, and synchronized breath and mudra. The flows are arranged by level and can be as gentle or as challenging as desired. In this style of yoga students may progress from basic to advance as they increase their flexibility, strength, endurance and knowledge of the flows.

Kripalu Yoga: It is also called the Yoga of consciousness. Kripalu puts great emphasis on Proper Breath, alignment, coordination of breath and movement, and "honoring the wisdom of the body" — you work according to the limits of your individual flexibility and strength. In this style of Yoga students learn to focus on the physical and psychological reactions caused by various postures to develop their awareness of mind, body, emotion and spirit. There are three stages in Kripalu Yoga.

— Stage One focuses on learning the postures, proper breathing, and exploring your body's abilities.

— Stage Two involves holding the postures for an extended time, developing concentration and awareness of your thoughts and emotions.

— Stage Three is like Meditation in motion.

Kundalini Yoga: It was brought to the West by Yogi Bhajan in 1969. This style of yoga focuses on the controlled release of the Kundalini (serpent power) energy which is found at the base of your spine. The practice of Kundalini Yoga involves classic poses, chanting, coordination of breath and movement and Meditation. In this style of yoga the emphasis is on the Chanting and Breathing.

Meditation in Yoga and Vedanta

Meditation is keeping the mind focused uninterruptedly on a subject for a certain length of time. All spiritual practices, ceremonies, prayer, and pilgrimage reach their consummation in meditation. In Patanjali's Yoga system, meditation is the last step before the final goal, samadhi, or superconscious experience. Sri Sankaracharya describes meditation as maintaining steady awareness within of Atman, the focus of the all-pervading Self. Meditation on Atman, our true Self, is the highest form of yoga. According to the Kurma Purana:

> The fire of yoga burns the cage of sin which imprisons a man. Knowledge becomes purified and Nirvana is directly obtained. From yoga comes knowledge; knowledge, again, helps the yogi to obtain freedom. He who combines in himself both yoga and knowledge-with him the Lord is pleased. Those who practice maha-yoga [meditation on the Self] either once a day, or twice, or thrice, or always-know them to be gods.

Yoga is divided into two parts: one is called abhava-yoga, and the other, maha-yoga. That in which one's self is meditated upon as a void and without qualities is called abhava-yoga. That in which one sees one's self as blissful, bereft of all impurities, and as one with God is called maha-yoga.

Vedic sages maintain that our true identity is Atman, or our inmost Self. When we forget It and fail to realize It, we become victims of endless suffering. Knowledge of Atman or Self is the only way to put an end to all suffering and meditation is the only way to Self-Knowledge. In meditation our consciousness rises high, comes into contact with the Atman, or universal Consciousness, and finds connection with It. We expand, taste supreme Bliss, and attain the highest fulfillment of life.

The state of meditation is supported by concentration, concentration by withdrawal of mind, and withdrawal of mind by purity and self-control. Vedanta texts say that if you can concentrate 12 seconds on a subject uninterruptedly, it becomes one unit of concentration; 12 such units of concentration make one unit of meditation; 12 units of meditation lead to the first stage of samadhi; and 12 units of this samadhi lead to the highest samadhi, the supreme realization of Atman. But this achievement does not come of itself; it calls for repeated practice of meditation.

The three components of meditation are: the subject of meditation, the center of consciousness at which the mind is held, and the method employed to guide the mind to concentration. The subject of meditation may be the nondual all-pervading Self, any specific aspect of the divine, or any divine incarnation. The center of consciousness may be at the heart, or between the eyebrows, or at the crown of the head. The method employed to invoke concentration may be any of the following: japa, or repetition of a sacred word; discrimination between the real and the unreal; dispassion, which is knowing the evil effect of sense-enjoyment; pranayama, or control of breath; and ceremonial observances.

Some examples of guided meditation are the following:

Sit in a straight posture. The next thing to do is to send a current of holy thought to all creation. Mentally repeat: "Let all beings be happy; let all beings be peaceful; let all beings be blissful." So do to the east, south, north, and west. The more you practice this, the better you will feel. You will find at last that the easiest way to make ourselves healthy is to see that others are healthy, and the easiest way to make ourselves happy is to see that others are happy. After doing that, those who believe in God, should pray-not for money, not for health, nor for heaven. Pray for knowledge and light; every other prayer is selfish. Then the next thing to do is to think that your body is firm, strong, and healthy; for it is the best instrument you have. Think of it as being as strong as adamant, and that with the help of this body you will cross the ocean of life. Freedom is never to be reached by the weak; throw away all weakness. Tell your body that it is strong, tell your mind that it is strong, and have unbounded faith and hope in yourself.

Sit straight and look at the tip of your nose. Later on we shall come to know how that helps to concentrate the mind, how by controlling the two optic nerves one advances a long way towards the control of the arc of reaction, and so to the control of the will. Here is one specimen of meditation: Imagine a lotus upon the top of the head, several inches up, with virtue as its center and knowledge as its stalk. The eight petals of the lotus are the eight powers of the yogi. Inside, the stamens and pistils are renunciation. If the yogi refuses the external powers he will come to salvation. So the eight petals of the lotus are the eight powers, but the internals stamens and pistils are extreme renunciation, the renunciation of all these powers. Inside that lotus, think of the Golden One, the Almighty, the Intangible, whose name is Om, the Inexpressible, surrounded with effulgent light. Meditate on that.

Another meditation is given: Think of a space in your heart, and think that in the midst of that space a flame is burning. Think of that flame as your own soul. Inside the flame is another effulgent light, and that is the Soul of your soul, God. Meditate upon that in the heart.

Let your mind dwell on some holy personality-a Buddha, a Christ, a Ramakrishna. Then concentrate upon his heart. Try to imagine how it must feel to be a great saint; pure and untroubled by sense-objects, a knower of Brahman [supreme Reality]. Try to feel that the saint's heart has become your heart, within your own body. Here, again, the localization of the image will be found very hepful. Both Hindus and Chritians practice this form of meditation-concentrating not only upon the heart but also, sometimes upon the hands and the feet and the whole form.

Meditate on Vishnu, the Dweller in the hearts of all beings, seated on a lotus within the rays of the sun, his body luminous, adorned with diadem, necklace, earrings, and bracelets of great luster, and holding conch shell and mace in his hands.

Then the wise man should meditate upon the luminous, benign form of the Lord, without the conch shell and mace, but adorned with ornaments.

As the mind becomes concentrated on the form, he must then keep his mind on the form without ornaments.

Then he must meditate upon his oneness with the luminous form of the Lord.

Lastly, he must let the form vanish and meditate upon the Atman.

The benefits of meditation manifest on the physical, mental, and spiritual levels. On the physical level, the benefits are good voice, good health, and good complexion. On the mental level, they are emotional stability, clear vision, a sense of peace, freedom from worry and anxiety, and greater concentration. On the spiritual level, the seeker develops more faith, a taste of inner bliss, self-surrender to the divine, and spiritual enthusiasm. Practice is vital to actualize these benefits, and the practice must be right. Practice is considered right when the three components of meditation-subject of meditation, center of consciousness, and method to guide the mind to concentration-are kept unchanged and unaltered, and the practice is followed steadfastly with faith, devotion, and determination.

Meditation is cultivating a single thought reminiscent of the subject of meditation by repeating it over and over again. By following the same method and concentrating on the same subject at the same center of consciousness, that single thought becomes a giant thought-wave. In course of time the mind develops a channel for that thought-wave and the practice becomes effortless. No practice, however mechanical or intermittent, is ever lost. The Bhagavad Gita tells us that even very little of the practice of Yoga saves a person from the great fears of life.[viii]

Success in meditation is measured not by any attainment of occult powers, not by dreams or visions or miraculous happenings, but by glimpses of the divine that give the seeker a taste of inner bliss and permanent transformation of character.

Karma-Yoga

The word karma is derived from the Sanskrit kri, "to do." All action is karma. Technically this word also means the effects of actions. In connection with metaphysics it sometimes means the effects of which our past actions were the causes. But in karma-yoga we have simply to do with the word karma as meaning work.

The goal of man is knowledge. That is the one great ideal placed before us by Eastern philosophy. Not pleasure, but knowledge, is the goal of man. Pleasure and happiness come to an end. It is a mistake to suppose that pleasure is the goal; the cause of all the miseries we have in the world is that men foolishly think pleasure to be the ideal to strive for. After a time a man finds that it is not happiness, but knowledge, towards which he is going, and that both pleasure and pain are great teachers, and that he learns as much from pain as from pleasure. As pleasure and pain pass before his soul, they leave upon it different pictures, and the result of these combined impressions is what is called a man's "character." If you take the character of any man, it really is but the aggregate of tendencies, the sum total of the inclinations of his mind; you will find that misery and happiness are equal factors in the formation of that character. Happiness and misery have an equal share in moulding character, and in some instances misery is a better teacher than happiness. Were one to study the great characters the world has produced, I dare say it would be found, in the vast majority of cases, that misery taught them more than happiness, poverty taught them more than wealth, blows brought out their inner fire more than praise.

Now knowledge, again, is inherent in man. No knowledge comes from outside; it is all inside. What we say a man "knows" should, in strict psychological language, be what he discovers or unveils; what a man "learns" is really what he discovers by taking the cover off his own soul, which is a mine of infinite knowledge. We say that Newton discovered gravitation. Was it sitting anywhere in a corner waiting for him? It was in his own mind. The right time came and he found it out. All the knowledge that the world has ever received comes from the mind; the infinite library of the universe is in your own mind.

The external world is simply the suggestion, the occasion, which sets you to studying your own mind; but the object of your study is always your own mind. The falling of an apple gave the suggestion to Newton, and he studied his own mind; he rearranged all the previous links of thought in his mind and discovered a new link among them, which we call the law of gravitation. It was not in the apple nor in anything in the centre of the earth. All knowledge, therefore, secular or spiritual, is in the human mind. In many cases it is not discovered, but remains covered. When the covering is being slowly taken off we say that we are "learning, " and the advance of knowledge is made by the advance of this process of uncovering. The man from whom this veil is being lifted is the knowing man; the man upon whom it lies thick is ignorant; and the man from whom it has entirely gone is all-knowing, omniscient.

Like fire in a piece of flint, knowledge exists in the mind. Suggestion is the friction which brings it out. So with all our feelings and actions. Our tears and our smiles, our joys and our griefs, our weeping and our laughter, our curses and our blessings, our praises and our blamings-every one of these we shall find, if we calmly study our own selves, to have been brought out from within ourselves by so many blows. The result is what we are. All these blows taken together are called karma-work, action. Every mental and physical blow that is given to the soul, by which, as it were, fire is struck from it, and by which its own power and knowledge are discovered, is karma, using the word in its widest sense. Thus we are all doing karma all the time. I am talking to you: that is karma. You are listening: that is karma. We breathe: that is karma. We walk: that is karma Everything we do, physical or mental, is karma, and it leaves its marks on us.

There are certain works which are, as it were, the aggregate, the sum total, of a large number of smaller works. If we stand near the seashore and hear the waves dashing against the shingle, we think it is a great noise. And yet we know that one wave is really composed of millions and millions of minute waves: Each one of these is making a noise, and yet we do not hear it; it is only when they become the big aggregate that we hear them. Similarly every pulsation of the heart is work. Certain kinds of work we feel and they become tangible to us; they are, at the same time, the aggregate of a number of small works. If you really want to judge the character of a man, do not look at his great performances. Every fool can act as a hero at one time or another. Watch a man do his most common actions; those are indeed the things which will tell you the real character of a great man. Great occasions rouse even the lowest of human beings to some kind of greatness; but he alone is the really great man whose character is great always, the same wherever he may be.

Karma in its effect on character is the most tremendous power that man has to deal with. Man is, as it were, a centre and is attracting all the powers of the universe towards himself, and in this centre is fusing them all and again sending them off in a big current. Such a centre is the real man, the almighty and the omniscient. He draws the whole universe towards him; good and bad, misery and happiness, all are running towards him and clinging round him. And out of them he fashions the mighty stream of tendency called character and throws it outwards. As he has the power of drawing in anything, so has he the power of throwing it out.

All the actions that we see in the world, all the movements in human society, all the works that we have around us, are simply the display of thought, the manifestation of the will of man. Machines, instruments, cities, ships, men-of-war-all these are simply the manifestation of the will of man; and this will is caused by character, and character is manufactured from karma. As is the karma, so is the manifestation of the will. The men of mighty will the world has produced have all been tremendous workers-gigantic souls with wills powerful enough to overturn worlds, wills they got by persistent work through ages and ages. Such a gigantic will as that of a Buddha or a Jesus could not be obtained in one life, for we know who their fathers were. It is not known that their fathers ever spoke a word for the good of mankind. Millions and millions of carpenters like Joseph had come and gone; millions are still living.

Millions and millions of petty kings like Buddha's father had been in the world. If it was only a case of hereditary transmission, how do you account for the fact that this petty prince, who was not, perhaps, obeyed by his own servants, produced a son whom half the world worships? How do you explain the gulf between the carpenter and his son, whom millions of human beings worship as God? It cannot be solved by the theory of heredity. The gigantic will which manifested Buddha and Jesus -whence did it come? Whence came this accumulation of power? It must have been there through ages and ages, continually growing bigger and bigger until it burst on society as Buddha or Jesus, and it is rolling down even to the present day.

All this is determined by karma, work. No one can get anything unless he earns it; this is an eternal law. We may sometimes think it is not so, but in the long run we become convinced of it. A man may struggle all his life for riches; he may cheat thousands; but he finds at last that he does not deserve to become rich and his life becomes a trouble and a nuisance to him. We may go on accumulating things for our physical enjoyment, but only what we earn is really ours. A fool may buy all the books in the world, and they will be in his library; but he will be able to read only those that be deserves to. This deserving is produced by karma.

Our karma determines what we deserve and what we can assimilate. We are responsible for what we are; and whatever we wish ourselves to be, we have the power to make ourselves. If what we are now has been the result of our own past actions, it certainly follows that whatever we wish to be in the future can be produced by our present actions. So we have to know how to act. You will say: "What is the use of learning how to work? Everyone works in some way or other in this world." But there is such a thing as frittering away our energies. Karma-yoga, the Bhagavad Gita says, is doing work with cleverness and as a science. By knowing how to work one can obtain the greatest results. You must remember that the aim of all work is simply, to bring out the power of the mind which is already there, to wake up the soul. The power is inside every man; and so is knowledge. Different works are like blows to bring them out, to cause these giants to wake up.

Man works with various motives; there cannot be work without motive. Some people want to get fame and they work for fame. Others want money and they work for money. Some want to have power and they work for power. Others want to get to heaven and they work for that. Still others want to earn a name for their ancestors, as in China, where no man gets a title until he is dead; and that is a better way, after all, than ours. When a man does something very good there, they give a title of nobility to his dead father or grandfather. Some people work for that. Some of the followers of certain Mohammedan sects work all their lives to have a big tomb built for them when they die.

There are some who are really the salt of the earth, who work for work's sake, who do not care for name or fame or even to go to heaven. They work just because good will come of it. There are others who do good to the poor and help mankind from still higher motives, because they believe in doing good and they love good. As a rule, the desire for name and fame seldom brings quick results; they come to us when we are old and have almost done with life. If a man works without any selfish motive, does he not gain something? Yes, he gains the highest benefit.

Unselfishness is more paying; only people have not the patience to practice it. It is more paying from the point of view of health also. Love, truth, and unselfishness are not merely figures of speech used by moralists, but they form our highest ideal, because in them lies such a manifestation of power. In the first place, a man who can work for five days, or even five minutes, without any selfish motive whatever, without thinking of the future, of heaven, of punishment, or anything of the kind, has in him the capacity to become a powerful moral giant. It is hard to do it, but in our heart of hearts we know its value and the good it brings.

It is the greatest manifestation of power, this tremendous restraint; self-restraint is a manifestation of greater power than any selfish action. A carriage with four horses may rush down a hill unrestrained, or the coachman may curb the horses. Which is the greater display of power-to let the horses go or to hold them? A cannon-ball flying through the air goes a long distance and falls. Another is cut short in its flight by striking against a wall, and the impact generates intense heat. All outgoing energy following from a selfish motive is frittered away; it will not cause power to return to you; but if selfishness is restrained, it will result in the development of power.

This self-control will tend to produce a mighty will, a character which makes a Christ or a Buddha. Foolish men do not know this secret; they nevertheless want to rule mankind. Even a fool may rule the whole world if he works and waits. Let him wait a few years, restrain that foolish idea of governing, and when that idea is wholly gone, he will be a power in the world. The majority of us cannot see beyond a few years, as some animals cannot see beyond a few steps. just a little narrow circle-that is our world. We have not the patience to look beyond, and thus we become immoral and wicked. This is our weakness, our powerlessness.

Even the lowest forms of work are not to be despised. Let the man who knows no better work for selfish ends, for name and fame; but everyone should always try to move towards higher and higher motives and to understand them. "To work we have the right, but not to the fruits thereof." Leave the fruits alone. Why care for results? If you wish to help a man, never think what that man's attitude should be towards you. If you want to do a great or a good work, do not trouble to think what the result will be.

There arises a difficult question in this ideal of work. Intense activity is necessary; we must always work. We cannot live a minute without work. What then becomes of rest? Here is one side of life: struggle and work by which we are whirled rapidly round. And here is the other: calm, retiring renunciation everything is peaceful around, there is very little of noise and show, only nature with her animals and flowers and mountains. Neither of them is a perfect picture. A man used to solitude, if brought in contact with the surging whirlpool of the world, will be crushed by it, just as the fish that lives in deep-sea water, as soon as it is brought to the surface, breaks into pieces, deprived of the weight of water on it that kept it together.

Can a man who has been used to the turmoil and the rush of life live at ease if he comes to a quiet place? He suffers and perchance may lose his mind. The ideal man is he who in the midst of the greatest silence and solitude finds the intensest activity, and in the midst of the intensest activity, the silence and solitude of the desert. He has learnt the secret of restraint; he has controlled himself. He goes through the streets of a big city with all its traffic, and his mind is calm as if he were in a cave where not a sound could reach him; but he is intensely working all the time. That is the ideal of karma-yoga; and if you have attained to that you have really learnt the secret of work.

But we have to start from the beginning, to take up works as they come to us and slowly make ourselves more unselfish every day. We must do the work and find out the motive that prompts us; and in the first years we shall find that almost without exception our motives are selfish. But gradually this selfishness will melt through persistence, and at last will come the time when we shall be able to do really unselfish work. We may all hope that some day or other, as we struggle through the paths of life, there will come a time when we shall become perfectly unselfish; and the moment we attain to that, all our powers will be concentrated and the knowledge which is ours will be manifest.

Bhakti Yoga

Bhakti Yoga is a real, genuine search after the Lord, a search beginning, continuing, and ending in love. One single moment of the madness of extreme love of God brings us eternal freedom. "Bhakti is intense love of God," says Narada in his bhakti aphorisms. "When a man gets it he loves all, hates none; he becomes satisfied for ever." "This love cannot be reduced to any earthly benefit"- because so long as worldly desires last that kind of love does not arise. "Bhakti is greater than karma, greater than jnana, and greater than yoga," because these have in view the attainment' of an object, while bhakti is its own fruition, "its own means, and its own end."

Bhakti has been the one constant theme of our sages. Apart from the special writers on bhakti such as Sandilya or Narada, the great commentators on the Vyasa Sutras, evident advocates of jnana, have also something very suggestive to say about love. Even when those commentators are anxious to explain many, if not all, of the texts so as to make them impart a sort of dry knowledge, the sutras, in the chapter on worship especially, do not lend themselves to be easily manipulated in that fashion.

There is not really so much difference between jnana and bhakti as people sometimes imagine. We shall see, as we go on, that in the end they converge and finally meet in the same point. So also is it with raja-yoga, which, when pursued as a means to attain liberation and not (as unfortunately it has frequently become in the hands of charlatans and mystery-mongers) as an instrument to hoodwink the unwary, leads us to the same goal.

The one great advantage of bhakti is that it is the easiest and the most natural way to reach the great divine end in view. Its great disadvantage is that in its lower forms it oftentimes degenerates into hideous fanaticism. The fanatical crew in Hinduism or Mohammedanism or Christianity have always been almost exclusively recruited from these worshippers on the lower planes of bhakti. That singleness of attachment (nishtha) to a loved object, without which no genuine love can grow, is very often also the cause of the denunciation of everything else. All the weak and undeveloped minds in every religion or country have only one way of loving their own ideal, and that is to hate every other ideal. Herein is the explanation of why the same man who is so lovingly attached to his own ideal of God, so devoted to his own ideal of religion, becomes a howling fanatic as soon as he sees or hears anything of any other ideal.

This kind of love is somewhat like the canine instinct of guarding the master's property from intruders; only the instinct of the dog is better than the reason of man, for the dog never mistakes its master for an enemy, in whatever dress he may come before it. Again, the fanatic loses all power of judgement. Personal considerations are in his case of such absorbing interest that to him it is no question at all of what a man says-whether it is right or wrong; but the one thing he is always particularly careful to know is, who says it. The same man who is kind, good, honest, and loving to people of his own opinion will not hesitate to do the vilest deeds against persons beyond the pale of his own religious brotherhood.

But this danger exists only in that stage of bhakti which is called the gauni or preparatory stage. When bhakti has become ripe and has passed into that form which is called the para or supreme, no more is there any fear of these hideous manifestations of fanaticism. That soul which is overpowered by this higher form of bhakti is too near the God of Love to become an instrument for the diffusion of hatred.

It is not given to all of us to be harmonious in the building up of our characters in this life; yet we know that that character is of the noblest type in which all these three-knowledge and love and raja-yoga-are harmoniously fused. Three things are necessary for a bird to fly: the two wings, and the tail as a rudder for steering. jnana is the one wing, bhakti is the other, and raja-yoga is the tail that maintains the balance. For those who cannot pursue all these three forms of worship together in harmony, and take up, therefore, bhakti alone as their way, it is necessary always to remember that forms and ceremonials, though absolutely necessary for the progressing soul, have no other value than to lead us on to that state in which we feel the most intense love of God.

There is a little difference in opinion between the teachers of knowledge and those of love, though both admit the power of bhakti. The jnanis hold bhakti to be an instrument of liberation; the bhaktas look upon it as both the instrument and the thing to be attained. To my mind this is a distinction without much difference. In fact, bhakti, when used as an instrument really means a lower form of worship; and when this lower form is further cultivated it becomes inseparable from the higher form of bhakti. Each seems to lay great stress upon his own peculiar method of discipline, forgetting that with perfect love true knowledge is bound to come unsought, and that, at the end, true love is inseparable from perfect knowledge.

Bearing this in mind, let us try to understand what the great Vedantic commentators have to say on the subject. In explaining an aphorism of the Vedanta Sutras, Sankara says: "Thus people say, 'He is devoted to the king' or 'He is devoted to the guru. They say this of him who follows his king or his guru, and does so, having that following as the one end in view. Similarly they say, 'The loving wife meditates on her loving husband away in a foreign land.' Here also a kind of eager and continuous remembrance is meant." This is devotion according to Sankara

Bhagavan Ramanuja, in his commentary on the first aphorism of the Vedanta Sutras, says:

> "Meditation, again, is a constant remembrance [of the thing meditated upon], flowing like an unbroken stream of oil poured from one vessel to another. When this kind of remembering has been attained [in relation to God], all bondages break, Thus it is said in the scriptures regarding constant remembering as a means to liberation. This

remembering, again, is of the same form as seeing, because it has the same meaning, as in the passage: 'When He who is far and near is seen, the bonds of the heart are broken, all doubts vanish, and all effects of work disappear. He who is near can be seen, but he who is far can only be remembered. Nevertheless the scriptures say that we have to see Him who is near as well as far, thereby indicating to us that the above kind of remembering is as good as seeing. This remembrance, when exalted, assumes the same form as seeing. . . . Worship is constant remembering, as may be seen from the principal texts of the scriptures. Knowing, which is the same as repeated worship, has been described as constant remembering. . . . Thus the memory which has attained to the height of what is as good as direct perception is spoken of in the Sruti as a means of liberation. 'This Atman is not to be reached through various sciences, nor by intellect, nor by much study of the Vedas. Whomsoever this Atman desires-by him is Atman attained; unto him Atman reveals Itself. Here, after saying that mere hearing, thinking, and meditating are not the means of attaining this Atman, the Sruti says: 'Whomsoever this Atman desires-by him is Atman attained.' The extremely beloved is desired. He by whom this Atman is extremely beloved becomes the most beloved of the Atman. So that this beloved may attain the Atman, the Lord Himself helps. For it has been said by the Lord: 'Those who are constantly attached to Me and worship Me with love-I give that direction to their will by which they come to Me.' Therefore it is said that he to whom this remembering, which is of the same nature as direct perception, is very dear, because it is dear to the object of such memory perception-he is desired by the Supreme Atman and by him the Supreme Atman is attained. This constant remembrance is denoted by the word bhakti.

In commenting on the sutra of Patanjali, "Or by the worship of the Supreme Lord," Bhoja says: "Pranidhana ('worship') is that sort of bhakti in which, without one's seeking results, such as sense enjoyments and so forth, all works are dedicated to the Lord, who is the Teacher of teachers." Bhagavan Vyasa also, when commenting on the same sutra, defines pranidhana as "the form of bhakti by which the mercy of the Supreme Lord comes to the yogi and blesses him by granting him his desires." According to

Sandilya "bhakti is intense love of God." The best idea of bhakti, however, is given by the king of bhaktas, Prahlada: "May that intense and deathless love which ignorant people have for the fleeting objects of the senses not slip away from my heart as I keep meditating on Thee!"

Love for whom? For the Supreme Lord Isvara. Love for any other being, however great, cannot be bhakti; for, as Ramanuja says in his Sri Bhashya, quoting an ancient acharya, or great teacher: "From Brahma to a clump of grass, all things that live in the world are slaves of birth and death caused by karma; therefore they cannot be helpful as objects of meditation, because they are all in ignorance and subject to change." In commenting on the word anurakti used by Sandilya, the commentator Svapnesvara says that it means anu, after, and rakti, attachment; that is to say, the attachment which comes after the knowledge of the nature and glory of God -else a blind attachment to anyone, such as wife or children, would be bhakti. We plainly see, therefore, that bhakti is a series or succession of mental efforts at religious realization, beginning with ordinary worship and ending in a supreme intensity of love for Isvara.

8

Karma Yoga

Karma in its Effect on Character

The word Karma is derived from the Sanskrit Kri, to do; all action is Karma. Technically, this word also means the effects of actions. In connection with metaphysics, it sometimes means the effects, of which our past actions were the causes. But in Karma-Yoga we have simply to do with the word Karma as meaning work. The goal of mankind is knowledge. That is the one ideal placed before us by Eastern philosophy. Pleasure is not the goal of man, but knowledge. Pleasure and happiness come to an end. It is a mistake to suppose that pleasure is the goal. The cause of all the miseries we have in the world is that men foolishly think pleasure to be the ideal to strive for. After a time man finds that it is not happiness, but knowledge, towards which he is going, and that both pleasure and pain are great teachers, and that he learns as much from evil as from good. As pleasure and pain pass before his soul they have upon it different pictures, and the result of these combined impressions is what is called man's "character". If you take the character of any man, it really is but the aggregate of tendencies, the sum total of the bent of his mind; you will find that misery and happiness are equal factors in the formation of that character. Good and evil have an equal share in moulding character, and in some instances misery is a greater teacher than happiness. In studying the great characters the world has produced, I dare say, in the vast majority of cases, it would be found that it was misery that taught more than happiness, it was poverty that taught more than wealth, it was blows that brought out their inner fire more than praise.

Now this knowledge, again, is inherent in man. No knowledge comes from outside; it is all inside. What we say a man "knows", should, in strict psychological language, be what he "discovers" or "unveils"; what a man "learns" is really what he "discovers", by taking the cover off his own soul, which is a mine of infinite knowledge.

We say Newton discovered gravitation. Was it sitting anywhere in a corner waiting for him? It was in his own mind; the time came and he found it out. All knowledge that the world has ever received comes from the mind; the infinite library of the universe is in your own mind. The external world is simply the suggestion, the occasion, which sets you to study your own mind, but the object of your study is always your own mind. The falling of an apple gave the suggestion to Newton, and he studied his own mind. He rearranged all the previous links of thought in his mind and discovered a new link among them, which we call the law of gravitation. It was not in the apple nor in anything in the centre of the earth.

All knowledge, therefore, secular or spiritual, is in the human mind. In many cases it is not discovered, but remains covered, and when the covering is being slowly taken off, we say, "We are learning," and the advance of knowledge is made by the advance of this process of uncovering. The man from whom this veil is being lifted is the more knowing man, the man upon whom it lies thick is ignorant, and the man from whom it has entirely gone is all-knowing, omniscient. There have been omniscient men, and, I believe, there will be yet; and that there will be myriads of them in the cycles to come. Like fire in a piece of flint, knowledge exists in the mind; suggestion is the friction which brings it out. So with all our feelings and action — our tears and our smiles, our joys and our griefs, our weeping and our laughter, our curses and our blessings, our praises and our blames — every one of these we may find, if we calmly study our own selves, to have been brought out from within ourselves by so many blows. The result is what we are. All these blows taken together are called Karma — work, action. Every mental and physical blow that is given to the soul, by which, as it were, fire is struck from it, and by which its own power and knowledge are discovered, is Karma, this word being used in its widest sense. Thus we are all doing Karma all the time. I am talking to you: that is Karma. You are listening: that is Karma. We breathe: that is Karma. We walk: Karma. Everything we do, physical or mental, is Karma, and it leaves its marks on us.

There are certain works which are, as it were, the aggregate, the sum total, of a large number of smaller works. If we stand near the seashore and hear the waves dashing against the shingle, we think it is such a great noise, and yet we know that one wave is really composed of millions and millions of minute waves. Each one of these is making a noise, and yet we do not catch it; it is only when they become the big aggregate that we hear. Similarly, every pulsation of the heart is work. Certain kinds of work we feel and they become tangible to us; they are, at the same time, the aggregate of a number of small works. If you really want to judge of the character of a man, look not at his great performances. Every fool may become a hero at one time or another. Watch a man do his most common actions; those are indeed the things which will tell you the real character of a great man. Great occasions rouse even the lowest of human beings to some kind of greatness, but he alone is the really great man whose character is great always, the same wherever he be.

Karma in its effect on character is the most tremendous power that man has to deal with. Man is, as it were, a centre, and is attracting all the powers of the universe towards himself, and in this centre is fusing them all and again sending them off in a big current. Such a centre is the *real* man — the almighty, the omniscient — and he draws the whole universe towards him. Good and bad, misery and happiness, all are running towards him and clinging round him; and out of them he fashions the mighty stream of tendency called character and throws it outwards. As he has the power of drawing in anything, so has he the power of throwing it out.

All the actions that we see in the world, all the movements in human society, all the works that we have around us, are simply the display of thought, the manifestation of the will of man. Machines or instruments, cities, ships, or men-of-war, all these are simply the manifestation of the will of man; and this will is caused by character, and character is manufactured by Karma. As is Karma, so is the manifestation of the will. The men of mighty will the world has produced have all been tremendous workers — gigantic souls, with wills powerful enough to overturn worlds, wills they got by persistent work, through ages, and ages. Such a gigantic will as that of a Buddha or a Jesus could not be obtained in one life, for we know who their fathers were. It is not known that their fathers ever spoke a word for the good of mankind. Millions and millions of carpenters like Joseph had gone; millions are still living. Millions and millions of petty kings like Buddha's father had been in the world. If it was only a case of hereditary transmission, how do you account for this petty prince, who was not, perhaps, obeyed by his own servants, producing this son, whom half a world worships? How do you explain the gulf between the carpenter and his son, whom millions of human beings worship as God? It cannot be solved by the theory of heredity. The gigantic will which Buddha and Jesus threw over the world, whence did it come? Whence came this accumulation of power? It must have been there through ages and ages, continually growing bigger and bigger, until it burst on society in a Buddha or a Jesus, even rolling down to the present day.

All this is determined by Karma, work. No one can get anything unless he earns it. This is an eternal law. We may sometimes think it is not so, but in the long run we become convinced of it. A man may struggle all his life for riches; he may cheat thousands, but he finds at last that he did not deserve to become rich, and his life becomes a trouble and a nuisance to him. We may go on accumulating things for our physical enjoyment, but only what we earn is really ours. A fool may buy all the books in the world, and they will be in his library; but he will be able to read only those that he deserves to; and this deserving is produced by Karma. Our Karma determines what we deserve and what we can assimilate. We are responsible for what we are; and whatever we wish ourselves to be, we have the power to make ourselves. If what we are now has been the result of our own past actions, it certainly follows that whatever we wish to be in future can be produced by our present actions; so we have to know how to act. You will say, "What is the use of learning how to work? Everyone works in some way or other in this world." But there is such a thing as frittering away our energies. With regard to Karma-Yoga, the Gita says that it is doing work with cleverness and as a science; by knowing how to work, one can obtain the greatest results. You must remember that all work is simply to bring out the power of the mind which is already there, to wake up the soul. The power is inside every man, so is knowing; the different works are like blows to bring them out, to cause these giants to wake up.

Man works with various motives. There cannot be work without motive. Some people want to get fame, and they work for fame. Others want money, and they work for money. Others want to have power, and they work for power. Others want to get to heaven, and they work for the same. Others want to leave a name when they die, as they do in China, where no man gets a title until he is dead; and that is a better way, after all, than with us. When a man does something very good there, they give a title of nobility to his father, who is dead, or to his grandfather. Some people work for that. Some of the followers of certain Mohammedan sects work all their lives to have a big tomb built for them when they die. I know sects among whom, as soon as a child is born, a tomb is prepared for it; that is among them the most important work a man has to do, and the bigger and the finer the tomb, the better off the man is supposed to be. Others work as a penance; do all sorts of wicked things, then erect a temple, or give something to the priests to buy them off and obtain from them a passport to heaven. They think that this kind of beneficence will clear them and they will go scot-free in spite of their sinfulness. Such are some of the various motives for work.

Work for work's sake. There are some who are really the salt of the earth in every country and who work for work's sake, who do not care for name, or fame, or even to go to heaven. They work just because good will come of it. There are others who do good to the poor and help mankind from still higher motives, because they believe in doing good and love good. The motive for name and fame seldom brings immediate results, as a rule; they come to us when we are old and have almost done with life. If a man works without any selfish motive in view, does he not gain anything? Yes, he gains the highest. Unselfishness is more paying, only people have not the patience to practice it. It is more paying from the point of view of health also. Love, truth, and unselfishness are not merely moral figures of speech, but they form our highest ideal, because in them lies such a manifestation of power. In the first place, a man who can work for five days, or even for five minutes, without any selfish motive whatever, without thinking of future, of heaven, of punishment, or anything of the kind, has in him the capacity to become a powerful moral giant. It is hard to do it, but in the heart of our hearts we know its value, and the good it brings. It is the greatest manifestation of power — this tremendous restraint; self-restraint is a manifestation of greater power than all outgoing action. A carriage with four horses may rush down a hill unrestrained, or the coachman may curb the horses. Which is the greater manifestation of power, to let them go or to hold them? A cannonball flying through the air goes a long distance and falls. Another is cut short in its flight by striking against a wall, and the impact generates intense heat. All outgoing energy following a selfish motive is frittered away; it will not cause power to return to you; but if restrained, it will result in development of power. This self-control will tend to produce a mighty will, a character which makes a Christ or a Buddha. Foolish men do not know this secret; they nevertheless want to rule mankind. Even a fool may rule the whole world if he works and waits. Let him wait a few years, restrain that foolish idea of governing; and when that idea is wholly gone, he will be a power in the world. The majority of us cannot see beyond a few years, just as some animals cannot see beyond a few steps. Just a little narrow circle — that is our world. We have not the patience to look beyond, and thus become immoral and wicked. This is our weakness, our powerlessness.

Even the lowest forms of work are not to be despised. Let the man, who knows no better, work for selfish ends, for name and fame; but everyone should always try to get towards higher and higher motives and to understand them. "To work we have the right, but not to the fruits thereof:" Leave the fruits alone. Why care for results? If you wish to help a man, never think what that man's attitude should be towards you. If you want to do a great or a good work, do not trouble to think what the result will be.

There arises a difficult question in this ideal of work. Intense activity is necessary; we must always work. We cannot live a minute without work. What then becomes of rest? Here is one side of the life-struggle — work, in which we are whirled rapidly round. And here is the other — that of calm, retiring renunciation: everything is peaceful around, there is very little of noise and show, only nature with her animals and flowers and mountains. Neither of them is a perfect picture. A man used to solitude, if brought in contact with the surging whirlpool of the world, will be crushed by it; just as the fish that lives in the deep sea water, as soon as it is brought to the surface, breaks into pieces, deprived of the weight of water on it that had kept it together. Can a man who has been used to the turmoil and the rush of life live at ease if he comes to a quiet place? He suffers and perchance may lose his mind. The ideal man is he who, in the midst of the greatest silence and solitude, finds the intensest activity, and in the midst of the intensest activity finds the silence and solitude of the desert. He has learnt the secret of restraint, he has controlled himself. He goes through the streets of a big city with all its traffic, and his mind is as calm as if he were in a cave, where not a sound could reach him; and he is intensely working all the time. That is the ideal of Karma-Yoga, and if you have attained to that you have really learnt the secret of work.

But we have to begin from the beginning, to take up the works as they come to us and slowly make ourselves more unselfish every day. We must do the work and find out the motive power that prompts us; and, almost without exception, in the first years, we shall find that our motives are always selfish; but gradually this selfishness will melt by persistence, till at last will come the time when we shall be able to do really unselfish work. We may all hope that some day or other, as we struggle through the paths of life, there will come a time when we shall become perfectly unselfish; and the moment we attain to that, all our powers will be concentrated, and the knowledge which is ours will be manifest

According to the Sânkhya philosophy, nature is composed of three forces called, in Sanskrit, Sattva, Rajas, and Tamas. These as manifested in the physical world are what we may call equilibrium, activity, and inertness. Tamas is typified as darkness or inactivity; Rajas is activity, expressed as attraction or repulsion; and Sattva is the equilibrium of the two.

In every man there are these three forces. Sometimes Tamas prevails. We become lazy, we cannot move, we are inactive, bound down by certain ideas or by mere dullness. At other times activity prevails, and at still other times that calm balancing of both. Again, in different men, one of these forces is generally predominant. The characteristic of one man is inactivity, dullness and laziness; that of another, activity, power, manifestation of energy; and in still another we find the sweetness, calmness, and gentleness, which are due to the balancing of both action and inaction. So in all creation — in animals, plants, and men — we find the more or less typical manifestation of all these different forces.

Karma-Yoga has specially to deal with these three factors. By teaching what they are and how to employ them, it helps us to do our work better. Human society is a graded organization. We all know about morality, and we all know about duty, but at the same time we find that in different countries the significance of morality varies greatly. What is regarded as moral in one country may in another be considered perfectly immoral. For instance, in one country cousins may marry; in another, it is thought to be very immoral; in one, men may marry their sisters-in-law; in another, it is regarded as immoral; in one country people may marry only once; in another, many times; and so forth. Similarly, in all other departments of morality, we find the standard varies greatly — yet we have the idea that there must be a universal standard of morality.

So it is with duty. The idea of duty varies much among different nations. In one country, if a man does not do certain things, people will say he has acted wrongly; while if he does those very things in another country, people will say that he did not act rightly — and yet we know that there must be some universal idea of duty. In the same way, one class of society thinks that certain things are among its duty, while another class thinks quite the opposite and would be horrified if it had to do those things. Two ways are left open to us — the way of the ignorant, who think that there is only one way to truth and that all the rest are wrong, and the way of the wise, who admit that, according to our mental constitution or the different planes of existence in which we are, duty and morality may vary. The important thing is to know that there are gradations of duty and of morality — that the duty of one state of life, in one set of circumstances, will not and cannot be that of another.

To illustrate: All great teachers have taught, "Resist not evil," that non-resistance is the highest moral ideal. We all know that, if a certain number of us attempted to put that maxim fully into practice, the whole social fabric would fall to pieces, the wicked would take possession of our properties and our lives, and would do whatever they liked with us. Even if only one day of such non-resistance were practiced, it would lead to disaster. Yet, intuitively, in our heart of hearts we feel the truth of the teaching "Resist not evil." This seems to us to be the highest ideal; yet to teach this doctrine only would be equivalent to condemning a vast portion of mankind. Not only so, it would be making men feel that they were always doing wrong, and cause in them scruples of conscience in all their actions; it would weaken them, and that constant self-disapproval would breed more vice than any other weakness would. To the man who has begun to hate himself the gate to degeneration has already opened; and the same is true of a nation.

Our first duty is not to hate ourselves, because to advance we must have faith in ourselves first and then in God. He who has no faith in himself can never have faith in God. Therefore, the only alternative remaining to us is to recognise that duty and morality vary under different circumstances; not that the man who resists evil is doing what is always and in itself wrong, but that in the different circumstances in which he is placed it may become even his duty to resist evil.

In reading the Bhagavad-Gita, many of you in Western countries may have felt astonished at the second chapter, wherein Shri Krishna calls Arjuna a hypocrite and a coward because of his refusal to fight, or offer resistance, on account of his adversaries being his friends and relatives, making the plea that non-resistance was the highest ideal of love. This is a great lesson for us all to learn, that in all matters the two extremes are alike. The extreme positive and the extreme negative are always similar. When the vibrations of light are too slow, we do not see them, nor do we see them when they are too rapid. So with sound; when very low in pitch, we do not hear it; when very high, we do not hear it either. Of like nature is the difference between resistance and non-resistance. One man does not resist because he is weak, lazy, and cannot, not because he will not; the other man knows that he can strike an irresistible blow if he likes; yet he not only does not strike, but blesses his enemies. The one who from weakness resists not commits a sin, and as such cannot receive any benefit from the non-resistance; while the other would commit a sin by offering resistance. Buddha gave up his throne and renounced his position, that was true renunciation; but there cannot be any question of renunciation in the case of a beggar who has nothing to renounce. So we must always be careful about what we really mean when we speak of this non-resistance and ideal love. We must first take care to understand whether we have the power of resistance or not. Then, having the power, if we renounce it and do not resist, we are doing a grand act of love; but if we cannot resist, and yet, at the same time, try to deceive ourselves into the belief that we are actuated by motives of the highest love, we are doing the exact opposite. Arjuna became a coward at the sight of the mighty array against him; his "love" made him forget his duty towards his country and king. That is why Shri Krishna told him that he was a hypocrite: Thou talkest like a wise man, but thy actions betray thee to be a coward; therefore stand up and fight!

Such is the central idea of Karma-Yoga. The Karma-Yogi is the man who understands that the highest ideal is non-resistance, and who also knows that this non-resistance is the highest manifestation of power in actual possession, and also what is called the resisting of evil is but a step on the way towards the manifestation of this highest power, namely, non-resistance. Before reaching this highest ideal, man's duty is to resist evil; let him work, let him fight, let him strike straight from the shoulder. Then only, when he has gained the power to resist, will non-resistance be a virtue.

I once met a man in my country whom I had known before as a very stupid, dull person, who knew nothing and had not the desire to know anything, and was living the life of a brute. He asked me what he should do to know God, how he was to get free. "Can you tell a lie?" I asked him. "No," he replied. "Then you must learn to do so. It is better to tell a lie than to be a brute, or a log of wood. You are inactive; you have not certainly reached the highest state, which is beyond all actions, calm and serene; you are too dull even to do something wicked." That was an extreme case, of course, and I was joking with him; but what I meant was that a man must be active in order to pass through activity to perfect calmness.

Inactivity should be avoided by all means. Activity always means resistance. Resist all evils, mental and physical; and when you have succeeded in resisting, then will calmness come. It is very easy to say, "Hate nobody, resist not evil," but we know what that kind of thing generally means in practice. When the eyes of society are turned towards us, we may make a show of non-resistance, but in our hearts it is canker all the time. We feel the utter want of the calm of non-resistance; we feel that it would be better for us to resist. If you desire wealth, and know at the same time that the whole world regards him who aims at wealth as a very wicked man, you, perhaps, will not dare to plunge into the struggle for wealth, yet your mind will be running day and night after money. This is hypocrisy and will serve no purpose. Plunge into the world, and then, after a time, when you have suffered and enjoyed all that is in it, will renunciation come; then will calmness come. So fulfil your desire for power and everything else, and after you have fulfilled the desire, will come the time when you will know that they are all very little things; but until you have fulfilled this desire, until you have passed through that activity, it is impossible for you to come to the state of calmness, serenity, and self-surrender. These ideas of serenity and renunciation have been preached for thousands of years; everybody has heard of them from childhood, and yet we see very few in the world who have really reached that stage. I do not know if I have seen twenty persons in my life who are really calm and non-resisting, and I have travelled over half the world.

Every man should take up his own ideal and endeavour to accomplish it. That is a surer way of progress than taking up other men's ideals, which he can never hope to accomplish. For instance, we take a child and at once give him the task of walking twenty miles. Either the little one dies, or one in a thousand crawls the twenty miles, to reach the end exhausted and half-dead. That is like what we generally try to do with the world. All the men and women, in any society, are not of the same mind, capacity, or of the same power to do things; they must have different ideals, and we have no right to sneer at any ideal. Let every one do the best he can for realising his own ideal. Nor is it right that I should be judged by your standard or you by mine. The apple tree should not be judged by the standard of the oak, nor the oak by that of the apple. To judge the apple tree you must take the apple standard, and for the oak, its own standard.

Unity in variety is the plan of creation. However men and women may vary individually, there is unity in the background. The different individual characters and classes of men and women are natural variations in creation. Hence, we ought not to judge them by the same standard or put the same ideal before them. Such a course creates only an unnatural struggle, and the result is that man begins to hate himself and is hindered from becoming religious and good. Our duty is to encourage every one in his struggle to live up to his own highest ideal, and strive at the same time to make the ideal as near as possible to the truth.

In the Hindu system of morality we find that this fact has been recognised from very ancient times; and in their scriptures and books on ethics different rules are laid down for the different classes of men — the householder, the Sannyâsin (the man who has renounced the world), and the student.

The life of every individual, according to the Hindu scriptures, has its peculiar duties apart from what belongs in common to universal humanity. The Hindu begins life as a student; then he marries and becomes a householder; in old age he retires; and lastly he gives up the world and becomes a Sannyasin. To each of these stages of life certain duties are attached. No one of these stages is intrinsically superior to another. The life of the married man is quite as great as that of the celibate who has devoted himself to religious work. The scavenger in the street is quite as great and glorious as the king on his throne. Take him off his throne, make him do the work of the scavenger, and see how he fares. Take up the scavenger and see how he will rule. It is useless to say that the man who lives out of the world is a greater man than he who lives in the world; it is much more difficult to live in the world and worship God than to give it up and live a free and easy life. The four stages of life in India have in later times been reduced to two — that of the householder and of the monk. The householder marries and carries on his duties as a citizen, and the duty of the other is to devote his energies wholly to religion, to preach and to worship God. I shall read to you a few passages from the Mahâ-Nirvâna-Tantra, which treats of this subject, and you will see that it is a very difficult task for a man to be a householder, and perform all his duties perfectly:

The householder should be devoted to God; the knowledge of God should be his goal of life. Yet he must work constantly, perform all his duties; he must give up the fruits of his actions to God.

It is the most difficult thing in this world to work and not care for the result, to help a man and never think that he ought to be grateful, to do some good work and at the same time never look to see whether it brings you name or fame, or nothing at all. Even the most arrant coward becomes brave when the world praises him. A fool can do heroic deeds when the approbation of society is upon him, but for a man to constantly do good without caring for the approbation of his fellow men is indeed the highest sacrifice man can perform. The great duty of the householder is to earn a living, but he must take care that he does not do it by telling lies, or by cheating, or by robbing others; and he must remember that his life is for the service of God, and the poor.

Knowing that mother and father are the visible representatives of God, the householder, always and by all means, must please them. If the mother is pleased, and the father, God is pleased with the man. That child is really a good child who never speaks harsh words to his parents.

Before parents one must not utter jokes, must not show restlessness, must not show anger or temper. Before mother or father, a child must bow down low, and stand up in their presence, and must not take a seat until they order him to sit.

If the householder has food and drink and clothes without first seeing that his mother and his father, his children, his wife, and the poor, are supplied, he is committing a sin. The mother and the father are the causes of this body; so a man must undergo a thousand troubles in order to do good to them.

Even so is his duty to his wife. No man should scold his wife, and he must always maintain her as if she were his own mother. And even when he is in the greatest difficulties and troubles, he must not show anger to his wife.

He who thinks of another woman besides his wife, if he touches her even with his mind — that man goes to dark hell.

Before women he must not talk improper language, and never brag of his powers. He must not say, "I have done this, and I have done that."

The householder must always please his wife with money, clothes, love, faith, and words like nectar, and never do anything to disturb her. That man who has succeeded in getting the love of a chaste wife has succeeded in his religion and has all the virtues.

The following are duties towards children:

A son should be lovingly reared up to his fourth year; he should be educated till he is sixteen. When he is twenty years of age he should be employed in some work; he should then be treated affectionately by his father as his equal. Exactly in the same manner the daughter should be brought up, and should be educated with the greatest care. And when she marries, the father ought to give her jewels and wealth.

Then the duty of the man is towards his brothers and sisters, and towards the children of his brothers and sisters, if they are poor, and towards his other relatives, his friends and his servants. Then his duties are towards the people of the same village, and the poor, and any one that comes to him for help. Having sufficient means, if the householder does not take care to give to his relatives and to the poor, know him to be only a brute; he is not a human being.

Excessive attachment to food, clothes, and the tending of the body, and dressing of the hair should be avoided. The householder must be pure in heart and clean in body, always active and always ready for work.

To his enemies the householder must be a hero. Them he must resist. That is the duty of the householder. He must not sit down in a corner and weep, and talk nonsense about non-resistance. If he does not show himself a hero to his enemies he has not done his duty. And to his friends and relatives he must be as gentle as a lamb.

It is the duty of the householder not to pay reverence to the wicked; because, if he reverences the wicked people of the world, he patronizes wickedness; and it will be a great mistake if he disregards those who are worthy of respect, the good people. He must not be gushing in his friendship; he must not go out of the way making friends everywhere; he must watch the actions of the men he wants to make friends with, and their dealings with other men, reason upon them, and then make friends.

These three things he must not talk of. He must not talk in public of his own fame; he must not preach his own name or his own powers; he must not talk of his wealth, or of anything that has been told to him privately.

A man must not say he is poor, or that he is wealthy — he must not brag of his wealth. Let him keep his own counsel; this is his religious duty. This is not mere worldly wisdom; if a man does not do so, he may be held to be immoral.

The householder is the basis, the prop, of the whole society. He is the principal earner. The poor, the weak, the children and the women who do not work — all live upon the householder; so there must be certain duties that he has to perform, and these duties must make him feel strong to perform them, and not make him think that he is doing things beneath his ideal. Therefore, if he has done something weak, or has made some mistake, he must not say so in public; and if he is engaged in some enterprise and knows he is sure to fail in it, he must not speak of it. Such self-exposure is not only uncalled for, but also unnerves the man and makes him unfit for the performance of his legitimate duties in life. At the same time, he must struggle hard to acquire these things — firstly, knowledge, and secondly, wealth. It is his duty, and if he does not do his duty, he is nobody. A householder who does not struggle to get wealth is immoral. If he is lazy and content to lead an idle life, he is immoral, because upon him depend hundreds. If he gets riches, hundreds of others will be thereby supported.

If there were not in this city hundreds who had striven to become rich, and who had acquired wealth, where would all this civilization, and these alms-houses and great houses be?

Going after wealth in such a case is not bad, because that wealth is for distribution. The householder is the centre of life and society. It is a worship for him to acquire and spend wealth nobly, for the householder who struggles to become rich by good means and for good purposes is doing practically the same thing for the attainment of salvation as the anchorite does in his cell when he is praying; for in them we see only the different aspects of the same virtue of self-surrender and self-sacrifice prompted by the feeling of devotion to God and to all that is His.

He must struggle to acquire a good name by all means. He must not gamble, he must not move in the company of the wicked, he must not tell lies, and must not be the cause of trouble to others.

Often people enter into things they have not the means to accomplish, with the result that they cheat others to attain their own ends. Then there is in all things the time factor to be taken into consideration; what at one time might be a failure, would perhaps at another time be a very great success.

The householder must speak the truth, and speak gently, using words which people like, which will do good to others; nor should he talk of the business of other men.

The householder by digging tanks, by planting trees on the roadsides, by establishing rest-houses for men and animals, by making roads and building bridges, goes towards the same goal as the greatest Yogi.

This is one part of the doctrine of Karma-Yoga — activity, the duty of the householder. There is a passage later on, where it says that "if the householder dies in battle, fighting for his country or his religion, he comes to the same goal as the Yogi by meditation," showing thereby that what is duty for one is not duty for another. At the same time, it does not say that this duty is lowering and the other elevating. Each duty has its own place, and according to the circumstances in which we are placed, we must perform our duties.

One idea comes out of all this — the condemnation of all weakness. This is a particular idea in all our teachings which I like, either in philosophy, or in religion, or in work. If you read the Vedas, you will find this word always repeated — fearlessness — fear nothing. Fear is a sign of weakness. A man must go about his duties without taking notice of the sneers and the ridicule of the world.

If a man retires from the world to worship God, he must not think that those who live in the world and work for the good of the world are not worshipping God: neither must those who live in the world, for wife and children, think that those who give up the world are low vagabonds. Each is great in his own place. This thought I will illustrate by a story.

A certain king used to inquire of all the Sannyasins that came to his country, "Which is the greater man — he who gives up the world and becomes a Sannyasin, or he who lives in the world and performs his duties as a house holder?" Many wise men sought to solve the problem. Some asserted that the Sannyasin was the greater, upon which the king demanded that they should prove their assertion. When they could not, he ordered them to marry and become householders. Then others came and said, "The householder who performs his duties is the greater man." Of them, too, the king demanded proofs. When they could not give them, he made them also settle down as householders.

At last there came a young Sannyasin, and the king similarly inquired of him also. He answered, "Each, O king, is equally great in his place." "Prove this to me," asked the king. "I will prove it to you," said the Sannyasin, "but you must first come and live as I do for a few days, that I may be able to prove to you what I say." The king consented and followed the Sannyasin out of his own territory and passed through many other countries until they came to a great kingdom. In the capital of that kingdom a great ceremony was going on. The king and the Sannyasin heard the noise of drums and music, and heard also the criers; the people were assembled in the streets in gala dress, and a great proclamation was being made. The king and the Sannyasin stood there to see what was going on. The crier was proclaiming loudly that the princess, daughter of the king of that country, was about to choose a husband from among those assembled before her.

It was an old custom in India for princesses to choose husbands in this way. Each princess had certain ideas of the sort of man she wanted for a husband. Some would have the handsomest man, others would have only the most learned, others again the richest, and so on. All the princes of the neighbourhood put on their bravest attire and presented themselves before her. Sometimes they too had their own criers to enumerate their advantages and the reasons why they hoped the princess would choose them. The princess was taken round on a throne, in the most splendid array, and looked at and heard about them. If she was not pleased with what she saw and heard, she said to her bearers, "Move on," and no more notice was taken of the rejected suitors. If, however, the princess was pleased with any one of them, she threw a garland of flowers over him and he became her husband.

The princess of the country to which our king and the Sannyasin had come was having one of these interesting ceremonies. She was the most beautiful princess in the world, and the husband of the princess would be ruler of the kingdom after her father's death. The idea of this princess was to marry the handsomest man, but she could not find the right one to please her. Several times these meetings had taken place, but the princess could not select a husband. This meeting was the most splendid of all; more people than ever had come to it. The princess came in on a throne, and the bearers carried her from place to place. She did not seem to care for any one, and every one became disappointed that this meeting also was going to be a failure. Just then came a young man, a Sannyasin, handsome as if the sun had come down to the earth, and stood in one corner of the assembly, watching what was going on. The throne with the princess came near him, and as soon as she saw the beautiful Sannyasin, she stopped and threw the garland over him. The young Sannyasin seized the garland and threw it off, exclaiming, "What nonsense is this? I am a Sannyasin. What is marriage to me?" The king of that country thought that perhaps this man was poor and so dared not marry the princess, and said to him, "With my daughter goes half my kingdom now, and the whole kingdom after my death!" and put the garland again on the Sannyasin. The young man threw it off once more, saying, "Nonsense! I do not want to marry," and walked quickly away from the assembly.

Now the princess had fallen so much in love with this young man that she said, "I must marry this man or I shall die"; and she went after him to bring him back. Then our other Sannyasin, who had brought the king there, said to him, "King, let us follow this pair"; so they walked after them, but at a good distance behind. The young Sannyasin who had refused to marry the princess walked out into the country for several miles. When he came to a forest and entered into it, the princess followed him, and the other two followed them. Now this young Sannyasin was well acquainted with that forest and knew all the intricate paths in it. He suddenly passed into one of these and disappeared, and the princess could not discover him. After trying for a long time to find him she sat down under a tree and began to weep, for she did not know the way out. Then our king and the other Sannyasin came up to her and said, "Do not weep; we will show you the way out of this forest, but it is too dark for us to find it now. Here is a big tree; let us rest under it, and in the morning we will go early and show you the road."

Now a little bird and his wife and their three little ones lived on that tree, in a nest. This little bird looked down and saw the three people under the tree and said to his wife, "My dear, what shall we do? Here are some guests in the house, and it is winter, and we have no fire." So he flew away and got a bit of burning firewood in his beak and dropped it before the guests, to which they added fuel and made a blazing fire. But the little bird was not satisfied. He said again to his wife, "My dear, what shall we do? There is nothing to give these people to eat, and they are hungry. We are householders; it is our duty to feed any one who comes to the house. I must do what I can, I will give them my body." So he plunged into the midst of the fire and perished. The guests saw him falling and tried to save him, but he was too quick for them.

The little bird's wife saw what her husband did, and she said, "Here are three persons and only one little bird for them to eat. It is not enough; it is my duty as a wife not to let my husband's effort go in vain; let them have my body also." Then she fell into the fire and was burned to death.

Then the three baby-birds, when they saw what was done and that there was still not enough food for the three guests, said, "Our parents have done what they could and still it is not enough. It is our duty to carry on the work of our parents; let our bodies go too." And they all dashed down into the fire also.

Amazed at what they saw, the three people could not of course eat these birds. They passed the night without food, and in the morning the king and the Sannyasin showed the princess the way, and she went back to her father.

Then the Sannyasin said to the king, "King, you have seen that each is great in his own place. If you want to live in the world, live like those birds, ready at any moment to sacrifice yourself for others. If you want to renounce the world, be like that young man to whom the most beautiful woman and a kingdom were as nothing. If you want to be a householder, hold your life a sacrifice for the welfare of others; and if you choose the life of renunciation, do not even look at beauty and money and power. Each is great in his own place, but the duty of the one is not the duty of the other.

The Secret of Work

Helping others physically, by removing their physical needs, is indeed great, but the help is great according as the need is greater and according as the help is far reaching. If a man's wants can be removed for an hour, it is helping him indeed; if his wants can be removed for a year, it will be more help to him; but if his wants can be removed for ever, it is surely the greatest help that can be given him. Spiritual knowledge is the only thing that can destroy our miseries for ever; any other knowledge satisfies wants only for a time. It is only with the knowledge of the spirit that the faculty of want is annihilated for ever; so helping man spiritually is the highest help that can be given to him. He who gives man spiritual knowledge is the greatest benefactor of mankind and as such we always find that those were the most powerful of men who helped man in his spiritual needs, because spirituality is the true basis of all our activities in life.

A spiritually strong and sound man will be strong in every other respect, if he so wishes. Until there is spiritual strength in man even physical needs cannot be well satisfied. Next to spiritual comes intellectual help. The gift of knowledge is a far higher gift than that of food and clothes; it is even higher than giving life to a man, because the real life of man consists of knowledge. Ignorance is death, knowledge is life. Life is of very little value, if it is a life in the dark, groping through ignorance and misery. Next in order comes, of course, helping a man physically. Therefore, in considering the question of helping others, we must always strive not to commit the mistake of thinking that physical help is the only help that can be given. It is not only the last but the least, because it cannot bring about permanent satisfaction. The misery that I feel when I am hungry is satisfied by eating, but hunger returns; my misery can cease only when I am satisfied beyond all want. Then hunger will not make me miserable; no distress, no sorrow will be able to move me. So, that help which tends to make us strong spiritually is the highest, next to it comes intellectual help, and after that physical help.

The miseries of the world cannot be cured by physical help only. Until man's nature changes, these physical needs will always arise, and miseries will always be felt, and no amount of physical help will cure them completely. The only solution of this problem is to make mankind pure. Ignorance is the mother of all the evil and all the misery we see. Let men have light, let them be pure and spiritually strong and educated, then alone will misery cease in the world, not before. We may convert every house in the country into a charity asylum, we may fill the land with hospitals, but the misery of man will still continue to exist until man's character changes.

We read in the Bhagavad-Gita again and again that we must all work incessantly. All work is by nature composed of good and evil. We cannot do any work which will not do some good somewhere; there cannot be any work which will not cause some harm somewhere. Every work must necessarily be a mixture of good and evil; yet we are commanded to work incessantly. Good and evil will both have their results, will produce their Karma. Good action will entail upon us good effect; bad action, bad. But good and bad are both bondages of the soul. The solution reached in the Gita in regard to this bondage-producing nature of work is that, if we do not attach ourselves to the work we do, it will not have any binding effect on our soul. We shall try to understand what is meant by this "non-attachment to" to work.

This is the on central idea in tile Gita: work incessantly, but be not attached to it. Samskâra can be translated very nearly by "inherent tendency". Using the simile of a lake for the mind, every ripple, every wave that rises in the mind, when it subsides, does not die out entirely, but leaves a mark and a future possibility of that wave coming out again. This mark, with the possibility of the wave reappearing, is what is called Samskâra. Every work that we do, every movement of the body, every thought that we think, leaves such an impression on the mind-stuff, and even when such impressions are not obvious on the surface, they are sufficiently strong to work beneath the surface, subconsciously. What we are every moment is determined by the sum total of these impressions on the mind. What I am just at this moment is the effect of the sum total of all the impressions of my past life. This is really what is meant by character; each man's character is determined by the sum total of these impressions. If good impressions prevail, the character becomes good; if bad, it becomes bad. If a man continuously hears bad words, thinks bad thoughts, does bad actions, his mind will be full of bad impressions; and they will influence his thought and work without his being conscious of the fact. In fact, these bad impressions are always working, and their resultant must be evil, and that man will be a bad man; he cannot help it. The sum total of these impressions in him will create the strong motive power for doing bad actions. He will be like a machine in the hands of his impressions, and they will force him to do evil. Similarly, if a man thinks good thoughts and does good works, the sum total of these impressions will be good; and they, in a similar manner, will force him to do good even in spite of himself. When a man has done so much good work and thought so many good thoughts that there is an irresistible tendency in him to do good in spite of himself and even if he wishes to do evil, his mind, as the sum total of his tendencies, will not allow him to do so; the tendencies will turn him back; he is completely under the influence of the good tendencies. When such is the case, a man's good character is said to be established.

As the tortoise tucks its feet and head inside the shell, and you may kill it and break it in pieces, and yet it will not come out, even so the character of that man who has control over his motives and organs is unchangeably established. He controls his own inner forces, and nothing can draw them out against his will. By this continuous reflex of good thoughts, good impressions moving over the surface of the mind, the tendency for doing good becomes strong, and as the result we feel able to control the Indriyas (the sense-organs, the nerve-centres). Thus alone will character be established, then alone a man gets to truth. Such a man is safe for ever; he cannot do any evil. You may place him in any company, there will be no danger for him. There is a still higher state than having this good tendency, and that is the desire for liberation. You must remember that freedom of the soul is the goal of all Yogas, and each one equally leads to the same result. By work alone men may get to where Buddha got largely by meditation or Christ by prayer. Buddha was a working Jnâni, Christ was a Bhakta, but the same goal was reached by both of them. The difficulty is here. Liberation means entire freedom — freedom from the bondage of good, as well as from the bondage of evil. A golden chain is as much a chain as an iron one. There is a thorn in my finger, and I use another to take the first one out; and when I have taken it out, I throw both of them aside; I have no necessity for keeping the second thorn, because both are thorns after all. So the bad tendencies are to be counteracted by the good ones, and the bad impressions on the mind should be removed by the fresh waves of good ones, until all that is evil almost disappears, or is subdued and held in control in a corner of the mind; but after that, the good tendencies have also to be conquered. Thus the "attached" becomes the "unattached". Work, but let not the action or the thought produce a deep impression on the mind. Let the ripples come and go, let huge actions proceed from the muscles and the brain, but let them not make any deep impression on the soul.

How can this be done? We see that the impression of any action, to which we attach ourselves, remains. I may meet hundreds of persons during the day, and among them meet also one whom I love; and when I retire at night, I may try to think of all the faces I saw, but only that face comes before the mind — the face which I met perhaps only for one minute, and which I loved; all the others have vanished. My attachment to this particular person caused a deeper impression on my mind than all the other faces. Physiologically the impressions have all been the same; every one of the faces that I saw pictured itself on the retina, and the brain took the pictures in, and yet there was no similarity of effect upon the mind. Most of the faces, perhaps, were entirely new faces, about which I had never thought before, but that one face of which I got only a glimpse found associations inside. Perhaps I had pictured him in my mind for years, knew hundreds of things about him, and this one new vision of him awakened hundreds of sleeping memories in my mind; and this one impression having been repeated perhaps a hundred times more than those of the different faces together, will produce a great effect on the mind.

Therefore, be "unattached"; let things work; let brain centres work; work incessantly, but let not a ripple conquer the mind. Work as if you were a stranger in this land, a sojourner; work incessantly, but do not bind yourselves; bondage is terrible. This world is not our habitation, it is only one of the many stages through which we are passing. Remember that great saying of the Sânkhya, "The whole of nature is for the soul, not the soul for nature." The very reason of nature's existence is for the education of the soul; it has no other meaning; it is there because the soul must have knowledge, and through knowledge free itself. If we remember this always, we shall never be attached to nature; we shall know that nature is a book in which we are to read, and that when we have gained the required knowledge, the book is of no more value to us. Instead of that, however, we are identifying ourselves with nature; we are thinking that the soul is for nature, that the spirit is for the flesh, and, as the common saying has it, we think that man "lives to eat" and not "eats to live". We are continually making this mistake; we are regarding nature as ourselves and are becoming attached to it; and as soon as this attachment comes, there is the deep impression on the soul, which binds us down and makes us work not from freedom but like slaves.

The whole gist of this teaching is that you should work like a *master* and not as a *slave;* work incessantly, but do not do slave's work. Do you not see how everybody works? Nobody can be altogether at rest; ninety-nine per cent of mankind work like slaves, and the result is misery; it is all selfish work. Work through freedom! Work through love! The word "love" is very difficult to understand; love never comes until there is freedom. There is no true love possible in the slave. If you buy a slave and tie him down in chains and make him work for you, he will work like a drudge, but there will be no love in him. So when we ourselves work for the things of the world as slaves, there can be no love in us, and our work is not true work. This is true of work done for relatives and friends, and is true of work done for our own selves. Selfish work is slave's work; and here is a test. Every act of love brings happiness; there is no act of love which does not bring peace and blessedness as its reaction. Real existence, real knowledge, and real love are eternally connected with one another, the three in one: where one of them is, the others also must be; they are the three aspects of the One without a second — the Existence - Knowledge - Bliss. When that existence becomes relative, we see it as the world; that knowledge becomes in its turn modified into the knowledge of the things of the world; and that bliss forms the foundation of all true love known to the heart of man. Therefore true love can never react so as to cause pain either to the lover or to the beloved. Suppose a man loves a woman; he wishes to have her all to himself and feels extremely jealous about her every movement; he wants her to sit near him, to stand near him, and to eat and move at his bidding. He is a slave to her and wishes to have her as his slave. That is not love; it is a kind of morbid affection of the slave, insinuating itself as love. It cannot be love, because it is painful; if she does not do what he wants, it brings him pain. With love there is no painful reaction; love only brings a reaction of bliss; if it does not, it is not love; it is mistaking something else for love. When you have succeeded in loving your husband, your wife, your children, the whole world, the universe, in such a manner that there is no reaction of pain or jealousy, no selfish feeling, then you are in a fit state to be unattached.

Krishna says, "Look at Me, Arjuna! If I stop from work for one moment, the whole universe will die. I have nothing to gain from work; I am the one Lord, but why do I work? Because I love the world." God is unattached because He loves; that real love makes us unattached. Wherever there is attachment, the clinging to the things of the world, you must know that it is all physical attraction between sets of particles of matter — something that attracts two bodies nearer and nearer all the time and, if they cannot get near enough, produces pain; but where there is *real* love, it does not rest on physical attachment at all. Such lovers may be a thousand miles away from one another, but their love will be all the same; it does not die, and will never produce any painful reaction.

To attain this unattachment is almost a life-work, but as soon as we have reached this point, we have attained the goal of love and become free; the bondage of nature falls from us, and we see nature as she is; she forges no more chains for us; we stand entirely free and take not the results of work into consideration; who then cares for what the results may be?

Do you ask anything from your children in return for what you have given them? It is your duty to work for them, and there the matter ends. In whatever you do for a particular person, a city, or a state, assume the same attitude towards it as you have towards your children — expect nothing in return. If you can invariably take the position of a giver, in which everything given by you is a free offering to the world, without any thought of return, then will your work bring you no attachment. Attachment comes only where we expect a return.

If working like slaves results in selfishness and attachment, working as master of our own mind gives rise to the bliss of non-attachment. We often talk of right and justice, but we find that in the world right and justice are mere baby's talk. There are two things which guide the conduct of men: might and mercy. The exercise of might is invariably the exercise of selfishness. All men and women try to make the most of whatever power or advantage they have. Mercy is heaven itself; to be good, we have all to be merciful. Even justice and right should stand on mercy. All thought of obtaining return for the work we do hinders our spiritual progress; nay, in the end it brings misery. There is another way in which this idea of mercy and selfless charity can be put into practice; that is, by looking upon work as "worship" in case we believe in a Personal God. Here we give up all the fruits our work unto the Lord, and worshipping Him thus, we have no right to expect anything from man kind for the work we do. The Lord Himself works incessantly and is ever without attachment. Just as water cannot wet the lotus leaf, so work cannot bind the unselfish man by giving rise to attachment to results. The selfless and unattached man may live in the very heart of a crowded and sinful city; he will not be touched by sin.

This idea of complete self-sacrifice is illustrated in the following story: After the battle of Kurukshetra the five Pândava brothers performed a great sacrifice and made very large gifts to the poor. All people expressed amazement at the greatness and richness of the sacrifice, and said that such a sacrifice the world had never seen before. But, after the ceremony, there came a little mongoose, half of whose body was golden, and the other half brown; and he began to roll on the floor of the sacrificial hall. He said to those around, "You are all liars; this is no sacrifice." "What!" they exclaimed, "you say this is no sacrifice; do you not know how money and jewels were poured out to the poor and every one became rich and happy? This was the most wonderful sacrifice any man ever performed." But the mongoose said, "There was once a little village, and in it there dwelt a poor Brahmin with his wife, his son, and his son's wife. They were very poor and lived on small gifts made to them for preaching and teaching. There came in that land a three years' famine, and the poor Brahmin suffered more than ever. At last when the family had starved for days, the father brought home one morning a little barley flour, which he had been fortunate enough to obtain, and he divided it into four parts, one for each member of the family. They prepared it for their meal, and just as they were about to eat, there was a knock at the door. The father opened it, and there stood a guest. Now in India a guest is a sacred person; he is as a god for the time being, and must be treated as such. So the poor Brahmin said, 'Come in, sir; you are welcome,' He set before the guest his own portion of the food, which the guest quickly ate and said, 'Oh, sir, you have killed me; I have been starving for ten days, and this little bit has but increased my hunger.' Then the wife said to her husband, 'Give him my share,' but the husband said, 'Not so.' The wife however insisted, saying, 'Here is a poor man, and it is our duty as householders to see that he is fed, and it is my duty as a wife to give him my portion, seeing that you have no more to offer him.' Then she gave her share to the guest, which he ate, and said he was still burning with hunger. So the son said, 'Take my portion also; it is the duty of a son to help his father to fulfil his obligations.' The guest ate that, but remained still unsatisfied; so the son's wife gave him her portion also. That was sufficient, and the guest departed, blessing them. That night those four people died of starvation. A few granules of that flour had fallen on the floor; and when I rolled my body on them, half of it became golden, as you see. Since then I have been travelling all over the world, hoping to find another sacrifice like that, but nowhere have I found one; nowhere else has the other half of my body been turned into gold. That is why I say this is no sacrifice."

This idea of charity is going out of India; great men are becoming fewer and fewer. When I was first learning English, I read an English story book in which there was a story about a dutiful boy who had gone out to work and had given some of his money to his old mother, and this was praised in three or four pages. What was that? No Hindu boy can ever understand the moral of that story. Now I understand it when I hear the Western idea — every man for himself. And some men take everything for themselves, and fathers and mothers and wives and children go to the wall. That should never and nowhere be the ideal of the householder.

Now you see what Karma-Yoga means; even at the point of death to help any one, without asking questions. Be cheated millions of times and never ask a question, and never think of what you are doing. Never vaunt of your gifts to the poor or expect their gratitude, but rather be grateful to them for giving you the occasion of practicing charity to them. Thus it is plain that to be an ideal householder is a much more difficult task than to be an ideal Sannyasin; the true life of work is indeed as hard as, if not harder than, the equally true life of renunciation.

What is Duty

It is necessary in the study of Karma-Yoga to know what duty is. If I have to do something I must first know that it is my duty, and then I can do it. The idea of duty again is different in different nations. The Mohammedan says what is written in his book, the Koran, is his duty; the Hindu says what is in the Vedas is his duty; and the Christian says what is in the Bible is his duty. We find that there are varied ideas of duty, differing according to different states in life, different historical periods and different nations. The term "duty", like every other universal abstract term, is impossible clearly to define; we can only get an idea of it by knowing its practical operations and results. When certain things occur before us, we have all a natural or trained impulse to act in a certain manner towards them; when this impulse comes, the mind begins to think about the situation. Sometimes it thinks that it is good to act in a particular manner under the given conditions; at other times it thinks that it is wrong to act in the same manner even in the very same circumstances. The ordinary idea of duty everywhere is that every good man follows the dictates of his conscience. But what is it that makes an act a duty? If a Christian finds a piece of beef before him and does not eat it to save his own life, or will not give it to save the life of another man, he is sure to feel that he has not done his duty. But if a Hindu dares to eat that piece of beef or to give it to another Hindu, he is equally sure to feel that he too has not done his duty; the Hindu's training and education make him feel that way. In the last century there were notorious bands of robbers in India called thugs; they thought it their duty to kill any man they could and take away his money; the larger the number of men they killed, the better they thought they were. Ordinarily if a man goes out into the street and shoots down another man, he is apt to feel sorry for it, thinking that he has done wrong. But if the very same man, as a soldier in his regiment, kills not one but twenty, he is certain to feel glad and think that he has done his duty remarkably well. Therefore we see that it is not the thing done that defines a duty. To give an objective definition of duty is thus entirely impossible. Yet there is duty from the subjective side. Any action that makes us go Godward is a good action, and is our duty; any action that makes us go downward is evil, and is not our duty. From the subjective standpoint we may see that certain acts have a tendency to exalt and ennoble us, while certain other acts have a tendency to degrade and to brutalise us. But it is not possible to make out with certainty which acts have which kind of tendency in relation to all persons, of all sorts and conditions. There is, however, only one idea of duty which has been universally accepted by all mankind, of all ages and sects and countries, and that has been summed up in a Sanskrit aphorism thus: "Do not injure any being; not injuring any being is virtue, injuring any being is sin."

The Bhagavad-Gita frequently alludes to duties dependent upon birth and position in life. Birth and position in life and in society largely determine the mental and moral attitude of individuals towards the various activities of life. It is therefore our duty to do that work which will exalt and ennoble us in accordance with the ideals and activities of the society in which we are born. But it must be particularly remembered that the same ideals and activities do not prevail in all societies and countries; our ignorance of this is the main cause of much of the hatred of one nation towards another. An American thinks that whatever an American does in accordance with the custom of his country is the best thing to do, and that whoever does not follow his custom must be a very wicked man. A Hindu thinks that his customs are the only right ones and are the best in the world, and that whosoever does not obey them must be the most wicked man living. This is quite a natural mistake which all of us are apt to make. But it is very harmful; it is the cause of half the uncharitableness found in the world. When I came to this country and was going through the Chicago Fair, a man from behind pulled at my turban. I looked back and saw that he was a very gentlemanly-looking man, neatly dressed. I spoke to him; and when he found that I knew English, he became very much abashed. On another occasion in the same Fair another man gave me a push. When I asked him the reason, he also was ashamed and stammered out an apology saying, "Why do you dress that way?" The sympathies of these men were limited within the range of their own language and their own fashion of dress. Much of the oppression of powerful nations on weaker ones is caused by this prejudice. It dries up their fellow feeling for fellow men. That very man who asked me why I did not dress as he did and wanted to ill-treat me because of my dress may have been a very good man, a good father, and a good citizen; but the kindliness of his nature died out as soon as he saw a man in a different dress. Strangers are exploited in all countries, because they do not know how to defend themselves; thus they carry home false impressions of the peoples they have seen. Sailors, soldiers, and traders behave in foreign lands in very queer ways, although they would not dream of doing so in their own country; perhaps this is why the Chinese call Europeans and Americans "foreign devils". They could not have done this if they had met the good, the kindly sides of Western life.

Therefore the one point we ought to remember is that we should always try to see the duty of others through their own eyes, and never judge the customs of other peoples by our own standard. I am not the standard of the universe. I have to accommodate myself to the world, and not the world to me. So we see that environments change the nature of our duties, and doing the duty which is ours at any particular time is the best thing we can do in this world. Let us do that duty which is ours by birth; and when we have done that, let us do the duty which is ours by our position in life and in society. There is, however, one great danger in human nature, viz that man never examines himself. He thinks he is quite as fit to be on the throne as the king. Even if he is, he must first show that he has done the duty of his own position; and then higher duties will come to him. When we begin to work earnestly in the world, nature gives us blows right and left and soon enables us to find out our position. No man can long occupy satisfactorily a position for which he is not fit. There is no use in grumbling against nature's adjustment. He who does the lower work is not therefore a lower man. No man is to be judged by the mere nature of his duties, but all should be judged by the manner and the spirit in which they perform them.

Later on we shall find that even this idea of duty undergoes change, and that the greatest work is done only when there is no selfish motive to prompt it. Yet it is work through the sense of duty that leads us to work without any idea of duty; when work will become worship — nay, something higher — then will work be done for its own sake. We shall find that the philosophy of duty, whether it be in the form of ethics or of love, is the same as in every other Yoga — the object being the attenuating of the lower self, so that the real higher Self may shine forth — the lessening of the frittering away of energies on the lower plane of existence, so that the soul may manifest itself on the higher ones. This is accomplished by the continuous denial of low desires, which duty rigorously requires. The whole organisation of society has thus been developed, consciously or unconsciously, in the realms of action and experience, where, by limiting selfishness, we open the way to an unlimited expansion of the real nature of man.

Duty is seldom sweet. It is only when love greases its wheels that it runs smoothly; it is a continuous friction. otherwise. How else could parents do their duties to their children, husbands to their wives, and vice versa? Do we not meet with cases of friction every day in our lives? Duty is sweet only through love, and love shines in freedom alone. Yet is it freedom to be a slave to the senses, to anger, to jealousies and a hundred other petty things that must occur every day in human life? In all these little roughnesses that we meet with in life, the highest expression of freedom is to forbear. Women, slaves to their own irritable, jealous tempers, are apt to blame their husbands, and assert their own "freedom", as they think, not knowing that thereby they only prove that they are slaves. So it is with husbands who eternally find fault with their wives.

Chastity is the first virtue in man or woman, and the man who, however he may have strayed away, cannot be brought to the right path by a gentle and loving and chaste wife is indeed very rare. The world is not yet as bad as that. We hear much about brutal husbands all over the world and about the impurity of men, but is it not true that there are quite as many brutal and impure women as men? If all women were as good and pure as their own constant assertions would lead one to believe, I am perfectly satisfied that there would not be one impure man in the world. What brutality is there which purity and chastity cannot conquer? A good, chaste wife, who thinks of every other man except her own husband as her child and has the attitude of a mother towards all men, will grow so great in the power of her purity that there cannot be a single man, however brutal, who will not breathe an atmosphere of holiness in her presence. Similarly, every husband must look upon all women, except his own wife, in the light of his own mother or daughter or sister. That man, again, who wants to be a teacher of religion must look upon every woman as his mother, and always behave towards her as such.

The position of the mother is the highest in the world, as it is the one place in which to learn and exercise the greatest unselfishness. The love of God is the only love that is higher than a mother's love; all others are lower. It is the duty of the mother to think of her children first and then of herself. But, instead of that, if the parents are always thinking of themselves first, the result is that the relation between parents and children becomes the same as that between birds and their offspring which, as soon as they are fledged, do not recognise any parents. Blessed, indeed, is the man who is able to look upon woman as the representative of the motherhood of God.

Blessed, indeed, is the woman to whom man represents the fatherhood of God. Blessed are the children who look upon their parents as Divinity manifested on earth.

The only way to rise is by doing the duty next to us, and thus gathering strength go on until we reach the highest state. A young Sannyâsin went to a forest; there he meditated, worshipped, and practiced Yoga for a long time. After years of hard work and practice, he was one day sitting under a tree, when some dry leaves fell upon his head. He looked up and saw a crow and a crane fighting on the top of the tree, which made him very angry. He said, "What! Dare you throw these dry leaves upon my head!" As with these words he angrily glanced at them, a flash of fire went out of his head — such was the Yogi's power — and burnt the birds to ashes. He was very glad, almost overjoyed at this development of power — he could burn the crow and the crane by a look. After a time he had to go to the town to beg his bread. He went, stood at a door, and said, "Mother, give me food." A voice came from inside the house, "Wait a little, my son." The young man thought, "You wretched woman, how dare you make me wait! You do not know my power yet." While he was thinking thus the voice came again: "Boy, don't be thinking too much of yourself. Here is neither crow nor crane." He was astonished; still he had to wait. At last the woman came, and he fell at her feet and said, "Mother, how did you know that?" She said, "My boy, I do not know your Yoga or your practices. I am a common everyday woman. I made you wait because my husband is ill, and I was nursing him. All my life I have struggled to do my duty. When I was unmarried, I did my duty to my parents; now that I am married, I do my duty to my husband; that is all the Yoga I practice. But by doing my duty I have become illumined· thus I could read your thoughts and know what you had done in the forest. If you want to know something higher than this, go to the market of such and such a town where you will find a Vyâdha (The lowest class of people in India who used to live as hunters and butchers.) who will tell you something that you will be very glad to learn." The Sannyasin thought, "Why should I go to that town and to a Vyadha?" But after what he had seen, his mind opened a little, so he went. When he came near the town, he found the market and there saw, at a distance, a big fat Vyadha cutting meat with big knives, talking and bargaining with different people. The young man said, "Lord help me! Is this the man from whom I am going to learn? He is the incarnation of a demon, if he is anything." In the meantime this man looked up and said, "O Swami, did that lady send you here? Take a seat until I have done my business." The Sannyasin thought, "What comes to me here?" He took his seat; the man went on with his work, and after he had finished he took his money and said to the Sannyasin, "Come sir, come to my home." On reaching home the Vyadha gave him a seat, saying, "Wait here," and went into the house. He then washed his old father and mother, fed them, and did all he could to please them, after which he came to the Sannyasin and said, "Now, sir, you have come here to see me; what can I do for you?" The Sannyasin asked him a few questions about soul and about God, and the Vyadha gave him a lecture which forms a part of the Mahâbhârata, called the *Vyâdha-Gitâ*. It contains one of the highest flights of the Vedanta. When the Vyadha finished his teaching, the Sannyasin felt astonished. He said, "Why are you in that body? With such knowledge as yours why are you in a Vyadha's body, and doing such filthy, ugly work?" "My son," replied the Vyadha, "no duty is ugly, no duty is impure. My birth placed me in these circumstances and environments. In my boyhood I learnt the trade; I am unattached, and I try to do my duty well. I try to do my duty as a householder, and I try to do all I can to make my father and mother happy. I neither know your Yoga, nor have I become a Sannyasin, nor did I go out of the world into a forest; nevertheless, all that you have heard and seen has come to me through the unattached doing of the duty which belongs to my position."

There is a sage in India, a great Yogi, one of the most wonderful men I have ever seen in my life. He is a peculiar man, he will not teach any one; if you ask him a question he will not answer. It is too much for him to take up the position of a teacher, he will not do it. If you ask a question, and wait for some days, in the course of conversation he will bring up the subject, and wonderful light will he throw on it. He told me once the secret of work, "Let the end and the means be joined into one." When you are doing any work, do not think of anything beyond. Do it as worship, as the highest worship, and devote your whole life to it for the time being. Thus, in the story, the Vyadha and the woman did their duty with cheerfulness and whole-heartedness; and the result was that they became illuminated, clearly showing that the right performance of the duties of any station in life, without attachment to results, leads us to the highest realisation of the perfection of the soul.

It is the worker who is attached to results that grumbles about the nature of the duty which has fallen to his lot; to the unattached worker all duties are equally good, and form efficient instruments with which selfishness and sensuality may be killed, and the freedom of the soul secured. We are all apt to think too highly of ourselves. Our duties are determined by our deserts to a much larger extent than we are willing to grant. Competition rouses envy, and it kills the kindliness of the heart. To the grumbler all duties are distasteful; nothing will ever satisfy him, and his whole life is doomed to prove a failure. Let us work on, doing as we go whatever happens to be our duty, and being ever ready to put our shoulders to the wheel. Then surely shall we see the Light!

9

Bhakti Yoga

The Preparation

The best definition given of Bhakti-Yoga is perhaps embodied in the verse: "May that love undying which the non-discriminating have for the fleeting objects of the senses never leave this heart of mine — of me who seek after Thee!" We see what a strong love men, who do not know any better, have for sense-objects, for money, dress, their wives, children, friends, and possessions. What a tremendous clinging they have to all these things! So in the above prayer the sage says, "I will have that attachment, that tremendous clinging, only to Thee." This love, when given to God, is called Bhakti. Bhakti is not destructive; it teaches us that no one of the faculties we have has been given in vain, that through them is the natural way to come to liberation. Bhakti does not kill out our tendencies, it does not go against nature, but only gives it a higher and more powerful direction. How naturally we love objects of the senses! We cannot but do so, because they are so real to us. We do not ordinarily see anything real about higher things, but when a man has seen something real beyond the senses, beyond the universe of senses, the idea is that he can have a strong attachment, only it should be transferred to the object beyond the senses, which is God. And when the same kind of love that has before been given to sense-objects is given to God, it is called Bhakti. According to the sage Ramanuja, the following are the preparations for getting that intense love.

The first is Viveka. It is a very curious thing, especially to people of the West. It means, according to Ramanuja, "discrimination of food". Food contains all the energies that go to make up the forces of our body and mind; it has been transferred, and conserved, and given new directions in my body, but my body and mind have nothing essentially different from the food that I ate. Just as the force and matter we find in the material world become body and mind in us, so, essentially, the difference between body and mind and the food we eat is only in manifestation. It being so, that out of the material particles of our food we construct the instrument of thought, and that from the finer forces lodged in these particles we manufacture thought itself, it naturally follows, that both this thought and the instrument will be modified by the food we take. There are certain kinds of food that produce a certain change in the mind; we see it every day. There are other sorts which produce a change in the body, and in the long run have a tremendous effect on the mind. It is a great thing to learn; a good deal of the misery we suffer is occasioned by the food we take. You find that after a heavy and indigestible meal it is very hard to control the mind; it is running, running all the time. There are certain foods which are exciting; if you eat such food, you find that you cannot control the mind. It is obvious that after drinking a large quantity of wine, or other alcoholic beverage, a man finds that his mind would not be controlled; it runs away from his control.

According to Ramanuja, there are three things in food we must avoid. First, there is Jâti, the nature, or species of the food, that must be considered. All exciting food should be avoided, as meat, for instance; this should not be taken because it is by its very nature impure. We can get it only by taking the life of another. We get pleasure for a moment, and another creature has to give up its life to give us that pleasure. Not only so, but we demoralise other human beings. It would be rather better if every man who eats meat killed the animal himself; but, instead of doing so, society gets a class of persons to do that business for them, for doing which, it hates them. In England no butcher can serve on a jury, the idea being that he is cruel by nature. Who makes him cruel? Society. If we did not eat beef and mutton, there would be no butchers. Eating meat is only allowable for people who do very hard work, and who are not going to be Bhaktas; but if you are going to be Bhaktas, you should avoid meat. Also, all exciting foods, such as onions, garlic, and all evil-smelling food, as "sauerkraut". Any food that has been standing for days, till its condition is changed, any food whose natural juices have been almost dried ups any food that is malodorous, should be avoided.

The next thing that is to be considered as regards food is still more intricate to Western minds — it is what is called Âshraya, i.e. the person from whom it comes This is rather a mysterious theory of the Hindus. The idea is that each man has a certain aura round him, and whatever thing he touches, a part of his character, as it were, his influence, is left on it. It is supposed that a man's character emanates from him, as it were, like a physical force, and whatever he touches is affected by it. So we must take care who touches our food when it is cooked; a wicked or immoral person must not touch it. One who wants to be a Bhakta must not dine with people whom he knows to be very wicked, because their infection will come through the food.

The other form of purity to be observed is Nimitta, or instruments. Dirt and dust must not be in food. Food should not be brought from the market and placed on the table unwashed. We must be careful also about the saliva and other secretions. The lips ought never, for instance, to be touched with the fingers. The mucous membrane is the most delicate part of the body, and all tendencies are conveyed very easily by the saliva. Its contact, therefore, is to be regarded as not only offensive, but dangerous. Again, we must not eat food, half of which has been eaten by someone else. When these things are avoided in food, it becomes pure; pure food brings a pure mind, and in a pure mind is a constant memory of God.

Let me tell you the same thing as explained by another commentator, Shankarâchârya, who takes quite another view. This word for food, in Sanskrit, is derived from the root, meaning to gather. Âhâra means "gathered in". What is his explanation? He says, the passage that when food is pure the mind will become pure really means that lest we become subject to the senses we should avoid the following: First as to attachment; we must not be extremely attached to anything excepting God. See everything, do everything, but be not attached. As soon as extreme attachment comes, a man loses himself, he is no more master of himself, he is a slave. If a woman is tremendously attached to a man, she becomes a slave to that man. There is no use in being a slave. There are higher things in this world than becoming a slave to a human being. Love and do good to everybody, but do not become a slave. In the first place, attachment degenerates us, individually, and in the second place, makes us extremely selfish. Owing to this failing, we want to injure others to do good to those we love. A good many of the wicked deeds done in this world are really done through attachment to certain persons. So all attachment excepting that for good works should be avoided; but love should be given to everybody. Then as to jealousy. There should be no jealousy in regard to objects of the senses; jealousy is the root of all evil, and a most difficult thing to conquer. Next, delusion. We always take one thing for another, and act upon that, with the result that we bring misery upon ourselves. We take the bad for the good. Anything that titillates our nerves for a moment we think; as the highest good, and plunge into it immediately, but find, when it is too late, that it has given us a tremendous blow. Every day, we run into this error, and we often continue in it all our lives. When the senses, without being extremely attached, without jealousy, or without delusion, work in the world, such work or collection of impressions is called pure food, according to Shankaracharya. When pure food is taken, the mind is able to take in objects and think about them without attachment, jealousy or delusion; then the mind becomes pure, and then there is constant memory of God in that mind.

It is quite natural for one to say that Shankara's meaning is the best, but I wish to add that one should not neglect Ramanuja's interpretation either. It is only when you take care of the real material food that the rest will come. It is very true that mind is the master, but very few of us are not bound by the senses. We are all controlled by matter; and as long as we are so controlled, we must take material aids; and then, when we have become strong, we can eat or drink anything we like. We have to follow Ramanuja in taking care about food and drink; at the same time we must also take care about our mental food. It is very easy to take care about material food, but mental work must go along with it; then gradually our spiritual self will become stronger and stronger, and the physical self less assertive. Then will food hurt you no more. The great danger is that every man wants to jump at the highest ideal, but jumping is not the way. That ends only in a fall. We are bound down here, and we have to break our chains slowly. This is called Viveka, discrimination.

The next is called Vimoka, freedom from desires. He who wants to love God must get rid of extreme desires, desire nothing except God. This world is good so far as it helps one to go to the higher world. The objects of the senses are good so far as they help us to attain higher objects. We always forget that this world is a means to an end, and not an end itself. If this were the end we should be immortal here in our physical body; we should never die. But we see people every moment dying around us, and yet, foolishly, we think we shall never die; and from that conviction we come to think that this life is the goal. That is the case with ninety-nine per cent of us. This notion should be given up at once. This world is good so far as it is a means to perfect ourselves; and as soon as it has ceased to be so, it is evil. So wife, husband, children, money and learning, are good so long as they help us forward; but as soon as they cease to do that, they are nothing but evil. If the wife help us to attain God, she is a good wife; so with a husband or a child. If money help a man to do good to others, it is of some value; but if not, it is simply a mass of evil, and the sooner it is got rid of, the better.

The next is Abhyâsa, practice. The mind should always go towards God. No other things have any right to withhold it. It should continuously think of God, though this is a very hard task; yet it can be done by persistent practice. What we are now is the result of our past practice. Again, practice makes us what we shall be. So practice the other way; one sort of turning round has brought us this way, turn the other way and get out of it as soon as you can. Thinking of the senses has brought us down here — to cry one moment, to rejoice the next, to be at the mercy of every breeze, slave to everything. This is shameful, and yet we call ourselves spirits. Go the other way, think of God; let the mind not think of any physical or mental enjoyment, but of God alone. When it tries to think of anything else, give it a good blow, so that it may turn round and think of God. As oil poured from one vessel to another falls in an unbroken line, as chimes coming from a distance fall upon the ear as one continuous sound, so should the mind flow towards God in one continuous stream. We should not only impose this practice on the mind, but the senses too should be employed. Instead of hearing foolish things, we must hear about God; instead of talking foolish words, we must talk of God. Instead of reading foolish books, we must read good ones which tell of God.

The greatest aid to this practice of keeping God in memory is, perhaps, music. The Lord says to Nârada, the great teacher of Bhakti, "I do not live in heaven, nor do I live in the heart of the Yogi, but where My devotees sing My praise, there am I". Music has such tremendous power over the human mind; it brings it to concentration in a moment. You will find the dull, ignorant, low, brute-like human beings, who never steady their mind for a moment at other times, when they hear attractive music, immediately become charmed and concentrated. Even the minds of animals, such as dogs, lions, cats, and serpents, become charmed with music.

The next is Kriyâ, work — doing good to others. The memory of God will not come to the selfish man. The more we come out and do good to others, the more our hearts will be purified, and God will be in them. According to our scriptures, there are five sorts of work, called the fivefold sacrifice. First, study. A man must study every day something holy and good. Second, worship of God, angels, or saints, as it may be. Third, our duty to our forefathers. Fourth, our duty to human beings. Man has no right to live in a house himself, until he builds for the poor also, or for anybody who needs it. The householder's house should be open to everybody that is poor and suffering; then he is a real householder.

If he builds a house only for himself and his wife to enjoy, he will never be a lover of God. No man has the right to cook food only for himself; it is for others, and he should have what remains. It is a common practice in India that when the season s produce first comes into the market, such as strawberries or mangoes, a man buys some of them and gives to the poor. Then he eats of them; and it is a very good example to follow in this country. This training will make a man unselfish, and at the same time, be an excellent object-lesson to his wife and children. The Hebrews in olden times used to give the first fruits to God. The first of everything should go to the poor; we have only a right to what remains. The poor are God's representatives; anyone that suffers is His representative. Without giving, he who eats and enjoys eating, enjoys sin. Fifth, our duty to the lower animals. It is diabolical to say that all animals are created for men to be killed and used in any way man likes. It is the devil's gospel, not God's. Think how diabolical it is to cut them up to see whether a nerve quivers or not, in a certain part of the body. I am glad that in our country such things are not countenanced by the Hindus, whatever encouragement they may get from the foreign government they are under. One portion of the food cooked in a household belongs to the animals also. They should be given food every day; there ought to be hospitals in every city in this country for poor, lame, or blind horses, cows, dogs, and cats, where they should be fed and taken care of.

Then there is Kalyâna, purity, which comprises the following: Satya, truthfulness. He who is true, unto him the God of truth comes. Thought, word, and deed should be perfectly true. Next Ârjava, straightforwardness, rectitude. The word means, to be simple, no crookedness in the heart, no double-dealing. Even if it is a little harsh, go straightforward, and not crookedly. Dayâ, pity, compassion. Ahimsâ, not injuring any being by thought, word, or deed. Dâna, charity. There is no higher virtue than charity. The lowest man is he whose hand draws in, in receiving; and he is the highest man whose hand goes out in giving. The hand was made to give always. Give the last bit of bread you have even if you are starving. You will be free in a moment if you starve yourself to death by giving to another. Immediately you will be perfect, you will become God. People who have children are bound already. They cannot give away. They want to enjoy their children, and they must pay for it. Are there not enough children in the world? It is only selfishness which says, "I'll have a child for myself".

The next is Anavasâda — not desponding, cheerfulness. Despondency is not religion, whatever else it may be. By being pleasant always and smiling, it takes you nearer to God, nearer than any prayer. How can those minds that are gloomy and dull love? If they talk of love, it is false; they want to hurt others. Think of the fanatics; they make the longest faces, and all their religion is to fight against others in word and act. Think of what they have done in the past, and of what they would do now if they were given a free hand. They would deluge the whole world in blood tomorrow if it would bring them power. By worshipping power and making long faces, they lose every bit of love from their hearts. So the man who always feels miserable will never come to God. It is not religion, it is diabolism to say, "I am so miserable." Every man has his own burden to bear. If you are miserable, try to be happy, try to conquer it.

God is not to be reached by the weak. Never be weak. You must be strong; you have infinite strength within you. How else will you conquer anything? How else will you come to God? At the same time you must avoid excessive merriment, Uddharsha, as it is called. A mind in that state never becomes calm; it becomes fickle.

Excessive merriment will always be followed by sorrow. Tears and laughter are near kin. People so often run from one extreme to the other. Let the mind be cheerful, but calm. Never let it run into excesses, because every excess will be followed by a reaction.

These, according to Ramanuja, are the preparations for Bhakti.

The First Steps

The philosophers who wrote on Bhakti defined it as extreme love for God. Why a man should love God is the question to be solved; and until we understand that, we shall not be able to grasp the subject at all. There are two entirely different ideals of life. A man of any country who has any religion knows that he is a body and a spirit also. But there is a great deal of difference as to the goal of human life.

In Western countries, as a rule, people lay more stress on the body aspect of man; those philosophers who wrote on Bhakti in India laid stress on the spiritual side of man; and this difference seems to be typical of the Oriental and Occidental nations. It is so even in common language. In England, when speaking of death it is said, a man gave up his ghost; in India, a man gave up his body. The one idea is that man *is* a body and *has* a soul; the other that man *is* a soul and *has* a body. More intricate problems arise out of this. It naturally follows that the ideal which holds that man is a body and has a soul lays all the stress on the body. If you ask why man lives, you will be told it is to enjoy the senses, to enjoy possessions and wealth. He cannot dream of anything beyond even if he is told of it; his idea of a future life would be a continuation of this enjoyment. He is very sorry that it cannot continue all the time here, but he has to depart; and he thinks that somehow or other he will go to some place where the same thing will be renewed. He will have the same enjoyments, the same senses, only heightened and strengthened. He wants to worship Cod, because God is the means to attain this end. The goal of his life is enjoyment of sense-objects, and he comes to know there is a Being who can give him a very long lease of these enjoyments, and that is why he worships God.

On the other hand the Indian idea is that God is the goal of life; there is nothing beyond God, and the sense-enjoyments are simply something through which we are passing now in the hope of getting better things. Not only so; it would be disastrous and terrible if man had nothing but sense-enjoyments. In our everyday life we find that the less the sense-enjoyments, the higher the life of the man. Look at the dog when he eats. No man ever ate with the same satisfaction. Observe the pig giving grunts of satisfaction as he eats; it is his heaven, and if the greatest archangel came and looked on, the pig would not even notice him. His whole existence is in his eating. No man was ever born who could eat that way. Think of the power of hearing in the lower animals, the power of seeing; all their senses are highly developed. Their enjoyment of the senses is extreme; they become simply mad with delight and pleasure. And the lower the man also, the more delight he finds in the senses. As he gets higher, the goal becomes reason and love. In proportion as these faculties develop, he loses the power of enjoying the senses.

For illustration's sake, if we take for granted that a certain amount of power is given to man, and that that can be spent either on the body, or the mind, or the spirit, then all the powers spent on any one of these leaves just so much less to be expended on the others. The ignorant or savage races have much stronger sensual faculties than the civilised races, and this is, in fact, one of the lessons we learn from history that as a nation becomes civilised the nerve organisation becomes finer, and they become physically weaker. Civilise a savage race, and you will find the same thing; another barbarian race comes up and conquers it. It is nearly always the barbarian race that conquers. We see then that if we desire only to have sense-enjoyments all the time, we degrade ourselves to the brute state. A man does not know what he is asking for when he says, he wants to go to a place where his sense-enjoyments will be intensified; that he can only have by going down to the brutes.

So with men desiring a heaven full of sense-pleasures. They are like swine wallowing in the mire of the senses, unable to see anything beyond. This sense-enjoyment is what they want, and the loss of it is the loss of heaven to them. These can never be Bhaktas in the highest sense of the word; they can never be true lovers of God. At the same time, though this lower ideal be followed for a time, it will also in course of time change, each man will find that there is something higher, of which he did not know, and so this clinging to life and to things of the senses will gradually die away. When I was a little boy at school, I had a fight with another schoolfellow about some sweetmeats, and he being the stronger boy snatched them from my hand. I remember the feeling I had; I thought that boy was the most wicked boy ever born, and that as soon as I grew strong enough I would punish him; there was no punishment sufficient for his wickedness. We have both grown up now, and we are fast friends. This world is full of babies to whom eating and drinking, and all these little cakes are everything. They will dream of these cakes, and their idea of future life is where these cakes will be plentiful. Think of the American Indian who believes that his future life will be in a place which is a very good hunting ground. Each one of us has an idea of a heaven just as we want it to be; but in course of time, as we grow older and see higher things, we catch higher glimpses beyond. But let us not dispense with our ideas of future life in the ordinary way of modern times, by not believing in anything — that is destruction. The agnostic who thus destroys everything is mistaken, the Bhakta sees higher. The agnostic does not want to go to heaven, because he has none; while the Bhakta does not want to go to heaven, because he thinks it is child's play. What he wants is God.

What can be a higher end than God? God Himself is the highest goal of man; see Him, enjoy Him. We can never conceive anything higher, because God is perfection. We cannot conceive of any higher enjoyment than that of love, but this word love has different meanings. It does not mean the ordinary selfish love of the world; it is blasphemy to call that love. The love for our children and our wives is mere animal love; that love which is perfectly unselfish is the only love, and that is of God. It is a very difficult thing to attain to. We are passing through all these different loves — love of children, father, mother, and so forth. We slowly exercise the faculty of love; but in the majority of cases we never learn anything from it, we become bound to one step, to one person. In some cases men come out of this bondage. Men are ever running after wives and wealth and fame in this world; sometimes they are hit very hard on the head, and they find out what this world really is. No one in this world can really love anything but God. Man finds out that human love is all hollow. Men cannot love though they talk of it. The wife says she loves her husband and kisses him; but as soon as he dies, the first thing she thinks about is the bank account, and what she shall do the next day. The husband loves the wife; but when she becomes sick and loses her beauty, or becomes haggard, or makes a mistake, he ceases to care for her. All the love of the world is hypocrisy and hollowness.

A finite subject cannot love, nor a finite object be loved. When the object of the love of a man is dying every moment, and his mind also is constantly changing as he grows, what eternal love can you expect to find in the world? There cannot be any real love but in God: why then all these loves? These are mere stages. There is a power behind impelling us forward, we do not know where to seek for the real object, but this love is sending us forward in search of it. Again and again we find out our mistake. We grasp something, and find it slips through our fingers, and then we grasp something else. Thus on and on we go, till at last comes light; we come to God, the only One who loves. His love knows no change and is ever ready to take us in. How long would any of you bear with me if I injured you? He in whose mind is no anger, hatred, or envy, who never loses his balance, dies, or is born, who is he but God? But the path to God is long and difficult, and very few people attain Him. We are all babies struggling. Millions of people make a trade of religion. A few men in a century attain to that love of God, and the whole country becomes blessed and hallowed. When a son of God appears, a whole country becomes blessed. It is true that few such are born in any one century in the whole world, but all should strive to attain that love of God. Who knows but you or I may be the next to attain? Let us struggle therefore.

We say that a wife loves her husband. She thinks that her whole soul is absorbed in him: a baby comes and half of it goes out to the baby, or more. She herself will feel that the same love of husband does not exist now. So with the father. We always find that when more intense objects of love come to us, the previous love slowly vanishes. Children at school think that some of their schoolfellows are the dearest beings that they have in life, or their fathers or mothers are so; then comes the husband or wife, and immediately the old feeling disappears, and the new love becomes uppermost. One star arises, another bigger one comes, and then a still bigger one, and at last the sun comes, and all the lesser lights vanish. That sun is God. The stars are the smaller loves. When that Sun bursts upon him, a man becomes mad what Emerson calls "a God-intoxicated man". Man becomes transfigured into God, everything is merged in that one ocean of love. Ordinary love is mere animal attraction. Otherwise why is the distinction between the sexes? If one kneels before an image, it is dreadful idolatry; but if one kneels before husband or wife, it is quite permissible!

The world presents to us manifold stages of love. We have first to clear the ground. Upon our view of life the whole theory of love will rest. To think that this world is the aim and end of life is brutal and degenerating. Any man who starts in life with that idea degenerates himself He will never rise higher, he will never catch this glimpse from behind, he will always be a slave to the senses. He will struggle for the dollar that will get him a few cakes to eat. Better die than live that life. Slaves of this world, slaves of the senses, let us rouse ourselves; there is something higher than this sense-life. Do you think that man, the Infinite Spirit was born to be a slave to his eyes, his nose, and his ears? There is an Infinite, Omniscient Spirit behind that can do everything, break every bond; and that Spirit we are, and we get that power through love. This is the ideal we must remember. We cannot, of course, get it in a day. We may fancy that we have it, but it is a fancy after all; it is a long, long way off. We must take man where he stands, and help him upwards. Man stands in materialism; you and I are materialists. Our talking about God and Spirit is good; but it is simply the vogue in our society to talk thus: we have learnt it parrot-like and repeat it. So we have to take ourselves where we are as materialists, and must take the help of matter and go on slowly until we become real spiritualists, and feel ourselves spirits, understand the spirit, and find that this world which we call the infinite is but a gross external form of that world which is behind.

But something besides that is necessary. You read in the Sermon on the Mount, "Ask, and it shall be given (to) you; seek, and ye shall find; knock, and it shall be opened unto you." The difficulty is, who seeks, who wants? We all say we know God. One man writes a book to disprove God, another to prove Him. One man thinks it his duty to prove Him all his life; another, to disprove Him, and he goes about to teach man there is no God. What is the use of writing a book either to prove or disprove God? What does it matter to most people whether there is a God or not ? The majority of men work just like a machine with no thought of God and feeling no need of Him. Then one day comes Death and says, "Come." The man says, "Wait a little, I want a little more time. I want to see my son grow a little bigger." But Death says, "Come at once." So it goes on. So goes poor John. What shall we say to poor John? He never found anything in which God was the highest; perhaps he was a pig in the past, and he is much better as a man. But there are some who get a little awakening. Some misery comes, someone whom we love most dies, that upon which we had bent our whole soul, that for which we had cheated the whole world and perhaps our own brother, that vanishes, and a blow comes to us. Perhaps a voice comes in our soul and asks, "What after this?" Sometimes death comes without a blow, but such cases are few. Most of us, when anything slips through our fingers, say, "What next?" How we cling to the senses! You have heard of a drowning man clutching at a straw; a man will clutch at a straw first, and when it fails, he will say someone must help him. Still people must, as the English phrase goes, "sow their wild oats", before they can rise to higher things.

Bhakti is a religion. Religion is not for the many, that is impossible. A sort of knee-drill, standing up and sitting down, may be suited for the many; but religion is for the few. There are in every country only a few hundreds who can be, and will be religious. The others cannot be religious, because they will not be awakened, and they do not want to be. The chief thing is to *want* God. We want everything except God, because our ordinary wants are supplied by the external world; it is only when our necessities have gone beyond the external world that we want a supply from the internal, from God. So long as our needs are confined within the narrow limits of this physical universe, we cannot have any need for God; it is only when we have become satiated with everything here that we look beyond for a supply. It is only when the need is there that the demand will come. Have done with this child's play of the world as soon as you can, and then you will feel the necessity of something beyond the world, and the first step in religion will come.

There is a form of religion which is fashionable. My friend has much furniture in her parlour; it is the fashion to have a Japanese vase, so she must have one even if it costs a thousand dollars. In the same way she will have a little religion and join a church. Bhakti is not for such. That is not *want*. Want is that without which we cannot live. We want breath, we want food, we want clothes; without them we cannot live. When a man loves a woman in this world, there are times when he feels that without her he cannot live, although that is a mistake. When a husband dies, the wife thinks she cannot live without him; but she lives all the same. This is the secret of necessity: it is that without which we cannot live; either it must come to us or we die. When the time comes that we feel the same about God, or in other words, we want something beyond this world, something above all material forces, then we may become Bhaktas. What are our little lives when for a moment the cloud passes away, and we get one glimpse from beyond, and for that moment all these lower desires seem like a drop in the ocean? Then the soul grows, and feels the want of God, and must have Him.

The first step is: *What* do we want? Let us ask ourselves this question every day, do we want God? You may read all the books in the universe, but this love is not to be had by the power of speech, not by the highest intellect, not by the study of various sciences. He who desires God will get Love, unto him God gives Himself. Love is always mutual, reflective. You may hate me, and if I want to love you, you repulse me. But if I persist, in a month or a year you are bound to love me. It is a wellknown psychological phenomenon. As the loving wife thinks of her departed husband, with the same love we must desire the Lord, and then we will find God, and all books and the various sciences would not be able to teach us anything. By reading books we become parrots; no one becomes learned by reading books. If a man reads but one word of love, he indeed becomes learned. So we want first to get that desire.

Let us ask ourselves each day, "Do we want Gods" When we begin to talk religion, and especially when we take a high position and begin to teach others, we must ask ourselves the same question. I find many times that I don't want God, I want bread more. I may go mad if I don't get a piece of bread; many ladies will go mad if they don't get a diamond pin, but they do not have the same desire for God; they do not know the only Reality that is in the universe. There is a proverb in our language — If I want to be a hunter, I'll hunt the rhinoceros; if I want to be a robber, I'll rob the king's treasury. What is the use of robbing beggars or hunting ants? So if you want to love, love God. Who cares for these things of the world? This world is utterly false; all the great teachers of the world found that out; there is no way out of it but through God. He is the goal of our life; all ideas that the world is the goal of life are pernicious. This world and this body have their own value, a secondary value, as a means to an end; but the world should not be the end. Unfortunately, too often we make the world the end and God the means. We find people going to church and saying, "God, give me such and such; God, heal my disease." They want nice healthy bodies; and because they hear that someone will do this work for them, they go and pray to Him. It is better to be an atheist than to have such an idea of religion. As I have told you, this Bhakti is the highest ideal; I don't know whether we shall reach it or not in millions of years to come, but we must make it our highest ideal, make our senses aim at the highest. If we cannot get to the end, we shall at least come nearer to it. We have slowly to work through the world and the senses to reach God.

The Teacher of Spirituality

Every soul is destined to be perfect, and every being, in the end, will attain to that state. Whatever we are now is the result of whatever we have been or thought in the past; and whatever we shall be in the future will be the result of what we do or think now. But this does not preclude our receiving help from outside; the possibilities of the soul are always quickened by some help from outside, so much so that in the vast majority of cases in the world, help from outside is almost absolutely necessary. Quickening influence comes from outside, and that works upon our own potentialities; and then the growth begins, spiritual life comes, and man becomes holy and perfect in the end. This quickening impulse which comes from outside cannot be received from books; the soul can receive impulse only from another soul, and from nothing else. We may study books all our lives, we may become very intellectual, but in the end we find we have not developed at all spiritually. It does not follow that a high order of intellectual development always shows an equivalent development of the spiritual side of man; on the other hand, we find cases almost every day where the intellect has become very highly developed at the expense of the spirit.

Now in intellectual development we can get much help from books, but in spiritual development, almost nothing. In studying books, sometimes we are deluded into thinking that we are being spiritually helped; but if we analyse ourselves, we shall find that only our intellect has been helped, and not the spirit. That is the reason why almost everyone of us can *speak* most wonderfully on spiritual subjects, but when the time of action comes, we find ourselves so woefully deficient. It is because books cannot give us that impulse from outside. To quicken the spirit, that impulse must come from another soul.

That soul from which this impulse comes is called the Guru, the teacher; and the soul to which the impulse is conveyed is called the disciple, the student. In order to convey this impulse, in the first place, the soul from which it comes must possess the power of transmitting it, as it were, to another; and in the second place, the object to which it is transmitted must be fit to receive it. The seed must be a living seed, and the field must be ready ploughed; and when both these conditions are fulfilled, a wonderful growth of religion takes place. "The speaker of religion must be wonderful, so must the hearer be"; and when both of these are really wonderful, extraordinary, then alone will splendid spiritual growth come, and not otherwise. These are the real teachers, and these are the real students. Besides these, the others are playing with spirituality — just having a little intellectual struggle, just satisfying a little curiosity — but are standing only on the outward fringe of the horizon of religion. There is some value in that; real thirst for religion may thus be awakened; all comes in course of time. It is a mysterious law of nature that as soon as the field is ready the seed *must* come, as soon as the soul *wants* religion, the transmitter of religious force *must* come. "The seeking sinner meeteth the seeking Saviour." When the power that attracts in the receiving soul is full and ripe, the power which answers to that attraction must come.

But there are great dangers in the way. There is the danger to the receiving soul of mistaking its momentary emotion for real religious yearning. We find that in ourselves. Many times in our lives, somebody dies whom we loved; we receive a blow; for a moment we think that this world is slipping between our fingers, and that we want something higher, and that we are going to be religious. In a few days that wave passes away, and we are left stranded where we were. We ofttimes mistake such impulses for real thirst after religion, but so long as these momentary emotions are thus mistaken, that continuous, real want of the soul will not come, and we shall not find the "transmitter".

So when we complain that we have not got the truth, and that we want it so much, instead of complaining, our first duty ought to be to look into our own souls and find whether we *really* want it. In the vast majority of cases we shall find that we are not fit; we do not want; there was no thirst after the spiritual.

There are still more difficulties for the "transmitter". There are many who, though immersed in ignorance, yet, in the pride of their hearts, think they know everything, and not only do not stop there, but offer to take others on their shoulders, and thus "the blind leading the blind, they both fall into the ditch". The world is full of these; everyone wants to be a teacher, every beggar wants to make a gift of a million dollars. Just as the latter is ridiculous, so are these teachers.

How are we to know a teacher then? In the first place, the sun requires no torch to make it visible. We do not light a candle to see the sun. When the sun rises, we instinctively become aware of its rising; and when a teacher of men comes to help us, the soul will instinctively know that it has found the truth. Truth stands on its own evidences; it does not require any other testimony to attest it; it is self-effulgent. It penetrates into the inmost recesses of our nature, and the whole universe stands up and says, "This is Truth." These are the very great teachers, but we can get help from the lesser ones also; and as we ourselves are not always sufficiently intuitive to be certain of our judgment of the man from whom we receive, there ought to be certain tests. There are certain conditions necessary in the taught, and also in the teacher.

The conditions necessary in the taught are purity, a real thirst after knowledge, and perseverance. No impure soul can be religious; that is the one great condition; purity in every way is absolutely necessary. The other condition is a real thirst after knowledge. Who *wants*? That is the question. We get whatever we want — that is an old, old law. He who wants, gets. To want religion is a very difficult thing, not so easy as we generally think. Then we always forget that religion does not consist in hearing talks, or in reading books, but it is a continuous struggle, a grappling with our own nature, a continuous fight till the victory is achieved. It is not a question of one or two days, of years, or of lives, but it may be hundreds of lifetimes, and we must be ready for that. It may come immediately, or it may not come in hundreds of lifetimes; and we must be ready for that. The student who sets out with such a spirit finds success.

In the teacher we must first see that he knows the secret of the scriptures. The whole world reads scriptures — Bibles, Vedas, Korans, and others; but they are only words, external arrangement, syntax, the etymology, the philology, the dry bones of religion. The teacher may be able to find what is the age of any book, but words are only the external forms in which things come. Those who deal too much in words and let the mind run always in the force of words lose the spirit. So the teacher must be able to know the *spirit* of the scriptures. The network of words is like a huge forest in which the human mind loses itself and finds no way out. The various methods of joining words, the various methods of speaking a beautiful language, the various methods of explaining the *dicta* of the scriptures, are only for the enjoyment of the learned. They do not attain perfection; they are simply desirous to show their learning, so that the world may praise them and see that they are learned men. You will find that no one of the great teachers of the world went into these various explanations of texts; on their part there is no attempt at "text-torturing", no saying, "This word means this, and this is the philological connection between this and that word." You study all the great teachers the world has produced, and you will see that no one of them goes that way. Yet they taught, while others, who have nothing to teach, will take up a word and write a three-volume book on its origin and use. As my Master used to say, what would you think of men who went into a mango orchard and busied themselves in counting the leaves and examining the colour of the leaves, the size of the twigs, the number of branches, and so forth, while only one of them had the sense to begin to eat the mangoes? So leave this counting of leaves and twigs and this note-taking to others. That work has its own value in its proper place, but not here in the spiritual realm. Men never become spiritual through such work; you have never once seen a strong spiritual man among these "leaf-counters". Religion is the highest aim of man, the highest glory, but it does not require "leaf-counting". If you want to be a Christian, it is not necessary to know whether Christ was born in Jerusalem or Bethlehem or just the exact date on which he pronounced the Sermon on the Mount; you only require to *feel* the Sermon on the Mount. It is not necessary to read two thousand words on when it was delivered. All that is for the enjoyment of the learned. Let them have it; say amen to that. Let *us* eat the mangoes.

The second condition necessary in the teacher is that he must be sinless. The question was once asked me in England by a friend, "Why should we look to the personality of a teacher? We have only to judge of what he says, and take that up." Not so. If a man wants to teach me something of dynamics or chemistry or any other physical science, he may be of any character; he can still teach dynamics or any other science. For the knowledge that the physical sciences require is simply intellectual and depends on intellectual strength; a man can have in such a case a gigantic intellectual power without the least development of his soul. But in the spiritual sciences it is impossible from first to last that there can be any spiritual light in that soul which is impure. What can such a soul teach? It knows nothing. Spiritual truth is purity. "Blessed are the pure in heart, for they shall see God". In that one sentence is the gist of all religions. If you have learnt that, all that has been said in the past and all that it is possible to say in the future, you have known; you need not look into anything else, for you have all that is necessary in that one sentence; it could save the world, were all the other scriptures lost. A vision of God, a glimpse of the beyond never comes until the soul is pure. Therefore in the teacher of spirituality, purity is the one thing indispensable; we must see *first* what he *is*, and *then* what he *says*. Not so with intellectual teachers; there we care more for what he says than what he is. With the teacher of religion we must first and foremost see what he is, and then alone comes the value of the words, because he is the transmitter. What will he transmit, if he has not flat spiritual power in him? To give a simile: If a heater is hot, it can convey heat vibrations, but if not, it is impossible to do so. Even so is the case with the mental vibrations of the religious teacher which he conveys to the mind of the taught. It is a question of transference, and not of stimulating only our intellectual faculties. Some power, real and tangible, goes out from the teacher and begins to grow in the mind of the taught. Therefore the necessary condition is that the teacher must be true.

The third condition is motive. We should see that he does not teach with any ulterior motive, for name, or fame, or anything else, but simply for love, pure love for you. When spiritual forces are transmitted from the teacher to the taught, they can only be conveyed through the medium of love; there is no other medium that can convey them. Any other motive, such as gain or name, would immediately destroy the conveying medium; therefore all must be done through love. One who has known God can alone be a teacher. When you see that in the teacher these conditions are fulfilled, you are safe; if they are not fulfilled, it is unwise to accept him. There is a great risk, if he cannot convey goodness, of his conveying wickedness sometimes. This must be guarded against; therefore it naturally follows that we cannot be taught by anybody and everybody.

The preaching of sermons by brooks and stones may be true as a poetical figure but no one can preach a single grain of truth until he has it in himself. To whom do the brooks preach sermons? To that human soul only whose lotus of life has already opened. When the heart has been opened, it can receive teaching from the brooks or the stones — it can get some religious teaching from all these; but the unopened heart will see nothing but brooks and rolling stones. A blind man may come to a museum, but he comes and goes only; if he is to see, his eyes must first be opened. This eye-opener of religion is the teacher. With the teacher, therefore, our relationship is that of ancestor and descendant; the teacher is the spiritual ancestor, and the disciple is the spiritual descendant. It is all very well to talk of liberty and independence, but without humility, submission, veneration, and faith, there will not be any religion. It is a significant fact that where this relation still exists between the teacher and the taught, there alone gigantic spiritual souls grow; but in those who have thrown it off religion is made into a diversion. In nations and churches where this relation between teacher and taught is not maintained spirituality is almost an unknown quantity. It never comes without that feeling; there is no one to transmit and no one to be transmitted to, because they are all independent. Of whom can they learn? And if they come to learn, they come to *buy* learning. Give me a dollar's worth of religion; cannot I pay a dollar for it? Religion cannot be got that way!

There is nothing higher and holier than the knowledge which comes to the soul transmitted by a spiritual teacher. If a man has become a perfect Yogi it comes by itself, but it cannot be got in books. You may go and knock your head against the four corners of the world, seek in the Himalayas, the Alps, the Caucasus, the Desert of Gobi or Sahara, or the bottom of the sea, but it will not come until you find a teacher. Find the teacher, serve him as a child, open your heart to his influence, see in him God manifested. Our attention should be fixed on the teacher as the highest manifestation of God; and as the power of attention concentrates there, the picture of the teacher as man will melt away; the frame will vanish, and the real God will be left there. Those that come to truth with such a spirit of veneration and love — for them the Lord of truth speaks the most wonderful words. "Take thy shoes from off thy feet, for the plaçe whereon thou standest is holy ground". Wherever His name is spoken, that place is holy. How much more so is a man who speaks His name, and with what veneration ought we to approach a man out of whom come spiritual truths! This is the spirit in which we are to be taught. Such teachers are few in number, no doubt, in this world, but the world is never altogether without them. The moment it is absolutely bereft of these, it will cease to be, it will become a hideous hell and will just drop. These teachers are the fair flowers of human life and keep the world going; it is the strength that is manifested from these hearts of life that keeps the bounds of society intact.

Beyond these is another set of teachers, the Christs of the world. These Teachers of all teachers represent God Himself in the form of man. They are much higher; they can transmit spirituality with a touch, with a wish, which makes even the lowest and most degraded characters saints in one second. Do you not read of how they used to do these things? They are not the teachers about whom I was speaking; they are the Teachers of all teachers, the greatest manifestations of God to man; we cannot see God except through them. We cannot help worshipping them, and they are the only beings we are bound to worship.

No man bath "seen" God but as He is manifested in the Son. We cannot see God. If we try to see Him, we make a hideous caricature of God. There is an Indian story that an ignorant man was asked to make an image of the God Shiva, and after days of struggle he made an image of a monkey. So whenever we attempt to make an image of God, we make a caricature of Him, because we cannot understand Him as anything higher than man so long as we are men. The time will come when we transcend our human nature and know Him as He is; but so long as we are men we must worship Him in man. Talk as we may, try as we may, we cannot see God except as a man. We may deliver great intellectual speeches, become very great rationalists, and prove that these tales of God as all nonsense, but let us come to practical common sense. What is behind this remarkable intellect? Zero, nothing, simply so much froth. When next you hear a man delivering great intellectual lectures against this worship of God, get hold of him and ask him what is his idea of God, what he means by "omnipotence", and "omniscience", and "omnipresent love", and so forth, beyond the spelling of the words. He means nothing, he cannot formulate an idea, he is no better than the man in the street who has not read a single book. That man in the street, however, is quiet and does not disturb the world, while the other man's arguments cause disturbance. He has no actual perception, and both are on the same plane.

Religion is realisation, and you must make the sharpest distinction between talk and realisation. What you perceive in your soul is realisation. Man has no idea of the Spirit, he has to think of it with the forms he has before him. He has to think of the blue skies, or the expansive fields, or the sea, or something huge. How else can you think of God? So what are you doing in reality? You are talking of omnipresence, and thinking of the sea. Is God the sea? A little more common sense is required. Nothing is so uncommon as common sense, the world is too full of talk. A truce to all this frothy argument of the world. We are by our present constitution limited and bound to see God as man. If the buffaloes want to worship God, they will see Him as a huge buffalo. If a fish wants to worship God, it will have to think of Him as a big fish. You and I, the buffalo, the fish, each represents so many different vessels. All these go to the sea to be filled with water according to the shape of each vessel. In each of these vessels is nothing but water. So with God. When men see Him, they see Him as man, and the animals as animal — each according to his ideal. That is the only way you can see Him; you have to worship Him as man, because there is no other way out of it. Two classes of men do not worship God as man — the human brute who has no religion, and the Paramahamsa (highest Yogi) who has gone beyond humanity, who has thrown off his mind and body and gone beyond the limits of nature. All nature has become his Self. He has neither mind nor body, and can worship God as God, as can a Jesus or a Buddha. They did not worship God as man. The other extreme is the human brute. You know how two extremes look alike. Similar is the case with the extreme of ignorance and the other extreme of knowledge; neither of these worships anybody. The extremely ignorant do not worship God, not being developed enough to feel the need for so doing. Those that have attained the highest knowledge also do not worship God — having realised and become one with God. God never worships God. Between these two poles of existence, if anyone tells you he is not going to worship God as man, take care of him. He is an irresponsible talker, he is mistaken; his religion is for frothy thinkers, it is intellectual nonsense.

Therefore it is absolutely necessary to worship God as man, and blessed are those races which have such a "God-man" to worship. Christians have such a God-man in Christ; therefore cling close to Christ; never give up Christ. That is the natural way to see God; see God in man. All our ideas of God are concentrated there. The great limitation Christians have is that they do not heed other manifestations of God besides Christ. He was a manifestation of God; so was Buddha; so were some others, and there will be hundreds of others. Do not limit God anywhere. Pay all the reverence that you think is due to God, to Christ; that is the only worship we can have. God cannot be worshipped; He is the immanent Being of the universe. It is only to His manifestation as man that we can pray. It would be a very good plan, when Christians pray, to say, "in the name of Christ". It would be wise to stop praying to God, and only pray to Christ. God understands human failings and becomes a man to do good to humanity. "Whenever virtue subsides and immorality prevails, then I come to help mankind", says Krishna. He also says, "Fools, not knowing that I, the Omnipotent and Omnipresent God of the universe, have taken this human form, deride Me and think that cannot be." Their minds have been clouded with demoniacal ignorance, so they cannot see in Him the Lord of the universe. These great Incarnations of God are to be worshipped. Not only so, they alone can be worshipped; and on the days of their birth, and on the days when they went out of this world, we ought to pay more particular reverence to them. In worshipping Christ I would rather worship Him just as He desires; on the day of His birth I would rather worship Him by fasting than by feasting — by praying. When these are thought of, these great ones, they manifest themselves in our souls, and they make us like unto them. Our whole nature changes, and we become like them.

But you must not mix up Christ or Buddha with hobgoblins flying through the air and all that sort of nonsense. Sacrilege! Christ coming into a spiritualistic seance to dance! I have seen that presence in this country. It is not in that way that these manifestations of God come. The very touch of one of them will be manifest upon a man; when Christ *touches*, the whole soul of man will change, that man will be transfigured just as He was.

His whole life will be spiritualised; from every pore of his body spiritual power will emanate. What were the great powers of Christ in miracles and healing, in one of his character? They were low, vulgar things that He could not help doing because He was among vulgar beings. Where was this miracle-making done? Among the Jews; and the Jews did not take Him. Where was it not done? In Europe. The miracle-making went to the Jews, who rejected Christ, and the Sermon on the Mount to Europe, which accepted Him. The human spirit took on what was true and rejected what was spurious. The great strength of Christ is not in His miracles or His healing. Any fool could do those things. Fools can heal others, devils can heal others. I have seen horrible demoniacal men do wonderful miracles. They seem to manufacture fruits out of the earth. I have known fools and diabolical men tell the past, present, and future. I have seen fools heal at a glance, by the will, the most horrible diseases.

These are powers, truly, but often demoniacal powers. The other is the spiritual power of Christ which will live and always has lived — an almighty, gigantic love, and the words of truth which He preached. The action of healing men at a glance is forgotten, but His saying, "Blessed are the pure in heart", that lives today. These words are a gigantic magazine of power — inexhaustible. So long as the human mind lasts, so long as the name of God is not forgotten, these words will roll on and on and never cease to be. These are the powers Jesus taught, and the powers He had. The power of purity; it is a definite power. So in worshipping Christ, in praying to Him, we must always remember what we are seeking. Not those foolish things of miraculous display, but the wonderful powers of the Spirit, which make man free, give him control over the whole of nature, take from him the badge of slavery, and show God unto him.

THE NEED OF SYMBOLS

Bhakti is divided into two portions. One is called Vaidhi, formal or ceremonial; the other portion is called Mukhyâ, supreme. The word Bhakti covers all the ground between the lowest form of worship and the highest form of life. All the worship that you have seen in any country in the world, or in any religion, is regulated by love. There is a good deal that is simple ceremony; there is also a good deal which, though not ceremony, is still not love, but a lower state. Yet these ceremonies are necessary. The external part of Bhakti is absolutely necessary to help the soul onward. Man makes a great mistake when he thinks that he can at once jump to the highest state. If a baby thinks he is going to be an old man in a day, he is mistaken; and I hope you will always bear in mind this one ideal, that religion is neither in books, nor in intellectual consent, nor in reasoning. Reason, theories, documents, doctrines, books, religious ceremonies, are all *helps* to religion: religion itself consists in *realisation*. We all say, "There is a God." Have you seen God? That is the question. You hear a man say, "There is God in heaven." You ask him if he has seen Him, and if he says he has, you would laugh at him and say he is a maniac. With most people religion is a sort of intellectual assent and goes no further than a document. I would not call it religion. It is better to be an atheist than to have that sort of religion. Religion does not depend on our intellectual assent or dissent. You say there is a soul. Have you seen the soul? How is it we all have souls and do not see them? You have to answer the question and find out the way to see the soul. If not, it is useless to talk of religion. If any religion is true, it must be able to show us the soul and show us God and the truth in ourselves. If you and I fight for all eternity about one of these doctrines or documents, we shall never come to any conclusion. People have been fighting for ages, and what is the outcome? Intellect cannot reach there at all. We have to go beyond the intellect; the proof of religion is in direct perception. The proof of the existence of this wall is that we see it; if you sat down and argued about its existence or non-existence for ages, you could never come to any conclusion; but directly you see it, it is enough. If all the men in the world told you it did not exist, you would not believe them, because you know that the evidence of your own eyes is superior to that of all the doctrines and documents in the world.

To be religious, you have first to throw books overboard. The less you read of books, the better for you; do one thing at a time. It is a tendency in Western countries, in these modern times, to make a hotchpotch of the brain; all sorts of unassimilated ideas run riot in the brain and form a chaos without ever obtaining a chance to settle down and crystallise into a definite shape. In many cases it becomes a sort of disease, but this is not religion. Then some want a sensation. Tell them about ghosts and people coming from the North Pole or any other remote place, with wings or in any other form, and that they are invisibly present and watching over them, and make them feel uncanny, then they are satisfied and go home; but within twenty-four hours they are ready for a fresh sensation. This is what some call religion. This is the way to the lunatic asylum, and not to religion. The Lord is not to be reached by the weak, and all these weird things tend to weakness. Therefore go not near them; they only make people weak, bring disorder to the brain, weaken the mind, demoralise the soul, and a hopeless muddle is the result. You must bear in mind that religion does not consist in talk, or doctrines, or books, but in realisation; it is not learning, but *being*. Everybody knows, "Do not steal", but what of it? That man has really known who has not stolen. Everybody knows, "Do not injure others", but of what value is it?

Those who have not done so have realised it, they know it and have built their character on it. Religion is realising; and I will call you a worshipper of God when you have become able to realise the Idea. Before that it is the spelling of the weird, and no more. It is this power of realisation that makes religion. No amount of doctrines or philosophies or ethical books, that you may have stuffed into your brain, will matter much, only what you *are* and what you have *realised*. So we have to realise religion, and this realisation of religion is a long process. When men hear of something very high and wonderful, they all think they will get that, and never stop for a moment to consider that they will have to work their way up to it; they all want to jump there. If it is the highest, we are for it. We never stop to consider whether we have the power, and the result is that we do not do anything. You cannot take a man with a pitchfork and push him up there; we all have to work up gradually. Therefore the first part of religion is Vaidhi Bhakti, the lower phase of worship.

What are these lower phases of worship? They are various. In order to attain to the state where we can realise, we must pass through the concrete — just as you see children learn through the concrete first — and gradually come to the abstract. If you tell a baby that five times two is ten, it will not understand; but if you bring ten things and show how five times two is ten, it will understand. Religion is a long, slow process. We are all of us babies here; we may be old, and have studied all the books in the universe, but we are all spiritual babies. We have learnt the doctrines and dogmas, but realised nothing in our lives. We shall have to begin now in the concrete, through forms and words, prayers and ceremonies; and of these concrete forms there will be thousands; one form need not be for everybody. Some may be helped by images, some may not. Some require an image outside, others one inside the brain. The man who puts it inside says, "I am a superior man. When it is inside it is all right; when it is outside, it is idolatry, I will fight it." When a man puts an image in the form of a church or a temple, he thinks it is holy; but when it is in a human form, he objects to it!

So there are various forms through which the mind will take this concrete exercise; and then, step by step, we shall come to the abstract understanding, abstract realisation. Again, the same form is not for everyone; there is one form that will suit you, and another will suit somebody else, and so on. All forms, though leading to the same goal, may not be for all of us. Here is another mistake we generally make. My ideal does not suit you; and why should I force it on you? My fashion of building churches or reading hymns does not suit you; why should I force it on you? Go into the world and every fool will tell you that his form is the only right one, that every other form is diabolical, and he is the only chosen man ever born in the universe. But in fact, all these forms are good and helpful. Just as there are certain varieties in human nature, so it is necessary that there should be an equal number of forms in religion; and the more there are, the better for the world. If there are twenty forms of religion in the world, it is very good; if there are four hundred, so much the better — there will be the more to choose from. So we should rather be glad when the number of religions and religious ideas increase and multiply, because they will then include every man and help mankind more. Would to God that religions multiplied until every man had his own religion, quite separate from that of any other! This is the idea of the Bhakti-Yogi.

The final idea is that my religion cannot be yours, or yours mine. Although the goal and the aim are the same, yet each one has to take a different road, according to the tendencies of his mind; and although these roads are various, they must all be true, because they lead to the same goal. It cannot be that one is true and the rest not. The choosing of one's own road is called in the language of Bhakti, Ishta, the chosen way.

Then there are words. All of you have heard of the power of words, how wonderful they are! Every book — the Bible, the Koran, and the Vedas — is full of the power of words. Certain words have wonderful power over mankind. Again, there are other forms, known as symbols. Symbols have great influence on the human mind. But great symbols in religion were not created indefinitely. We find that they are the natural expressions of thought. We think symbolically. All our words are but symbols of the thought behind, and different people have come to use different symbols without knowing the reason why. It was all behind, and these symbols are associated with the thoughts; and as the thought brings the symbol outside, so the symbol, on the contrary, can bring the thought inside. So one portion of Bhakti tells about these various subjects of symbols and words and prayers. Every religion has prayers, but one thing you must bear in mind — praying for health or wealth is not Bhakti, it is all Karma or meritorious action. Praying for any physical gain is simply Karma, such as a prayer for going to heaven and so forth. One that wants to love God, to be a Bhakta, must discard all such prayers. He who wants to enter the realms of light must first give up this buying and selling this "shopkeeping" religion, and then enter the gates. It is not that you do not get what you pray for; you get everything, but such praying is a beggar's religion. "Foolish indeed is he who, living on the banks of the Ganga, digs a little well for water. A fool indeed is the man who, coming to a mine of diamonds, seeks for glass beads." This body will die some time, so what is the use of praying for its health again and again? What is there in health and wealth? The wealthiest man can use and enjoy only a little portion of his wealth. We can never get all the things of this world; and if not, who cares? This body will go, who cares for these things? If good things come, welcome; if they go away, let them go. Blessed are they when they come, and blessed are they when they go. We are striving to come into the presence of the King of kings. We cannot get there in a beggar's dress. Even if we wanted to enter the presence of an emperor, should we be admitted? Certainly not. We should be driven out. This is the Emperor of emperors, and in these beggar's rags we cannot enter. Shopkeepers never have admission there; buying and selling have no place there. As you read in the Bible, Jesus drove the buyers and sellers out of the Temple. Do not pray for little things. If you seek only bodily comforts, where is the difference between men and animals? Think yourselves a little higher than that.

So it goes without saying that the first task in becoming a Bhakta is to give up all desires of heaven and other things. The question is how to get rid of these desires. What makes men miserable? Because they are slaves, bound by laws, puppets in the hand of nature, tumbled about like playthings. We are continually taking care of this body that anything can knock down; and so we are living in a constant state of fear. I have read that a deer has to run on the average sixty or seventy miles every day, because it is frightened. We ought to know that we are in a worse plight than the deer. The deer has some rest, but we have none. If the deer gets grass enough it is satisfied, but we are always multiplying our wants. It is a morbid desire with us to multiply our wants. We have become so unhinged and unnatural that nothing natural will satisfy us. We are always grasping after morbid things, must have unnatural excitement — unnatural food, drink, surroundings, and life. As to fear, what are our lives but bundles of fear? The deer has only one class of fear, such as that from tigers, wolves, etc. Man has the whole universe to fear.

How are we to free ourselves from this is the question. Utilitarians say, "Don't talk of God and hereafter; we don't know anything of these things, let us live happily in this world." I would be the first to do so if we could, but the world will not allow us. As long as you are a slave of nature, how can you? The more you struggle, the more enveloped you become. You have been devising plans to make you happy, I do not know for how many years, but each year things seem to grow worse. Two hundred years ago in the old world people had few wants; but if their knowledge increased in arithmetical progression, their wants increased in geometrical progression. We think that in salvation at least our desires will be fulfilled, so we desire to go to heaven. This eternal, unquenchable thirst! Always wanting something! When a man is a beggar, he wants money.

When he has money, he wants other things, society; and after that, something else. Never at rest. How are we to quench this? If we get to heaven, it will only increase desire. If a poor man gets rich, it does not quench his desires, it is only like throwing butter on the fire, increasing its bright flames. Going to heaven means becoming intensely richer, and then desire comes more and more. We read of many human things in heaven in the different Bibles of the world; they are not always very good there; and after all, this desire to go to heaven is a desire after enjoyment. This has to be given up. It is too little, too vulgar a thing for you to think of going to heaven. It is just the same as thinking, I will become a millionaire and lord it over people. There are many of these heavens, but through them you cannot gain the right to enter the gates of religion and love.

The Chief Symbols

There are two Sanskrit words, Pratika and Pratimâ. Pratika means coming towards, nearing. In all countries you find various grades of worship. In this country, for instance, there are people who worship images of saints, there are people who worship certain forms and symbols. Then there are people who worship different beings who are higher than men, and their number is increasing very rapidly — worshippers of departed spirits. I read that there are something like eight millions of them here. Then there are other people who worship certain beings of higher grade — the angels, the gods, and so forth. Bhakti-Yoga does not condemn any one of these various grades, but they are all classed under one name, Pratika. These people are not worshipping God, but Pratika, something which is near, a step towards God. This Pratika worship cannot lead us to salvation and freedom; it can only give us certain particular things for which we worship them. For instance, if a man worships his departed ancestors or departed friends, he may get certain powers or certain information from them. Any particular gift that is got from these objects of worship is called Vidyâ, particular knowledge; but freedom, the highest aim, comes only by worship of God Himself. Some Orientalists think, in expounding the Vedas, that even the Personal God Himself is a Pratika. The Personal God may be a Pratika, but the Pratikas are neither the Personal nor Impersonal God. They cannot be worshipped as God. So it would be a great mistake if people thought that by worshipping these different Pratikas, either as angels, or ancestors, or Mahâtmâs (holy men, saints), etc., or departed spirits, they could ever reach to freedom. At best they can only reach to certain powers, but God alone can make us free. But because of that they are not to be condemned, their worship produces some result. The man who does not understand anything higher may get some power, some enjoyment, by the worship of these Pratikas; and after a long course of experience, when he will be ready to come to freedom, he will of his own accord give up the Pratikas.

Of these various Pratikas the most prevalent form is the worship of departed friends. Human nature — personal love, love for our friends — is so strong in us that when they die, we wish to see them once more — clinging on to their forms. We forget that these forms while living were constantly changing, and when they die, we think they become constant, and that we shall see them so. Not only so, but if I have a friend or a son who has been a scoundrel, as soon as he dies, I begin to think he is the saintliest person in existence; he becomes a god. There are people in India who, if a baby dies, do not burn it, but bury it and build a temple over it; and that little baby becomes the god of that temple. This is a very prevalent form of religion in many countries, and there are not wanting philosophers who think this has been the origin of all religions. Of course they cannot prove it. We must remember, however, that this worship of Pratikas can never bring us to salvation or to freedom.

Secondly, it is very dangerous. The danger is that these Pratikas, "nearing-stages", so far as they lead us on to a further stage, are all right; but the chances are ninety-nine to one that we shall stick to the Pratikas all our lives. It is very good to be born in a church, but it is very bad to die there. To make it clearer, it is very good to be born in a certain sect and have its training — it brings out our higher qualities; but in the vast majority of cases we die in that little sect, we never come out or grow. That is the great danger of all these worships of Pratikas. One says that these are all stages which one has to pass, but one never gets out of them; and when one becomes old, one still sticks to them. If a young man does not go to church, he ought to be condemned. But if an old man goes to church, he also ought to be condemned; he has no business with this child's play any more; the church should have been merely a preparation for something higher. What business has he any more with forms and Pratikas and all these preliminaries?

Book worship is another strong form of this Pratika, the strongest form. You find in every country that the book becomes the God. There are sects in my country who believe that God incarnates and becomes man, but even God incarnate as man must conform to the Vedas, and if His teachings do not so conform, they will not take Him. Buddha is worshipped by the Hindus, but if you say to them, "If you worship Buddha, why don't you take His teachings?" they will say, because they, the Buddhists, deny the Vedas. Such is the meaning of book worship. Any number of lies in the name of a religious book are all right. In India if I want to teach anything new, and simply state it on my own authority, as what I think, nobody will come to listen to me; but if I take some passage from the Vedas, and juggle with it, and give it the most impossible meaning, murder everything that is reasonable in it, and bring out my own ideas as the ideas that were meant by the Vedas, all the fools will follow me in a crowd. Then there are men preaching a sort of Christianity that would frighten the ordinary Christian out of his wits; but they say, "This is what Jesus Christ meant", and many come round them. People do not want anything new, if it is not in the Vedas or the Bible It is a case of nerves: when you hear a new and striking thing, you are startled; or when you see a new thing, you are startled; it is constitutional. It is much more so with thoughts. The mind has been running in ruts, and to take up a new idea is too much of a strain; so the idea has to be put near the ruts, and then we slowly take it. It is a good policy, but bad morality. Think of the mass of incongruities that reformers, and what you call the liberal preachers, pour into society today. According to Christian Scientists, Jesus was a great healer; according to the Spiritualists, He was a great psychic; according to the Theosophists, He was a Mahâtmâ. All these have to be deduced from the same text. There is a text in the Vedas which says, "Existence (Sat) alone existed, O beloved, nothing else existed in the beginning". Many different meanings are given to the word Sat in this text. The Atomists say the word meant "atoms", and out of these atoms the world has been produced. The Naturalists say it meant "nature", and out of nature everything has come. The Shunyavâdins (maintainers of the Void) say it meant "nothing", "zero", and out of nothing everything has been produced. The Theists say it meant "God", and the Advaitists say it was "Absolute Existence", and all refer to the same text as their authority.

These are the defects of book worship. But there is, on the other hand, a great advantage in it: it gives strength. All religious sects have disappeared excepting those that have a book. Nothing seems to kill them. Some of you have heard of the Parsees. They were the ancient Persians, and at one time there were about a hundred millions of them. The majority of them were conquered by the Arabs, and converted to Mohammedanism. A handful fled from their persecutors with their book, which is still preserving them. A book is the most tangible form of God. Think of the Jews; if they had not had a book, they would have simply melted into the world. But that keeps them up; the Talmud keeps them together, in spite of the most horrible persecution. One of the great advantages of a book is that it crystallises everything in tangible and convenient form, and is the handiest of all idols. Just put a book on an altar and everyone sees it; a good book everyone reads. I am afraid I may be considered partial. But, in my opinion books have produced more evil than good. They are accountable for many mischievous doctrines. Creeds all come from books, and books are alone responsible for the persecution and fanaticism in the world. Books in modern times are making liars everywhere. I am astonished at the number of liars abroad in every country.

The next thing to be considered is the Pratima, or image, the use of images. All over the world you will find images in some form or other. With some, it is in the form of a man, which is the best form. If I wanted to worship an image I would rather have it in the form of a man than of an animal, or building, or any other form. One sect thinks a certain form is the right sort of image, and another thinks it is bad. The Christian thinks that when God came in the form of a dove it was all right, but if He comes in the form of a fish, as the Hindus say, it is very wrong and superstitious. The Jews think if an idol be made in the form of a chest with two angels sitting on it, and a book on it, it is all right, but if it is in the form of a man or a woman, it is awful. The Mohammedans think that when they pray, if they try to form a mental image of the temple with the Caaba, the black stone in it, and turn towards the west, it is all right, but if you form the image in the shape of a church it is idolatry. This is the defect of image-worship. Yet all these seem to be necessary stages.

In this matter it is of supreme importance to think what we ourselves believe. What we have realised, is the question. What Jesus, or Buddha, or Moses did is nothing to us, unless we too do it for ourselves. It would not satisfy our hunger to shut ourselves up in a room and think of what Moses ate, nor would what Moses thought save *us*. My ideas are very radical on these points. Sometimes I think that I am right when I agree with all the ancient teachers, at other times I think they are right when they agree with me. I believe in thinking independently. I believe in becoming entirely free from the holy teachers; pay all reverence to them, but look at religion as an independent research. I have to find my light, just as they found theirs. Their finding the light will not satisfy us at all. You have to *become* the Bible, and not to follow it, excepting as paying reverence to it as a light on the way, as a guide-post, a mark: that is all the value it has. But these images and other things are quite necessary. You may try to concentrate your mind, or even to project any thought. You will find that you naturally form images in your mind. You cannot help it. Two sorts of persons never require any image — the human animal who never thinks of any religion, and the perfected being who has passed through these stages. Between these two points all of us require some sort of ideal, outside and inside. It may be in the form of a departed human being, or of a living man or woman. This is clinging to personality and bodies, and is quite natural. We are prone to concretise. How could we be here if we did not concretise? We are concreted spirits, and so we find ourselves here on this earth. Concretisation has brought us here, and it will take us out. Going after things of the senses has made us human beings, and we are bound to worship personal beings, whatever we may say to the contrary. It is very easy to say "Don't be personal"; but the same man who says so is generally most personal. His attachment for particular men and women is very strong; it does not leave him when they die, he wants to follow them beyond death. That is idolatry; it is the seed, the very cause of idolatry; and the cause being there it will come out in some form. Is it not better to have a personal attachment to an image of Christ or Buddha than to an ordinary man or woman? In the West, people say that it is bad to kneel before images, but they can kneel before a woman. and say, "You are my life, the light of my eyes, my soul." That is worse idolatry. What ifs this talk about my soul my life? It will soon go away.

It is only sense-attachment. It is selfish love covered by a mass of flowers. Poets give it a good name and throw lavender-water and all sorts of attractive things over it. Is it not better to kneel before a statue of Buddha or the Jina conqueror and say, "*Thou* art my life"? I would rather do that.

There is another sort of Pratika which is not recognised in Western countries, bout is taught in our books. This teaches the worship of mind as God. Anything that is worshipped as God is a stage, a nearing, as it were. An example of this is the method of showing the fine star known as Arundhati, near the group Pleiades. One is shown a big star near to it, and when he has fixed his attention on this and has come to know it, he is shown a finer and still nearer star; and when he has fixed his attention on that, he is led up to Arundhati. So all these various Pratikas and Pratimas lead to God. The worship of Buddha and of Christ constitute a Pratika. a drawing near to the worship of God. But this worship of Buddha and of Christ will not save a man, he must go beyond them to Him who manifested Himself as Jesus Christ, for God alone can give us freedom. There are even some philosophers who say these should he regarded as God; they are not Pratikas, but God Himself. However, we can take all these different Pratikas, these different stages of approach, and not be hurt by them: but if we think while we are worshipping them that we are worshipping God, we are mistaken. If a man worships Jesus Christ, and thinks he will be saved by that, he is mistaken entirely. If a man thinks that by worshipping an idol or the ghosts or spirits of the departed he will be saved, he is entirely mistaken. We may worship anything by seeing God *in* it, if we can forget the idol and see God there. We must not project any image upon God. But we may fill any image with that Life which is God. Only forget the image, and you are right enough — for "Out of

Him comes everything". He is everything. We may worship a picture as God, but not God as the picture. God in the picture is right, but the picture as God is wrong. God *in* the image is perfectly right. There is no danger there. This is the real worship of God. But the image-God is a mere Pratika.

The next great thing to consider in Bhakti is the "word", the Nâmashakti, the power of the name. The whole universe is composed of name and form. Whatever we see is either a compound of name and form, or simply name with form which is a mental image. So, after all, there is nothing that is not name and form. We all believe God to be without form or shape, but as soon as we begin to *think* of Him, He acquires both name and form The Chitta is like the calm lake, thoughts being like waves upon this Chitta — and name and form are the normal ways in which these waves arise; no wave can rise without name and form. The uniform cannot be thought of; it is beyond thought; as soon as it becomes thought and matter, it must have name and form. We cannot separate these. It is said in many books that God created the universe out of the Word. Shabdabrahman, in Sanskrit, is the Christian theory of the Word. An old Indian theory, it was taken to Alexandria by Indian preachers and was planted there. Thus the idea of the Word and the Incarnation became fixed there.

There is deep meaning in the thought that God created everything out of the Word. God Himself being formless, this is the best way to describe the projection of forms, or the creation. The Sanskrit word for creation is Srishti, projection. What is meant by "God created things out of nothing"? The universe is projected out of God. He becomes the universe, and it all returns to Him, and again it proceeds forth, and again returns. Through all eternity it will go on in that way. We have seen that the projection of anything in the mind cannot be without name and form. Suppose the mind to be perfectly calm, entirely without thought; nevertheless, as soon as thought begins to rise it will immediately take name and form. Every thought has a certain name and a certain form. In the same way the very fact of creation, the very fact of projection is eternally connected with name and form. Thus we find that every idea that man has, or can have, must be connected with a certain name or word as its counterpart. This being so, it is quite natural to suppose that this universe is the outcome of mind, just as your body is the outcome of your idea — your idea, as it were, made concrete and externalised. If it be true, moreover, that the whole universe is built on the same plan, then, if you know the manner in which one atom is built, you can understand how the whole universe is built. If it is true that in you, the body forms the gross part outside and the mind forms the fine part inside, and both are eternally inseparable, then, when you cease to have the body, you will cease to have the mind also. When a man's brain is disturbed, his ideas also get disturbed, because they are but one, the finer and the grosser parts. There are not two such things as matter and mind. As in a high column of air there are dense and rarefied strata of one and the same element air, so it is with the body; it is one thing throughout, layer on layer, from grosser to finer. Again, the body is like the finger nails. As these continue growing even when they are cut, so from our subtle ideas grows body after body. The finer a thing the more persistent it is; we find that always. The grosser it is the less persistent. Thus, form is the grosser and name the finer state of a single manifesting power called thought. But these three are one; it is the Unity and the Trinity, the three degrees of existence of the same thing. Finer, more condensed, and most condensed. Wherever the one is, the others are there also. Wherever name is, there is form and thought.

It naturally follows that if the universe is built upon the same plan as the body, the universe also must have the same divisions of form, name, and thought. The "thought" is the finest part of the universe, the real motive power. The thought behind our body is called soul, and the thought behind the universe is called God. Then after that is the name, and last of all is the form which we see and feel. For instance, you are a particular person, a little universe in this universe, a body with a particular form; then behind that a name, John or Jane, and behind that again a thought; similarly there is this whole universe, and behind that is the name, what is called the "Word" in all religions, and behind that is God. The universal thought is Mahat, as the Sânkhyas call it, universal consciousness. What is that name? There must be some name. The world is homogeneous, and modern science shows beyond doubt that each atom is composed of the same material as the whole universe. If you know one lump of clay you know the whole universe. Man is the most representative being in the universe, the microcosm, a small universe in himself. So in man we find there is the form, behind that the name, and behind that the thought, the thinking being. So this universe must be on exactly the same plan. The question is: What is that name? According to the Hindus that word is Om. The old Egyptians also believed that. The Katha Upanishad says, "That, seeking which a man practices Brahmacharya, I will tell you in short what that is, that is Om. ... This is Brahman, the Immutable One, and is the highest; knowing this Immutable One, whatever one desires one gets."

This Om stands for the name of the whole universe, or God. Standing midway between the external world and God. it represents both. But then we can take the universe piecemeal, according to the different senses, as touch, as colour, as taste, and in various other ways. In each case we can make of this universe millions of universes from different standpoints, each of which will be a complete universe by itself, and each one will have a name, and a form, and a thought behind. These thoughts behind are Pratikas. Each of them has a name. These names of sacred symbols are used in Bhakti-Yoga. They have almost infinite power. Simply by repetition of these words we can get anything we desire, we can come to perfection. But two things are necessary. "The teacher must be wonderful, so also must be the taught", says the Katha Upanishad. Such a name must come from a person to whom it has descended through right succession. From master to disciple, the spiritual current has been coming; from ancient times, bearing its power. The person from whom such a word comes is called a Guru, and the person to whom it goes is called Shishya, the disciple. When the word has been received in the regular way, and when it has been repeated, much advance has been made in Bhakti-Yoga. Simply by the repetition of that word will come even the highest state of Bhakti. "Thou hast so many names. Thou understandest what is meant by them all these names are Thine, and in each is Thine infinite power; there is neither time nor place for repeating these names, for all times and places are holy. Thou art so easy, Thou art so merciful, how unfortunate am I, that I have no love for Thee!"

THE ISHTA

The theory of Ishta, which I briefly referred to before, is a subject requiring careful attention because with a proper understanding of this, all the various religions of the world can be understood. The word Ishta is derived from the root Ish, to desire, choose. The ideal of all religions, all sects, is the same — the attaining of liberty and cessation of misery. Wherever you find religion, you find this ideal working in one form or other. Of course in lower stages of religion it is not so well expressed; but still, well or ill-expressed, it is the one goal to which every religion approaches. All of us want to get rid of misery; we are struggling to attain to liberty — physical, mental, spiritual. This is the whole idea upon which the world is working. Through the goal is one and the same, there may be many ways to reach it, and these ways are determined by the peculiarities of our nature. One man's nature is emotional, another's intellectual, another's active, and so forth. Again, in the same nature there may be many subdivisions. Take for instance love, with which we are specially concerned in this subject of Bhakti. One man's nature has a stronger love for children; another has it for wife, another for mother, another for father, another for friends. Another by nature has love for country, and a few love humanity in the broadest sense; they are of course very few, although everyone of us talks of it as if it were the guiding motive power of our lives. Some few sages have experienced it. A few great souls among mankind feel this universal love, and let us hope that this world will never be without such men.

We find that even in one subject there are so many different ways of attaining to its goal. AH Christians believe in Christ; but think, how many different explanations they have of him. Each church sees him in a different light, from different standpoints. The Presbyterian's eyes are fixed upon that scene in Christ's life when he went to the money-changers; he looks on him as a fighter. If you ask a Quaker, perhaps he will say, "He forgave his enemies." The Quaker takes that view, and so on. If you ask a Roman Catholic, what point of Christ's life is the most pleasing to him, he, perhaps, will say, "When he gave the keys to Peter". Each sect is bound to see him in its own way.

It follows that there will be many divisions and subdivisions even of the same subject. Ignorant persons take one of these subdivisions and take their stand upon it, and they not only deny the right of every other man to interpret the universe according to his own light, but dare to say that others are entirely wrong, and they alone are right. If they are opposed, they begin to fight. They say that they will kill any man who does not believe as they believe, just as the Mohammedans do. These are people who think they are sincere, and who ignore all others. But what is the position we want to take in this Bhakti-Yoga? Not only that we would not tell others that they are wrong, but that we would tell them that they are right — all of these who follow their own ways. That way, which your nature makes it absolutely necessary for you to take, is the right way. Each one of us is born with a peculiarity of nature as the result of our past existence. Either we call it our own reincarnated past experience or a hereditary past; whatever way we may put it, we are the result of the past - that is absolutely certain, through whatever channels that past may have come. It naturally follows that each one of us is an effect, of which our past has been the cause; and as such, there is a peculiar movement, a peculiar train, in each one of us; and therefore each one will have to find way for himself.

This way, this method, to which each of us is naturally adapted, is called the "chosen way". This is the theory of Ishta, and that way which is ours we call our own Ishta. For instance, one man's idea of God is that He is the omnipotent Ruler of the universe. His nature is perhaps such. He is an overbearing man who wants to rule everyone; he naturally finds God an omnipotent Ruler. Another man, who was perhaps a schoolmaster, and severe, cannot see any but a just God, a God of punishment, and so on Each one sees God according to his own nature; and this vision, conditioned by our own nature, is our Ishta. We have brought ourselves to a position where we can see that vision of God, and that alone; we cannot see any other vision. You will perhaps sometimes think of the teaching of a man that it is the best and fits you exactly, and the next day you ask one of your friends to go and hear him; but he comes away with the idea that it was the worst teaching he had ever heard. He is not wrong, and it is useless to quarrel with him. The teaching was all right, but it was not fitted to that man. To extend it a little further, we must understand that truth seen from different standpoints can be truth, and yet not the same truth.

This would seem at first to be a contradiction in terms, but we must remember that an absolute truth is only one, while relative truths are necessarily various. Take your vision of this universe, for instance. This universe, as an absolute entity, is unchangeable, and unchanged, and the same throughout. But you and I and everybody else hear and see, each one his own universe. Take the sun. The sun is one; but when you and I and a hundred other people stand at different places and look at it, each one of us sees a different sun. We cannot help it. A very little change of place will change a man's whole vision of the sun. A slight change in the atmosphere will make again a different vision. So, in relative perception, truth always appears various. But the Absolute Truth is only one. Therefore we need not fight with others when we find they; are telling something about religion which is not exactly according to our view of it. We ought to remember that both of us may be true, though apparently contradictors. There may be millions of radii converging towards the same centre in the sun. The further they are from the centre, the greater is the distance between any two. But as they all meet at the centre, all difference vanishes. There is such a centre, which is the absolute goal of mankind. It is God. We are the radii. The distances between the radii are the constitutional limitations through which alone we can catch the vision of God. While standing on this plane, we are bound each one of us to have a different view of the Absolute Reality; and as such, all views are true, and no one of us need quarrel with another. The only solution lies in approaching the centre. If we try to settle our differences by argument or quarrelling, we shall find that we can go on for hundreds of years without coming to a conclusion. History proves that. The only solution is to march ahead and go towards the centre; and the sooner we do that the sooner our differences will vanish.

This theory of Ishta, therefore, means allowing a man to choose his own religion. One man should not force another to worship what he worships. All attempts to herd together human beings by means of armies, force, or arguments, to drive them pell-mell into the same enclosure and make them worship the same God have failed and will fail always, because it is constitutionally impossible to do so. Not only so, there is the danger of arresting their growth. You scarcely meet any man or woman who is not struggling for some sort of religion; and how many are satisfied, or rather how few are satisfied! How few find anything! And why? Simply because most of them go after impossible tasks. They are forced into these by the dictation of others. For instance, when I am a child, my father puts a book into my hand which says God is such and such. What business has he to put that into my mind? How does he know what way I would develop? And being ignorant of my constitutional development, he wants to force his ideas on my brain, with the result that my growth is stunted. You cannot make a plant grow in soil unsuited to it. A child teaches itself. But you can *help* it to go forward in its own way. What you can do is not of the positive nature, but of the negative. You can take away the obstacles, but knowledge comes out of its own nature. Loosen the soil a little, so that it may come out easily. Put a hedge round it; see that it is not killed by anything, and there your work stops. You cannot do anything else. The rest is a manifestation from *within* its own nature. So with the education of a child; a child educates itself. You come to hear me, and when you go home, compare what you have learnt, and you will find you have thought out the same thing; I have only given it expression. I can never teach you anything: you will have to teach yourself, but I can help you perhaps in giving expression to that thought.

So in religion — more so — I must teach myself religion. What right has my father to put all sorts of nonsense into my head? What right has my master or society to put things into my head? Perhaps they are good, but they may not be *my* way. Think of the appalling evil that is in the world today, of the millions and millions of innocent children perverted by wrong ways of teaching. How many beautiful things which would have become wonderful spiritual truths have been nipped in the bud by this horrible idea of a family religion, a social religion, a national religion, and so forth. Think of what a mass of superstition is in your head just now about your childhood's religion, or your country's religion, and what an amount of evil it does, or can do. Man does not know what a potent power lies behind each thought and action. The old saying is true that, "Fools rush in where angels fear to tread." This should be kept in view from the very first. How? By this belief in Ishta. There are so many ideals; I have no right to say what shall be your ideal, to force any ideal on you. My duty should be to lay before you all the ideals I know of and enable you to see by your own constitution what you like best, and which is most fitted to you. Take up that one which suits you best and persevere in it. This is your Ishta, your special ideal.

We see then that a congregational religion can never be. The *real* work of religion must be one's own concern.

I have an idea of my own, I must keep it sacred and secret, because I know that it need not be your idea. Secondly, why should I create a disturbance by wanting to tell everyone what my idea is? Other people would come and fight me. They cannot do so if I do not tell them; but if I go about telling them what my ideas are, they will all oppose me. So what is the use of talking about them? This Ishta should be kept secret, it is between you and God. All theoretical portions of religion can be preached in public and made congregational, but higher religion cannot be made public. I cannot get ready my religious feelings at a moment's notice. What is the result of this mummery and mockery? It is making a joke of religion, the worst of blasphemy. The result is what you find in the churches of the present day. How can human beings stand this religious drilling? It is like soldiers in a barrack. Shoulder arms, kneel down, take a book, all regulated exactly. Five minutes of feeling, five minutes of reason, five minutes of prayer, all arranged beforehand. These mummeries have driven out religion. Let the churches preach doctrines, theories, philosophies to their hearts' content, but when it comes to worship, the real practical part of religion, it should be as Jesus says, "When thou prayest, enter into thy closet, and when thou hast shut thy door, pray to thy Father which is in secret"

This is the theory of Ishta. It is the only way to make religion meet practically the necessities of different constitutions, to avoid quarrelling with others, and to make real practical progress in spiritual life. But I must warn you that you do not misconstrue my words into the formation of secret societies. If there were a devil, I would look for him within a secret society — as the invention of secret societies. They are diabolical schemes. The Ishta is *sacred*, not secret. But in what sense? Why should I not speak of my Ishta to others? Because it is my own most holy thing. It may help others, but how do I know that it will not rather hurt them? There may be a man whose nature is such that he cannot worship a Personal God, but can only worship as an Impersonal God his own highest Self. Suppose I leave him among you, and he tells you that there is no Personal God, but only God as the Self in you or me. You will be shocked. His idea is sacred, but not secret. There never was a great religion or a great teacher that formed secret societies to preach God's truths. There are no such secret societies in India. Such things are purely Western in idea, and merely foisted upon India. We never knew anything about them. Why indeed should there be secret societies in India? In Europe, people were not allowed to talk a word about religion that did not agree with the views of the Church. So they were forced to go about amongst the mountains in hiding and form secret societies, that they might follow their own kind of worship. There was never a time in India when a man was persecuted for holding his own views on religion. There were never secret religious societies in India, so any idea of that sort you must give up at once. These secret societies always degenerate into the most horrible things. I have seen enough of this world to know what evil they cause, and how easily they slide into free love societies and ghost societies, how men play into the hands of other men or women, and how their future possibilities of growth in thought and act are destroyed, and so on. Some of you may be displeased with me for talking in this way, but I must tell you the truth. Perhaps only half a dozen men and women will follow me in all my life; but they will be real men and women, pure and sincere, and I do not want a crowd. What can crowds do? The history of the world was made by a few dozens, whom you can count on your fingers, and the rest were a rabble. All these secret societies and humbugs make men and women impure, weak and narrow; and the weak have no will, and can never work. Therefore have nothing to do with them. All this false love of mystery should be knocked on the head the first time it comes into your mind. No one who is the least impure will ever become religious. Do not try to cover festering sores with masses of roses. Do you think you can cheat God? None can. Give me a straightforward man or woman; but Lord save me from ghosts, flying angels, and devils. Be common, everyday, nice people.

There is such a thing as instinct in us, which we have in common with the animals, a reflex mechanical movement of the body. There is again a higher form of guidance, which we call reason, when the intellect obtains facts and then generalises them. There is a still higher form of knowledge which we call inspiration, which does not reason, but knows things by flashes. That is the highest form of knowledge. But how shall we know it from instinct? That is the great difficulty. Everyone comes to you, nowadays and says he is inspired, and puts forth superhuman claims. How are we to distinguish between inspiration and deception? In the first place, inspiration must not contradict reason. The old man does not contradict the child, he is the development of the child. What we call inspiration is the development of reason. The way to intuition is through reason. Instinctive movements of your body do not oppose reason. As you cross a street, how instinctively you move your body to save yourself from the cars. Does your mind tell you it was foolish to save your body that way? It does not. Similarly, no genuine inspiration ever contradicts reason. Where it does it is no inspiration. Secondly, inspiration must be for the good of one and all, and not for name or fame, or personal gain. It should always be for the good of the world, and perfectly unselfish. When these tests are fulfilled, you are quite safe to take it as inspiration. You must remember that there is not one in a million that is inspired, in the present state of the world. I hope their number will increase. We are now only playing with religion. With inspiration we shall begin to have religion. Just as St. Paul says, "For now we see through a glass darkly, but then face to face." But in the present state of the world they are few and far between who attain to that state; yet perhaps at no other period were such false claims made to inspiration, as now. It is said that women have intuitive faculties, while men drag themselves slowly upward by reason. Do not believe it. There are just as many inspired men as women, though women have perhaps more claim to peculiar forms of hysteria and nervousness. You had better die as an unbeliever than be played upon by cheats and jugglers. The power of reasoning was given you for use. Show then that you have used it properly. Doing so, you will be able to take care of higher things.

We must always remember that God is Love. "A fool indeed is he who, living on the banks of the Ganga, seeks to dig a little well for water. A fool indeed is the man who, living near a mine of diamonds, spends his life in searching for beads of glass." God is that mine of diamonds. We are fools indeed to give up God for legends of ghosts or flying hobgoblins. It is a disease, a morbid desire. It degenerates the race, weakens the nerves and the brain, living in incessant morbid fear of hobgoblins, or stimulating the hunger for wonders; all these wild stories about them keep the nerves at an unnatural tension — a slow and sure degeneration of the race. It is degeneration to think of giving up God, purity, holiness, and spirituality, to go after all this nonsense! Reading other men's thoughts! If I must read everyone else's thoughts for five minutes at a time I shall go crazy. Be strong and stand up and seek the God of Love. This is the highest strength. What power is higher than the power of purity? Love and purity govern the world. This love of God cannot be reached by the weak; therefore, be not weak, either physically, mentally, morally or spiritually. The Lord alone is true. Everything else is untrue; everything else should be rejected for the salve of the Lord. Vanity of vanities, all is vanity. Serve the Lord and Him alone.

10

Quotes of Swami Vivekananda

ASPIRANTS

Seek only after one thing, and that, God! (Life of Swami Vivekananda by his Eastern and Western Disciples. First ed Vol 2 pg 374)

BHAKTI

To obtain Bhakti, seek the company of holy men who have Bhakti, and read books like the Gita and the *Imitation of Christ;* always think of the attributes of God.(Notes taken down in Madras 1892-1893)

Bhakti is a higher thing higher than even desiring heaven. The idea of heaven is of a place of intensified enjoyment How can that be God? (Notes from a lecture On Bhakti Yoga)

Bhakti-Yoga is the path of systematised devotion for the attainment of union with the Absolute. It is the easiest and surest path to religion or realisation.

BOOK LEARNING

Even he who has seen only a spook is more spiritual than book-learned pundits.

BUDDHA AND BUDDHISM

Buddha's Sermon on the Mount was, "As thou thinkest, so

art thou." *(Notes from a Lecture - On Bhakti Yoga)*

A religion invented by the Kshattriyas as a crushing rejoinder to Brahminism! (Notes of some wanderings with the Swami Vivekananda by Sister Nivedita)

I am the servant of the servants of the servants of Buddha. Who was there ever like Him ?—the Lord—who never performed one action for Himself—with a heart that embraced the whole world ! So full of pity that He—prince and monk—would give his life to save a little goat ! So loving that He sacrificed himself to the hunger of a tigress !—to the hospitality of a pariah and blessed him. (Notes of some wanderings with the Swami Vivekananda by Sister Nivedita)

Chastity

No force can be created; it can only be directed. Therefore, we must learn to control the grand powers that are already in our hands, and by will power make them spiritual, instead of merely animal. Thus it is clearly seen that chastity is the cornerstone of all morality and of all religion. (C.W. 8.46)

Competition

The day will come when men will study history from a different light and find that competition is neither the cause nor the effect, simply a thing on the way, not necessary to evolution at all.

Concentration

The mind has to be made malleable like clay. Just as clay sticks wherever you throw it, so the mind must be made to dwell upon whatever object you concentrate it.

Darjeeling

It is the most picturesque city in the world. (Letter to Mrs. Bull - April 4 1898)

Devotion

The devotion to God as seen in every religion is divided

into two parts: the devotion which works through forms and ceremonies and through words, and that which works through love. (Notes from a lecture Lessons on Bhakti yoga)

Education

We want that education by which character is formed, strength of mind is increased, the intellect is expanded, and by which one can stand on one's own feet.

Ethics

Renunciation is the very basis upon which ethics stands. There never was an ethical code preached which had not renunciation for its basis.

Ethics always says, "Not I, but thou." Its motto is, "Not self, but non-self." The vain ideas of individualism, to which man clings when he is trying to find that Infinite Power or that Infinite Pleasure through the senses, have to be given up—say the laws of ethics. You have to put yourself last, and others before you. The senses say, "Myself first." Ethics says, "I must hold myself last." Thus, all codes of ethics are based upon this renunciation; destruction, not construction, of the individual on the material plane.

Faith in Oneself

The old religions said that he was an atheist who did not believe in God. The new religion says that he is the atheist who does not believe in himself.

Fanatics and Fanaticism

In ninety cases out of a hundred, fanatics must have bad livers, or they are dyspeptics, or are in some way diseased. By degrees even physicians will find out that fanaticism is a kind of disease. *(Notes from a lecture On Fanaticism)*

Gita

This is the one central idea in the Gita: work incessantly, but be not attached to it.

That wonderful poem, without one note in it, of weakness or unmanliness. (Notes of some wanderings with the Swami Vivekananda by Sister Nivedita)

God

Some imaginations help to break the bondage of the rest. The whole universe is imagination, but one set of imaginations will cure another set. Those that tell us that there is sin and sorrow and death in the world are terrible. But the other set — thou art holy, there is God, there is no pain — these are good, and help to break the bondage of the others. The highest imagination that can break all the links of the chain is that of the Personal God. (Notes from a lecture On Bhakti Yoga)

Good and Evil

Who can say that God does not manifest Himself as Evil as well as Good ? But only the Hindu dares to worship Him in the evil. (Notes of some wanderings with the Swami Vivekananda by Sister Nivedita)

Greatness

Great occasions rouse even the lowest of human beings to some kind of greatness, but he alone is the really great man whose character is great always, the same wherever he be.

Hinduism

The three essentials of Hinduism are belief in God, in the Vedas as revelation, in the doctrine of Karma and transmigration. (*Notes taken down in Madras 1892-93)*

My religion is one of which Christianity is an offshoot and Buddhism a rebel child. (Notes taken down in Madras 1892-93)

There is no new religious idea preached anywhere which is not found in the Vedas. (Notes taken down in Madras 1892-93)

The Vedas contain not only the means how to obtain Bhakti but also the means for obtaining any earthly good or evil. Take whatever you want. (Notes taken down in Madras 1892-93)

Householders

Never forget, to say to yourself, and to teach to your children, as the difference between a firefly and the blazing sun, between the infinite ocean and a little pond, between a mustard-seed and the mountain of Meru, such is the difference between the householder and the Sannyasin. *(Notes of some wanderings with the Swami Vivekananda by Sister Nivedita)*

Italy

Greatest of the countries of Europe, land of religion and of art; alike of imperial organization and of Mazzini ;— mother of ideas, of culture, and of freedom ! *(Notes of some wanderings with the Swami Vivekananda by Sister Nivedita)*

Jnana (True Knowledge)

Jnâna (knowledge) is "creedlessness"; but that does not mean that it despises creeds. It only means that a stage above and beyond creeds has been gained. *(Notes from a lecture On Jnana Yoga)*

Judging Others

In criticising another, we always foolishly take one especially brilliant point as the whole of our life and compare that with the dark ones in the life of another. Thus we make mistakes in judging individuals. (Notes from a lecture On Bhakti Yoga)

Krishna

This was the great work of Krishna : to clear our eyes and make us look with broader vision upon humanity in its march upward and onward. His was the first heart that was large enough to see truth in all, his the first lips that uttered beautiful words for each and all.

Krishna talks of himself as God, as Christ does. He sees the Deity in himself. And he says, "None can go a day out of my path. All have to come to me. Whosoever wants to worship in whatsoever form, I give him faith in that form, and through that I meet him. ..."(Gita, IV. 12.) His heart is all for the masses. (From his lecture · Krishna)

Shri Krishna is the God of the poor, the beggar, the the sinner, the son, the father, the wife, and of everyone. He enters intimately into all our human relations and makes everything holy and in the end brings us to salvation. He is the God who hides himself from the philosopher and the learned and reveals himself to the ignorant and the children. He is the God of faith and love and not of learning. With the Gopis, love and God were the same thing — they knew Him to be love incarnate. *(Notes taken down in Madras 1892-93)*

Liberty

To care only for spiritual liberty and not for social liberty is a defect, but the opposite is a still greater defect. Liberty of both soul and body is to be striven for. *(Notes from a lecture Hindu and Greek)*

This life is a tremendous assertion of freedom; and this obedience to law, carried far enough, would make us simply matter — either in society, or in politics, or in religion. Too many laws are a sure sign of death. Wherever in any society there are too many laws, it is a sure sign that that society will soon die. (Notes from a lecture Law and Freedom)

Manhood

When the soul wants to depend upon nothing, not even upon life, that is the height of philosophy, the height of manhood. (From his lecture Krishna)

Marriage

Though the love of a mother is in some ways greater, yet the whole world takes the love of man and woman as the type. No other has such tremendous idealising power. The beloved actually becomes what he is imagined to be. This love transforms its obiect. *(Notes from some wanderings with the Swami Vivekananda by Sister Nivedita)*

Maya

He who knows the Real sees in Maya not illusion, but reality. He who knows not the Real sees in Maya illusion and thinks it real. (Notes from a lecture *The reality and shadow*)

Meditation

The greatest thing is meditation. It is the nearest approach to spiritual life — the mind meditating. It is the one moment in our daily life that we are not at all material — the Soul thinking of Itself, free from all matter — this marvellous touch of the Soul! (Notes from a lecture Sadhanas or preparations for higher life)

Misery

Unborn and uncreated, without beginning and without end, deathless, birthless and omnipresent — that is what I am; and all misery comes just because I think this little lump of clay is myself. I am identifying myself with matter and taking all the consequences. (Lecture The Practice of Religion)

Mistakes

Our mistakes have places here. Go on! Do not look back if you think you have done something that is not right. Now, do you believe you could be what you are today, had you not made those mistakes before? Bless your mistakes, then. They have been angels unawares. Blessed be torture! Blessed be happiness Do not care what be your lot. Hold on to the ideal. March on! Do not look back upon little mistakes and things. In this battlefield of ours, the dust of mistakes must be raised. Those who are so thin-skinned that they cannot bear the dust, let them get out of the ranks. (Notes from a lecture · Sadhanas or preparations for higher life)

Money and Fame

Fortune is like a flirt; she cares not for him who wants her, but she is at the feet of him who does not care for her.

Money comes and showers itself upon one who does not care for it; so does fame come in abundance until it is a trouble and a burden. They always come to the Master. The slave never gets anything. The Master is he who can live in spite of them, whose life does not depend upon the little, foolish things of the world. (Notes from a lecture Sadhanas or preparations for higher life)

Motherhood

The highest of all feminine types in India is mother, higher than wife. Wife and children may desert a man, but his mother never. Mother is the same or loves her child perhaps a little more. Mother represents colourless love that knows no barter, love that never dies. Who can have such love? — only mother, not son, nor daughter, nor wife. (*Notes from a lecture - Mother Worship*)

Mercy

Mercy is heaven itself; to be good, we have all to be merciful. Even justice and right should stand on mercy.

Ordinary Mankind

Ordinary mankind cannot understand anything that is subtle. Well has it been said that mobs would run after a lion that could kill a thousand lambs, and never for a moment think that it is death unto the lambs, although it may be a momentary triumph for the lion; because in that the mob finds the greatest manifestation of physical strength. Thus with the ordinary run of mankind, they understand and find pleasure in everything that is external. (The Necessity of Religion - Jnana Yoga 1902 edition)

Politics

In order to become a nation, it appears that *we need a common hate* as well as a common love. (Notes of some wanderings with the Swami Vivekananda by Sister Nivedita)

Race and Racism

If I am grateful to my white-skinned Aryan ancestor, I am far more so to my yellow-skinned Mongolian ancestor, and most so of all, to the black-skinned Negritoid! (As quoted by Sister Nivedita)

The Tartar is the wine of the race! He gives energy and power to every blood! (As quoted by Sister Nivedita)

Radha-Prema of the Vaishnavas

Look at this nation. Through the preaching of that love broadcast, the nation has become effeminate—a race of women! The whole of Orissa has been turned into a land of cowards, and Bengal, running high after the Radha-prema, these past four hundred years, has almost lost all sense of manliness. (As quoted by Surendranath Sen in his private diary)

Realisation

Do not accept anything because I have said so; but test everything for yourself. It is not in assent or dissent that the goal is to be attained, but in actual and concrete realization. (Life of Swami Vivekananda by Eastern and Western Disciples)

Religion

The ultimate goal of all mankind, the aim and end of all religions, is but one — re-union with God, or, what amounts to the same, with the divinity which is every man's true nature. (Notes from a lecture ·The goals and methods of realisation)

So long as religion was in the hands of a chosen few or of a body of priests, it was in the temples, it was in the churches, it was in the books, in dogmas, in ceremonials, forms, and rituals. When men have come to the real, universal, spiritual concept, then, and then alone, religion will become real and living; it will come into our very nature, live in every movement of the human being, it will penetrate every pore of society, and be infinitely more a power for good than it has ever been before. (The Necessity of Religion - Jnana Yoga 1902 edition)

The mainspring of the strength of every race lies in the spirituality manifested in religion and the death of that race begins the day that spirituality wanes and materialism begins. (The Necessity of Religion - Jnana Yoga 1902 edition)

It is good and very grand to conquer external nature, but grander still to conquer the internal nature of man. It is grand and good to know the laws that govern the stars and planets; it is infinitely grander and better to know the laws that govern the passions, the feelings, the will, of mankind. This conquering of the inner man, understanding the secrets of the subtle workings that are within the human mind, and knowing its wonderful secrets, belong entirely to religion. (The Necessity of Religion - ·Jnana Yoga 1902 edition)

Reniciation

This hideous world is Maya. Renounce and be happy. Give up the idea of sex and possessions. There is no other bond. Marriage and sex and money are the only living devils. All earthly love proceeds from the body. No sex, no possessions; as these fall off, the eyes open to spiritual vision. The soul regains its own infinite power. *(Letter to Mary Hale - July 9, 1897).*

Samadhi

Samadhi is perfect absorption of thought into the Supreme Spirit, when one realises. "I and my Father are one." (Notes from a lecture On Raja Yoga)

Sanyasins

Blessed be even the fraudulent *sadhus,* and those who have failed to carry out their vows, in as much as they also have witnessed to the ideal, and so are in some degree the cause of the success of others!

Let us never, never, forget our Ideal. (Notes from some wanderings with the Swami Vivekananda by Sister Nivedita)

Sense Control

There is but one way to control the senses — to see Him who is the Reality in the universe. Then and only then can we really conquer our senses. (*Notes from a lecture Concentration*)

The Soul

The soul lives and forever expands. Worlds must come into the soul. Worlds must disappear in the soul like drops in the ocean. (Lecture The practice of religion)

Evolution is in nature, not in the soul — evolution of nature, manifestation of the soul. (Notes from a lecture · The reality and shadow)

Strength

The highest manifestation of strength is to keep ourselves calm and on our own feet.

Whatever you think, that you will be. If you think yourselves weak, weak you will be; if you think yourselves strong, strong you will be.

Strength, strength it is that we want so much in this life, for what we call sin and sorrow have all one cause, and that is our weakness. With weakness comes ignorance, and with ignorance comes misery.

Everyone says, "Woe unto you people! !" Who says, "Woe unto me that I cannot help you?" The people are doing all right to the best of their ability and means and knowledge. Woe unto me that I cannot lift them to where I am! (From his lecture Krishna)

The only test of good things is that they make us strong. (CW, 8:185)

Unselfishness

Every successful man must have behind him somewhere tremendous integrity, tremendous sincerity, and that is the cause of his signal success in life. He may not have been perfectly unselfish; yet he was tending towards it. If he had been perfectly unselfish, his would have been as great a success as that of the Buddha or of the Christ. The degree of unselfishness marks the degree of success everywhere. (Notes from a lecture **On Karma Yoga)**

WORK

It is always good to give a few strong strokes and rest on your oars. (Letter to Sashi - March 1898)

WOMANHOOD

O India ! Forget not that the ideal of thy womanhood is Sita, Savitri, Damayanti. (CW, *IV, 479-80: Modern India*).

The women of India must grow and develop in the footprints of Sita, and that is the only way. (CW, III, 256: Vivekananda's lecture "The Sages of India" at Victoria Public Hall, Madras February 11, 1897).

Sita is the name in India for everything that is good, pure, and holy; everything that in women we call woman. (Notes from a lecture Fragmentary notes on the Ramayana)

WORSHIP

This is the gist of all worship – to be pure and to do good to others.

Various sorts of worship we see in this world. The sick man is very worshipful to God. ... There is the man who loses his fortune; he also prays very much — to get money. The highest worship is that of the man who loves God for God's sake. (From his lecture Krishna)

WORK

The best work is only done by alternate repose and work. (Letter to Sashi - March 1898)

THE YOGI

A mongoose is generally kept in a glass-case with a long chain attached to it, so that it may go about freely. When it scents danger as it wanders about, with one jump it goes into the glass-case. So is a Yogi in this world. (Notes taken down in Madras 1892-93)

11

Lectures and Discourses

Unity, the Goal of Religion, (Delivered in New York, 1896)

This universe of ours, the universe of the senses, the rational, the intellectual, is bounded on both sides by the illimitable, the unknowable, the ever unknown. Herein is the search, herein are the inquiries, here are the facts; from this comes the light which is known to the world as religion. Essentially, however, religion belongs to the supersensuous and not to the sense plane. It is beyond all reasoning and is not on the plane of intellect. It is a vision, an inspiration, a plunge into the unknown and unknowable, making the unknowable more than known for it can never be "known". This search has been in the human mind, as I believe, from the very beginning of humanity. There cannot have been human reasoning and intellect in any period of the world's history without this struggle, this search beyond. In our little universe, this human mind, we see a thought arise. Whence it arises we do not know; and when it disappears, where it goes, we know not either. The macrocosm and the microcosm are, as it were, in the same groove, passing through the same stages, vibrating in the same key.

I shall try to bring before you the Hindu theory that religions do not come from without, but from within. It is my belief that religious thought is in man's very constitution, so much so that it is impossible for him to give, up religion until he can give up his mind and body, until he can give up thought and life. As long as a man thinks, this struggle must go on, and so long man must have some form of religion. Thus we see various forms of religion in the world. It is a bewildering study; but it is not, as many of us think, a vain speculation. Amidst this chaos there is harmony, throughout these discordant sounds there is a note of concord; and he who is prepared to listen to it will catch the tone.

The great question of all questions at the present time is this: Taking for granted that the known and the knowable are bounded on both sides by the unknowable and the infinitely unknown, why struggle for that infinite unknown? Why shall we not be content with the known? Why shall we not rest satisfied with eating, drinking, and doing a little good to society? This idea is in the air. From the most learned professor to the prattling baby, we are told that to do good to the world is all of religion, and that it is useless to trouble ourselves about questions of the beyond. So much is this the case that it has become a truism.

But fortunately we *must* inquire into the beyond. This present, this expressed, is only one part of that unexpressed. The sense universe is, as it were, only one portion, one bit of that infinite spiritual universe projected into the plane of sense consciousness. How can this little bit of projection be explained, be understood, without. knowing that which is beyond? It is said of Socrates that one day while lecturing at Athens, he met a Brahmin who had travelled into Greece, and Socrates told the Brahmin that the greatest study for mankind is man. The Brahmir sharply retorted: "How can you know man until you know Gods" This God, this eternally Unknowable, or Absolute, or Infinite, or without name —

you may call Him by what name you like — is the rationale, the only explanation, the *raison d'être* of that which is known and knowable, this present life. Take anything before you, the most material thing — take one of the most material sciences, as chemistry or physics, astronomy or biology — study it, push the study forward and forward, and the gross forms will begin to melt and become finer and finer, until they come to a point where you are bound to make a tremendous leap from these material things into the immaterial. The gross melts into the fine, physics into metaphysics, in every department of knowledge.

Thus man finds himself driven to a study of the beyond. Life will be a desert, human life will be vain, if we cannot know the beyond. It is very well to say: Be contented with the things of the present. The cows and the dogs are, and so are all animals; and that is what makes them animals. So if man rests content with the present and gives up all search into the beyond, mankind will have to go back to the animal plane again. It is religion, the inquiry into the beyond, that makes the difference between man and an animal. Well has it been said that man is the only animal that naturally looks upwards; every other animal naturally looks down. That looking upward and going upward and seeking perfection are what is called salvation; and the sooner a man begins to go higher, the sooner he raises himself towards this idea of truth as salvation. It does not consist in the amount of money in your pocket, or the dress you wear, or the house you live in, but in the wealth of spiritual thought in your brain. That is what makes for human progress, that is the source of all material and intellectual progress, the motive power behind, the enthusiasm that pushes mankind forward.

Religion does not live on bread, does not dwell in a house. Again and again you hear this objection advanced:

"What good can religion do? Can it take away the poverty of the poor?" Supposing it cannot, would that prove the untruth of religion? Suppose a baby stands up among you when you are trying to demonstrate an astronomical theorem, and says, "Does it bring gingerbread?" "No, it does not", you answer. "Then," says the baby, "it is useless." Babies judge the whole universe from their own standpoint, that of producing gingerbread, and so do the babies of the world. We must not judge of higher things from a low standpoint. Everything must be judged by its own standard and the infinite must be judged by the standard of infinity. Religion permeates the whole of man's life, not only the present, but the past, present, and future. It is, therefore, the eternal relation between the eternal soul and the eternal God. Is it logical to measure its value by its action upon five minutes of human life? Certainly not. These are all negative arguments.

Now comes the question: Can religion really accomplish anything? It can. It brings to man eternal life. It has made man what he is, and will make of this human animal a god. That is what religion can do. Take religion from human society and what will remain? Nothing but a forest of brutes. Sense-happiness is not the goal of humanity. Wisdom (Jnâna) is the goal of all life. We find that man enjoys his intellect more than an animal enjoys its senses; and we see that man enjoys his spiritual nature even more than his rational nature. So the highest wisdom must be this spiritual knowledge. With this knowledge will come bliss. All these things of this world are but the shadows, the manifestations in the third or fourth degree of the real Knowledge and Bliss.

One question more: What is the goal? Nowadays it is asserted that man is infinitely progressing, forward and forward, and there is no goal of perfection to attain to. Ever approaching, never attaining, whatever that may mean and however wonderful it may be, it is absurd on the face of it. Is there any motion in a straight line? A straight line infinitely projected becomes a circle, it returns to the starting point. You must end where you begin; and as you began in God, you must go back to God. What remains? Detail work. Through eternity you have to do the detail work.

Yet another question: Are we to discover new truths of religion as we go on? Yea and nay. In the first place, we cannot know anything more of religion, it has all been known. In all religions of the world you will find it claimed that there is a unity within us. Being one with divinity, there cannot be any further progress in that sense. Knowledge means finding this unity. I see you as men and women, and this is variety. It becomes scientific knowledge when I group you together and call you human beings. Take the science of chemistry, for instance. Chemists are seeking to resolve all known substances into their original elements, and if possible, to find the one element from which all these are derived. The time may come when they will find one element that is the source of all other elements. Reaching that, they can go no further; the science of chemistry will have become perfect. So it is with the science of religion. If we can discover this perfect unity, there cannot be any further progress.

The next question is: Can such a unity be found? In India the attempt has been made from the earliest times to reach a science of religion and philosophy, for the Hindus do not separate these as is customary in Western countries. We regard religion and philosophy as but two aspects of one thing which must equally be grounded in reason and scientific truth.

The system of the Sânkhya philosophy is one of the most ancient in India, or in fact in the world. Its great exponent Kapila is the father of all Hindu psychology;

and the ancient system that he taught is still the foundation of all accepted systems of philosophy in India today which are known as the Darshanas. They all adopt his psychology, however widely they differ in other respects.

The Vedanta, as the logical outcome of the Sankhya, pushes its conclusions yet further. While its cosmology agrees with that taught by Kapila, the Vedanta is not satisfied to end in dualism, but continues its search for the final unity which is alike the goal of science and religion.

The Free Soul, (Delivered in New York, 1896)

The analysis of the Sânkhyas stops with the duality of existence — Nature and souls. There are an infinite number of souls, which, being simple, cannot die, and must therefore be separate from Nature. Nature in itself changes and manifests all these phenomena; and the soul, according to the Sankhyas, is inactive. It is a simple by itself, and Nature works out all these phenomena for the liberation of the soul; and liberation consists in the soul discriminating that it is not Nature.

At the same time we have seen that the Sankhyas were bound to admit that every soul was omnipresent. Being a simple, the soul cannot be limited, because all limitation comes either through time, space, or causation. The soul being entirely beyond these cannot have any limitation. To have limitation one must be in space, which means the body; and that which is body must be in Nature. If the soul had form, it would be identified with Nature; therefore the soul is formless, and that which is formless cannot be said to exist here, there, or anywhere. It must be omnipresent. Beyond this the Sankhya philosophy does not go.

The first argument of the Vedantists against this is that this analysis is not a perfect one. If their Nature be absolute and the soul be also absolute, there will be two absolutes, and all the arguments that apply in the case of the soul to show that it is omnipresent will apply in the case of Nature, and Nature too will be beyond all time, space, and causation, and as the result there will be no change or manifestation. Then will come the difficulty of having two absolutes, which is impossible. What is the solution of the Vedantist? His solution is that, just as the Sankhyas say, it requires some sentient Being as the motive power behind, which makes the mind think and Nature work, because Nature in all its modifications, from gross matter up to Mahat (Intelligence), is simply insentient.

Now, says the Vedantist, this sentient Being which is behind the whole universe is what we call *God,* and consequently this universe is not different from Him. It is He Himself who has become this universe. He not only is the instrumental cause of this universe, but also the material cause. Cause is never different from effect, the effect is but the cause reproduced in another form. We see that every day. So this Being is the cause of Nature. All the forms and phases of Vedanta, either dualistic, or qualified-monistic, or monistic, first take this position that God is not only the instrumental, but also the material cause of this universe, that everything which exists is He. The second step in Vedanta is that these souls are also a part of God, one spark of that Infinite Fire. "As from a mass of fire millions of small particles fly, even so from this Ancient One have come all these souls." So far so good, but it does not yet satisfy. What is meant by a part of the Infinite? The Infinite is indivisible; there cannot be parts of the Infinite. The Absolute cannot be divided. What is meant, therefore, by saying that all these sparks are from Him?

The Advaitist, the non-dualistic Vedantist, solves the problem by maintaining that there is really no part; that each soul is really not a part of the Infinite, but actually is the Infinite Brahman. Then how can there be so many? The sun reflected from millions of globules of water appears to be millions of suns, and in each globule is a miniature picture of the sun-form; so all these souls are but reflections and not real. They are not the real "I" which is the God of this universe, the one undivided Being of the universe. And all these little different beings, men and animals etc. are but reflections, and not real. They are simply illusory reflections upon Nature. There is but one Infinite Being in the universe, and that Being appears as you and as I; but this appearance of divisions is after all a delusion. He has not been divided, but only appears to be divided. This apparent division is caused by looking at Him through the network of time, space, and causation. When I look at God through the network of time, space, and causation, I see Him as the material world. When I look at Him from a little higher plane, yet through the same network, I see Him as an animal, a little higher as a man, a little higher as a god, but yet He is the One Infinite Being of the universe, and that Being we are. I am That, and you are That. Not parts of It, but the whole of It. "It is the Eternal Knower standing behind the whole phenomena; He Himself is the phenomena." He is both the subject and the object, He is the "I" and the "You". How is this? "How to know the Knower? The Knower cannot know Himself; I see everything but cannot see myself.

The Self, the Knower, the Lord of all, the Real Being, is the cause of all the vision that is in the universe, but it is impossible for Him to see Himself or know Himself, excepting through reflection. You cannot see your own face except in a mirror, and so the Self cannot see Its own nature until It is reflected, and this whole universe therefore is the Self trying to realise Itself. This reflection is thrown back first from the protoplasm, then from plants and animals, and so on and on from better and better reflectors, until the best reflector, the perfect man, is reached — just as a man who, wanting to see his face, looks first in a little pool of muddy water, and sees just an outline; then he comes to clear water, and sees a better image; then to a piece of shining metal, and sees a still better image; and at last to a looking-glass, and sees himself reflected as he is. Therefore the perfect man is the highest reflection of that Being who is both subject and object. You now find why man instinctively worships everything, and how perfect men are instinctively worshipped as God in every country. You may talk as you like, but it is they who are bound to be worshipped. That is why men worship Incarnations, such as Christ or Buddha. They are the most perfect manifestations of the eternal Self. They are much higher than all the conceptions of God that you or I can make. A perfect man is much higher than such conceptions. In him the circle becomes complete; the subject and the object become one. In him all delusions go away and in their place comes the realisation that he has always been that perfect Being. How came this bondage then? How was it possible for this perfect Being to degenerate into the imperfect? How was it possible that the free became bound? The Advaitist says, he was never bound, but was always free.

Various clouds of various colours come before the sky. They remain there a minute and then pass away. It is the same eternal blue sky stretching there for ever. The sky never changes: it is the cloud that is changing. So you are always perfect, eternally perfect. Nothing ever changes your nature, or ever will. All these ideas that I am imperfect, I am a man, or a woman, or a sinner, or I am the mind, I have thought, I will think — all are hallucinations; you never think, you never had a body;

you never were imperfect. You are the blessed Lord of this universe, the one Almighty ruler of everything that is and ever will be, the one mighty ruler of these suns and stars and moons and earths and planets and all the little bits of our universe. It is through you that the sun shines and the stars shed their lustre, and the earth becomes beautiful. It is through your blessedness that they all love and are attracted to each other. You are in all, and you are all. Whom to avoid, and whom to take? You are the all in all. When this knowledge comes delusion immediately vanishes.

I was once travelling in the desert in India. I travelled for over a month and always found the most beautiful landscapes before me, beautiful lakes and all that. One day I was very thirsty and I wanted to have a drink at one of these lakes; but when I approached that lake it vanished. Immediately with a blow came into my brain the idea that this was a mirage about which I had read all my life; and then I remembered and smiled at my folly, that for the last month all the beautiful landscapes and lakes I had been seeing were this mirage, but I could not distinguish them then. The next morning I again began my march; there was the lake and the landscape, but with it immediately came the idea, "This is a mirage." Once known it had lost its power of illusion. So this illusion of the universe will break one day. The whole of this will vanish, melt away. This is realization.

Philosophy is no joke or talk. It has to be realised; this body will vanish, this earth and everything will vanish, this idea that I am the body or the mind will for some time vanish, or if the Karma is ended it will disappear, never to come back; but if one part of the Karma remains, then as a potter's wheel, after the potter has finished the pot, will sometimes go on from the past momentum, so this body, when the delusion has vanished altogether, will go on for some time. Again this world will come, men and women and animals will come, just as the mirage came the next day, but not with the same force; along with it will come the idea that I know its nature now, and it will cause no bondage, no more pain, nor grief, nor misery. Whenever anything miserable will come, the mind will be able to say, "I know you as hallucination." When a man has reached that state, he is called Jivanmukta, living-free", free even while living.

The aim and end in this life for the Jnâna-Yogi is to become this Jivanmakta, "living-free". He is Jivanmukta who can live in this world without being attached. He is like the lotus leaves in water, which are never wetted by the water. He is the highest of human beings, nay, the highest of all beings, for he has realised his identity with the Absolute, he has realised that he is one with God. So long as you think you have the least difference from God, fear will seize you, but when you have known that you are He, that there is no difference, entirely no difference, that you are He, all of Him, and the whole of Him, all fear ceases. "There, who sees whom? Who worships whom? Who talks to whom? Who hears whom? Where one sees another, where one talks to another, where one hears another, that is little.

Where none sees none, where none speaks to none, that is the highest, that is the great, that is the Brahman." Being That, you are always That. What will become of the world then? What good shall we do to the world? Such questions do not arise "What becomes of my gingerbread if I become old?" says the baby! "What becomes of my marbles if I grow? So I will not grow," says the boy! "What will become of my dolls if I grow old?" says the little child! It is the same question in connection with this world, it has no existence in the past, present, or future. If we have known the Âtman as It is, if we have known that there is nothing else but this Atman, that everything else is but a dream, with no existence in reality, then this world with its poverties, its miseries, its wickedness, and its goodness will cease to disturb us. If they do not exist, for whom and for what shall we take trouble? This is what the Jnana-Yogis teach. Therefore, dare to be free, dare to go as far as your thought leads, and dare to carry that out in your life. It is very hard to come to Jnâna. It is for the bravest and most daring, who dare to smash all idols, not only intellectual, but in the senses. This body is not I; it must go. All sorts of curious things may come out of this.

A man stands up and says, "I am not the body, therefore my headache must be cured"; but where is the headache if not in his body? Let a thousand headaches and a thousand bodies come and go. What is that to me? I have neither birth nor death; father or mother I never had; friends and foes I have none, because they are all I. I am my own friend, and I am my own enemy. I am Existence-Knowledge-Bliss Absolute. I am He, I am He. If in a thousand bodies I am suffering from fever and other ills, in millions of bodies I am healthy. If in a thousand bodies I am starving, in other thousand bodies I am feasting. If in thousands of bodies I am suffering misery, in thousands of bodies I am happy. Who shall blame whom, who praise whom? Whom to seek, whom to avoid? I seek none, nor avoid any, for I am all the universe. I praise myself, I blame myself, I suffer for myself, I am happy at my own will, I am free. This is the Jnâni, the brave and daring. Let the whole universe tumble down; he smiles and says it never existed, it was all a hallucination. He sees the universe tumble down. Where was it! Where has it gone!

Before going into the practical part, we will take up one more intellectual question. So far the logic is tremendously rigorous. If man reasons, there is no place for him to stand until he comes to this, that there is but

One Existence, that everything else is nothing. There is no other way left for rational mankind but to take this view. But how is it that what is infinite, ever perfect, ever blessed, Existence-Knowledge-Bliss Absolute, has come under these delusions? It is the same question that has been asked all the world over. In the vulgar form the question becomes, "How did sin come into this world?" This is the most vulgar and sensuous form of the question, and the other is the most philosophic form, but the answer is the same. The same question has been asked in various grades and fashions, but in its lower forms it finds no solution, because the stories of apples and serpents and women do not give the explanation. In that state, the question is childish, and so is the answer. But the question has assumed very high proportions now: "How did this illusion come?" And the answer is as fine. The answer is that we cannot expect any answer to an impossible question. The very question is impossible in terms. You have no right to ask that question. Why? What is perfection? That which is beyond time, space, and causation — that is perfect. Then you ask how the perfect became imperfect. In logical language the question may be put in this form: "How did that which is beyond causation become caused?" You contradict yourself. You first admit it is beyond causation, and then ask what causes it. This question can only be asked within the limits of causation. As far as time and space and causation extend, so far can this question be asked. But beyond that it will be nonsense to ask it, because the question is illogical. Within time, space, and causation it can never be answered, and what answer may lie beyond these limits can only be known when we have transcended them; therefore the wise will let this question rest. When a man is ill, he devotes himself to curing his disease without insisting that he must first learn how he came to have it.

There is another form of this question, a little lower, but more practical and illustrative: What produced this delusion? Can any reality produce delusion? Certainly not. We see that one delusion produces another, and so on. It is delusion always that produces delusion. It is disease that produces disease, and not health that produces disease. The wave is the same thing as the water, the effect is the cause in another form. The effect is delusion, and therefore the cause must be delusion. What produced this delusion? Another delusion. And so on without beginning. The only question that remains for you to ask is: Does not this break your monism, because you get two existences in the universe, one yourself and the other the delusion? The answer is: Delusion cannot be called an existence. Thousands of dreams come into your life, but do not form any part of your life. Dreams come and go; they have no existence. To call delusion existence will be sophistry. Therefore there is only one individual existence in the universe, ever free, and ever blessed; and that is what you are. This is the last conclusion reached by the Advaitists.

It may then be asked: What becomes of all these various forms of worship? They will remain; they are simply groping in the dark for light, and through this groping light will come. We have just seen that the Self cannot see Itself. Our knowledge is within the network of Mâyâ (unreality), and beyond that is freedom. Within the network there is slavery, it is all under law; beyond that there is no law. So far as the universe is concerned, existence is ruled by law, and beyond that is freedom. As long as you are in the network of time, space, and causation, to say you are free is nonsense, because in that network all is under rigorous law, sequence, and consequence. Every thought that you think is caused, every feeling has been caused; to say that the will is free is sheer nonsense. It is only when the infinite existence comes, as it were, into this network of Maya that it takes the form of will. Will is a portion of that being, caught in the network of Maya, and therefore "free will" is a misnomer. It means nothing — sheer nonsense. So is all this talk about freedom. There is no freedom in Maya.

Every one is as much bound in thought, word, deed, and mind, as a piece of stone or this table. That I talk to you now is as rigorous in causation as that you listen to me. There is no freedom until you go beyond Maya. That is the real freedom of the soul. Men, however sharp and intellectual, however clearly they see the force of the logic that nothing here can be free, are all compelled to think they are free; they cannot help it. No work can go on until we begin to say we are free. It means that the freedom we talk about is the glimpse of the blue sky through the clouds and that the real freedom — the blue sky itself— is behind. True freedom cannot exist in the midst of this delusion, this hallucination, this nonsense of the world, this universe of the senses, body, and mind.

All these dreams, without beginning or end, uncontrolled and uncontrollable, ill-adjusted, broken, inharmonious, form our idea of this universe. In a dream, when you see a giant with twenty heads chasing you, and you are flying from him, you do not think it is inharmonious; you think it is proper and right. So is this law. All that you call law is simply chance without meaning. In this dream state you call it law. Within Maya, so far as this law of time, space and causation exists, there is no freedom; and all these various forms of worship are within this Maya. The idea of God and the ideas of brute and of man are within this Maya, and as such are equally hallucinations; all of them are dreams. But you must take care not to argue like some extraordinary men of whom we hear at the present time. They say the idea of God is a delusion, but the idea of this world is true. Both ideas stand or fall by the same logic. He alone has the right to be an atheist who denies this world, as well as the other. The same argument is for both.

The same mass of delusion extends from God to the lowest animal, from a blade of grass to the Creator. They stand or fall by the same logic. The same person who sees falsity in the idea of God ought also to see it in the idea of his own body or his own mind. When God vanishes, then also vanish the body and mind; and when both vanish, that which is the Real Existence remains for ever. "There the eyes cannot go, nor the speech, nor the mind. We cannot see it, neither know it." And we now understand that so far as speech and thought and knowledge and intellect go, it is all within this Maya within bondage. Beyond that is Reality. There neither thought, nor mind, nor speech, can reach.

So far it is intellectually all right, but then comes the practice. The real work is in the practice. Are any practices necessary to realise this Oneness? Most decidedly. It is not that you become this Brahman. You are already that. It is not that you are going to become God or perfect; you are already perfect; and whenever you think you are not, it is a delusion. This delusion which says that you are Mr. So-and-so or Mrs. So-and-so can be got rid of by another delusion, and that is practice. Fire will eat fire, and you can use one delusion to conquer another delusion. One cloud will come and brush away another cloud, and then both will go away. What are these practices then? We must always bear in mind that we are not going to be free, but are free already. Every idea that we are bound is a delusion. Every idea that we are happy or unhappy is a tremendous delusion; and another delusion will come — that we have got to work and worship and struggle to be free — and this will chase out the first delusion, and then both will stop.

The fox is considered very unholy by the Mohammedans and by the Hindus. Also, if a dog touches any bit of food, it has to be thrown out, it cannot be eaten by any man. In a certain Mohammedan house a fox entered and took a little bit of food from the table, ate it up, and fled. The man was a poor man, and had prepared a very nice feast for himself, and that feast was made unholy, and he could not eat it. So he went to a Mulla, a priest, and said, "This has happened to me; a fox came and took a mouthful out of my meal. What can be done? I had prepared a feast and wanted so much to eat it, and now comes this fox and destroys the whole affair."

The Mulla thought for a minute and then found only one solution and said, "The only way for you is to get a dog and make him eat a bit out of the same plate, because dogs and foxes are eternally quarrelling. The food that was left by the fox will go into your stomach, and that left by the dog will go there too, and both will be purified." We are very much in the same predicament. This is a hallucination that we are imperfect; and we take up another, that we have to practice to become perfect. Then one will chase the other, as we can use one thorn to extract another and then throw both away. There are people for whom it is sufficient knowledge to hear, "Thou art That". With a flash this universe goes away and the real nature shines, but others have to struggle hard to get rid of this idea of bondage.

The first question is: Who are fit to become Jnana-Yogis? Those who are equipped with these requisites: First, renunciation of all fruits of work and of all enjoyments in this life or another life. If you are the creator of this universe, whatever you desire you will have, because you will create it for yourself. It is only a question of time. Some get it immediately; with others the past Samskâras (impressions) stand in the way of getting their desires. We give the first place to desires for enjoyment, either in this or another life. Deny that there is any life at all; because life is only another name for death. Deny that you are a living being. Who cares for life? Life is one of these hallucinations, and death is its counterpart. Joy is one part of these hallucinations, and misery the other part, and so on. What have you to do with life or death ? These are all creations of the mind. This is called giving up desires of enjoyment either in this life or another.

Then comes controlling the mind, calming it so that it will not break into waves and have all sorts of desires, holding the mind steady, not allowing it to get into waves from external or internal causes, controlling the mind perfectly, just by the power of will. The Jnana-Yogi does not take any one of these physical helps or mental helps: simply philosophic reasoning, knowledge, and his own will, these are the instrumentalities he believes in. Next comes Titikshâ, forbearance, bearing all miseries without murmuring, without complaining. When an injury comes, do not mind it. If a tiger comes, stand there. Who flies? There are men who practice Titiksha, and succeed in it. There are men who sleep on the banks of the Ganga in the midsummer sun of India, and in winter float in the waters of the Ganga for a whole day; they do not care. Men sit in the snow of the Himalayas, and do not care to wear any garment.

What is heat? What is cold? Let things come and go, what is that to me, I am not the body. It is hard to believe this in these Western countries, but it is better to know that it is done. Just as your people are brave to jump at the mouth of a cannon, or into the midst of the battlefield, so our people are brave to think and act out their philosophy. They give up their lives for it. "I am Existence-Knowledge-Bliss Absolute; I am He, I am He." Just as the Western ideal is to keep up luxury in practical life, so ours is to keep up the highest form of spirituality, to demonstrate that religion is riot merely frothy words, but can be carried out, every bit of it, in this life. This is Titiksha, to bear everything, not to complain of anything. I myself have seen men who say, "I am the soul; what is the universe to me? Neither pleasure nor pain, nor virtue nor vice, nor heat nor cold is anything to me." That is Titiksha; not running after the enjoyments of the body. What is religion? To pray, "Give me this and that"? Foolish ideas of religion! Those who believe them have no true idea of God and soul. My Master used to say, "The vulture rise higher and higher until he becomes a speck, but his eye is always on the piece of rotten carrion on the earth." After all, what is the result of your ideas of religion? To cleanse the streets and have more bread and clothes? Who cares for bread and clothes? Millions come and go every minute. Who cares? Why care for the joys and vicissitudes of this little world? Go beyond that if you dare; go beyond law, let the whole universe vanish, and stand alone. "I am Existence-Absolute, Knowledge-Absolute, Bliss-Absolute; I am He, I am He."

One Existence Appearing as Many, (Delivered in New York, 1896)

Vairâgya or renunciation is the turning point in all the various Yogas. The Karmi (worker) renounces the fruits of his work. The Bhakta (devotee) renounces all little loves for the almighty and omnipresent love. The Yogi renounces his experiences, because his philosophy is that the whole Nature, although it is for the experience of the soul, at last brings him to know that he is not in Nature, but eternally separate from Nature. The Jnâni (philosopher) renounces everything, because his philosophy is that Nature never existed, neither in the past, nor present, nor will It in the future. The question of utility cannot be asked in these higher themes. It is very absurd to ask it; and even if it be asked, after a proper analysis, what do we find in this question of utility?

The ideal of happiness, that which brings man more happiness, is of greater utility to him than these higher things which do not improve his material conditions or bring him such great happiness. All the sciences are for this one end, to bring happiness to humanity; and that which brings the larger amount of happiness, man takes and gives up that which brings a lesser amount of happiness. We have seen how happiness is either in the body, or in the mind, or in the Âtman. With animals, and in the lowest human beings who are very much like animals, happiness is all in the body. No man can eat with the same pleasure as a famished dog or a wolf; so in the dog and the wolf the happiness is entirely in the body. In men we find a higher plane of happiness, that of thought; and in the Jnani there is the highest plane of happiness in the Self, the Atman. So to the philosopher this knowledge of the Self is of the highest utility, because it gives him the highest happiness possible.

Sense-gratifications or physical things cannot be of the highest utility to him, because he does not find in them the same pleasure that he finds in knowledge itself; and after all, knowledge is the one goal and is really the highest happiness that we know. All who work in ignorance are, as it were, the draught animals of the Devas. The word Deva is here used in the sense of a wise man. All the people that work and toil and labour like machines do not really enjoy life, but it is the wise man who enjoys. A rich man buys a picture at a cost of a hundred thousand dollars perhaps, but it is the man who understands art that enjoys it; and if the rich man is without knowledge of art, it is useless to him, he is only the owner. All over the world, it is the wise man who enjoys the happiness of the world. The ignorant man never enjoys; he has to work for others unconsciously.

Thus far we have seen the theories of these Advaitist philosophers, how there is but one Atman; there cannot be two. We have seen how in the whole of this universe there is but One Existence; and that One Existence when seen through the senses is called the world, the world of matter. When It is seen through the mind, It is called the world of thoughts and ideas; and when It is seen as it is, then It is the One Infinite Being. You must bear this in mind; it is not that there is a soul in man, although I had to take that for granted in order to explain it at first, but that there is only One Existence, and that one the Atman, the Self; and when this is perceived through the senses, through sense-imageries, It is called the body. When It is perceived through thought, It is called the mind. When It is perceived in Its own nature, It is the Atman, the One Only Existence. So it is not that there are three things in one, the body and the mind and the Self, although that was a convenient way of putting it in the course of explanation; but all is that Atman, and that one Being is sometimes called the body, sometimes the mind, and sometimes the Self, according to different vision.

There is but one Being which the ignorant call the world. When a man goes higher in knowledge, he calls the very same Being the world of thought. Again, when knowledge itself comes, all illusions vanish, and man finds it is all nothing but Atman. I am that One Existence. This is the last conclusion. There are neither three nor two in the universe; it is all One. That One, under the illusion of Maya, is seen as many, just as a rope is seen as a snake. It is the very rope that is seen as a snake. There are not two things there, a rope separate and a snake separate. No man sees these two things there at the same time. Dualism and non-dualism are very good philosophic terms, but in perfect perception we never perceive the real and the false at the same time. We are all born monists, we cannot help it. We always perceive the one. When we perceive the rope, we do not perceive the snake at all; and when we see the snake, we do not see the rope at all — it has vanished. When you see illusion, you do not see reality.

Suppose you see one of your friends coming at a distance in the street; you know him very well, but through the haze and mist that is before you, you think it is another man. When you see your friend as another man, you do not see your friend at all, he has vanished. You are perceiving only one. Suppose your friend is Mr. A; but when you perceive Mr. A as Mr. B. you do not see Mr. A at all. In each case you perceive only one. When you see yourself as a body, you are body and nothing else; and that is the perception of the vast majority of mankind. They may talk of soul and mind, and all these things, but what they perceive is the physical form, the touch, taste, vision, and so on. Again, with certain men in certain states of consciousness, they perceive themselves as thought. You know, of course, the story told of Sir Humphrey Davy, who has making experiments before his class with laughing-gas, and suddenly one of the tubes broke, and the gas escaping, he breathed it in. For some moments he remained like a statue.

Afterwards he told his class that when he was in that state, he actually perceived that the whole world is made up of ideas. The gas, for a time, made him forget the consciousness of the body, and that very thing which he was seeing as the body, he began to perceive as ideas. When the consciousness rises still higher, when this little puny consciousness is gone for ever, that which is the Reality behind shines, and we see it as the One Existence-Knowledge-Bliss, the one Atman, the Universal. "One that is only Knowledge itself, One that is Bliss itself, beyond all compare, beyond all limit, ever free, never bound, infinite as the sky, unchangeable as the sky. Such a One will manifest Himself in your heart in meditation."

How does the Advaitist theory explain these various phases of heaven and hells and these various ideas we find in all religions? When a man dies, it is said that he goes to heaven or hell, goes here or there, or that when a man dies he is born again in another body either in heaven or in another world or somewhere. These are all hallucinations. Really speaking nobody is ever born or dies. There is neither heaven nor hell nor this world; all three never really existed. Tell a child a lot of ghost stories, add let him go out into the street in the evening. There is a little stump of a tree. What does the child see? A ghost, with hands stretched out, ready to grab him. Suppose a man comes from the corner of the street, wanting to meet his sweetheart; he sees that stump of the tree as the girl.

A policeman coming from the street corner sees the stump as a thief. The thief sees it as a policeman. It is the same stump of a tree that was seen in various ways. The stump is the reality, and the visions of the stump are the projections of the various minds. There is one Being, this Self; It neither comes nor goes. When a man is ignorant, he wants to go to heaven or some place, and all his life he has been thinking and thinking of this; and when this earth dream vanishes, he sees this world as a heaven with Devas and angels flying about, and all such things. If a man all his life desires to meet his forefathers, he gets them all from Adam downwards, because he creates them. If a man is still more ignorant and has always been frightened by fanatics with ideas of hell, with all sorts of punishments, when he dies, he will see this very world as hell.

All that is meant by dying or being born is simply changes in the plane of vision. Neither do you move, nor does that move upon which you project your vision. You are the permanent, the unchangeable. How can you come and go? It is impossible; you are omnipresent. The sky never moves, but the clouds move over the surface of the sky, and we may think that the sky itself moves, just as when you are in a railway train, you think the land is moving. It is not so, but it is the train which is moving. You are where you are; these dreams, these various clouds move. One dream follows another without connection. There is no such thing as law or connection in this world, but we are thinking that there is a great deal of connection. All of you have probably read *Alice in Wonderland*. It is the most wonderful book for children that has been written in this century When I read it, I was delighted; it was always in my head to write that sort of a book for children. What pleased me most in it was what you think most incongruous, that there is no connection there. One idea comes and jumps into another, without any connection.

When you were children, you thought that the most wonderful connection. So this man brought back his thoughts of childhood, which were perfectly connected to him as a child, and composed this book for children. And all these books which men write, trying to make children swallow their own ideas as men, are nonsense. We too are grown-up children, that is all. The world is the same unconnected thing — *Alice in Wonderland* — with no connection whatever. When we see things happen a number of times in a certain sequence, we call it cause and effect, and say that the thing will happen again. When this dream changes, another dream will seem quite as connected as this. When we dream, the things we see all seem to be connected; during the dream we never think they are incongruous; it is only when we wake that we see the want of connection. When we wake from this dream of the world and compare it with the Reality, it will be found all incongruous nonsense, a mass of incongruity passing before us, we do not know whence or whither, but we know it will end; and this is called

Maya, and is like masses of fleeting fleecy clouds. They represent all this changing existence, and the sun itself, the unchanging, is you. When you look at that unchanging Existence from the outside, you call it God; and when you look at it from the inside, you call it yourself. It is but one.

There is no God separate from you, no God higher than you, the real "you". All the gods are little beings to you, all the ideas of God and Father in heaven are but your own reflection. God Himself is your image. "God created man after His own image." That is wrong. Man creates God after his own image. That is right. Throughout the universe we are creating gods after our own image. We create the god and fall down at his feet and worship him; and when this dream comes, we love it!

This is a good point to understand — that the sum and substance of this lecture is that there is but One Existence, and that One-Existence seen through different constitutions appears either as the earth, or heaven, or hell, or gods, or ghosts, or men, or demons, or world, or all these things. But among these many, "He who sees that One in this ocean of death, he who sees that One Life in this floating universe, who realises that One who never changes, unto him belongs eternal peace; unto none else, unto none else." This One existence has to be realised. How, is the next question. How is it to be realised? How is this dream to be broken, how shall we wake up from this dream that we are little men and women, and all such things? We are the Infinite Being of the universe and have become materialised into these little beings, men and women, depending upon the sweet word of one man, or the angry word of another, and so forth.

What a terrible dependence, what a terrible slavery! I who am beyond all pleasure and pain, whose reflection is the whole universe, little bits of whose life are the suns and moons and stars — I am held down as a terrible slave! If you pinch my body, I feel pain. If one says a kind word, I begin to rejoice. See my condition — slave of the body, slave of the mind, slave of the world, slave of a good word, slave of a bad word, slave of passion, slave of happiness, slave of life, slave of death, slave of everything! This slavery has to be broken. How? "This Atmàn has first to be heard, then reasoned upon, and then meditated upon." This is the method of the Advaita Jnâni. The truth has to be heard, then reflected upon, and then to be constantly asserted. Think always, "I am Brahman". Every other thought must be cast aside as weakening. Cast aside every thought that says that you are men or women. Let body go, and mind go, and gods go, and ghosts go. Let everything go but that One Existence. "Where one hears another, where one sees another, that is small; where one does not hear another, where one does not see another, that is Infinite." That is the highest when the subject and the object become one. When I am the listener and I am the speaker, when I am the teacher and I am the taught, when I am the creator and I am the created — then alone fear ceases; there is not another to make us afraid. There is nothing but myself, what can frighten me?

This is to be heard day after day. Get rid of all other thoughts. Everything else must be thrown aside, and this is to be repeated continually, poured through the ears until it reaches the heart, until every nerve and muscle, every drop of blood tingles with the idea that I am He, I am He. Even at the gate of death say, "I am He". There was a man in India, a Sannyâsin, who used to repeat "Shivoham" — "I am Bliss Eternal"; and a tiger jumped on him one day and dragged him away and killed him; but so long as he was living, the sound came, "Shivoham, Shivoham". Even at the gate of death, in the greatest danger, in the thick of the battlefield, at the bottom of the ocean, on the tops of the highest mountains, in the thickest of the forest, tell yourself, "I am He, I am He". Day and night say, "I am He". It is the greatest strength; it is religion. "The weak will never reach the Atman." Never say, "O Lord, I am a miserable sinner." Who will help you? You are the help of the universe. What in this universe can help you? Where is the man, or the god, or the demon to help you? What can prevail over you? You are the God of the universe; where can you seek for help?

Never help came from anywhere but from yourself. In your ignorance, every prayer that you made and that was answered, you thought was answered by some Being, but you answered the prayer yourself unknowingly. The help came from yourself, and you fondly imagined that some one was sending help to you. There is no help for you outside of yourself; you are the creator of the universe. Like the silkworm you have built a cocoon around yourself. Who will save you? Burst your own cocoon and come out as the beautiful butterfly, as the free soul. Then alone you will see Truth. Ever tell yourself, "I am He." These are words that will burn up the dross that is in the mind, words that will bring out the tremendous energy which is within you already, the infinite power which is sleeping in your heart. This is to be brought out by constantly hearing the truth and nothing else. Wherever there is thought of weakness, approach not the place. Avoid all weakness if you want to be a Jnani.

Before you begin to practice, clear your mind of all doubts. Fight and reason and argue; and when you have established it in your mind that this and this alone can be the truth and nothing else, do not argue any more; close your mouth. Hear not argumentation, neither argue yourself. What is the use of any more arguments? You have satisfied yourself, you have decided the question. What remains? The truth has now to be realised, therefore why waste valuable time in vain arguments? The truth has now to be meditated upon, and every idea that strengthens you must be taken up and every thought that weakens you must be rejected. The Bhakta meditates upon forms and images and all such things and upon God. This is the natural process, but a slower one. The Yogi meditates upon various centres in his body and manipulates powers in his mind. The Jnani says, the mind does not exist, neither the body. This idea of the body and of the mind must go, must be driven off; therefore it is foolish to think of them. It would be like trying to cure one ailment by bringing in another. His meditation therefore is the most difficult one, the negative; he denies everything, and what is left is the Self. This is the most analytical way. The Jnani wants to tear away the universe from the Self by the sheer force of analysis. It is very easy to say, "I am a Jnani", but very hard to be really one. "The way is long", it is, as it were, walking on the sharp edge of a razor; yet despair not. "Awake, arise, and stop not until the goal is reached", say the Vedas.

So what is the meditation of the Jnani? He wants to rise above every idea of body or mind, to drive away the idea that he is the body. For instance, when I say, "I Swami", immediately the idea of the body comes. What must I do then? I must give the mind a hard blow and say, "No, I am not the body, I am the Self." Who cares if disease comes or death in the most horrible form? I am not the body. Why make the body nice? To enjoy the illusion once more? To continue the slavery? Let it go, I am not the body. That is the way of the Jnani. The Bhakta says, "The Lord has given me this body that I may safely cross the ocean of life, and I must cherish it until the journey is accomplished." The Yogi says, "I must be careful of the body, so that I may go on steadily and finally attain liberation." The Jnani feels that he cannot wait, he must reach the goal this very moment. He says, "I am free through eternity, I am never bound; I am the God of the universe through all eternity. Who shall make me perfect? I am perfect already." When a man is perfect, he sees perfection in others. When he sees imperfection, it is his own mind projecting itself. How can he see imperfection if he has not got it in himself? So the Jnani does not care for perfection or imperfection. None exists for him. As soon as he is free, he does not see good and evil. Who sees evil and good? He who has it in himself. Who sees the body? He who thinks he is the body. The moment you get rid of the idea that you are the body, you do not see the world at all; it vanishes for ever. The Jnani seeks to tear himself away from this bondage of matter by the force of intellectual conviction. This is the negative way — the "Neti, Neti" — "Not this, not this."

On Karma Yoga

Isolation of the soul from all objects, mental and physical, is the goal; when that is attained, the soul will find that it was alone all the time, and it required no one to make it happy. As long as we require someone else to make us happy, we are slaves. When the Purusha finds that It is free, and does not require anything to complete Itself, that this nature is quite unnecessary, then freedom (Kaivalya) is attained.

Men run after a few dollars and do not think anything of cheating a fellow-being to get those dollars; but if they would restrain themselves, in a few years they would develop such characters as would bring them millions of dollars — if they wanted them. Then their will would govern the universe. But we are all such fools!

What is the use of talking of one's mistakes to the world? They cannot thereby be undone. For what one has done one must suffer; one must try and do better. The world sympathises only with the strong and the powerful.

It is only work that is done as a free-will offering to humanity and to nature that does not bring with it any binding attachment.

Duty of any kind is not to be slighted. A man who does the lower work is not, for that reason only, a lower man than he who does the higher work; a man should not be judged by the nature of his duties, but by the manner in which he does them. His manner of doing them and his pourer to do them are indeed the test of a man. A shoemaker who can turn out a strong, nice pair of shoes in the shortest possible time is a better man, according to his profession and his work, than a professor who talks nonsense every day of his life.

Every duty is holy, and devotion to duty is the highest form of the worship of God; it is certainly a source of great help in enlightening and emancipating the deluded and ignorance-encumbered souls of the Baddhas — the bound ones.

By doing well the duty which is nearest to us, the duty which is in our hands now, we make ourselves stronger and improving our strength in this manner step by step, we may even reach a state in which it shall be our privilege to do the most coveted and honoured duties in life and in society.

Nature's justice is uniformly stern and unrelenting.

The most practical man would call life neither good nor evil.

Every successful man must have behind him somewhere tremendous integrity, tremendous sincerity, and that is the cause of his signal success in life. He may not have been perfectly unselfish; yet he was tending towards it. If he had been perfectly unselfish, his would have been as great a success as that of the Buddha or of the Christ. The degree of unselfishness marks the degree of success everywhere.

The great leaders of mankind belong to higher fields than the field of platform work.

However we may try, there cannot be any action which is perfectly pure or any which is perfectly impure, taking purity or impurity in the sense of injury or non-injury. We cannot breathe or live without injuring others, and every morsel of food we eat is taken from another's mouth; our very lives are crowding out some other lives. It may be those of men, or animals, or small fungi, but someone somewhere we have to crowd out. That being the case, it naturally follows that perfection can never be attained by work. We may work through all eternity, but there will be no way out of this intricate maze: we may work on and on and on, but there will be no end.

The man who works through freedom and love cares nothing for results. But the slave wants his whipping; the servant wants his pay. So with all life; take for instance the public life. The public speaker wants a little applause or a little hissing and hooting. If you keep him in a corner without it, you kill him, for he requires it. This is working through slavery. To expect something in return, under such conditions, becomes second nature. Next comes the work of the servant, who requires some pay; I give this, and you give me that. Nothing is easier to say, "I work for work's sake", but nothing is so difficult to attain. I would go twenty miles on my hands and knees to look on the face of the man who can work for work's sake. There is a motive somewhere. If it is not money, it is power. If it is not power, it is gain. Somehow, somewhere, there is a motive power. You are my friend, and I want to work for you and with you. This is all very well, and every moment I may make protestation of my sincerity. But take care, you must be sure to agree with me! If you do not, I shall no longer take care of you or live for you! This kind of work for a motive brings misery. That work alone brings unattachment and bliss, wherein we work as masters of our own minds.

The great lesson to learn is that I am not the standard by which the whole universe is to be judged; each man is to be judged by his own idea, each race by its own standard and ideal, each custom of each country by its own reasoning and conditions. American customs are the result of the environment in which the Americans live and Indian customs are the result of the environment in which the Indians are; and so of China, Japan, England, and every other country.

We all find ourselves in the position for which we are fit, each ball finds its own hole; and if one has some capacity above another, the world will find that out too, in this universal adjusting that goes on. So it is no use to grumble. There may be a rich man who is wicked, yet there must be in that man certain qualities that made him rich; and if any other man has the same qualities, he will also become rich. What is the use of fighting and complaining? That will not help us to better things. He who grumbles at the little thing that has fallen to his lot to do will grumble at everything. Always grumbling, he will lead a miserable life, and everything will be a failure. But that man who does his duty as he goes, putting, his shoulder to the wheel, will see the light, and higher and higher duties will fall to his share.

On Fanaticism

There are fanatics of various kinds. Some people are wine fanatics and cigar fanatics. Some think that if men gave up smoking cigars, the world would arrive at the millennium. Women are generally amongst these fanatics. There was a young lady here one day, in this class. She was one of a number of ladies in Chicago who have built a house where they take in the working people and give them music and gymnastics. One day this young lady was talking about the evils of the world and said she knew the remedy. I asked, "How do you know?" and she answered, "Have you seen Hull House?" In her opinion, this Hull House is the one panacea for all the evils that flesh is heir to. This will grow upon her. I am sorry for her. There are some fanatics in India who think that if a woman could marry again when her husband died, it would cure all evil. This is fanaticism.

When I was a boy I thought that fanaticism was a great element in work, but now, as I grow older, I find out that it is not.

There may be a woman who would steal and make no objection to taking someone else's bag and going away with it. But perhaps that woman does not smoke. She becomes a smoke fanatic, and as soon as she finds a man smoking, she strongly disapproves of him, because he smokes a cigar. There may be a man who goes about cheating people; there is no trusting him; no woman is safe with him. But perhaps this scoundrel does not drink wine. If so, he sees nothing good in anyone who drinks wine. All these wicked things that he himself does are of no consideration. This is only natural human selfishness and one-sidedness.

You must also remember that the world has God to govern it, and He has not left it to our charity. The Lord God is its Governor and Maintainer, and in spite of these wine fanatics and cigar fanatics, and all sorts of marriage fanatics, it would go on. If all these persons were to die, it would go on none the worse.

Do you not remember in your own history how the "Mayflower" people came out here, and began to call themselves Puritans? They were very pure and good as far as they went, until they began to persecute other people; and throughout the history of mankind it has been the same. Even those that run away from persecution indulge in persecuting others as soon as a favourable opportunity to do so occurs.

In ninety cases out of a hundred, fanatics must have bad livers, or they are dyspeptics, or are in some way diseased. By degrees even physicians will find out that fanaticism is a kind of disease. I have seen plenty of it. The Lord save me from it!

My experience comes to this, that it is rather wise to avoid all sorts of fanatical reforms. This world is slowly going on; let it go slowly. Why are you in a hurry? Sleep well and keep your nerves in good order; eat right food, and have sympathy with the world. Fanatics only make hatred. Do you mean to say that the temperance fanatic loves these poor people who become drunkards? A fanatic is a fanatic simply because he expects to get something for himself in return. As soon as the battle is over, he goes for the spoil. When you come out of the company of fanatics you may learn how really to love and sympathise. And the more you attain of love and sympathy, the less will be your power to condemn these poor creatures; rather you will sympathise with their faults. It will become possible for you to sympathise with the drunkard and to know that he is also a man like yourself. You will then try to understand the many circumstances that are dragging him down, and feel that if you had been in his place you would perhaps have committed suicide. I remember a woman whose husband was a great drunkard, and she complained to me of his becoming so. I replied, "Madam, if there were twenty millions of wives like yourself, all husbands would become drunkards." I am convinced that a large number of drunkards are manufactured by their wives. My business is to tell the truth and not to flatter anyone.

These unruly women from whose minds the words *bear* and *forbear* are gone for ever, and whose false ideas of independence lead them to think that men should be at their feet, and who begin to howl as soon as men dare to say anything to them which they do not like — such women are becoming the bane of the world, and it is a wonder that they do not drive half the men in it to commit suicide. In this way things should not go on. Life is not so easy as they believe it to be; it is a more serious business!

A man must not only have faith but intellectual faith too. To make a man take up everything and believe it, would be to make him a lunatic. I once had a book sent me, which said I must believe everything told in it. It said there was no soul, but that there were gods and goddesses in heaven, and a thread of light going from each of our heads to heaven! How did the writer know all these things? She had been inspired, and wanted me to believe it too; and because I refused, she said, "You must be a very bad man; there is no hope for you!" This is fanaticism.

Work is Worship

The highest man *cannot* work, for there is no binding element, no attachment, no ignorance in him. A ship is said to have passed over a mountain of magnet ore, and all the bolts and bars were drawn out, and it went to pieces. It is in ignorance that struggle remains, because we are all really atheists. Real theists cannot work. We are atheists more or less. We do not see God or believe in Him. He is G-O-D to us, and nothing more. There are moments when we think He is near, but then we fall down again. When you see Him, who struggles for whom? Help the Lord! There is a proverb in our language, "Shall we teach the Architect of the universe how to build?" So those a· e highest of mankind who do not work. The next time you see these silly phrases about the world and how we must all help God and do this or that for Him, remember this. Do not think such thoughts; they are too selfish. All the work you do is subjective, is done for your own benefit. God has not fallen into a ditch for you and me to help Him out by building a hospital or something of that sort. He allows you to work. He *allows* you to exercise your muscles in this great gymnasium, not in order to help Him but that you may help yourself. Do you think even an ant will die for want of your help? Most arrant blasphemy! The world does not need you at all. The world goes on you are like a drop in the ocean. A leaf does not move, the wind does not blow without Him. Blessed are we that we are given the privilege of working for Him, not of helping Him. Cut out this word "help" from your mind. You cannot help; it is blaspheming. You are here yourself at His pleasure. Do you mean to say, you help Him? You worship. When you give a morsel of food to the dog, you worship the dog as God. God is in that dog. He is the dog. He is all and in all. We are allowed to worship Him. Stand in that reverent attitude to the whole universe, and then will come perfect non-attachment. This should be your duty. This is the proper attitude of work. This is the secret taught by Karma-Yoga.

Work without Motive

At the forty-second meeting of the Ramakrishna Mission held at the premises No. 57 Râmkânta Bose Street, Baghbazar, Calcutta, on the 20th March, 1898, Swami Vivekananda gave an address on "Work without Motive", and spoke to the following effect:

When the Gita was first preached, there was then going on a great controversy between two sects. One party considered the Vedic Yajnas and animal sacrifices and such like Karmas to constitute the whole of religion.

The other preached that the killing of numberless horses and cattle cannot be called religion. The people belonging to the latter party were mostly Sannyâsins and followers of Jnâna. They believed that the giving up of all work and the gaining of the knowledge of the Self was the only path to Moksha By the preaching of His great doctrine of work without motive, the Author of the Gita set at rest the disputes of these two antagonistic sects.

Many are of opinion that the Gita was not written at the time of the Mahâbhârata, but was subsequently added to it. This is not correct. The special teachings of the Gita are to be found in every part of the Mahabharata, and if the Gita is to be expunged, as forming no part of it, every other portion of it which embodies the same teachings should be similarly treated.

Now, what is the meaning of working without motive? Nowadays many understand it in the sense that one is to work in such a way that neither pleasure nor pain touches his mind. If this be its real meaning, then the animals might be said to work without motive. Some animals devour their own offspring, and they do not feel any pangs at all in doing so. Robbers ruin other people by robbing them of their possessions; but if they feel quite callous to pleasure or pain, then they also would be working without motive. If the meaning of it be such, then one who has a stony heart, the worst of criminals, might be considered to be working without motive. The walls have no feelings of pleasure or pain, neither has a stone, and it cannot be said that they are working without motive. In the above sense the doctrine is a potent instrument in the hands of the wicked. They would go on doing wicked deeds, and would pronounce themselves as working without a motive. If such be the significance of working without a motive, then a fearful doctrine has been put forth by the preaching of the Gita. Certainly this is not the meaning. Furthermore, if we look into the lives of those who were connected with the preaching of the Gita, we should find them living quite a different life. Arjuna killed Bhishma and Drona in battle, but withal, he sacrificed all his self-interest and desires and his lower self millions of times.

Gita teaches Karma-Yoga. We should work through Yoga (concentration). In such concentration in action (Karma-Yoga), there is no consciousness of the lower ego present. The consciousness that I am doing this and that is never present when one works through Yoga. The Western people do not understand this. They say that if there be no consciousness of ego, if this ego is gone, how then can a man work? But when one works with concentration, losing all consciousness of oneself the work that is done will be infinitely better, and this every one may have experienced in his own life. We perform many works subconsciously, such as the digestion of food etc., many others consciously, and others again by becoming immersed in Samâdhi as it were, when there is no consciousness of the smaller ego. If the painter, losing the consciousness of his ego, becomes completely immersed in his painting, he will be able to produce masterpieces. The good cook concentrates his whole self on the food-material he handles he loses all other consciousness for the time being. But they are only able to do perfectly a single work in this way, to which they are habituated. The Gita teaches that all works should be done thus. He who is one with the Lord through Yoga performs all his works by becoming immersed in concentration, and does not seek any personal benefit. Such a performance of work brings only good to the world, no evil can come out of it. Those who work thus never do anything for themselves.

The result of every work is mixed with good and evil. There is no good work that has not a touch of evil in it. Like smoke round the fire, some evil always clings to work. We should engage in such works as bring the largest amount of good and the smallest measure of evil. Arjuna killed Bhishma and Drona; if this had not been done Duryodhana could not have been conquered, the force of evil would have triumphed over the force of good, and thus a great calamity would have fallen on the country. The government of the country would have been usurped by a body of proud unrighteous kings, to the great misfortune of the people. Similarly, Shri Krishna killed Kamsa, Jarâsandha, and others who were tyrants, but not a single one of his deeds was done for himself. Every one of them was for the good of others. We are reading the Gita by candle-light, but numbers of insects are being burnt to death. Thus it is seen that some evil clings to work. Those who work without any consciousness of their lower ego are not affected with evil, for they work for the good of the world. To work without motive, to work unattached, brings the highest bliss and freedom. This secret of Karma-Yoga is taught by the Lord Shri Krishna in the Gita.

12

Inspired Talks

WEDNESDAY, *JUNE 19, 1895.*

(This day marks the beginning of the regular teaching given daily by Swami Vivekananda to his disciples at Thousand Island Park. We had not yet all assembled there, but the Master's heart was always in his work, so he commenced at once to teach the three or four who were with him. He came on this first morning with the Bible in his hand and opened to the Book of John, saying that since we were all Christians, it was proper that he should begin with the Christian scriptures.)

"In the beginning was the Word, and the Word was with God, and the Word was God." The Hindu calls this Mâyâ, the manifestation of God, because it is the power of God. The Absolute reflecting through the universe is what we call nature. The Word has two manifestations — the general one of nature, and the special one of the great Incarnations of God — Krishna, Buddha, Jesus, and Ramakrishna. Christ, the special manifestation of the Absolute, is known and knowable. The absolute cannot be known: we cannot know the Father, only the Son. We can only see the Absolute through the "tint of humanity", through Christ.

In the first five verses of John is the whole essence of Christianity: each verse is full of the profoundest philosophy.

The Perfect never becomes imperfect. It is in the darkness, but is not affected by the darkness. God's mercy goes to all, but is not affected by their wickedness. The sun is not affected by any disease of our eyes which may make us see it distorted. In the twenty-ninth verse, "taketh away the sin of the world" means that Christ would show us the way to become perfect. God became Christ to show man his true nature, that we too are God. We are human coverings over the Divine; but as the divine Man, Christ and we are one.

The Trinitarian Christ is elevated above us; the Unitarian Christ is merely a moral man; neither can help us. The Christ who is the Incarnation of God, who has not forgotten His divinity, that Christ can help us, in Him there is no imperfection. These Incarnations are always conscious of their own divinity; they know it from their birth. They are like the actors whose play is over, but who, after their work is done, return to please others. These great Ones are untouched by aught of earth; they assume our form and our limitations for a time in order to teach us; but in reality they are never limited, they are ever free. . . .

Good is near Truth, but is not yet Truth. After learning not to be disturbed by evil, we have to learn not to be made happy by good. We must find that we are beyond both evil and good; we must study their adjustment and see that they are both necessary.

The idea of dualism is from the ancient Persians.* Really good and evil are one (Because they are both chains and products of Maya.) and are in our own mind. When the mind is self-poised, neither good nor bad affects it. Be perfectly free; then neither can affect it, and we enjoy freedom and bliss. Evil is the iron chain, good is the gold one; both are chains. Be free, and know once for all that there is no chain for you. Lay hold of the golden chain to loosen the hold of the iron one, then throw both away. The thorn of evil is in our flesh; take another thorn from the same bush and extract the first thorn; then throw away both and be free. . . .

In the world take always the position of the giver. Give everything and look for no return. Give love, give help, give service, give any little thing you can, but *keep out barter*. Make no conditions, and none will be imposed. Let us give out of our own bounty, just as God gives to us.

The Lord is the only Giver, all the men in the world are only shopkeepers. Get His cheque, and it must be honoured everywhere.

"God is the inexplicable, inexpressible essence of love", to be known, but never defined.

SUNDAY, *JUNE 23, 1895.*

Be brave and be sincere; then follow any path with devotion, and you *must* reach the Whole. Once lay hold of one link of the chain, and the whole chain must come by degrees. Water the roots of the tree (that is, reach the Lord), and the whole tree is watered; getting the Lord, we get all.

One-sidedness is the bane of the world. The more sides you can develop the more souls you have, and you can see the universe through all souls — through the Bhakta (devotee) and the Jnâni (philosopher). Determine your own nature and stick to it. Nishthâ (devotion to one ideal) is the only method for the beginner; but with devotion and sincerity it will lead to all. Churches, doctrines, forms, are the hedges to protect the tender plant, but they must later be broken down that the plant may become a tree. So the various religions, Bibles, Vedas, dogmas — all are just tubs for the little plant; but it must get out of the tub. Nishthâ is, in a manner, placing the plant in the tub, shielding the struggling soul in its path. . . .

Look at the "ocean" and not at the "wave"; see no difference between ant and angel. Every worm is the brother of the Nazarene. How say one is greater and one less? Each is great in his own place. We are in the sun and in the stars as much as here. Spirit is beyond space and time and is everywhere. Every mouth praising the Lord is my mouth, every eye seeing is my eye. We are confined nowhere; we are not body, the universe is our body. We are magicians waving magic wands and creating scenes before us at will. We are the spider in his huge web, who can go on the varied strands wheresoever he desires. The spider is now only conscious of the spot where he is, but he will in time become conscious of the whole web. We are now conscious only where the body is, we can use only one brain; but when we reach ultraconsciousness, we know all, we can use all brains. Even now we can "give the push" in consciousness, and it goes beyond and acts in the superconscious.

We are striving "to be" and nothing more, no "I" ever — just pure crystal, reflecting all, but ever the same, When that state is reached, there is no more doing; the body becomes a mere mechanism, pure without care for it; it cannot become impure.

Know you are the Infinite, then fear must die. Say ever, "I and my Father are one."

MONDAY, *JUNE 24, 1895.*

(The reading today was from the Bhakti-Sutras by Nârada.)

"Extreme love to God is Bhakti, and this love is the real immortality, getting which a man becomes perfectly satisfied, sorrows for no loss, and is never jealous; knowing which man becomes mad."

My Master used to say, "This world is a huge lunatic asylum where all men are mad, some after money, some after women, some after name or fame, and a few after God. I prefer to be mad after God. God is the philosophers' stone that turns us to gold in an instant; the form remains, but the nature is changed — the human form remains, but no more can we hurt or sin."

"Thinking of God, some weep, some sing, some laugh, some dance, some say wonderful things, but all speak of nothing but God."

Prophets preach, but the Incarnations like Jesus, Buddha, Ramakrishna, can give religion; one glance, one touch is enough. That is the power of the Holy Ghost, the "laying on of hands"; the power was actually transmitted to the disciples by the Master — the "chain of Guru-power". That, the real baptism, has been handed down for untold ages.

"Bhakti cannot be used to fulfil any desires, itself being the check to all desires." Narada gives these as the signs of love: "When all thoughts, all words, and all deeds are given up unto the Lord, and the least forgetfulness of God makes one intensely miserable, then love has begun."

"This is the highest form of love because therein is no desire for reciprocity, which desire is in all human love."

"A man who has gone beyond social and scriptural usage, he is a Sannyâsin. When the whole soul goes to God, when we take refuge only in God, then we know that we are about to get this love."

Obey the scriptures until you are strong enough to do without them; then go beyond them. Books are not an end-all. Verification is the only proof of religious truth. Each must verify for himself; and no teacher who says, "I have seen, but *you* cannot", is to be trusted, only that one who says, "You can see too". All scriptures, all truths are Vedas in all times, in all countries; because these truths are to be *seen*, and any one may discover them.

"When the sun of Love begins to break on the horizon, we want to give up all our actions unto God; and when we forget Him for a moment, it grieves us greatly."

Let nothing stand between God and your love for Him. Love Him, love Him, love Him; and let the world say what it will. Love is of three sorts — one demands, but gives nothing; the second is exchange; and the third is love without thought of return — love like that of the moth for the light.

"Love is higher than work, than Yoga, than knowledge."

Work is merely a schooling for the doer; it can do no good to others. We must work out our own problem; the prophets only show us how to work. *"What you think, you become"*, so if you throw your burden on Jesus, you will have to think of Him and thus become like Him — you *love* Him.

"Extreme love and highest knowledge are one."

But theorising about God will not do; we must love and work. Give up the world and all worldly things, especially while the "plant" is tender. Day and night think of God and think of nothing else as far as possible. The daily necessary thoughts can all be thought through God. Eat to Him, drink to Him, sleep to Him, see Him in all. Talk of God to others; this is most beneficial.

Get the mercy of God and of His greatest children: these are the two chief ways to God. The company of these children of light is very hard to get; five minutes in their company will change a whole life; and if you really want it enough, one will come to you. The presence of those who love God makes a place holy, "such is the glory of the children of the Lord". They are He; and when they speak, their words are scriptures. The place where they have been becomes filled with their vibrations, and those going there feel them and have a tendency to become holy also.

"To such lovers there is no distinction of caste, learning, beauty, birth, wealth, or occupation; because all are His."

Give up all evil company, especially at the beginning. Avoid worldly company, that will distract your mind. *Give up all "me and mine"*. To him who has nothing in the universe the Lord comes. Cut the bondage of all worldly affections; go beyond laziness and all care as to what becomes of you. Never turn back to see the result of what you have done. Give all to the Lord and go on and think not of it. The whole soul pours in a continuous current to God; there is no time to seek money, or name, or fame, no time to think of anything but God; then will come into our hearts that infinite, wonderful bliss of Love. All desires are but beads of glass. Love of God increases every moment and is ever new, to be known only by feeling it. Love is the easiest of all, it waits for no logic, it is natural. We need no demonstration, no proof. Reasoning is limiting something by our own minds. We throw a net and catch something, and then say that we have demonstrated it; but never, never can we catch God in a net.

Love should be unrelated. Even when we love wrongly, it is of the true love, of the true bliss; the power is the same, use it as we may. Its very nature is peace and bliss. The murderer when he kisses his baby forgets for an instant all but love. Give up all self, all egotism s get out of anger, lust, give *all* to God. "I am not, but Thou art; the old man is all gone, only Thou remainest." "I am

Thou." Blame none; if evil comes, know the Lord is playing with you and be exceeding glad.

Love is beyond time and space, it is absolute.

TUESDAY, *JUNE 25, 1895.*

After every happiness comes misery; they may be far apart or near. The more advanced the soul, the more quickly does one follow the other. *What we want is neither happiness nor misery.* Both make us forget our true nature; both are chains — one iron, one gold; behind both is the Atman, who knows neither happiness nor misery. These are *states* and states must ever change; but the nature of the Soul is bliss, peace, unchanging. We have not to get it, we have it; only wash away the dross and see it.

Stand upon the Self, then only can we truly love the world. Take a very, very high stand; knowing out universal nature, we must look with perfect calmness upon all the *panorama* of the world. It is but baby's play, and we know that, so cannot be disturbed by it. If the mind is pleased with praise, it will be displeased with blame. All pleasures of the senses or even of the mind are evanescent but within ourselves is the one true unrelated pleasure, dependent upon nothing. It is perfectly free, it is bliss. *The more our bliss is within, the more spiritual we are.* The pleasure of the Self is what the world calls religion.

The internal universe, the *real,* is infinitely greater than the external, which is only a shadowy projection of the true one. This world is neither true nor untrue, it is the shadow of truth. "Imagination is the gilded shadow of truth", says the poet.

We enter into creation, and then for us it becomes living. Things are dead in themselves; only we give them life, and then, like fools, we turn around and are afraid of them, or enjoy them. But be not like certain fisher-women, who, caught in a storm on their way home from market, took refuge in the house of a florist. They were lodged for the night in a room next to the garden where the air was full of the fragrance of flowers. In vain did they try to rest, until one of their number suggested that they wet their fishy baskets and place them near their heads. Then they all fell into a sound sleep.

The world is our fish basket, we must not depend upon it for enjoyment. Those who do are the Tâmasas or the bound. Then there are the Râjasas or the egotistical, who talk always about "I", "I". They do good work sometimes and may become spiritual. But the highest are the Sâttvikas, the introspective, those who live only in the Self. These three qualities, Tamas, Rajas, and Sattva (idleness, activity, and illumination), are in everyone, and different ones predominate at different times.

Creation is not a "making" of something, it is the struggle to regain the equilibrium, as when atoms of cork are thrown to the bottom of a pail of water and rush to rise to the top, singly or in clusters. *Life is and must be accompanied by evil.* A little evil is the source of life; the little wickedness that is in the world is very good; for when the balance is regained, the world will end, because sameness and destruction are one. When this world goes, good and evil go with it; but when we can transcend this world, we get rid of both good and evil and have bliss.

There is no possibility of ever having pleasure without pain, good without evil; for living itself is just the lost equilibrium. What we want is freedom, not life, nor pleasure, nor good. Creation is infinite, without beginning and without end — the ever-moving ripple in an infinite lake. There are yet unreached depths and others where the equilibrium has been regained; but the ripple is always progressing, the struggle to regain the balance is eternal. Life and death are only different names for the same fact, the two sides of the one coin. Both are

Maya, the inexplicable state of striving at one time to live, and a moment later to die. Beyond this is the true nature, the Atman. While we recognise a God, it is really only the Self which we have separated ourselves from and worship as outside of us; but it is our true Self all the time — the one and only God.

To regain the balance we must counteract Tamas by Rajas; then conquer Rajas by Sattva, the calm beautiful state that will grow and grow until all else is gone. Give up bondage; become a son, be free, and then you can "see the Father", as did Jesus. Infinite strength is religion and God. Avoid weakness and slavery. You are only a soul, *if* you are free; there is immortality for you, *if* you are free; there is God, *if* He is free. . . .

The world for me, not I for the world. Good and evil are our slaves, not we theirs. It is the nature of the brute to remain where he is (not to progress); it is the nature of man to seek good and avoid evil; it is the nature of God to seek neither, but just to be eternally blissful. Let us be God! Make the heart like an ocean, go beyond all the trifles of the world, be mad with joy even at evil; see the world as a picture and then enjoy its beauty, knowing that nothing affects you. Children finding glass beads in a mud puddle, that is the good of the world. Look at it with calm complacency; see good and evil as the same — both are merely "God's play"; enjoy all.

WEDNESDAY, *JUNE 26, 1895.*

Our best work is done, our greatest influence is exerted, when we are without thought of self. All great geniuses know this. Let us open ourselves to the one Divine Actor, and let Him act, and do nothing ourselves. *"O Arjuna! I have no duty in the whole world"*, says Krishna. Be perfectly resigned, perfectly unconcerned; then alone can you do any true work. No eyes can see the real forces, we can only see the results. Put out self, lose it, forget it; just let God work, it is His business. We have nothing to do but stand aside and let God work. The more we go away, the more God comes in. Get rid of the little "I", and let only the great "I" live.

We are what our thoughts have made us; so take care of what you think. Words are secondary. Thoughts live, they travel far. Each thought we think is tinged with our own character, so that for the pure and holy man, even his jests or abuse will have the twist of his own love and purity and do good.

Desire nothing; think of God and look for no return. It is the desireless who bring results. The begging monks carry religion to every man's door; but they think that they do nothing, they claim nothing, their work is unconsciously done. If they should eat of the tree of knowledge, they would become egoists, and all the good they do would fly away. As soon as we say "I", we are humbugged all the time; and we call it "knowable", but it is only going round and round like a bullock tied to a tree. The Lord has hidden Himself best, and His work is best; so he who hides himself best, accomplishes most. Conquer *yourself,* and the whole universe is yours.

In the state of Sattva we see the very nature of things, we go beyond the senses and beyond reason. The adamantine wall that shuts us in is egoism; we refer everything to ourselves, thinking. "I do this, that, and the other." Get rid of this puny "I"; kill this diabolism in us; "Not I, but Thou" — say it, feel it, live it. Until we give up the world manufactured by the ego, never can we enter the kingdom of heaven. None ever did, none ever will. To give up the world is to forget the ego, to know it not at all — living *in* the body, but not *of* it. This rascal ego must be obliterated. Bless men when they revile you. Think how much good they are doing you; they can only hurt themselves. Go where people hate you, let them thrash the ego out of you, and you will get nearer to the Lord. Like the mother-monkey, we hug our "baby", the world, as long as we can, but at last when we are driven to put it under our feet and step on it* then we are ready to come to God. Blessed it is to be persecuted for the sake of righteousness. Blessed are we if we cannot read, we have less to take us away from God.

Enjoyment is the million-headed serpent that we must tread under foot. We renounce and go on, then find nothing and despair; but hold on, *hold on*. The world is a demon. It is a kingdom of which the puny ego is king. Put it away and stand firm. Give up lust and gold and fame and hold fast to the Lord, and at last we shall reach a state of perfect indifference. The idea that the gratification of the senses constitutes enjoyment is purely materialistic. There is not one spark of real enjoyment there; all the joy there is, is a mere reflection of the true bliss.

Those who give themselves up to the Lord do more for the world than all the so-called workers. One man who has purified himself thoroughly accomplishes more than a regiment of preachers. *Out of purity and silence comes the word of power.*

"Be like a lily — stay in one place and expand your petals; and the bees will come of themselves." There was a great contrast between Keshab Chandra Sen and Shri Ramakrishna. The second never recognised any sin or misery in the world, no evil to fight against. The first was a great ethical reformer, leader, and founder of the Brahmo-Samaj. After twelve years the quiet prophet of Dakshineswar had worked a revolution not only in India, but in the world. The power is with the silent ones, who only live and love and then withdraw their personality. They never say "me" and "mine"; they are only blessed in being instruments. Such men are the makers of Christs and Buddhas, ever living fully identified with God, ideal existences, asking nothing, and not consciously doing anything. They are the real movers, the Jivanmuktas, (Literally, free even while living.) absolutely selfless, the little personality entirely blown away, ambition non-existent. They are all principle, no personality.

Thursday, *June 27, 1895.* (*The Swami brought the New Testament this morning and talked again on the book of John.*)

Mohammed claimed to be the "Comforter" that Christ promised to send. He considered it unnecessary to claim a supernatural birth for Jesus. Such claims have been common in all ages and in all countries. All great men have claimed gods for their fathers.

Knowing is only relative; we can be God, but never *know* Him. Knowledge is a lower state; Adam's fall was when he came to "know". Before that he was God, he was truth, he was purity. We are our own faces, but can see only a reflection, never the real thing. We are love, but when we think of it, we have to use a phantasm, which proves that matter is only externalised thought.

Nivritti is turning aside from the world. Hindu mythology says that the four first-created (The four first-created were Sanaka, Sanandana, Sanâtana, and Sanatkumâra.) were warned by a Swan (God Himself) that manifestation was only secondary; so they remained without creating. The meaning of this is that expression is degeneration, because Spirit can only be expressed by the letter and then the "letter killeth" (Bible, 2 Cor. III. 6.); yet principle is bound to be clothed in matter, though we know that later we shall lose sight of the real in the covering. Every great teacher understands this, and that is why a continual succession of prophets has to come to show us the principle and give it a new covering suited to the times. My Master taught that religion is one; all prophets teach the same; but they can only present the principle in a form; so they take it out of the old form and put it before us in a new one. When we free ourselves from name and form, especially from a body — when we need no body, good or bad — then only do we escape from bondage. Eternal progression is eternal bondage; annihilation of form is to be preferred. We must get free from any body, even a "god-body". God is the only real existence, there cannot be two. There is but One Soul, and I am That.

Good works are only valuable as a means of escape; they do good to the doer, never to any other.

Knowledge is mere classification. When we find many things of the same kind we call the sum of them by a certain name and are satisfied; we discover "facts", never "why". We take a circuit in a wider field of darkness and think we know something! No "why" can be answered in this world; for that we must go to God. The Knower can never be expressed; it is as when a grain of salt drops into the ocean, it is at once merged in the ocean.

Differentiation creates; homogeneity or sameness is God. Get beyond differentiation; then you conquer life and death and reach eternal sameness and are in God, are God. Get freedom, even at the cost of life. All lives belong to us as leaves to a book; but we are unchanged, the Witness, the Soul, upon whom the impression is made, as when the impression of a circle is made upon the eyes when a firebrand is rapidly whirled round and round. The Soul is the unity of all personalities, and because It is at rest, eternal, unchangeable. It is God, Atman. It is not life, but It is coined into life. It is not pleasure, but It is manufactured into pleasure. . . .

Today God is being abandoned by the world because He does not seem to be doing enough for the world. So they say, "Of what good is He?" Shall we look upon God as a mere municipal authority?

All we can do is to put down all desires, hates, differences; put down the lower self, commit mental suicide, as it were; keep the body and mind pure and healthy, but only as instruments to help us to God; that is their only true use. Seek truth for truth's sake alone, look not for bliss. It may come, but do not let that be your incentives. Have no motive except God. Dare to come to Truth even through hell.

FRIDAY, *JUNE 28, 1895*

(The entire party went on a picnic for the day, and although the Swami taught constantly, as he did wherever he was, no notes were taken and no record, therefore, of what he said remains. As he began his breakfast before setting out, however, he remarked:)

Be thankful for all food, it is Brahman. His universal energy is transmuted into our individual energy and helps us in all that we do.

SATURDAY, *JUNE 29, 1895.*

(The Swami came this morning with a Gita in his hand.)

Krishna, the "Lord of souls", talks to Arjuna or Gudâkesha, "lord of sleep" (he who has conquered sleep). The "field of virtue" (the battlefield) is this world; the five brothers (representing righteousness) fight the hundred other brothers (all that we love and have to contend against); the most heroic brother, Arjuna (the awakened soul), is the general. We have to fight all sense-delights, the things to which we are most attached, to kill them. We have to stand alone; we are Brahman, all other ideas must be merged in this one.

Krishna did everything but without any attachment; he was in the world, but not of it. "Do all work but without attachment; work for work's sake, never for yourself."

Freedom can never be true of name and form; it is the clay out of which we (the pots) are made; then it is limited and not free, so that freedom can never be true of the related. One pot can never say "I am free" as a pot; only as it loses all ideas of form does it become free. The whole universe is only the Self with variations, the one tune made bearable by variation; sometimes there are discords, but they only make the subsequent harmony more perfect. In the universal melody three ideas stand out — freedom, strength, and sameness.

If your freedom hurts others, you are not free there. You must not hurt others.

"To be weak is to be miserable", says Milton. Doing and suffering are inseparably joined. (Often, too, the man who laughs most is the one who suffers most.) "To work you have the right, not to the fruits thereof."

SUNDAY, *JUNE 30, 1895.*

To try to think without a phantasm is to try to make the impossible possible. We cannot think "mammalia" without a concrete example. So with the idea of God.

The great abstraction of ideas in the world is what we call God.

Each thought has two parts — the thinking and the word; and we must have both. Neither idealists nor materialists are right; we must take both idea and expression.

All knowledge is of the reflected, as we can only see our face in a mirror. No one will ever know his own Self or God; but we are that own Self, we are God.

In Nirvana you are when *you* are not. Buddha said, "You are best, you are real, when you are not" — when the little self is gone.

The Light Divine within is obscured in most people. It is like a lamp in a cask of iron, no gleam of light can shine through. Gradually, by purity and unselfishness we can make the obscuring medium less and less dense, until at last it becomes as transparent as glass. Shri Ramakrishna was like the iron cask transformed into a glass cask through which can be seen the inner light as it is. We are all on the way to become the cask of glass and even higher and higher reflections. As long as there is a "cask" at all, we must think through material means. No impatient one can ever succeed.

13

Swami Vivekananda and Modern Problems

He was one of the "Seven Sages", brought down by Sri Ramakrishna for the good of the world. What are the implications of this, for our society today? Swami Vivekananda, however, was more than a traditional monk: he was patriot and prophet as well, and in this respect joined in his own body of thought both Eastern and Western elements.

Swami Vivekananda is one of the very few sannyasins to turn his mind to more than just "religion," and he has spoken on many of the issues of his day which remain issues for ours. Importantly, he looked upon religion itself as "the fulfillment of the perfection in man." He was a great humanist, who picked up European social ideas and fleshed them out with philosophic underpinning and implication.

As a prophet he foresaw the twentieth century as the age "of labor and the *sudras* and of women", predicting the rise of Russia and China. He also said the Indian ideas would go to every country under the sun and, before long, become a component of their many forces. It should be obvious by now that the Western world's dream of attaining happiness or permanent success through materialism has been a failure. Certainly Vivekananda did say, "Bread first; then religion," but for those who have too much bread? What about them? It is fine to have computers and color television, but do we not see that it is the Orient alone which has understood the finer dimensions of happiness? It is never in the machine; it is in the human mind. This was his message.

Today we find ourselves in a world beset with horrendous problems and dilemmas, and we have not yet evaded the threat of nuclear war. What does Swamiji have to say to us? It plays out on two levels: first as he addressed the problem on the level of the problem; and later, how he made us look behind it.

Crime and Public Morality

The facts are that punishment for crime often foments more crime than it prevents. The enforcers of law are as often corrupt and unlawful as not. And we could go on and on. "If it is social opinion that makes us moral, then really we are little better than animals," he said. "It is inner strength only that can curb the vicious tendencies." He told Indian boys, "You will be nearer to God by playing football than by studying the *Gita*." "Strength is the medicine for the world's disease." He encouraged athletic and bodily development in all who were effete. How sad he would feel, now, to see the dearth of Indian Olympians at the Games, and the commercializing of sports!

Swamiji saw crime as the result, not only of the injustices of society, but more the lack of self-esteem in the individual, and the impoverishment of higher ideals. He compared the social fabric of India with that of America, and felt that the Indian marriage system, in spite of its glaring injustices, was superior to the promiscuity (already rampant in his day) of the romantic

West. He was getting wind of the license Freudianism was going to bring. He did not try to be a Manu, defining particular codes of conduct. Following his Master, he could prescribe for human nature only turning our base impulses in a higher direction: there was no other solution. "Consciously or unconsciously," he said, "that Indian idea of the divinity within everyone will express itself even in other countries." Behind the drunkard, behind the abuser, he saw the crushed and struggling divinity. "Do not seek help from anyone. There is only one sin: weakness. Be strong, physically, mentally, morally."

Family Breakdown

We have known for long that just producing valedictorians and spelling geniuses in not enough to warranty the continuity of high culture. Hear Vivekananda: "It is the culture of the heart, really, not that of the intellect, that will lessen the misery of the world." "It is culture that withstands shocks, not learning! And we are finding that our children face many shocks, more every day. To the Christians he said, "Make yourselves decent people...Be chaste and pure...There is no other way. Did Christ find any other way? 'Except ye become as a little child, ye may not enter the Kingdom of Heaven.'"

He told us how to love a wife or a husband: "It is not our love that makes us miserable, but the fact that we want love in return." Always give, do not demand, he said. Swamiji was not a "reformer" in the sense of pulling down social systems. He approved the idea of a caste system, but not the latter-day applications of it; with proper amendments he thought it good for a society. As to family coherence, he knew that "those who cannot discipline themselves cannot control their children and pointed out the folly of expecting the offspring not to follow their parents' conduct. What we would like others to do, we had better do, ourselves.

Health Care

Sri Ramakrishna had been eclectic in his resort to methods of medical practice. He used to say that the Ayur Vedic treatments were good for the "Satya Yuga", the days of the *rishis* when time was abundant. They worked too slowly for modern times. But when stricken by cancer at the end, he would let all the schools of medicine try their hand! Swami Vivekananda too, in his approach to health and treatment, felt that all types of health management could be tried. He had no high opinion of what governments could do in the matter; they had to take a role, of course, but when all the evils of corruption, inefficiency, waste and callousness which attend bureaucracy were taken into account, how much could health be improved? Again, that idea of strength: "No disease can get a hold in you unless you are weak, and allow it to do so." We do not know for sure, but can surmise that in today's health controversies he would encourage prevention over cure, immunity over medicine, natural alternatives over pills, and spiritual practice to eliminate mental and physical dependence. There are hints of these, throughout the Swami's conversations.

Environmental Pollution and Denigration

The problem was scarcely recognized at the end of the nineteenth century, but one can extrapolate from nearly all that Swamiji said about life styles and conspicuous consumption. He was a realist and knew very well that we cannot have something for nothing. "The misery of the world is like chronic rheumatismchase it from one area, it shows up in another, " he said. If he were here today to face the problem in its ripest stage, there is little doubt that he would be an "environment-alist", and surely would remind us that we are going to be the inheritors of our own mess, allowing the Hindu doctrine of reincarnation. And one may imagine the almost acid tones with which he would refer to the population explosion and accent the role of self-control in its solution.

The same is true of fiscal irresponsibility. Do you remember that he upheld the value of the caste system as regards its original ideal and concept? That the caste member who attained to wealth or status was under the *dharmic* obligation to help raise the whole community from which he had risen and which had launched his struggle? Then how can we provide only for our own offspring? That would be adopting the nuclear family framework of the West, not the best to emulate, in his mind. "Freedom is the first condition of growth;" he forcefully remarked one day, "what you do not make free can never grow." This applies to employees and dependents as well.

The question of male dominance and woman's status. This defect the Hindus share with all the world's peoples, he acknowledged, as there is scarcely a culture which has not succumbed to it. He was one of the first of his era in the field of religion to recognize the indignity and oppression which woman was subject to, in this world of men. He had seen and studied the misery of his own sister, a suicide, and it had deeply affected his thinking. "If woman cannot act, neither can man suffer," he said; a fact now well-known in the statistics of psychology.

There were times when Vivekananda's mind was dwelling in a transcendental realm, and those times gave rise to expressions like these: "There is neither man nor woman [in Vedanta] , for the soul is sexless... It is a lie to say that I am a man or a woman, or I belong to this country or that. All the world is my country, because I have clothed myself with it as my body." Such was his sense of identity at that moment. He never tired of brushing off the well-meaning concerns of men who would ask him about "women's problems" "Hands off! " he exclaimed, "women will solve their own problems." Men had no business attempting to solve them for them.

In the United States he made a very interesting comment. He said, "American men profess to worship woman, but in my opinion they simply worship youth and beauty. They never fall in love with wrinkles and grey hair." By worship of woman, Sri Ramakrishna had meant, he assured us, that to him every woman's face was that of the Blissful Mother and nothing else. At the same time he could clearly see that in America alone there was now the social freedom to rise up and take equality with men. Swamiji met many women in the West, patrons, admirers, helpers, disciples and with all of them he dealt in his own natural and spontaneous way. They sometimes expected of him the gallant chivalry of that Victorian era, but he flatly refused. "You can take care of yourself, " he would say; "you are as able as I am, if not more." Swami Vivekananda was prophet enough to foresee what the twentieth century would bring. We can sum up the subject in his broad but telling generality: "Asia laid the germs of civilization. Europe developed man. America is developing woman and the masses."

Lack of Religious Identity

On this subject Swamiji had much to say. His years of wandering over his Motherland brought him to summarize what he considered the "Common Bases of Hinduism." These were: Belief in God (he once said with a bit of exasperation, "The Hindus can never give up His Majesty, the Lord of the Universe!"), belief in the Vedas as "revealed," the cyclic nature of time (*yugas* and *kalpas* in the macrocosm, reincarnation in the microcosm), and belief in all religions as valid paths because of the divinity of the human soul. Rather a minimal list, when one stops to think about it.

As regards scripture, Swamiji declared: "The proof of religion depends on the constitution of man, not on any books." What was the role of religion for a Hindu? "Religion, to help mankind, must be ready and able to help him in whatever condition he is." Then is there any place there for caste?

Above all, the Hindu is certain that we never go from falsehood to truth, but only from truth to truth. Be convinced of these and you are a Hindu.

Bibliography

Ann Myren and Dorothy Madison, eds., *Living at the Source: Yoga Teachings of Vivekananda.*

Harish C. Gupta, tr., *Swami Vivekananda Studies in the Soviet Union.*

His Eastern and Western Admirers, *Reminiscences of Swami Vivekananda.*

His Eastern and Western Disciples, *The Life of Swami Vivekananda,* Two vols. Hardback.

His Eastern and Western Disciples, *Vivekananda: The Man and His Message,* 1914-1918.

Marcus Toyne, *Involved in Mankind.*

Marie Lousie Burke, *Swami Vivekananda in the West: New Discoveries,* Six vols.

Pravrajika Atmaprana, ed., *Western Women in the Footsteps of Swami Vivekananda.*

Pravrajika Prabuddhaprana, *Tantine: The Life of Joesephine MacLeod.*

Romain Rolland and E.F. Malcom-Smith, tr., *The Life of Vivekananda and the Universal Gospel.*

Sarat Chandra Chakravarty, *Talks with Swami Vivekananda,* 1897 to 1902.

Shailendranath Dhar, *Comprehensive Biography of Swami Vivekananda,* 2 vols. Hardback.

Sister Nivedita, *Notes of Some Wanderings with the Swami Vivekananda.*

Sister Nivedita, *The Master as I Saw Him,* 1895-1902.

Swami Ashokananda, *Swami Vivekananda in San Francisco.*

Swami Chetanananda, ed., *Vedanta Voice of Freedom,* Paperback/ Hardcover.

Swami Chetanananda, *Vivekananda: A Biography in Pictures.*

Swami Chetanananda, *Vivekananda: East Meets West, A Pictorial Biography,* Hardback.

Swami Chetanananda. ed., *Meditation and Its Methods According to Swami Vivekananda.*

Swami Jyotirmayananda, *Vivekananda: His Gospel of Man-Making.*

Swami Nikhilananda, ed., *Vivekananda, the Yogas and Other Works.*

Swami Nikhilananda, *Vivekananda: A Biography.*

Swami Shraddhananda and others, *Facets of Vivekananda.*

Swami Tapasyananda, *The Four Yogas of Swami Vivekananda,* Condensed and Retold.

Swami Tejasananda, *A Short Life of Swami Vivekananda,* A good introductory biography.

Swami Vidyatmananda, ed., *What Religion Is In the Words of Swami Vivekananda.*

Index